THE TREK—

Once in a generation the Trek to prove fitness for rulership was undertaken, that arduous, nearly impossible journey over the two towering ridges and seemingly impassable chasm that split the major continent of Bear Ridge in half. Many had left their bones to bleach in the sun on the first and lesser ridge. A few had made it past the dread chasm. But in modern memory, only T.J. Shepherd, Master of the Terk and ruler of Bear Ridge, had survived to reach the lands of the Webbines, the mysterious, nonhuman natives of this world.

Only T.J. had returned to claim the crown, and only he knew the truth about the Webbines, a truth he had sworn to keep from the Federation's representatives at all costs. For it was this knowledge that might forever bar Bear Ridge from membership in the Federation Council. . . .

WE BUY AND SELL
THE BOOK STORE
243 NORTH FRONT ST.
BELLEVILLE, ONT.
966-8227

TREKMASTER

JAMES B. JOHNSON

DAW BOOKS, INC.
DONALD A. WOLLHEIM, PUBLISHER

Copyright © 1987 by James B. Johnson.

All Rights Reserved.

Cover art by Michael R. Whelan.

For color prints of Michael Whelan paintings, please contact:

Glass Onion Graphics
P.O. Box 88
Brookfield, CT 06804

DAW Book Collectors No. 719.

First Printing, September, 1987

2 3 4 5 6 7 8 9

PRINTED IN CANADA

COVER PRINTED IN THE U.S.A.

Dedicated to my mother Elouise, who taught me how to type before I learned handwriting.

1: THE KING

The seeds of rebellion were strewn this day, though, at the time, he did not know it—he only suspected it. Thomas Jefferson (family name Shepherd) Rex enjoyed his birthday celebration anyway.

". . . only living Master of the Trek, King of Bear Ridge, Supreme Commander of the Armies and the Gyrenes of the Palace Guard, Lord of Crimson Sapphire, Protector of the Faith . . ." TJ snorted to himself at this one as the herald continued to chant his titles. He noted the herald's calm cadence and felt a grudging admiration for the man's ability to wade through the necessary formalities. ". . . Unbeaten Swordmaster, Admiral of all the Navies, the Conqueror, Prime Chancellor, Lord of all Nobles, Father to all His Peoples . . ."

The herald Seemed to Talk in Capitals. TJ admitted that reciting the list of his titles was boring. He'd delete most of them—rather, the formal reading of them. The herald would hem and haw and disagree, for he liked the formality of the court. Alfred, the herald, was an administrative genius but he had his flaws. At least he was almost finished.

". . . paying homage to His Majesty, Thomas Jefferson Rex, King of Bear Ridge, on this his forty-second birthday."

Would this never end? TJ could see bored faces throughout the cavernous formal throne room. The court sycophants gathered together up front practiced bland exteriors though even they had to be bored. Throat clearing and coughing began in earnest. More than a thousand present, he thought, and all dressed in their finest. To his right was a section dedicated to the nobility; several of the two hundred or so present there could not conceal hostile glances at him. To his left, an equal sized section contained the clergy where an equal number of hostile looks favored him. In the center sat or stood almost a thousand of his subjects, mostly those from the city without. At the far walls stood members of the Gyrenes, ever alert, eyes constantly scanning. Random squads of these palace guards stood amongst the spectators and individual soldiers peppered the front rows of the crowd.

The jester must have sensed the unrest for he suddenly whooped and flew into a series of nimble cartwheels in the open space below the throne. The herald missed a beat of his chant.

Finally the opening ceremonies were complete and TJ smiled benevolently down at a group of tertiary school girls as they serenaded him. A team of jugglers followed. TJ sneaked a glance at the Fed's Envoy, Sharon Gold. She stood with rapt attention observing everything. Even though she was a xenobiologist, she couldn't conceal her interest in the supposed quaint ways of a backward planet like Bear Ridge. TJ admired Sharon. She was a tall, lithe young lady with golden brown skin. And she was from Olde Earthe. TJ found it surprising that the Federation Council had appointed one so young to be the final judge in the upcoming drama so important to him and his planet. Politics? Possibly. He'd have to study on it. The Fed Council could well be as full of intrigue as his own court. How the hell did an Olde Earthe Oriental get a Jewish name? He'd asked himself this question ten times since her arrival on Bear Ridge.

A team of tumblers cavorted now, bodies flying indiscriminately about and threatening to plunge into the crowd. The court jester hopped and flew amongst them, holding his talents in reserve, TJ knew, so as to not embarrass the tumblers.

Uncertainty struck at him. What if he turned out to be wrong? He began to fidget and a mood of depression settled over him. Push doubts aside. Birthdays were cause for celebration. Wasn't all of Bear Ridge on holiday just because of his birthday? And TJ knew that creeping age wasn't the sole cause of his lethargy. Two decades of fighting. Twenty years of blood, of agony, of battle after battle, of planning, of sweating and shaking nerves, of death and, worse, the rotting stench of it, of living on the knife-edge—after all that, life was too tame. He recognized his unrest as the curse of peace, a curse that many soldiers bear. He felt as if he were waiting for something to happen. It had been this way since the euphoria of war had passed. He shook his body. Pursue dreams of the future; do not revel in the past, learn from it. Christ, a philosopher now?

Gwen, sitting at his side on a smaller and less pretentious throne, patted him on the arm, sensing his mood.

". . . from the Ethnarchy of Bexar," the herald was announcing, "and the town of Lonestar, the selected representative of the Ethnarch and the people of Bexar, may I present to His Majesty the musician, Kellen Sing." The herald stepped back.

Somehow he knew it. This was a turning point. The young man's eyes glinted fire. Kellen Sing? TJ noted his stiff back, the shock of unruly black hair, the directness of focus from the coal black eyes, and the controlled energy. As he stared into the young man's eyes, TJ saw a direct threat. Maybe not. Try to read him? He should have mastered aura-control, but knew his stubborn personality was a hindrance to the self-integration. Yet his gut feelings were generally correct: they had to be.

"Welcome." TJ cut the formal greeting.

"Your Majesty," said Kellen Sing, "we are but a poor province and cannot afford expensive gifts. Thus the people of the Ethnarchy of Bexar have dispatched me to entertain you and your court." Sing followed the proper form while speaking, then knelt on one knee, touching his forehead to the other knee.

TJ signaled for him to rise, but Kellen Sing shook his head. From one wrist he detached a connected pair of thumb drums and secured them to his knee. He flicked his hair out of his eyes and lowered the lids halfway. His head angled back and he began to tap out a haunting melody.

The entire hall fell quiet. The throb of the thumb drums filled every inch of the crowded room. Each about the size of a fist, the drums were tuned in compliment.

TJ saw the mesmerizing effect the music had on most of those in the court. The people present were unnaturally silent. Occasionally, one of his palace guard would catch himself as if just coming awake. TJ recognized a few chords of "Death March" hidden within the framework of the piece. Gwendlyon stared in fascination, leaning forward so as to not miss a beat. The rhythm captured his blood beat, striking notes deep within. He tore his attention away, afraid to reveal himself. Much of the crowd seemed hypnotized.

Kellen Sing finished, and the hall remained dead silent with mental echoes of the music remaining.

Kellen's head dropped to his knee again, nudging the drums, and remained in that position. A spontaneous roar of approval,burst from the thousand present and shook the palace itself. The applause lasted for many minutes. TJ could see Kellen smiling into his knee.

TJ felt a sudden affinity for this young man, perhaps the age of his and Gwen's son, or perhaps a year or two older. Would that Michale commanded the presence that Kellen Sing did, and would that he manifested less antagonism. Ah, well, he could only hope that things would change.

The applause died slowly, a huge wave receding, leaving isolated spots of noisy approval. Gradually, all quieted and anticipation rose. It was the King's custom to handsomely reward outstanding performances. On his birthday, the royal coffers dropped in proportion to both the King's mood and his magnanimity.

TJ again signaled for Kellen to rise.

"I trust Your Majesty was pleased," Sing said, not asked.

The court gasped. One only replied to the King in court, not address him.

TJ had to hide his appreciation for the kid's spunk. "Yes, it pleased me. My dear?"

Gwen nodded deeply, and not a silver hair on her carefully prepared coiffure fell out of place. She turned to him and whispered, "TJ, he was magnificent!" and her face broke into the Queen's famous smile as she returned her gaze to Kellen and the court. "Yes, M'Lord. I would hear more, later."

TJ addressed Kellen, who continued to kneel, but was now looking up at TJ and Gwen. "Rise, and approach."

In one fluid motion, Kellen rose and began climbing the wide marble steps. The herald motioned him to stop on the second from the top.

"How came you to be so proficient?" asked TJ.

"Your Majesty, I am but a poor shepherd who has little formal schooling." TJ knew then the scene was orchestrated to the best of Kellen's ability. "My flocks are calmed by my playing. I have spent many hours practicing in front of sheepaloe. Sire."

TJ noted the careful brashness, the slightly off-kilter manner of address, and took an immediate liking to the boy. He wished there were more like him about the court.

"Are you aware, Kellen Sing, that it is the custom for the throne to reward the best of the day?" The crowd murmured at his words. All except the nobles who had little love for TJ and his ways. He could tell that most present expected Kellen Sing to receive the highest praise. And riches would overwhelm this poor shepherd boy.

"No. Sire."

The boy was not practiced enough to fool Thomas Jefferson (Shepherd) Rex, TJ told himself. As he detected the lie, it strengthened that sense of kinship with Kellen. He thought about baiting the boy, verbally tripping him to show that you didn't lie to the King of Bear Ridge and remain unexposed. But he chose not to, deciding instead to play along, perhaps to discover Sing's real objective.

"Awards are given," TJ said, "to those I deem worthy." He had selected those specific words rather than saying something about "the best performances."

Kellen Sing raised an eyebrow.

"Your weight in coin of the realm would be ample recognition, don't you think?" The kid would play hell trying to carry all that loot back to Lonestar on foot. Anyway, the bait was there and he was curious as to what Sing would say as he took the bait from the hook.

"More than ample," said Kellen. "Your generosity is overwhelming," he finished off-key.

And TJ knew that Sing's tone of voice was calculated to tell him that money wasn't what he wanted.

Gwen sensed this subtle byplay and took her cue. "Perhaps Kellen Sing has something else in mind? A mount from the King's stables? And a fancy carriage? Temporary lodgings in the palace, for he has obviously never visited the capital?"

TJ caught the slight disapproval in her voice. She didn't like any strayings from the strict formality of the official court. And she well knew TJ's penchant for variation, for mockery, and his sometimes childish sense of humor, as well as his impatience. Maybe that's why I have this liking for Kellen Sing, he thought; we both have a disdain for formal procedure crap.

"If Your Majesties please," Kellen said, "is not my weight in coin sufficient to exchange for formal learning?"

"What?" TJ had not expected this.

"Sire, I have no one left in Lonestar. My family is dead . . . well, there is one sister, but she cares for herself. I have spent my life upon the hills with sheepaloe and predators . . . and my thumb drums. Out there, I have dreamed of stars; but more, I have dreamed of learning, of books I could not possibly afford, of knowledge I could not obtain by seeking in the province, er, Ethnarchy of Bexar. Surely, with your intervention, I could attend one of the superior schools here in Crimson Sapphire? I know this is asking much. I thumb my drums. I herd sheepaloe. I am from the country and the hills in the country. But even there your graciousness and fondness for education are widely known." He paused. "Sire."

TJ watched Kellen watch him. He knew his presence had to be imposing to a country boy. Yet Kellen seemed relaxed, enjoying the obvious pressure of the game he had initiated with the King. Kellen's eyes catalogued him, taking his measure. TJ knew what Kellen saw. The monarch was more than a head taller than average, large boned, with a strong nose. There was a hint of stomach being held in by tight clothing. His scarlet tunic was braided about the sleeves in five rows near the cuffs and around the neckpiece. Epaulets topped the shoulders, and winding from underneath the right epaulet came a white satin sash. Decorations, medals and ribbons adorned the left chest and hung from his neck. TJ saw the shock hit Kellen when his eyes came to the symbol of the Muster hanging from his neck. His eyes stopped and he was obviously shaken by this discovery. TJ only wore the symbol on occasions such as these—and none that were present on that fateful day ever spoke of it. Those few that lived through it. Finally, Kellen's eyes left the medallion and reluctantly moved on. TJ's tunic hung loosely over solid black trousers which in turn were tucked into glass-polished high boots. He knew that overshadowing the whole effect was Thomas Jefferson Shepherd, the face, the face that fronted the mind which ran the planet. His hair was thick, tinged with shards of gray, as was his Prince Albert beard— though this was carefully trimmed. Finally, TJ saw Kellen's black eyes meet his own gray eyes, gray eyes tinged by battle and blood, steadily regarding Kellen. TJ read Kellen well enough now to know what he thought at this moment. Kellen must be awed, standing there in his simple tunic. Then TJ saw something change in Kellen's eyes, and a hardening glint came into them.

Abruptly, TJ broke the silence. "All right." Here he was toying with a damn kid when there were matters of supreme importance waiting for his attention. He wished he could scratch under his collar, but of course Gwen would notice and raise hell with him later.

The jester began to do back flips, and TJ knew he was

spending too much time with Kellen Sing. TJ sighed. His plans for himself and Bear Ridge were close to being realized, and he should be concentrating on them. Would Bear Ridge pass the test? Could he convince Sharon Gold that Bear Ridge was ready? But the presence of this Kellen Sing seemed to cloud the clarity of his purpose.

"It shall be as you wish," he said to Kellen. "Remain. The herald will arrange an audience at the conclusion of the ceremonies."

The jester tumbled and cavorted, grinning like a cheshire of the highlands, his makeup holding up under occasional drooling of the apparent idiot.

TJ sat back to watch tamed snarves dance and tried to ease his belt. He thought that it was a good thing the tunic was worn outside the trousers. He blamed the incipient middle age spread on a lack of action and immediately missed times past.

An uproar of hilarity came from the front rows as one of the beasts messed on the floor and attendants hurried to clean it up. TJ took the opportunity to tug his belt line down a bit.

Gwen touched him lightly on the arm, reminding him of form.

He turned to her and said in a low voice, "At least I'm not as raunchy as that bastard Tirano."

"This is your day, Thomas. Do not let politics spoil it for you."

Guiltily, he glanced at Sharon Gold. It had probably taken her less time to travel from Federation Central to Bear Ridge, dozens of light years, than it took Kellen Sing to walk from Lonestar to Crimson Sapphire, and he thought that was criminal.

2: KELLEN SING

Kellen Sing wasn't ready for the suddenness of the action, the fierceness of response, the quickness of the King, or the smell of blood.

As he watched the continuation of festivities, Kellen re-

flected that the court of Thomas Jefferson Rex was alien.
He was now seated in a semi-official section, one with
legitimate bench seats, apparently grouped among those
favored few in front. He reflected that this wasn't his world
at all.

He looked about. Palace guards, sometimes known as the
Gyrenes, stood about, all armed with polished swords, oiled
crossbows, and the deadly assegais. They were inhibiting:
there was something about a group of men who all looked
alike, their backs militarily stiff, their hair cut the same, the
deadly look to their eyes, the firm, uniform set of jaws, and
the bodily precision. Each seemed to be a walking arsenal
and each was positioned for the King's protection. Kellen
could not identify it, but he knew there was a pattern in
their placement and in their apparently random movement
about the crowded court.

The King must love the trappings of his office. Kellen
watched as a team of dark men presented the King with a
pair of wild snarves, one male and one female. They were
going through the motions of formal presentation, with the
King's own handler hovering obviously about. The beasts'
powerful necks were circled by metal collars from which
four chains ran to bolts secured to a heavy cart. Like most
snarves, these made little noise when aroused. Kellen shivered. He had encountered snarves before: if they growled
almost silently, then trouble was at hand. Of course these
snarves were angry. Their neutral, rock-gray fur bristled,
running in waves up and down their hides.

Kellen looked around to see if the guards were aware of
some danger but found no evidence of it. Should he warn
someone? Of what? A suspicion? If so, he would have to
explain why he thought he knew. Anxiously, he looked
around to see if anyone seemed capable of combating a
loose snarv. No. Only the King seemed large enough—way
up there on his throne, he seemed larger than life. The King
did have a sword, but Kellen couldn't tell if it was a cere-mo-
nial sword or a functional one. Could that specific sword
actually be "The Widow-Maker?"

He guessed that the male snarv outweighed the King by
three times. He watched the snarves' feral eyes dart in
panic. Snouts nervously jerked from side to side, snouts that
topped mouths which were long enough to hold a man's arm
without swallowing. The teeth, he knew, were razor sharp
and angled toward the gullet of the snarv. And the beasts

were built close to the ground for quicker movement. Six powerful legs with splayed, hide-tough, gripping feet showed the animals were designed for the mountains. The short legs gave them a crocodilian advantage over any other beast on the planet.

Some of the people in the front of the audience became apprehensive. Kellen could feel fear begin to seep into those near him. No human of Olde Earthe stock was ever comfortable in the presence of snarves. The nearby palace guard didn't seem outwardly bothered, though. Kellen felt the first stirrings of alarm in those close to him. But with no visible threat, they had nothing on which to hang their suspicions. Ha, let them sweat! The Gyrenes, he could see, were more concerned with the crowd than with the threat of the snarves.

Kellen didn't understand the military mind. He looked again at the King as he sat there so complacently, probably contemplating what he would have for lunch. Shortly after this King had subordinated the other nations and city-states on Bear Ridge, he had instituted a planet-wide government service program: two years, spent either in the military or in public service. Kellen thought this cunning, as the program required more education than most people possessed and therefore increased the academic level of all humans on the planet. And, not incidentally, made them available to the garbage propaganda of Thomas Jefferson Shepherd.

Kellen had not chosen military service. Instead, he had worked with the poor folk of his province. Poor himself, he thought it appropriate for the monarchy to pay him to help the poor. He embraced the idea of all young people serving before their twentieth birthdays and giving of themselves to others. The service, he thought, induced humility and a better view of life under this King. On the other hand, he frequently argued, it allowed this King to poison or put his particular brand of propaganda out to all young people. His determination reasserted itself and the court no longer overwhelmed him with its largeness and its strangeness.

What happened next occurred faster than most people present could follow.

The jester had foolishly placed himself in front of the low-snarling snarves, as if challenging them. He sat upon the third step up to the throne, resting as if tired by his exertions. Oddly, Kellen could not read anything about the jester save he was wary.

Then the female snarv reared up, exposing her hard underbelly, inviting attack, challenging. All eyes went to her. The jester leapt up and whirled past her, obviously trying to distract her attention until the trainers could calm her. But Kellen felt something else happening. Then he saw the collar holding the male's four chains snap.

Suddenly, the male was loose and baying a challenge that rang throughout the chamber. The beast whirled, and glared at the front row of robed padres. Just to the side of the padres stood the favored group of tertiary school girls who had serenaded the King. Where would the beast attack? It jumped again, landing on the top stair to the throne.

Simultaneously, Kellen saw the jester scrambling toward the beast and several Gyrenes drawing their swords and crossbows.

But before anyone else could move, the King leaped and drew his not-so-ceremonial sword as he landed in front of the Queen. The swiftness of the movement stunned not only Kellen and the beast, but those nearby quick enough to follow the action. As the male snarv darted at the Queen, the King's sword pierced the top right eye. Then the King kicked the beast's snout upward, his sword following the kick with a twisting motion cleaving into the snarv's throat. Bloody ichor erupted and the beast reared. The King swung his sword with both hands now, the flat of the blade slamming into the torso of the screaming beast and knocking him off balance. The scream of the snarv paralyzed almost everyone in the room.

Except the King, Kellen amended. The damnfool jester was still scurrying up the stairs in a panic, both hands outstretched as if he didn't know where he was. The snarv struck in front of him and the jester leaped over him to the feet of the King. The King shoved the jester aside, almost throwing him in the lap of the Queen, and ran down the stairs toward the wounded snarv, sword positioned for another strike. The sword must be Widow-Maker.

By then the palace guards had recovered and the male snarv was suddenly transfixed with a dozen crossbow bolts. Kellen saw an officer signal and the female snarv was also shot to death—even though she was still attached to the holding cart. The same officer made another motion and a squad of the Gyrenes surrounded the hapless snarv trainers. Kellen did not envy them. This King had a reputation. And the conditions under which the snarv had escaped were suspicious.

The scene seemed to freeze for a moment, then some of the more fainthearted in front began shouting and those far back finally responded. Kellen noted that now all of the palace guards held their weapons at ready and most had been deployed around the King. The crowd noise swelled and the King held his bloody and dripping sword above his head in a commanding manner. The great hall fell immediately silent. The specter of the blood-splattered King was riveting. The only sound was the sobbing of the men who had brought the snarves into the court. They were being escorted through a side door as attendants were dragging off the slain snarves. Kellen marveled at the excellent organization. The herald, pale but efficient, was directing the operation.

The King glared a challenge and casually returned his sword to its scabbard. He turned to converse with the Queen as the jester moved from his kneeling position in front of her. The fool began a series of motions which Kellen suddenly recognized as an exaggerated mime of the drama that had just unfolded. Kellen knew instinctively that the legend of Thomas Jefferson Shepherd would swell to new dimensions this day. The King ignored the mess on his formal uniform, casually wiping the gore off his Muster medallion with his braided sleeve.

Kellen watched as the king finished the ceremonies. You'd never know anything had happened except that the main floor was covered with sand and the King was splattered with blackening ichor.

The ceremonies completed, Kellen found himself walking beside the herald, following the royal party at a respectful distance. They stopped momentarily when a general in the palace guard intercepted the party. The King took him aside and spoke with him. Kellen saw the general standing at attention and not replying. The King spoke harshly in his face for moments, and only by straining could Kellen hear any words at all. He knew that the general—Vero, he picked the name up—was being lambasted. ". . . could've killed, goddamnit . . . kind of cheap security . . . Jesus, a bunch of young girls, for Chrissake," and ". . . take them apart, no damned accident . . ."

The King dismissed General Vero and turned to join the party. He walked next to the off-worlder named Sharon Gold. Kellen didn't know her purpose, but could guess some of it. The story went that Bear Ridge had recently been rediscovered by the Federation. The centuries-long separation from other worlds was now over. This was one of the main reasons Kellen had come to Crimson Sapphire.

They continued down the long corridor and Kellen eavesdropped on the King's conversation with Gold. He towered over her, talking and waving his hands about as if saying something important.

". . . and I have been an avid student of Olde Earthe history," the King was telling her. Kellen felt a twinge of jealousy. There was so much he wanted to learn—for without knowledge, without the learning skills, he would not be able to better himself, to reach further. . . .

They entered an antechamber. This room was more businesslike, not the ostentatious display Kellen had expected; spacious offices fed off from this reception area.

The King waved everyone to a seat, but no one sat. Kellen started to sit down when a cold glance from the herald told him no one sat before the King did.

The jester had accompanied the procession and slumped unceremoniously into a corner, scratching his rear end. Nobody seemed to notice.

The King disengaged himself from the envoy and addressed the herald. "Well, Alfred, what is the order of business?"

Sharon Gold stepped back and stood beside Kellen. She was taller than he. Her eyes remained on the King.

The herald said, "Sire, the calendar is clear for both the celebration and the staff meeting this afternoon. Besides this young man here," Alfred nodded toward Kellen, "there is only one pressing matter of business."

"Well, Hark, what is it?"

"Sire, the Ethnarch of Juarez requests an immediate determination regarding an ecological problem."

"This is pressing business?" demanded the King.

"It is, Sire."

"Shall we see if the facts bear out your judgment, then, Hark?"

"Yes, Sire." Alfred spoke aside to a guard who stepped into a side room. Soon he returned with two men. The first was formally garbed with the tunic insignia of a province official. The second was a young man, about Kellen's age, dressed in many bright colors like a young nobleman.

"Sire," said the herald, indicating the official, "this is Hammond Wouk, the representative of the Ethnarch of

Juarez." The man bowed. "And this young man is a representative of the Juarez Ecological Society, Franco Valdez."

"Well, what's the situation? Can the Ethnarch not handle
his own problems these days?"

"Sire," said Wouk, "that he can. However, there is a
conflict between two different royal decrees. Thus it is not
resolvable at our level."

"It is so urgent that it could not wait for a business day?"

"Time passes and money is lost."

"Tell me what the hell the problem is, then. Let's get this
over with."

"Yes, Sire. Construction was to have begun three days
ago on the long awaited aqueduct from the lake to the city
of Figgeredwrong. Running water for the first time. The
Juarez Ecological Society has prevented its start."

"How?"

"May I, Sir?" asked Valdez.

"I wish somebody would."

Valdez visibly blanched, gulped and started. "Sire, the
royal decree regarding ecology will be thwarted. They plan
to cut through a large forest, despoiling wild life and ruining
thousands of trees."

"Your Highness, the aqueduct is necessary for sanitation
and public welfare, all found in another royal decree—plus
it is in accordance with your modernization drive," Wouk
put in.

"Ah, I see it now. The conflict." The King nodded.

"The crews are waiting in place and it's costing the provincial treasury daily to have them sit thusly," said Wouk.
"And, by extension, the royal treasury."

"Good thinking. Any other ancillary problems? Like, for
instance, Mr. Valdez, would not the people of the province
require the cut timber for building and winter heating?"

"Yes, Sire, but that could be done more judiciously, more
selectively. And not harm the wild life."

"Did it occur to you, Valdez, that people are a form of
life and deserve to be considered under an ecological order?" The King was standing over Valdez and glaring down
at him.

"Er, yes, Sire. People can think for themselves, choose
their own habitats without disturbing the natural scheme of
things."

The King's eyebrows went up. "And the sheepaloe your
province lives off, are they in the natural scheme of things?"

"Er, yes, Sire."

"Negative, Valdez. Our ancestors introduced them from Olde Earthe. Ever wonder why one animal is so useful? From the wool to the meat to the hooves? Wonder why sheepaloe grow fat on the sparse vegetation of the hills?" Valdez looked bewildered. The King stepped back and looked around him. He rubbed his hands as if approaching a favorite subject. Kellen saw the Queen stifle a groan. "In vitro mean anything to you? No, I can tell it doesn't. When you're settling a planet, you can't take everything you want with you. So the genetic engineers on Earthe stole from the sheep, the longhorn steer and the buffalo, the toughest and most adaptable animals, and developed an animal that would not only live on Bear Ridge, but thrive on its harsh conditions. Once they had the sheepaloe perfected, they preserved sufficient sperm and ovae. So they only had to ship a few of the animals to act as host mothers. Fortunately, the herds were building well when the Rollback came and the wars separated Earthe from its former colonies. All the time we spent regressing to almost a primitive state the sheepaloe thrived. When we finally turned around and began advancing again, the sheepaloe provided sufficient food and clothing.

"Now you see how our ancestors changed things. Can we not also?"

Valdez stammered. "My group, Sire, understands, but we have tasked ourselves with preservation. It is all important."

"How many in your group?"

"Nearly a hundred, Sire. We have an enclave just outside Figgeredwrong."

"Ah."

Kellen watched Wouk bursting to respond. But the King didn't seem to notice.

The King turned to the herald. "Have your scribes amend those royal decrees mentioned. I want them sprinkled liberally with the words 'common sense' and like that."

The herald motioned and a secretary hastily wrote down the King's words.

"Also, I want the following: the aqueduct to begin construction as soon as possible. The sons of ecology or whatever the hell their name is," he glared at Valdez, who seemed to be shrinking in place, "shall gather buggaloes and dry them and sell them for heating and cooking fires. They will turn in the receipts to the province until those monies equal the amount spent on idle construction crews. Lastly, there is to be no connection of running water to their enclave. If they choose to remain together as a group in that place and do not maintain minimum sanitary conditions, they are to be taxed enough money to pay for cleanup. If, after all this, they still be recalcitrant, then come and see me again."

Wouk appeared both pleased with his victory and frightened by the King's wrath. Valdez looked crestfallen.

Sharon Gold leaned toward Kellen and asked in a low voice, "Whatever are buggaloes?"

"Chips," he said and when she shook her head she still didn't understand, he added, "manure." She looked startled and nodded understanding.

It seemed to Kellen that even though the King might have been right, he could have handled the situation far more delicately, and at least commend Valdez and his group for their interest in the well-being of Bear Ridge. But obviously, this monarch had no patience, no tact, no diplomacy. Thinking this merely hardened Kellen's resolve.

As Wouk and Valdez left, Kellen saw the King brighten as though disposing of something distasteful.

"And now," the King said, "Kellen Sing." He smiled.

Momentarily awed by the sheer presence of the man, Kellen drew himself up straighter. He could not help but remember what had happened to Valdez. Was that a subtle warning to him by the King? Did the King suspect? Of course he suspected something, his eyes showed it. Kellen knew he must follow his original plans. He bowed. The King is a formidable opponent to engage, thought Kellen Sing and swallowed with difficulty.

The King stepped over to him and reached out his hand. Kellen grasped the hand in return, surprised by the gesture. The King's hand was tough and callused, and not for the first time did Kellen glance at the not-so-ceremonial sword. In a detached portion of his mind, Kellen realized that the King's calluses matched the ridges on the hilt of the sword. Kellen smelled the sour odor from the snarv.

"Sire," Kellen responded, finding he had to apply more pressure than usual in his handshake to match the King's grip. Queen Gwendlyon approached with a formal smile and held out her hand.

Kellen sensed the test and bent and brushed his lips just above the back of her hand. The Queen nodded, which told him he'd done the right thing.

The King introduced him to the Federation Envoy. "Kellen Sing, may I present Ambassador Plenipotentiary Gold?"

The willowy lady from off-planet stretched her arm and Kellen sensed that he should shake her hand, not kiss it. He'd passed another test.

"You play most beautifully," she said. Her accent was strange: nonetheless, her voice seemed to call to him personally.

"Thank you."

"The thumb drum is new to me," she said. "I've seen nothing like it on any of the Federation worlds I've visited."

"Special wood, my lady, hewn from the yowel tree peculiar to my province; and the skin is from the hide of the volv." He didn't want to tell her that the volv's testicle pack was the skin used. "It is dried and cured and stretched over the yowel wood base."

"The wood also makes fine bows," the King pointed out.

"Found only on the planet of Bear Ridge, Your Majesty?" asked Sharon Gold.

"A mutation caused by the atmospheric conditions of Bear Ridge," replied the King. "There are similarities between the yowel tree and others originally transported from Earthe."

She looked questioningly at the King.

He shrugged. "Our science—biological, chemical, physical—is not as advanced as we would have it. All those centuries in rebuilding—but with admission to the Fed, well . . ."

"That is yet to be determined, Your Highness," said Sharon Gold.

"It is, isn't it?" the King said enigmatically.

Kellen wished he knew what the byplay was about. He felt forgotten.

Queen Gwendlyon said, "Thomas, about the boy . . ."

"Ah, yes. Schooling it is you wish?"

"Yes, Your Majesty."

"Most would take the coin and hustle back to their province and become a local celebrity, building their status, milking it for everything."

Kellen again became uncomfortable as the King's hand rested on the hilt of his sword and his eyes bored into Kellen's. Kellen knew he was supposed to answer, but how could he answer what the King had just said?

"Sire, I do not seek recognition for something I have

found to be a simple achievement. Thumb drumming is easy." His courage grew as he spoke. "It is my dream, Sire, to learn; this I consider significant above all else. What good is money if you have few needs? And my needs are to expand my mind, to discover new ideas and concepts, to learn of my heritage through history, to seek mathematical relationships." Kellen was serious but knew it sounded like he was piling it on too thick.

"I believe he means it," the King said to nobody in particular. He glanced at the Queen, who nodded almost imperceptively. "May I speak with you alone for a moment?" He took Kellen's arm and guided him into the corner next to the jester who seemed to stare vacantly up at them.

In a low voice that no one could hear, Thomas Jefferson Rex said, "Cut the crap, fellow. What is it you want?"

Kellen was taken aback. The jester seemed to tense. "But . . . but . . . Your Majesty . . ." He thought swiftly. Kellen knew little of psychology, but he knew he had an inner grasp of how to handle people and situations that was almost preternatural and he didn't hesitate to use it here. He drew himself up and with a cold, formal voice, said, "Sire. If you think I have been playing some game, you are in error." He projected sincerity. He well knew that he shouldn't have called the King "in error." Framed by the beard, the King's face froze.

Suddenly, the King grinned. "You'll never make a good sycophant, boy." He glanced at the jester, who scratched his right ear with his thumb. "All right then, you got it. Learning a trade. A fine technical school. That shall give you entry to a trade union and security for life. Something to contribute to your community."

"Sire, as I tried to point out earlier, and I am not able to articulate so well, I prefer the academic subjects."

"A learned sheepaloe herder?" the King reflected. "Well, I've heard of stranger things." He turned and addressed the group. "So be it. Herald, ensure Kellen Sing is enrolled in the Francisco Shepherd University. Give him a temporary room in the palace. For pocket change, Kellen, you shall play your wizard drums at Our request." He looked at Kellen, who could only nod, unable to trust himself to speak—again flaunting convention, but this time not by choice.

"And, Hark, insure he studies."

"Yes, Sire."

"And now," the King said, "we have business of the realm to conduct: we must plan and determine a way to convince this beautiful young lady here to give us admission to the Fed so that we may bring it to its knees." He grinned wolfishly.

Everyone laughed at his joke. Thomas Jefferson Shepherd was known for his ribald sense of humor.

Sharon Gold appeared stunned until she understood it was a joke, then tried to laugh along with the others.

Kellen Sing saw that the King's eyes did not smile.

3: THE ENVOY

Before she began her briefing, she didn't know she was going to antagonize the King. She looked at the man with the eye patch and the scars and thought him an executioner.

Sharon Gold was waiting for quiet. She found standing on a raised podium in front of the hierarchy of an entire planet intimidating despite her training and when she saw the King watching her she felt unusually disquieted. As things settled she saw a bug scurrying across the floor. Durn, she thought, the only constant in the universe: a roach. Had the pioneers brought them to Bear Ridge or had they already existed here? She'd never been to a planet where roaches did not exist.

"Herald," the King grunted. The herald, Alfred, nodded politely and stepped to the door past the two stone-faced sentries. Soon he was back with an attendant who scurried to the front of the room and scattered leaves along the wall.

"Bay leaves," murmured the herald to her as the attendant left the conference room.

Gradually, everyone found the proper seat, yet the King had not signaled her to start. Her confidence was fleeing fast, and she glanced around and saw the King's gaze steady on her. She knew that he sensed her nervousness, her apprehension. She closed her eyes for a moment and forced her breathing to a slower pace. When she looked at him again his gaze seemed to be steadying, a comfort in her isolation.

She couldn't help but be attracted to him.

She forced her eyes from him and looked about the crowded room. Besides the guards, some twenty people sat around the formal conference table. The King occupied the central position at the head of the table and was surrounded by all of his ministers and department heads. No round table of equals, this one. To one side sat the Queen, Gwendlyon, and the Queen Mother, Felicia, and the King's son by Gwendlyon, Michale. Looking at Prince Michale, she saw that he'd gotten his good looks—soft beauty—from his mother. Both mother and son were tall, though TJ must have contributed some height to Michale; both stood and sat straight; rounded faces, ovals contrasting TJ's occluded but sharper visage. And unlike the King's, their noses fit their faces. Gwen's hair seemed prematurely silver, Michale's still thick and dark, curls hanging over his forehead.

LET'S GET ON WITH IT! she screamed silently. She'd practiced this presentation all the way to Bear Ridge and she was becoming flustered.

The Chief Padre gave her a sour smile. He sat at the foot of the table, chair turned so that he could watch her presentation. A Catholic planet, her data base had told her, but she was not entirely certain whether this was a significant fact or not.

She avoided looking at the man in black, the man with the eye patch and the sword? knife? scars upon his face.

The jester slouched in the corner near her. The King had introduced everyone formally and, regardless of her mnemonic training, she couldn't remember all of them; but with time, she'd get to know them. She didn't understand why Prince Michale seemed unhappy and she did understand why the Chief Padre seemed unhappy. The Profane King? Or was there more to the Chief Padre's discontent?

The King nodded and the room fell silent. He smiled at her. "Miz Gold?" Apparently he felt there was no need to formally introduce her to the assembly.

She decided to eliminate the formal introductory remarks that she'd copied out of the Federation Etiquette data base. She cleared her mind.

"Your Majesty," she said, "as the Envoy of the Federation of Planets, it is my task to evaluate the planet of Bear Ridge and its people, and specifically its governmental structure to determine whether it meets the criteria for entrance to the Federation of Planets. The application by Thomas Jefferson Shepherd Rex to the Federation Council was well received, and thus Bear Ridge has been placed on a list of possible entrants. As you know, the Council sits for ten Federation standard years as constituted without membership change or addition of other planets—and the beginning of that session is not far off."

As the King nodded agreement with her words, she knew the time compression factor weighed heavily on his mind. "We're all familiar with this introductory stuff," the King said in a tone of dismissal. "Who are we up against?" He looked around the room. "I'm not going to wait ten years and go through this test again just to get generated power and indoor plumbing." He received a polite laugh. An expression of pain streaked across Prince Michale's face.

Sharon stared at the King, wanting to repay his impatience with a tart word. Diplomatic? Hardly, but—blast it! She'd really practiced her presentation. And on another level she was fighting a growing attraction to this demanding man. He was pushing her, testing her. She simply stared at him. She could hold her own with men, people trying to push her. Had this man grown up in adversity? No, he'd been born to royalty. She had grown up in an Israeli refugee camp in a stinking valley edged off the Shan plateau in Burma country. A tributary of the Salween River was the only running water they had. The daughter of a Burmese general out of favor because he'd married an anglo-jewess. She squared her shoulders.

"Who are we up against?" the King asked again.

"Your Highness, only a dozen planets have been recontacted this session, and not all of those are far enough advanced to meet the criteria yet. The wars of the Rollback struck when Earthe was stretched too thin, colonizing planets faster than they could plan for and almost faster than they could logistically support."

"Almost as if they knew the Rollback was coming," the King finished for her. "Who's against us?"

"Eight planets have been evaluated thus far," she said, "seven have failed."

"You don't really want to tell me, do you?" the King said, drawing himself straighter. "Lookit here, girl, I know there is only one slot open for the next Fed Council session. I want it. They can play their politics and do whatever the hell they want with their damned slots, but I want my planet admitted, and I want all the modern technologies here and here damn quick. I want aircars, indoor plumbing, air conditioning, instant communications . . ." He looked about and obviously realized that everyone in the room had heard it all before. Sharon simply watched and listened. "Okay, okay," he said. "They are going to dilute their Council strength only by one this time. I want to be that one. I don't want Bear Ridge to have to wait ten more years for TODAY to arrive. No contact for ten more years? Think of the diseases that could be conquered in that time, think of . . ." He hesitated. "I'm doing it again, aren't I?"

The Queen Mother nodded enthusiastically and Sharon felt an immediate liking for the old woman. She had the same craggy face the King must have under his beard. But there was something tough and smiling underneath Felicia's put-down of her son. Entry to the Federation was as important to Felicia as it was to the King. Sharon did not agree with the Federation "hands-off" or quarantine of planets not yet admitted, but as part of that organization, she had to support the policy.

The King was still staring directly at Sharon and she felt antagonism rise in her, displacing the attraction she'd felt earlier. He was challenging her.

"If Bear Ridge passes my evaluation, you are up against only one other possible entrant to the Federation Council, Sire."

"Which one?"

Sharon hesitated. Should she answer? She didn't think it was required and wasn't covered in her instructions. And since this was her first major assignment, she was unfamiliar with the form. The King continued to stare at her.

"Two Tongues." There, she had said it.

"Tirano?" demanded the King, naming the ruler of Two Tongues.

"Yes, Your Majesty."

"Christ."

The Chief Padre frowned.

"Christ," the King said again as if to upset the priest. "Two Tongues is technologically more advanced than we are," he pointed out, his voice sounding depressed.

Sharon sensed his disappointment. She also thought there might be more to his anger about Two Tongues than met the eye. "One seat, Your Majesty. Two potential applicants. Those odds are not bad."

"Tyrannical Tirano? Tyrannosaurus Rex? That lard-ass, son of a . . ."

Felicia cleared her throat.

The King of the planet of Bear Ridge looked guilty, shook his head and stopped. Everyone else in the room seemed to be inspecting either the ceiling or the floor. The Prince shook his head and made a disapproving, dour face at his father.

"You know Tirano?" Sharon asked, curiosity overcoming diplomatic caution. Two Tongues was in this solar system, a rarity for two habitable planets to be located in the same system. But with only horsepower on Bear Ridge, how could . . . ?

"Yeah," said the King. "Met him a couple of times. Fed Fed sponsored conferences, here, on Two Tongues, at Fed-central

Sharon failed to understand the animosity about Tirano. "May I continue?" Her voice came out more haughty than she'd intended.

"Sure, go ahead."

"How I make the evaluations is all organized. By checklist. I shall observe, I shall investigate, I shall interview. There are certain mandatory requirements for entry to the Federation that must be met. For example, I must personally review everything about your military and observe a series of predetermined, complicated maneuvers. I must go through each governmental department to insure Bear Ridge is sound and able to adapt to Federation organization and regulations—if admitted."

"Besides all that," TJ interrupted again, "do you foresee any special problems?" He'd changed from his ruined formal court garb into a simple, almost military, skyblue tunic which was reflected in his gray eyes.

"The mysterious inhabitants," she said.

The King seemed to withdraw into himself. "In what manner?" he said, and she thought you could ice-skate on his words.

"Your relationship to them, their relationship to you, their position after—and if—you've gained Federation admission."

"Why should anything change? What the hell difference does it make?"

Couldn't she take a step without mashing his toes in some manner? She regretted it. But it was her job. "Mechanization, industrialization, technology, all these invariably and drastically change a planet. And the Federation is concerned with intelligent life—for we have yet to discover another space-faring race."

"The Webbines are not space-faring. They should not enter into the question," the King said adamantly.

Was the King trying to hide something? "We'll see when we get to that point, Your Majesty." Appease 'em, avoid confrontations. Cost her nothing. Just do her job. She was trained as a xenobiologist, and thus chosen for this mission. Fortunately for her, the others in that department at Federation Central were not available for the time span of this mission, and the task fell to her almost by default. Yet . . . that sounded almost too easy. Was she a political pawn? A sacrifice? Suppose she denied Bear Ridge admission to the Federation? Fine, the Council would back her up, no sweat. But if she said yes to TJ Shepherd, and that was not what the Council really wanted, couldn't they simply overrule her, point out her inexperience and youth? Was that how her appointment to this important mission had occurred? And she had been so confident that circumstances and her outstanding job performance had provided her this opportunity.

As a xenobiologist, she'd jumped at the chance. In fact, she was itching to meet one of the mysterious inhabitants of Bear Ridge, to study one, to communicate with one.

"I hope you aren't going to want to visit them?" the King asked in counterpoint to her thoughts.

"Yes."

"Impossible."

"Why?"

"Seldom are they seen. No one can speak to them if they *are* seen. They're just there, mysterious and unaffected, going about their business, whatever that is."

Now she knew he was hiding something. "Nevertheless, I shall attempt it."

"Lady, your ship is gone. Did you perchance observe this continent from above on the way down?"

"Yes, sir."

"Then you saw the two great ridges splitting the continent?"

"Teddy Bear Ridge and Big Bear Ridge? Yes, I saw them."

"Well, you can't get there from here. Unless you still have access to a ship."

"No, I don't."

"That settles that. You see, they stay on the far side of the two ridges and we're stuck over here. Hell, a damn monkeybird couldn't climb Teddy Bear Ridge and live, much less the bigger one after that, Big Bear Ridge itself."

Everyone in the room looked at the King and the jester snorted.

He shrugged. "Well, it *is* done, but perhaps only once in a generation."

"By whom?" Sharon demanded, thinking she was the recipient of the old "dazzle 'em with fancy footwork and baffle 'em with bullshit" routine. Animosity rose in her voice and reflected in her posture. Damn, she couldn't help it.

"You're talking to him," said Thomas Jefferson (Shepherd) Rex, "and sure as hell, *I'm* not going to do it again."

Sharon regarded TJ. Her initial briefing had been scattered, some hard intelligence, some good background, but with notable holes in the "PERSONAL INFO" seg. Why hadn't she known this fact about the King? A data clerk filtering items which seemed unbelievable or myth? What else was missing? TJ Shepherd had surmounted the two ridges and crossed the bottomless chasm between? Impossible . . . yet no one here had taken issue with his claim. The shuttle pilot had shown her the ridges from above. Both ridges circled the globe from pole to pole, even emerging higher than the ocean surface in places, and neatly divided this continent in half. At the time she'd thought the ridges and the immense canyon between them so forbidding that not even a professional hillary from the Planet of Mountains could surmount either. The shuttle pilot had told her: "You could shave yourself on some of that lava." Still not satisfied, she asked, "The ocean?"

"Sure," the King responded, grinning. "If somehow you could make your way almost to the pole, then fight a continuing blizzard in storm seas and then cross the Cut. The Cut is where two oceans meet. From stories handed down, it is not a Sunday School picnic. That's to the north. Legend has it that the south is the same; however, no one has been that way to confirm it in generations. Otherwise, to get over the ridges, you need your airship. Or else climb them," he added, a slight challenge in his voice.

No thanks, she thought. "We'll see," she said.

Again, he seemed to read her mind. "Should you desire to try—as many others have—I'll point the right way, and then you simply follow the bones until they run out. Then you're on your own."

Sharon tried to suppress a shiver, but knew what he had said so bluntly was true. The man was just stating fact, solid fact, and had no real need to drag the old male-dominance business out. No, he was definitely protecting or hiding something.

The Queen said, "Thomas, I think we should get on with this."

"That we shall. In fact, I'm canceling the rest of this meeting." He looked a challenge at Sharon but she held her expression in check. "Miz Gold can brief each department chief separately when she interviews them," he continued. "And, Miz Gold, all the ministers and department chiefs have been instructed to cooperate fully and provide any information you request. Nothing is to be withheld." He reinforced this statement with a royal glare around the room.

Sure, TJ, thought Sharon. I might be young but I ain't dumb. As he continued instructing his ministers, Sharon couldn't help but wonder about him. Were the rumors about the King's affairs—liaisons?—true? If so, it didn't jibe with his background nor the social and Roman Catholic background of the planet. Bear Ridge had been settled, mostly, by dissatisfied United Statesers, French Canadians, Amerind, Mexish, and Mexind. If there were any discontinuity in the society of Bear Ridge, it was her job to ferret it out for investigation. Many planets had changed during the Rollback. Like most of the rest, Bear Ridge, not being self-supporting at the time, was stuck on its own. Machinery wore out and humanity reverted to basics. An old story. And Bear Ridge had had a more difficult time reclimbing the ladder of human advancement: the weather on the planet was unfathomable. Only in certain areas, such as the alluvial valley around Crimson Sapphire, could the weather be counted on. And then, at times, it was disastrous. Sharon was amazed by the progress of humanity on the planet of Bear Ridge.

The King was still talking, giving her a short history of the planet. Why? His ministers already knew it and her briefing was at least well prepared in that area. He was now talking about the recent separation of Church and state and Sharon detected a sour grimace from the Chief Padre. But it reminded her of the changes TJ Shepherd had made since he had united the planet with his governance. He'd changed the face of the monarchy. Oh, it was still a one-man rule, dependent on his whims; yet it appeared to be more streamlined, more efficient, and most important, breaking free of rule by petty nobility.

". . . after the Consolidation Wars, we divided the planet into provinces run by governors, or Ethnarchs. This leaves the governing to professionals and the nobles go about their business as farmers, industrialists, land owners, whatever." And, Sharon knew, it was a well policed planet. This King had an answer for every problem: the dreaded taxman. She remembered well the fate of the ecological group this morning. The Revenue Service Extension consisted of quiet, businesslike men and women who enforced the King's laws and directives, not by force, but by fear. It saved a lot of money on standing armies, though there was one of the latter. The King was beginning to speak to the individual functions of each department, and he'd passed right by the Revenue Service (once known as Ancillary Revenue Service Extension, she recalled, until the King had tired of the joke).

"Your Majesty," she interrupted, "I would like to hear about the Revenue Service in depth."

The King frowned. "Hell with it. Everybody is dismissed. Reginald, you stay."

The man with the scars and eyepatch nodded. The Queen Mother looked relieved and marched out, followed by the Queen and the rest of the ministers. Soon Sharon was alone with the Taxman, the Prince and the King—and the jester in the corner.

The Prince sprawled in his chair and looked the King a challenge.

"All right, Ambassador, what do you want to know?" The King's voice was all business.

"How? What? Why?" She had to tear herself away from the undercurrents here.

"Reginald?" the King prompted.

"Madam," Reginald said with a deep voice, face failing to react to any of his own words, "when the King consolidated the planet, there had been many kingdoms, many citystates, many feudal holdings, so there was very much needed a source of funds; something other than the royal coffers from which to pay for governmental services. Thus came into being the Revenue Service Extension. The word Extension is there to show that it is indeed a part of the King's planetary government." He tried to smile and failed.

Sharon knew that the RSE also served the King as a secret police function, one so insidious and effective he needed no other.

"Our job," continued Reginald sounding like an accountant reciting a well rehearsed lecture, "is to provide funds for the operation of the Royal and provincial governments."

Prince Michale snorted.

The King favored his son with a glare. "You see, Sharon, after Consolidation, I gave up most of my recently won and already held income-producing property and thus cannot support, personally or royally, the necessary functions of government. I still have a few farms, a mine or two, and interest in a few paltry commercial ventures. These I've kept for the security of my family and they aren't sufficient for the vast payroll."

So she was Sharon now?

Reginald was drawing an organizational chart: offices in each province reporting to him at the palace and he in turn reporting to the King. She noted that the Ethnarchs had no control over the tax agencies. "And the tax courts work independently also, with the King as the final arbiter, if necessary."

An org chart? On a planet with swords and crossbows? Next thing you know, they'll be trotting out their "Management By Objectives." If they got MBOs, God help 'em.

All right, she had stalled long enough to make them uncomfortable. Play a card and see what happens. "And that is all?"

She saw the King knew immediately what her point was. Michale nodded enthusiastically. Reginald eased his eye patch.

"Miz Gold," the King became formal again, "you must understand this is a monarchy. Instead of using the traditional spies and secret police and military to insure my word is carried out, we do it more subtly. Instead of imprisoning nonviolent offenders, we merely insure their cooperation by taxing the hell out of them. We even tax cities and ethnarchies. For instance, should a city not comply with a new sanitation code, the taxes start to rise until those standards are met. It works wonders."

"If those standards are still not met?" she asked.

The King waved a hand, dismissing the problem. "We change officials. At any rate, once people began to realize we meant business, an amazing transformation occurred: the standard of living on Bear Ridge rose, the taxes dropped, and there was little trouble with people following royal decrees."

Sure, sure, Sharon interpreted. A group shows a trend toward disloyalty, and its taxes rise until they can't afford them, then they're disbanded and jailed for nonpayment. She'd seen it this morning with that fellow Valdez. On the other hand, she had to admit, it was an effective system. Much better than public hangings and medieval oppression. Yet, it was a system that could explode. "Your Majesty, perhaps it would be better if I went ahead with my interviews and research?"

"Certainly. You need but to say it, and whatever you require shall be provided."

"Sure," said Prince Michale.

Sure, thought Sharon simultaneously.

4: TJ

TJ was bored. He would rather review troops or do anything military than this.

The throne room was three-quarters full. Petitioners gathered in one group to be brought forward by the herald. As this was an open session, those with complaints against local officials, ethnarchs, or tax courts stood waiting. TJ looked at the jester.

Delancy Camp, the jester, squatted momentarily at the foot of the stairs to the throne. Other than the King, none of the royal family were present. TJ groaned as the pace of petitioners slowed even more. It was the jester's job to be present when the King appeared in public, at any occasion: meetings (staff, ministerial, military), at group meals, during military formations and maneuvers, and all court sessions.

Camp was a well-muscled man given to eating thousands of extra calories daily to counter the physical effort spent.

His favorite quick energy producer was a chocolate wine, a secret recipe from his home town of Lonestar in the Ethnarchy of Bexar. Strange, TJ thought, Kellen Sing also came from Lonestar. When TJ asked, Camp replied he had been gone from the town for too many years, since he was a younster not even into his teens, and so hadn't recalled a child named Kellen. Or the family Sing.

A new petitioner came forward, and the herald, reading from a paper, introduced him. The herald glanced distastefully at Camp. TJ grinned, knowing the jester's rest period had ended. After all, he had a job to do.

He sprang about in the open space in front of the King. To one side stood the petitioners and other claimants; to the other stood the general public who wished to view the proceedings, friends of the petitioners, and other interested parties, such as students observing.

Camp stopped, folded lightly backward onto his hands, and began hand-walking along the edge of the crowd. TJ watched as the herald completed the formalities. A few women lurched backward when they realized the jester could see too much—those with taste enough to wear short dresses, TJ amended. But that wasn't Camp's purpose. From his vantage point he could see more than one would think. Weapons concealed from head-height might be visible to him. Muscles bulged and his bulky pantaloons threatened to rip at the crotch from his scissoring legs.

By now all were so used to his presence they failed to see him.

An ex-attorney was complaining to TJ about a prostitute.

"Prostitutes are honest and hard working," pointed out the King. "Lawyers are not. What have you to say about that?"

"Well, Your Majesty, I . . ."

The jester bounced away. Almost weekly some ex-lawyer would come to court to complain about the King's royal proclamation outlawing the profession. It used to be daily, but those were in the good old days. Before he had decided to try for the Fed Council seat.

"What?" the King demanded.

"Sire, people need protection, advice, procedural expertise."

"From other attorneys, you mean." TJ's voice had taken on a threatening tone, but this ex-attorney did not know it.

"But, Sire . . ."

"But nothing. You and your cronies almost wrecked this planet. Royal decrees, laws, provincial regulations are now written so that any normal person can understand them—and are not written by lawyers. Let me tell you one thing, mister." TJ was off on his favorite subject. "You know Bear Ridge was settled by North Americans. You know why? I'll tell you why. The North American economy went to hell. So the smart ones left. So-called experts messed it up. Just a bunch of honest attorneys tying up every system, from their own legal system to the economy, unions, the military. Just great. The Japanese ruled the economic world. Why? There were fewer than twenty thousand attorneys in Japan at the time, and over a million attorneys in North America. That tell you anything?"

"But, Sire . . ."

"Appeal denied," the King said, "and a fine to you, one hundred Shepherd unit coins, or the equivalent, to the orphanage fund of your ethnarchy." He glanced at the herald. "See to it." He'd conveniently ignored pointing out that lawyers somehow manage to turn into legislators and constitution-writers; besides making money, what lawyers like to do most is tell people what to do and how to do it.

TJ sighed. Wouldn't they ever learn? Make a legal nuisance of yourself and lose your case, you pay heavy. Nowadays, most people were certain of themselves and their cases before they petitioned the King.

The man had not moved.

"Out," said the King.

As the man hesitated, two Gyrenes moved forward and he sullenly turned and stalked off.

"Who's next?" asked the King.

This time the jester didn't rest between petitioners. In a whirl, he cartwheeled across the floor and partway up the open center aisle.

A woman had stepped out of the crowd at the herald's signal and was walking down the center lane.

As she reached the front line of spectators, the jester spun past her rudely, and his feet, swinging high, intercepted an object flying over her shoulder.

The knife clattered against a ridged column and fell within an arm's length of the King.

The jester continued his cartwheel and slammed into a bearded man. The man tried to turn and flee, but somehow got tangled up with the jester. Before anyone could realize what had happened, two Gyrenes leaped into the fray.

The jester picked himself up ruefully and bounded to the King's side. Other palace guards immediately surrounded them. The crowd found its voice and started with a buzz and ended with a conglomeration of voices and queries. The Gyrenes dragged off the assailant.

"Silence," commanded the King. The hall fell immediately quiet, yet an air of expectancy remained. "Get on with business," the King told the herald.

And the jester began tumbling around the room again.

After the court session, the King stood in an outer chamber to his suite of offices talking to the herald and his administrative assistant. "Any new NOPEs?"

The entire palace knew the King's fondness for buzz words. NOPE was an acronym for "number one problem entity," meaning immediate problems. So what if it was a cutesy acronym? He'd changed ARSE, for Ancillary Revenue Service Extension, to RSE, hadn't he?

"No, sire," said the herald's exec.

"Then leave us, I have paperwork to do."

"Yes, Sire," Alfred the herald glanced at Camp with more respect than usual. Both knew what "paperwork" meant. The King only signed. He almost never read. Of course, the last time a mistake had been made and the King had signed the order unknowingly was perhaps two years ago. And those responsible were still guarding isolated mountain passes against nonexistent enemies—or were they the ones cleaning latrines for the palace guard? Regardless, administrative efficiency was always at its peak in TJ's palace.

"Let's go into my office," said the King.

As they entered, Camp said, "Sure, boss."

"Thanks," said the King, acknowledging Camp's swift action in the throne room.

"It was my job." Camp closed the door behind him and then collapsed on a leather couch. The King pulled a bottle from a plain cabinet and poured two wide-mouthed glasses almost full. He took one over to Delancy Camp and handed it to him.

"Any speculation as to who or why?" TJ took a long drink.

Camp gulped his sour mash and shook his head. "A possible. But I'll wager the commandant will arrive within

ten minutes with all the information wrung out of the
assassin—but I doubt we'll learn anything of substance."

"So do I. Probably a disgruntled fellow lawyer."

"Or an opponent of joining the Fed," said Delancy Camp
pointedly.

"Summer, it's come to that, has it?" With his strange
sense of humor, the King was wont to refer to Delancy as
"Summer, my aide de camp."

"TJ, it's gonna get a hell of a lot worse." He drained his
glass and rose to refill it.

"I shan't turn back. Goddamn, Summer, indoor plumbing, real doctors and medicine, ground and air travel? Give
that up? Hell, no."

Camp shrugged. "It's your life. Go ahead and throw it
away."

"Measured against those benefits, my life is nothing."

"Look, TJ, you pulled this planet together and up almost
single-handedly. You hold it together now by the mere force
of your presence and personality. There is much to measure
your life against."

The King rubbed his forehead with his left hand. "You do
not say the words, Summer; you imply Prince Michale is not
yet capable of donning the robes of power."

"Of filling your shoes, TJ. He is a difficult one to figure,"
he added diplomatically.

"Damn it, I know that."

"It was in my thoughts, *Your Majesty,* to punch the button on that secret transponder and have one Jean-Claude
Laffitte Fitzroy pay us a visit. A few protective devices
only."

"A million Fed credits worth of gold just to turn on a red
light in a starship?"

Camp handed the King a refilled glass. "There are relay
satellites throughout occupied space. He would receive the
summons almost immediately. Or as fast as a ship could
travel the distance—as I understand it. And the cost would
be more than the million. The million is just to have Fitzroy
show up here in response to our call. The merchandise
would also be prohibitively expensive. Where else could we
buy it? Without political connections, smuggling doesn't pay
in the long run. Except in death from the Federation Navy."

"Too expensive," said TJ. And damned the Federation
system that kept Bear Ridge isolated until tested, passed
and accepted into the Fed.

"You can afford it. Have Reginald skim a little more off the top. Or put an extra shift on that secret gold mine. We've got enough condemned prisoners stored up."

"The idea is distasteful to me."

"So is dying, boss."

"Your point. We'll see."

"You don't want to push that button and call Fitzroy because you're afraid the Fed might detect the smuggler's ship and thus jeopardize your chance at the Council seat, no?"

"The thought had crossed my mind. Break their foolish rules and we are quarantined for ten years and our entry into the Fed postponed for at least that long." The King slumped into his high back chair behind a cluttered desk. He propped his feet on a clear space. Camp leaned back on the couch's arm rest and set his glass on his chest.

"We ought to retire," the King continued. "I'm getting too old for these games. And you aren't getting any younger either, Summer. Why don't you find a nice girl and settle down on your lands? I'll draft someone else for this job."

"Hell, TJ."

"Yeah, I know. Me, too. And thanks. But you can be commandant, or chief of staff, High Minister, I'll think of something. You've already got a couple of thousand hectares of prime grape lands. I'll stack a few titles on and make it official."

"If I ever find a nice girl, I'll think about it. And I ain't so old either, a mere decade less than you!"

"Yes, but you've packed a lot into those years."

"Had a ball, too. And I somehow have the notion that we ain't done raising hell yet either."

TJ grinned.

"When are you going to let me in on. . . ?" Camp began.

A knock came to the closed door. Instantly, Camp drained his glass, tossed it under the couch, plucked three rubber balls from his pocket, scurried to a corner, crouched, and began to juggle.

TJ picked up a quill and said, "Enter."

General Manuel Vero, commandant of the Gyrenes, came in and saluted. "Sire, the prisoner has been interrogated." He stood stiffly at attention, almost muscle bound. His accoutrements glittered, his sword swung loosely at his side. The only decoration he wore was the insignia of the Muster.

"At ease, Manny. Nobody here but us chickens," said the King.

Camp rose and retrieved his glass from under the couch. "Want one, Manny?"

"No thanks, Camp. *I'm* on duty." To the King, he said, "My resignation, Sire. At your convenience."

"Your men cannot be everywhere within the crowd. Nor," TJ held up his hand to stop Vero's protest, "can we strip search everyone who attends an open court session. What did you find out?"

"The blade was poisoned, Sire."

"And?"

"The assassin said he was hired at night by someone in thick robes using an obviously disguised voice. Also, the man had no real future: he was free on bail awaiting a hearing for murder. Conviction was certain. So he traded his life for enough money to support his family for many years."

"Could be a plot," observed Camp.

"On your way out, Manny," TJ said, "tell the herald to find out what idiot judge allowed bail for a murder suspect, have him fire her, and the usual—slap her in prison for five years and award her property and possessions to the victim relief fund of whatever ethnarchy that is. I'll sign the papers when he has them prepared—which will be immediately. What happened to the prisoner?"

Vero shrugged. "There was only one quick way to determine if the dagger actually had poison on it."

"Good. That is all."

After the general had left, TJ said, "If I'm now a target, how about my possible successor? How is the Prince's training coming along?"

"TJ, I'm tired and my diplomacy is gone. Want it straight?"

"Yes," the King said, already knowing the answer.

"Academics, fine. He will never be a quality swordsman of our class. But he does have an eye. A bowman he might make. Part of the reason he can't refine his swordsmanship may be his balance. His toes have grown that skin between them again. Do either your or Gwen's families have a history of attached toes?" TJ shook his head. Summer shrugged. "Strange. Maybe we can have your surgeon cut the skin one more time." TJ looked sour and Summer shrugged again, obviously not wanting to pursue that line of thought. He continued, "Yet I do not know whether Michale will kill or not, for that is the final test. I'll tell you right now, he doesn't have the thirst for blood that some have." He glanced at TJ.

"Some of *us* do have that problem, do we not?"

Camp grinned. "At any rate, he hasn't had to come up the hard way."

"I couldn't very well make a slave of him, Summer. My mother and Gwen had a great deal to do with his upbringing. Too much."

"You could spend more time with him, TJ."

"He'd rather compose poetry and read and study than attend me at my duties. I cannot let him ignore his education."

"Hell, boss. *I* would rather read and study than attend you, but I don't. And there are more ways to receive an education than from instructors and books." Summer paused. "And Mike will have to make the Trek one of these days."

TJ bowed his head. "I know," he whispered.

"If he's not prepared and killing tough, the Trek will kill him," Summer said.

"Yes."

"Unless he chooses to challenge the system and not take the Trek." Summer's voice was soft.

TJ whipped his head up, shaking off the possible shame. "No!" he shouted, slamming his fist onto the desk and scattering papers. "He shall take the Trek when it is time. He would not shame the family."

TJ knew Summer had accomplished his purpose: he'd gotten the King's attention focused onto the matter.

Damn, TJ thought. What happened to the child I raised so carefully? The child who almost died before life was realized? The child whom I nursed in the broadest sense, sending the governesses and maids off when Gwen was still ill and colic and sickness raged within him? The child who used to lie in his wrap and smile up at my beard? The child whom I treated with a proper amount of discipline as he grew, binding him to Gwen first and myself second; but more importantly, instilling in him the welfare of the kingdom, the welfare of Bear Ridge. Whatever happened to *that* child? Where did he go wrong? Or was it just me who went wrong? Had not other influences warped his character? Aye, did I not raise him to be a warrior prince? What happened to the bond to me? Certainly, he thinks for himself and does not have to echo me.

But. But why is he the way he is?

5: A:ALPHA

Face up, they lay staring through perfectly round eyes; occasionally, membranes flicked. Two body lengths of ocean flowed above them. A human-introduced dolphin swam leisurely past and A:alpha caressed her gently. O:chacka smiled and spoke to the dolphin. They exchanged thoughts and good wishes and the dolphin lazily spun away. A pup tagged along behind her, echoing her every movement.

A:alpha's fin-foot flipped randomly to keep him abreast of O:chacka as they encountered far off-shore currents.

/Would it please you if I roiled the surface with a T'storm? The practice would aid me,/ said A:alpha.

/No. Sunlight filtered is fine for the moment,/ replied O:chacka.

They communicated as they had with the dolphin: an inborn ability to interpret sounds, movements, body position, aura waves, and intent—a conglomeration of all the senses, save taste underwater. Scent was important both in the water and out. On land, long distance communication was accomplished by a complex series of auras and whistles.

/Dolphins please me,/ said A:alpha.

/'Tis a fact, young one, 'tis a fact. A noble human experiment to bring such here. Yet there is regret within me that dolphins are not as we, for they are primarily carnivores./

/Some are changing . . ./ replied A:alpha.

/Affirm. But 'tis a long process. Yet, time we possess. Though: is it proper?/

/It is not natural to them, no, I think,/ said A:alpha. /However, it is not natural for them to reside in these oceans, alien to them./

/Well thought, my young friend,/ O:chacka said. /'Twas the humans who introduced them here. From that point natural forces had their ways. Who knows what shall come of it all?

/I do not understand these humans,/ A:alpha said.

/'Tis not simple, that is granted,/ replied O:chacka. /As

42

you are a revered young one, 'tis my duty to aid in your instructions, your inhalation of life and knowledge; yet at times, there come things and situations not easily grasped. I still study the matter myself./

A:alpha snatched a string of kelp and sucked it in through his intake organ. /That humans are here—does this fact not presuppose a technology or life-style that should grow, much as our growth has been along different paths?/

/Affirm./

/Then why is it not so?/ asked A:alpha. /Especially considering their life-basis is similar to ours, else this planet would not support them./

/Thinkers attribute it,/ said O:chacka slowly as if considering a deep philosophical question, /to some inborn racial trait. The human species is a strange one. They appear to progress in leaps forward and jumps backward./

/I do not understand,/ said A:alpha after some study. Applying historical and cultural perspective to an alien race was difficult.

/'Tis not an easy task, granted; nor do many of us understand, and of those, not all comprehend fully. It merits the long-term study, the intent of which I sense from your aura./ O:chacka stretched the webs between his many toes in reflex and continued. /'Tis a worthy life-goal./

/Perhaps the humans themselves can tell us why, why they act so . . . so contradictory to nature, why they treat each other the way they do,/ said A:alpha, not willing to drop the discussion yet.

/'Tis a thought which has been acted on. Upon his visit many years ago, the current Trekmaster, my stone-mate, was queried and his answer was not satisfying to us, more enigmatic than specific. Though, it will be admitted, he was no great philosopher or academician. To balance, though, he had a consuming drive, unusual for a human, for it burned inside of him and his aura fairly danced with undirected energy./

/What did he say, learned one?/

/Perhaps it was a riddle? I know not. His answer was simple. "Who knows?" he said. "Maybe we don't get along. Or maybe common sense ain't so fuckin' common, and you can quote me on that." Those were his exact words and worthy of study in cultural context. He followed with, "Maybe we just don't like each other." More enigma. There is a school of thought that the human mystery is coded within their genes, a racial trait that has been augmented by circumstance and environment rather than submerged by nature for the good of their race./ He rolled in a mass of drifting weed.

A:alpha retuned his hearing more accurately to compensate.

/So far, the Trekmaster has justified our efforts in him,/ O:chacka finished.

/What humans do on this planet could have an altering effect on our lives,/ A:alpha said, knowing that was the tip of his life-goal. Finally, a starting-point.

/From your aura, I sense you might consider that effect adverse,/ said O:chacka. /Does adversity necessarily follow from what we know?/

/Most probably./

/Yet not a definite conclusion. Additionally, this conclusion depends on the point of view of the one doing the considering,/ said O:chacka.

Thinking, A:alpha noted the warning. There were no requirements for objectivity. On the other web, if he could not understand the human past, how could he extrapolate a future? He said as much to O:chacka.

/Point is well taken, young one. For now, we have no *acceptable* answers./

/This does not bode well for us,/ said A:alpha.

/Aye. We live within our environment and ecosystem. There is no requirement to change this to provide food or shelter. Aesthetics aside, of course. Yet we see already the alarming growth rate of humanity. Many years of war, now their population has doubled. And with this current Trekmaster in control, there promises to be more humans and more expansion. Room enough? Sufficient now on this globe . . ./

/And in the future?/ A:alpha prompted.

/For a while./

/Action should be taken,/ A:alpha stated.

/Ah, the impetuosity and impatience of youth. The rock-certainty./ O:chacka's aura colored to indulgent.

/Perhaps I shall be the one to accomplish the honor./

/An honor?/ asked O:chacka.

/The possibilities include that permutation./

/Not highly, young one./

/Nevertheless, it shall befall my lot./

/In what manner?/

/This I know not yet. However, I have learned to study before taking action./

/You shall be a wise old one, young one. To learn is to conquer. Knowledge to become the end in itself./

/Knowledge can also be a bridge,/ mused A:alpha. /Perhaps therein lies the problem. Knowledge can lead to understanding and thus preclude the necessity for action./

/You swim a long way to reach a short goal in your words, young one. But what you say is true. On the other web, action could become desirable should we wish to avoid the onslaught of humanity. And that, young one, is what we face. And sooner than it would seem. To quote again the current Trekmaster, "If you don't want to know the answer, don't ask the question."/

They floated over a chasm and spiraled down until the sunlight no longer illuminated their surroundings. A:alpha always found the absolute dark restful, the silence mind-expanding.

From below, a pinpoint glow floated straight up at them, gaining in speed as it ascended.

/A flash worm,/ said O:chacka.

Soon they could see the length of the creature. It was one of their body lengths long. And it glowed the entire surface of its body. A:alpha knew that humans feared this electrical killer.

/He shall try us before reaching the surface to recharge,/ said O:chacka.

/It would seem so, though I would hope not./

The flash worm accelerated and, when near, sent out an expanding flash that rippled through the water at them.

At the last moment, A:alpha tightened his aura, ballooned it, and deflected the charge. The resultant clash of the two forces enveloped the flash worm and it reacted by going into convulsions, curling within itself, and floating off into the depths.

/Why did you not act, learned one? I abhor violence and your aura is more powerful./

/'Tis obvious, A:alpha. I accomplished my duty. Perhaps you have learned something this day./

6: TJ

"You don't tell me how to rule and I won't tell you how to write poetry," TJ said. Doesn't matter anyway, he thought ruefully; poetry doesn't have to rhyme any more. Don't even think it, he told himself, don't ruin the academia you have so carefully built. Just because some scholars had poisoned his son's mind, he shouldn't think seriously about interfering with the university system he was so proud of. Prince Michale stood beside him watching the executioner take the hood off his battle axe. "The hell with that poetry and book learning anyway. Your education ought to be about the fine art of war and politics, of economics and leadership." He'd wanted so badly a warrior-prince for a son.

"Taking a life is your idea of leadership?" Michale demanded.

"Son, you're going to rule, you've got to be willing to make decisions, big and little. Life or death." That's one reason he'd instituted the system whereby the monarch must approve a death sentence, must determine method of execution, and must be present during the execution. He'd insisted this day that Mick accompany him.

Michale looked at him with disgust. TJ noted that the last body had been dragged off. He'd decreed slow-hanging for that one, a repeat offender who had done an S and M rape/murder. The execution due was another murderer who had killed quickly and cleanly—thus his own death would be merciful and in the twinkling of an axe.

The King and the Prince stood facing the platform where the executions were accomplished, in a flat area on the side of the palace, within eyesight of the city of Crimson Sapphire and facing out on the amaranth grain fields that covered the alluvial plain. The public was invited. TJ felt that if his executions were public, they would have both warning value to others who would rape and murder, and also they might vicariously give some the taste of death so that they

46

would not have to murder for their own gratification. TJ knew there were some who killed for pleasure. Not for money, sex, power, jealousy, or revenge, the good, old fashioned values you were supposed to kill for.

A struggling man, short and thin, was brought up the stairs to the platform. Two guards wrestled him to his knees and locked him in the wooden mechanism which held him bent over a block, neck bared to the axeman.

The executioner shouldered his axe and walked to the edge of the platform. "Shall I carry out my duty, Sire?"

TJ nodded curtly. "Carry out your duty, executioner." He noted Mick's intake of breath and slight tremble. He paid no attention. The axeman wasted no time, and strode swiftly and silently to the front of the blindfolded man. His axe went high, paused, and sliced down. The only sound was a solid "thunk" as the blade cut into the timber. The killer's head barely twitched, and rolled over on its side, an ear crumpling beneath it. TJ noted Mick blanch again. This was the third execution in a row. You'd think the kid would get used to death by now. "Just goes to show you," he mused, thinking of an old saying, "you gonna run with the big dogs, you got to expect to get some of them big fleas."

Michale shot a look of pure horror at him. TJ saw Summer Camp squatting next to him trying to keep a straight face.

"How can you be so callous?" Mick demanded.

"A learned trait," he replied. "Leadership isn't only being the host of royal dances and poetry contests."

"Next," came the executioner's formal voice. A woman, kicking and struggling, appeared at the stairs. A gag muffled her screams. Her eyes were wild.

"Sire," the herald, Alfred, spoke from his position at the foot of the stairs, "a plea for mercy has been lodged."

"What was her crime?" TJ replied, knowing full well what her crime and those of all the others were.

"Murder of her child by neglect and abuse," the herald fairly shouted—as he had been instructed to.

"Who asks for mercy in her behalf?" TJ said.

"Her mother."

"What is the method of her execution?"

"You determined slow-hanging at the hearing, Sire."

There were a few things on which TJ would never change his attitude, like barracks thieves in the army, and child abusers and rapists. This woman's child had been consistently beaten and not sufficiently nourished. For once, TJ was glad he hadn't seen the body (he ordinarily wished he could view the crime victim to reinforce his decisions).

He spoke loudly, voice grim. "Appeal denied, method of execution changed," he said, and paused. The hundreds of people present would expect him to change to a more humane execution. "Method of execution changed from slow-hanging to starvation and thirst. Lock her up. No water, no food. In four days, see that she has a dull knife in her cell with her." There. He'd done it. A new form of capital punishment. One that fit the crime, too.

Camp looked startled. "The Fed," he whispered, "Sharon Gold."

Michale spoke, not hiding his anger. "Yes, what about that, father?"

TJ spoke low. "They aren't interested in individuals. They want to know about systems, cultures, governments. If they work, and how. Effectiveness is the key."

"Barbarity is the key," Michale said.

"Justice," spoke TJ, his voice fraught with warning. "Perhaps we won't have any more child abuse, no?"

"Thought you would have considered the envoy, boss," said Camp. "Had to make sure."

"May I leave now?" Michale asked.

"No, Mick, you stay." Michale preferred to be called Mike. Maybe you can't raise a son this way, TJ told himself. But he had gotten his experience the hard way, learned by bleeding and watching men die. Was that right for Michale, though? Had his own experiences of twenty bloody years perverted his outlook on life? On justice? Had he lost his concern for his fellow man? Was he too callous? And, Summer had a point. Changing the method of execution on a woman was a calculated risk. On the one hand, Sharon Gold might not notice—though he doubted that. But the hell with that, there were certain principles he would not sacrifice or compromise even for Fed entry. On the other hand, it was possible that the Fed would approve of his strong reprisals against criminals. (And, he hoped, any possible rebels within his kingdom would take equal note of his swift and deadly justice.) He wanted the strongest deterrent to crime and threats to his rule he could devise.

On the third hand, he wanted Michale to realize that being King meant hard decisions. It was time Mick learned what it was all about. Hell of a way to learn. That woman would pay a terrible price just so his son could learn a lesson. Maybe some day in the future this lesson would make a difference.

Guards led the silent woman away. But her body reflected her fear with an uncontrolled trembling and moisture stained the rags she wore.

Clouds obscured the sun and TJ glanced up. He hoped it would rain. There was something amusing about blood washing off the platform and thinning out until it colored the rivulets among the spectators. That would really be effective crowd participation. A quick wind blew those thick clouds off. Never knew what to expect from the weather, he reflected. Looking at the fields that fed off from the palace, he knew that heavy rains would turn the alluvial plain to a quagmire. That was one of the reasons he intended to build his spaceport right there—should he have the opportunity.

Another woman appeared between two soldiers at the foot of the stairs to the platform. She was scarred about the neck and had only one arm. He felt Michale tense.

"God," whispered Michale. "Not this. I am leaving."

Casually, TJ linked his arm with Michale's and closed it with an iron grip. Michale gave him a startled glance and after a brief but unsuccessful tug to remove his arm, said, "I'll stay."

In the crowd below them, TJ saw Kellen Sing, the thumb drummer, watching him and Michale.

The woman shook loose her captors and climbed the stairs unaided. A brave one. Briefly he considered commuting the death sentence, but, observing her bearing, he knew that life imprisonment would be more cruel than the axe. To the executioner's question, he said, "Carry out your duty." The woman was too handy with poisons, anyway.

Prince Michale started away from whatever he was thinking with the thud of the axe. Would he never learn? TJ wondered if other monarchs had the same problems with their offspring? Or was it all fathers?

7: THE OTHER KING

"One kilogram!"

"My price, I say again, is one kilogram . . . Majesty," said the renegade captain.

"One kilogram is many months' production," said Tirano. This goddamn pervert was robbing him. A kilogram of Tirano's Dust for this smuggler's services? Ridiculous.

"That is your problem, Majesty. Have you alternatives?" Shawn appeared undisturbed. Little did he know of the anger of Tirano—not enough to realize his life was in danger. But Tirano needed Shawn. And the stakes were enormous. So, Tirano knew he'd have to pay the one kilogram.

Another bird flew by in the private audience chamber and Shawn slapped at it.

"Do not!" Tirano commanded.

Shawn shook his head. "Mites," he said, as if he couldn't believe it. By weight, the most valuable commodity ever known to humanity. Tirano knew that Shawn was thinking the question, why? Why Two Tongues? Why the Birdking and Two Tongues of any planet in all the Federation and associated planets not yet admitted? Tirano snorted. He cared not for the wonder of this homofreak. But he couldn't be choosy. He needed Shawn.

The bird flew past again and Shawn merely ducked his head. Three other birds were free within the room, but only this one was airborne. The special species. The only organism that would support the valuable, but parasitic, mites. The dark gray bird settled on his perch. The two men were alone in this room of the sprawling, ranch-style summer palace of a ten-thousand-square-kilometer plantation.

Tirano began the obligatory lecture he'd given so many times before. "Birds. Mites at the feather root. Picked from the bird by hand or a miniature suction tool. Then frozen. Processed by a special manner I am not at liberty to discuss. All hard, dirty, time consuming labor. And the bird must be kept alive." He paused. "Think you that you ask too much now?" Tirano liked to sell high and buy low, and Shawn wanted to trade too little of his ships' time for too much of Tirano's Dust.

"The price remains one kilogram, Majesty."

Tirano was short and obese. To many, he knew he appeared the jolly king and he did nothing to dissuade this reputation. But to those who knew him intimately, he was short tempered, harsh, quick to judge. The antithesis of his outward appearance. Nor did he attempt to change this lesser known image. Tirano was clean shaven and his hair fell in a bowl-trimmed mop, which, by decree, no other could sport. He saw Shawn's eyes drop to his legs again. For once, Tirano regretted shaving his legs. This sexoff queen couldn't keep his eyes off them. "I must study on this."

"You provide the men, I provide the transports," Shawn said. "And I require sufficient lead time to assemble crews and find legitimate reasons to gather that many transports."

Tirano glared at him. "Not all at one place and one destination?"

"I am more subtle than that. I will get them from different ports on different worlds, ostensibly to bring mined materials from some distant asteroids." He waved a hand. "That's really no problem. The point remains that it shall take time."

"One kilogram of mite dust will make you a wealthy man." Tirano couldn't hide the sneer in his voice.

"And insure *you* are no less wealthy yourself, Majesty."

Tirano knew he could afford it. Was not wealth one reason why he and Two Tongues were technologically superior to that dolt Shepherd and Bear Ridge? An old folk remedy found during the Rollback on Two Tongues. And now, specially treated, the only genuine non-synthesizable aphrodisiac, organic or inorganic, in the scope of human existence.

Shawn interrupted his thoughts. "What have you got against this fellow, the one over there on Bear Ridge?"

"He is a fool and a childbrain."

"Doesn't seem to me sufficient reason to mount an invasion," Shawn observed, scratching through his jump suit.

Tirano remembered the instant enmity between Shepherd and himself. They'd argued and fought from the beginning. First at the conference on Bear Ridge, gaining intensity at the sector capital years later. Then he had thought himself free from Shepherd until it was his turn to sponsor the conference; the Federation had flown Shepherd to Two Tongues and the animosity exploded. Tirano thought that he'd had the last laugh by humiliating Shepherd when he could, but after the conference and Shepherd had left, Tirano discovered the miserable bastard had placed a laxative candy in his palace bird feed supply. It had taken weeks of investigation to figure that one out and rectify the problem. Weeks of birds which could not be caged and were used to the run of the palace actually having the runs all over the palace. The mess! Guano, slippery and runny, everywhere.

"The bird-shit episode doesn't qualify as important enough for revenge to invade another planet," chuckled Shawn.

"Does the entire universe know of my humiliation?"

"Laughs are hard to come by," Shawn said evasively and looked again at Tirano's legs.

But Tirano knew that Shawn knew the bird guano incident wasn't enough to cause an invasion. An illegal invasion. Fleetingly, Tirano thought of the long-legged, lithe-limbed, star-eyed beauty named Gwendlyon. Then he thought of her in bed with that animal Shepherd. She could have been mine, he thought. He had been younger and thinner then. It had all been arranged with her father. Gwen had caught his eye during the conference on Bear Ridge. He made a quick agreement with Gwen's father and all was set. Until an upstart young king of Bear Ridge's largest kingdom had taken a notion in his head to unite the planet. Shepherd was a scheming conniver, always sneaking about, planning some mischief, grabbing what he wanted. Grabbing, always grabbing. No flair, no subtlety. Always driving for something. Well, Tirano thought, he'd take a page from Shepherd's book. Talk about audacity. They'd never expect this move; and especially since Two Tongues had the upper hand in the race for admission to the one vacant Federation Council seat.

He'd planned this for years. The timing had to be precise. He'd present the Federation with a fait accompli; and, by their own foolish rules, they would have to admit Two Tongues and give him the Council seat. But there was a weak point in his plans: in transit. His troops would be vulnerable and his plans could fail should the Fed discover the illicit freighters transporting an army to a neighboring planet. After they arrived, and the ships were gone, there was nothing the Fed could do. The cunning manner in which

he alone pulled off the coup would be a high recommendation to those political asses on the Council. And then his
power would be amplified. No longer would he have to fret
over the loyalty of his kingdom, his planet, his people.

Of course, he already had the under-the-table support of
several on the Council; money goes a long way—and with it,
power. Those on the Council smart enough to realize his
worth secretly backed him. In fact, one had dispatched this
distasteful man Shawn. He scarcely wanted to admit to
himself one more reason for his invasion of Bear Ridge. It
was a castro. When you're in charge and have problems,
blame your social ills on some outside agency. Redirect
attention elsewhere and thus submerge internal problems in
a larger, more significant action. When he became *emperor*
of both planets, he could play one off against the other.
After, he amended, he looted Bear Ridge. He knew of
Shepherd's secret gold mine. That would become his.

"You have highly placed agents to insure . . ." Shawn
was saying.

"I said I have an agent or agents, and I did not say how
placed," Tirano corrected. No one save himself knew of the
spy. One who was disenchanted with Shepherd. They communicated in code by clandestine comm sets, two of which
his wealth had bought, and were hidden well, unknown to
the Fed. The whole invasion hinged on timing and the agent
was the crux of the matter. Two Tongues had already been
reviewed by a Federation envoy, thus Tirano knew precisely
what procedures were required of the applicant being reviewed. And this knowledge he would use. He stroked a
bird which landed on his shoulder. "Ah, TJ, count your
days."

"Majesty?"

"Nothing. Get your ships, Shawn. My general will brief
you on the requirements before your departure. And have
caution. Do not let the Fed observe your ship, or else . . ."

"It's my ass, too," Shawn said.

"Your political connections, they'll save you, Shawn."

"I doubt they could."

"A kilogram of mite dust should buy a lot of Federation
bureaucrats."

Shawn shrugged.

Tirano briefly worried that Shawn would discover that a
Federation envoy was currently on Bear Ridge observing
and evaluating. Further complications could arise. He'd have

to neutralize the envoy or at least remove the envoy's comm
gear. Yes, a little sabotage was in order—not too early, just
at the right time. On the other hand, suppose something
bad happened to the envoy? Like death, for instance. Would
not the Federation hold Shepherd responsible? A point
worth considering. Along with the removal of Shepherd
himself. Decapitate the Dragon of Bear Ridge and the planet
was his. Tirano shuddered when he remembered Shepherd
carried the Muster medallion. He had to admit that Shepherd was one fighting son of a bitch.

And if Shepherd were dead, then Gwendlyon would be a
widow. Tirano found he still wanted her. After all these
years. She could remain queen, and help him consolidate
power—almost a coup d'etat rather than an invasion. No
matter what other promises had been made.

But Thomas Jefferson Shepherd had to die.

Maybe he wouldn't marry Gwendlyon, maybe he'd just
use her; humiliate her for turning him down against her
father's wishes.

Tirano looked at Shawn, the politically connected, sexoff,
renegade captain. Was Shawn really a renegade? Or was he
merely acting a role? Could someone at the Federation or
on the Council be playing his own game for his own ends,
using Tirano? Possibly. It bore close watching. Even though
the plan was his own conception, someone could be using it.
It was a tricky situation since the Fed had express regulations against member planets and their people having any
contact with non-member planets. Only Fed controlled occasions, such as necessary conferences, were the exceptions.
No, he was protected by the Federation itself, and no one
planet was strong enough to challenge those odds. Of course,
there were factions among the Council members and there
could be power plays, but the Council performed its function so well that none had any intentions of changing the
Council system at all. Which was one reason why so many
rediscovered planets tried so hard to gain membership.
"Shawn?"

The captain jumped upright.

"Your terms are accepted. Half on loading of the ships,
half on arrival on Bear Ridge."

"How do I know you'll pay the latter half?"

"You want guarantees? Captain, we do not wish to walk
home. It would be distasteful."

"Logical, Majesty. I agree."

Hah! thought Tirano. Those troops will remain as an occupation force. And after Bear Ridge is under my control, the Fed Council seat will automatically fall to me. Fortunate that Bear Ridge and Two Tongues are the final competing applicants. Thus, as a Council member, I can command my own transport. So Shawn is out. "And, Shawn?"

Shawn shifted nervously. "Sir?"

"Let *me* explain about treachery. The mite dust is carried in a glass container. In the center of that container rests another container filled with acid. There is a button on the side connecting to a spring-loaded plunger. Touch the button and the acid is released. The dust destroyed. Fear not, for it is a common method of shipment, effectively safeguarding the material."

"I see."

"One other thing, Shawn. I also have friends at the sector capital and at Federation Central. Betrayal signs your death warrant. If you so intend, think seriously, for you are now a dead man breathing my air."

Tirano knew his reputation would assure Shawn ran scared. And it might send a message to Shawn's contact on the Council—should there be trickery afoot.

8: TJ

The surgeon's lance struck and TJ felt immediate relief. TJ lay back on the couch in his office and sighed. The royal surgeon, Nora Ahimsa, drained the infection into a bowl. TJ's left foot was bare and propped over the arm rest of the couch. Nora sat on a stool ministering to his foot.

"Formal occasions," TJ grunted. "So formal boots, not comfortable, everyday, well-worn, loyal, easy boots. No. Got to have *formal* boots to wear with formal uniforms and formal court garb. Well, formal boots lead to formal blisters."

"Had you not ignored the problem, it would not have developed into this bad an infection," Nora Ahimsa said. "Why, the military doctors would pull the lowest soldier off duty for the same." She was only a few years younger than

TJ, but showed her wear. Her hair was red and full, and her complexion wan.

TJ noted the tone of reproof in her voice and ignored it. She poured a disinfectant over his heel and TJ winced. Damn foot really hurt, he suddenly realized. He started to laugh aloud, but remembered his audience. He was about to say that every king ought to have a foot infection to remind him of his humanity.

Nora lifted the needle again and caressed his foot almost lovingly with a swab. TJ averted his eyes. He glared at Alfred, the herald, and General Manuel Vero, commandant of the palace guard—and thus highest ranking military officer in the kingdom. The two stood casually in front of him. The jester rested quietly in his corner.

"I'm about decided," TJ said, "to raise some hell. Stir the pot. Maybe the rats and roaches will jump ship, who knows?" Nora cut gingerly about his infection with a razor-like tool. TJ glanced at her and looked away uncomfortably. "Anyway, I can't have people keep trying to kill me. I just won't have it. Somebody's behind these attempts, and I shall find who it is. Your reaction, Alfred?"

"What do you mean 'stir the pot,' Sire?"

"Raise hell with somebody. Point fingers to watch reactions."

The herald fidgeted. "Uh, Sire, I, as is my wont, recommend subtlety, caution. I have people looking for the answers quietly."

"You do? Ah, I expected no less. Where are they looking?"

"In the city, at the palace."

"Specific targets?" TJ asked.

"The nobility," said the herald.

"Ah, the disenfranchised. Good. Any other formal organizations?"

"No, Sire."

"How about the priesthood?"

"I did not think that within my purview," said Alfred.

Like hell you didn't, TJ thought. And he knew that Alfred knew that he knew. He shook his head and smiled at the herald. "Any results?"

"None."

"Figgers." Nora's fingers seemed to caress his foot again, and he felt the old attraction returning. He remembered those fingers, those sensuous instruments. God, he'd like to bury his fist in her hair again and pull her head back and

. . . pain slammed his foot and ran along his leg. "Agh. Pour me some wine."

The herald did so.

"General Vero," TJ's eyes rested on him, "you are strangely silent. What is your opinion?"

"My opinion, Your Majesty, is that when you start asking questions, your mind is already made up. You merely seek confirmation of what you are going to do anyway."

"Humpf," muttered TJ. Manny Vero said that? Unlike him. He didn't want to admit, thinking about it, that Manny was right. Nora drained more pus and dabbed at the wound with another swab. "Alfred, find out who made those 'formal' boots and double their business taxes." He knew Alfred would ignore the comment. "Opinions," he demanded. "Who should be the prime suspect. Manny?"

"The nobility, Sire." TJ knew Vero didn't like the nobility since his family had suffered at their hands in the past.

"Alfred?"

"The same, Sire. Most likely candidates. Money, motive, position, ability to do it, but . . ."

"But what?" TJ knew all were skirting the other possibilities. Nobody wanted to come right out and accuse the Church of complicity in attempted murder of the monarch.

The herald hesitated. "There are other groups who are not enamored of your rule. Geographically removed people whom you subjugated during the Consolidation wars. Disenchanted groups that have allegedly suffered from your rule, such as lawyers, some educators, traders in human flesh, people whose friends and relatives died as a result of your commands."

TJ thought that Alfred was excessively diplomatic today. He'd said everything but "the priesthood." "Don't mealymouth, Hark," he told the herald. "Say what you think."

"Certainly, Sire," the herald smiled. "There is a relatively new 'interest' group about nowadays. Young people. What with the emphasis on education, they are now thrown together, and since they are not out earning a living, they have time. Along with the time, they have some new-found freedoms. They are groping at this time, but have the possibility of organizing."

"That's obvious, Alfred. I knew that. Why do you bring it up now?" Nora was applying ointment to his heel and he felt the immediate soothing relief. Gently, she began wrapping a light bandage around his foot.

"Frankly, Sire, it's gone further than I intimated. This boy, Kellen Sing . . ."

"The thumb drummer?"

"Yes, Sire. He is slowly making a name for himself. His music gives him crowds. The crowds give him an audience. Other students are beginning to gather around his banner."

"You talking about the kid that I rewarded for that fine performance in court?"

"Yes, Sire."

"Well, I'll be damned."

Nora slipped a sock over his foot. "Wear this instead of your boots for a day or two. Do I need to tell you the other instructions?"

"No. Thank you, Nora. I'll stay off my feet." She nodded and left as he glared up at Vero and Alfred. "And when I'm well, I shall go and find who is trying to kill me." He had already disregarded Kellen Sing as a likely candidate. "Everybody's excused," he said suddenly.

The general and the herald left.

When the door had closed, TJ finished his wine with a gulp, leaned back and closed his eyes.

Summer Camp stood, and looked at TJ's sock covered foot. "You'd think the Trekmaster who conquered the mountains of Teddy Bear Ridge and Big Bear Ridge on foot and Bear Ridge the planet also on foot and horseback, could ignore a little boil on his foot and do his job as king."

"Infected wound," TJ corrected.

"And the legend grows?" said Camp.

"Take the rest of the day off, Summer."

9: THE PRINCE

Where was it? Part of the Trekmaster Log was missing.

Only this day had his father authorized Prince Michale to read the Log. Probably because he felt mortal nowadays, Michale thought. He'd always thought his father invincible, but now? He felt guilty because his realization that the King was mortal did not change his opinion of his father, the

Royal Ass. The pomp*ass* braggart who knew everything. (Always saying, "I understand you, Mick, hell, I was young once myself, you know.") God, Michale thought, if I've heard that once, I've heard it ten times a day. And Mick. Why can't father say Mike like everyone else? Does even a name have to be tough to meet his satisfaction?

His eyes returned to the tattered parchment. He'd never suspected the existence of the Trekmaster Log. But here it was: continuity of Crimson Sapphire since . . . since when? Since its establishment? It showed how this part of Bear Ridge began its disorderly progression from isolated spots of humanity surviving only, to modern times. And from a peculiar perspective. The Log also explained specifically some history he'd learned in academics. And it included information not generally known—and a flavor he'd not expected.

Michale sat in the security of his parents' suite, in their comfortable and private sitting room. His eyes skimmed back over what he'd read.

The first pages were brittle, written on beaten bark, the words fading, some illegible. A few pages had been traced over with newer ink, others copied on fresher paper where one Trekmaster or another had striven to maintain the continuity of the document. As time and pages progressed, the quality of paper improved. Apparently, one individual, a certain Joshua Jones, had gone on a quest for some obscure reason (a woman's urging?). As time went on and the humans of Bear Ridge began to regain some of their lost heritage, others followed in Jones' footsteps. Thousands. Only a few of these questers survived. Sometimes two generations went by without any quester returning alive.

Michale did not understand all he'd read, nor did he understand how the Trek became the prime criterion—besides royal blood—for a man to grasp the reins of royalty—and nowadays, the kingship. His eyes returned to the page. He realized he'd been staring at a weapons display on the wall. One which, because of a disagreement between his parents, alternated every month with local art.

"It was a bear of a ridge, I thought," wrote Joshua Jones. "Until I surmounted the damned thing and there, in the distance across this enormous gorge, was another ridge. This one dwarfed the one I'd somehow managed to climb. Almost then did I turn back. But *she* had challenged me and they had ostracized me and I required to accomplish some feat, so on went I. When, after many days, I reached the bottom of the gorge from descending the first ridge, I saw one of those creatures the old folks tell stories about. Tall they were, weird feet with webs and things on them. Faces long with a passingly alien mouth which looked like it was made for straining spinach with and I tell you when they whistled at me (there were two of Them) I turned right around and climbed that ridge fastern I went down it."

Michale scanned excerpts.

—from Chief Mathiew Bearpaw:

I write not well for it was a difficult thing which to learn and my teachers cared not to teach when there was no food in the lodges. But this man Joshua Jones and his people who we chased from this land bid me on his deathpad to continue with learning and with maintaining of this book. Some of the others of my tribe had heard that over the ridge—Bear Ridge, Jones had called it—was much food. For the drout had crapped onto this grate plain and we discussing moving our lodges again toward the west and the coast where it is said that crops grow better and the hunting too is better. The shadow of Bear Ridge looms large upon the land, seems like a mysterious malady, bringing wrath upon us and our people. Lone George claims he seen one of the creatures Jones talked about here lately and I shall clamber the ridge to see if there is food and meat animals before we move the many kilometers or miles I can never keep them straight with baggage and women and children and lodges to the west to look for better hunting grounds.

The sharp lava had cut my feet through the hide sandals, and I feared I would lose the left foot. Nor did I make it to the bottom of the gorge as Jones had done. An encounter with a killer snarv took my left eye. I saw no food and I could not go any farther so I returned and we moved our long-time encampment.

—from Commandante Walter Hernadez Fernando Coronado:

Yep, we run them injuns off and took this fine farm land. Some little distance from the west coast, but upon a fine plain of its own. Protected on two sides by mountains with a river running between them across our plain. My servant, old Bearpaw, tells tales of strange creatures which we've heard was our legacy from the Before Time when our ancestores flew here from the stars and earthe and all, not real interesting if you got to go out and slaughter a sheepalo for evening chow and all, but what the hell, I got Bearpaw for that work, don't I? Anyway, Bearpaw's a good old boy and him and me we get along fine, he's almost convinced me to goto see myself for the adventure. He acts like it's something he's gotta do before he ups and dies, but I am tired of working the fields and making other people work them fields so I just might take him up on it.

. . . so together, me and Bearpaw made it up the *second* ridge. I'll tell you, hadn't it been for Bearpaw, may he rest in peace, I'd of never made it half that far, but I couldn't very well let a injun do something that I couldn't do, could I?? That there gorge—a real devil's dip—was full of snarves, and so was about the first third of the big ridge. The second third of the big ridge was strange vapors, killing vapors, some of which burned eternally flames. No single one man could have lived through that alone. Bear Ridge grows some tough hombres, but . . . Anyway, the third tier was hell on weather. Stuff I din't really understand. But on we went and Christ it was cold as the cellars of hell. Bearpaw was like a man driven by hordes of deevils. Atop Big Bear Ridge, there was this flat place, see? Wind blowing like God was awailing. !But the view! On the other side of the big ridge, what land!! Looked like you could drop seeds on the ground and they'd grow right there without no supervision or any of that farming crap. But clouds and weather moved in 'tween and couldn't see no more.

. . . damn near frozen when we sat to rest it was so high a altitude and Bearpaw, he just stood there and here came these whistles and Bearpaw dropped the vine ropes he was reweaving and ran to them and I never saw him again. Frightening apparitions, the devil's work. Fat, like inflated sheepalo bladders. Strangest thing I ever seen. I started to follow but they was all gone quick, the two of Them and old Bearpaw, who I'd really got to like even if he was a injun and all. Would of liked to see them better.

. . . one of Them had dropped this stone, see? It was blue with red fire in it and seemed to dance about . . . or was it red with blue fire dancing? It seemed to change so often, you coun't really tell . . .

—from Chief Mathiew Mohammed Bearpaw II:

My grandfather had called from the dreamworld and I knew what I had to do. First we hunters gathered and provided food for our people for weeks then we burned their crops and scared them off and out of our land. This old mexican man made me take this book and read it. He said I'd know what to do with it. And then I read it and was amazed and had to retrace some of the writings to see 'em, will add pages later it is so interesting.

. . . on this day I go out to find my grandfather. Or his spirit.

. . . never did find him, but there was this gem, just like old Coronado had and we had buried with him for it was our and his customs, and the people thought that it was okay since maybe it contained his spirit and nobody wanted to cart around another man's spirit and all.

. . . though the snarv had almost disembowled me, I found this stream and the minnows ate most of the maggots out that I hadn't ate and I healed well enough . . . never did understand, for I sensed them around me when I lay unconscious and almost dying. It could have been them for I crossed the first ridge with the help of God and in Devil's Dip that damn snarv got me—and then I woke and found myself back on *this* the human side of the ridges . . . grandfather Bearpaw's spirit?????

—from Alyouishes Longstreet:

I was the only one who climbed the mother of the mountain, and they'll probably try again next year when the season is right, but knowing what I do, none of those wimpish limp-dicks will ever return, you gotta be tough, and I mean mean.

—from Sir Lance Phillips:

. . . of my brothers, I saw nothing after I surpast them in the climbing. Doubtless, their bones add to the soil on the ridges or in the gorge. And the stone? Well and fine it was, almost a gift and I had nothing to give in return, but he seemed, if it was a he, a right fine fellow. And you know? I sort of understood what he was telling me, though the grunts and motions and whistles and sniffs he seemed to be using to communicate were certainly out of my experience. But I felt good about our companionship, you know? Too bad there ain't a lot of them poor indians left, maybe they coulda helped explain. His eyes, like some fish, capable of seeing 2 ways at once. Do their minds register 2 pictures? He . . . (Note: remainder of this section obliterated with black substance which could have been blood. Francisco Shepherd)

—from Mark Trevan:

. . . so my father, the King, dispatched all his children—

save the girls—and whoever came back first would be King after him. But we had to have proof and obviously the proof is in the gem.

. . . would have made it too, goddamn their tough hides. Damn sister hadn't beaten me to it. Amazing Grace had disobeyed father. Maybe old Aygee had talked or communicated better with them, those strange ones, weather was horrible, poor sister, and she fell down on this side of Teddy Bear ridge and broke her neck. I buried her there, and took her gem, for I was certain father wouldn't want a girl to take over the kingdom, which he renamed for the stone I then carried to Crimson Sapphire. And I was correct, he believed I had made the Trek, which I had, and I told the truth. After all, I could have lied, could I not?

. . . and both my sons, the twins, returned alive, too, which was unusual since I had not completed the Trek myself and knew what it was like? Now I am pressed with making a decision about a successor before I allow them to write in this here log?

—from Francisco Shepherd:

Forced out of the mountains, we migrated to Crimson Sapphire, and brought our books with us. The joint rule of the twins had torn the kingdom asunder and there were no further entries in the Log. I, the youngest son, had worked my way up in the army for a while and, then discovering my book learning (for did not our family religiously maintain secret and sacred tomes for our children?) the generals took me as an advisor. In that capacity, I was able to locate more written word. My position became quite secure. Because of the fine army, we had no competitors within our territory now—but the twins were ruining the kingdom with their bickering. The generals asked me for a solution and did not like my answer. Learning? Education? These qualifications for the Kingship? Not hardly, they replied. These were fine fighting men and understood only the sword and bow and tactics. I could, at least, applaud their loyalty to Crimson Sapphire in not overthrowing the twins. For they were smart men and saw the example of what had happened to the twins. The Trek book interested them and they were intelligent enough to choose from royal blood or at least blood of nobility for continuity of the crown. Unfortunately, by that time, I was a nobleman, and when the plan was announced, my son determined to go.

Though I am not a Trekmaster myself, I make these

entries in the interest of both history and continuity since the twins failed to carry out their responsibilities in these pages.

My son, I am now proud to say, stole off in the dead of the night.

Along with the sons of many other noblemen, he crossed the great plain. He climbed T. Bear Ridge, fought his way through the gorge called Devil's Dip, surmounted Big Bear Ridge and spoke with the mysterious inhabitants. His account follows.

—from Thornton Shepherd:

It was the mountain training my father gave me which gifted me with the techniques and abilities to climb the ridges. Out of many, I alone survived. And talked to the people, or whatever they are, over there. And they gave me a stone, this thing the kingdom was named after. They seemed to actually understand me. And I got some of the concepts they expressed. One day, I would return for study and leisure to communicate further. My observations of the Webbines are attached on separate sheets. (NOT FOUND: perhaps my father was updating these pages when he passed on? Solomon Shepherd)

But going back there may be a bit difficult for there are other kingdoms now encroaching upon my territory and I must prepare the army and make arrangements. Fools. Civilization is returning, and so must wars? I have heard that all over this vast continent, at least on this west side of the great divide provided by the two Bear ridges, that other towns and villages are growing and joining, becoming feudal kingdoms of which I've read from books of Olde Earthe. I foresee that these next years shall be trying to our people. Fortunate that we've built a fine kingdom, a strong people, and common goals. (Save those pesky priests.) Personal tragedy aside, I still look at the stone, the badge of office won, and become calm again and am able to plan. I see that the future holds much, and should be accounted for in any actions I take as King.

—from Solomon Shepherd:

. . . but my father insisted, else the people and particularly the army would not follow me. I used the landmarks he told me of: the spire atop Teddy Bear ridge called The Finger of God, and the peak dwarfing Big Bear ridge, seen by few men only. (INSERT NOTE: this latter peak has since been named Forty-K. TJ Shepherd) And when I returned with my stone, he was dead in battle. How could I forgive myself for not being there? Only Felicia could console me. Now I understand. I face the same problem my ancestors did: I must commit my sons, one of which I hope will master the Trek as I did. But so many have died making the Trek. Should I not consider ordering it ended? My advisors counsel against it. Not knowing what to do, I asked one of my sons, Thomas Jefferson, for his opinion. "Opinions are like assholes, father," he told me. "Everybody's got one. Yet it seems to me that there is value within the doing," he said enigmatically, and I saw this was true. Did not taking the Trek make me a better, more understanding man? Perhaps. But to balance this off with the death of one's fine sons? TJ seemed to have a grasp of man's inner nature. But the hordes press in upon us and our isolated little kingdom. And TJ is a fine warrior already—those in the army who personally know him idolize him. He is one of them more than one of us, the royalty. Thinking upon it, I realize that TJ recognized the value of the Trek, not just in personal terms to those who have conquered it, but in importance to the people of Crimson Sapphire. We are the most stable and strongest community that I am aware of now. And for that reason, and our natural wealth of tillable soil, others clamor on our borders. The entire continent is seething with battle. Armies and raiders are all about and it takes much of our energy and production to maintain safe borders. It is draining us. Unfortunately, this is giving the Church new life; that entity is resurging in importance, political importance. They want to return to the days of church domination. Hang infidels, nonbelievers, and blasphemers (being "Jerked for Jesus" they call it, an old SowestAm tradition, they claim). What with the external threats to the integrity of Crimson Sapphire (I'm beginning to sound like an officious monarch, part of the bureaucracy—TJ will fix that when I see him next. If.), I believe the crown is temporarily safe from the priesthood for they need warriors to protect the kingdom they wish to manage.

—from Felicia Shepherd:

My husband, the King Solomon Shepherd Rex, died in battle before he completed his obligatory entries. Currently, the army suffers my rule, for is there another option in this time of crisis?

It saddened me to send my three young sons across the plains to the mountains and chilling ridges to those strange peoples whom I read about in these pages. Odds are against any returning. But the eldest, Thomas, shows promise. Stonewall Jackson has a slim chance. But the youngest, Theodore Roosevelt, though the most agile of the three, is not sufficiently cunning, I fear, to complete the Trek. What will I do should none live through it? Am I up to handling the crown? But my money is on Thomas. The rogue. Many young ladies about Crimson Sapphire will miss his presence, even though he was most of the time with the troops and fighting. Even as a child, he was a fighter. Tossed off pneumonia and other illness. Frankly, he was a hardheaded little rascal whom I called Rowdy. The other two? Fine sons, aye, that they were. (Were? A mother knows.) I sent them off with nary a tear. They took my heart with them; for you see, I knew I'd never see them again. Is this a job for a mother? To bear sons to die? But go they did, for the kingdom my husband was trying to save, and for our heritage. I had no choice. The more I write, the more confident I become that Thomas shall return. I shall have one son left to me. (Should The Good Lord be Willing and Give Blessings.) Thomas is a natural leader of men and an expert swordsman. Expert with almost any weapon. Though he does not seem to be growing into a philosopher-king like the other Shepherds, he is worth reckoning. Our land needs men, leaders and fighters and builders like Thomas. It can do without a philosopher-king for a generation or two.

I find I ramble. There are matters of the realm to attend to.

Respectfully signed and submitted, Felicia Shepherd, Queen Regent.

Addendum: The men from the stars have arrived. Thank God they landed on our countryside, and not that of some others. Oh, I do so wish Thomas would return from the Trek. FS.

Mike knew that after his father had finished the Trek, he had conquered the planet of Bear Ridge. That simple—ignoring the twenty or so years it took. Possibly the richest entry was not here in the log: that of Thomas Jefferson Shepherd. He was irritated and relieved at the same time. Relieved so that he would not have to read how tough things had been for his father and thus have to empathize some with the old bastard. And irritated because he wanted to know what the King had gone through. How did his father complete the Trek? Did he go only to the top of the first ridge? Or did he continue and cross the gorge and climb the second ridge and reach the home of those mysterious inhabitants? Mike felt somehow cheated.

"Michale?"

Visions of ridges, volcanic remains, monstrous jigsaws of ruined terrain, snarves, ice, burning gas, bleeding fingers, dead Trekkers, and mysterious inhabitants faded. He looked up sharply. "Mother. Hello."

Gwen had come into the sitting room. "Your grandmother's entries always fascinate me," she said, "more from what she doesn't write in them than what she logs."

"After all, she is a Shepherd," Michale said and immediately regretted his caustic tongue. He saw that his mother understood. "Where is father's book? His pages?"

Gwen shrugged. "He is still working on them."

"Naaah," Mike stretched the sound out. "It's been many years, mother. And one as fond of administrative matters as he is would not fail to accomplish so sacred a duty."

"Michale, sometimes I think you are part volv the way your tongue flickers and hisses."

"Mmm sorree," he mimicked himself when he was a child.

She smiled at the memory. "I'll tell you about the Trek— what little I know."

He looked questioningly at her.

"Yes, he does not confide totally in me."

Mike snorted.

She ignored. "Your father was the first one, the first Trekmaster—they were called Trekkers while doing it—to reach the Webbines' Home Ground. Except perhaps the first Bearpaw, and nobody will likely ever know what happened to him. TJ actually spent some time there at their Home Ground, communicating, talking, or whatever they do. He doesn't feel right in putting his thoughts about the episode and all the data he learned on paper yet."

"God, wouldn't Sharon Gold just rape him for that information . . . oops, sorry, mother but you know what I mean." He felt a compulsion to cross the ridges himself and meet with the mysterious inhabitants, the Webbines. But he wasn't ready to make the Trek. "Perhaps it is a foolish custom, mother. Grown men dying for the sake of a throne? A throne which may be much diminished in importance soon should we gain entry into the Federation."

Her voice took on a strained tone. "The Federation will leave us alone. Planetary matters are internal, and there will be no interference. At least that's the way I understand it. Sharon Gold said that's why they still use the archaic term 'Federation.' "

"And if Sharon Gold doesn't recommend us for the Council seat, then what?"

"It is all academic then," she answered.

"Mother, I don't think I like the idea of a high percentage chance of dying in order to become King."

"I've told you," she almost shouted at him, "the Trek is custom. It will be honored."

Mike saw the strained look on her face and understood for the first time. She didn't want him to go on the Trek either. But she had no choice. She was more bound than he was by custom and tradition.

She slumped to a stool and her shoulders dropped. "What do you want me to say?" she demanded.

Michale's resentment grew. He could not stop himself. "So, one day, TJ Shepherd is going to turn me loose with a bunch of his illegitimate children he calls 'kinglets' to make some insane trek and probably get killed?" Instantly, he wished he could have said it differently. He knew he'd hurt her. "Mother." He shook his head. "That wasn't fair of me. Forgive me, formally, mother. I didn't intend to hurt you. It was foolish of me to say." The subject was an unspoken taboo. Mike knew his father would do anything to insure the continuity of the Shepherd rule and prevent the re-emergence of the nobility as a ruling class.

"Don't you see he had to do it?"

"No," Mike said flatly, still understanding only partly. But he knew it was one of the many crosses she had to carry. After his own birth, she had been unable to have other children. A price she had to pay. One taken from her heart every time her husband fathered another child to insure Shepherd succession to the throne of Crimson Sapphire. A self-sacrificing concept TJ had come up with. Or so he said. Mike knew these things instinctively, and felt closer to his mother than a few minutes before when he was faulting her for his father's shortcomings. At least, he thought ruefully, the crusty old bastard hadn't dumped her like he could have. Could TJ really love her? She must love him, for why else would she put up with him, and his foibles? His profanity, his "official" affairs, his boorishness. Mike felt a pang of jealousy. Always had he fought for his mother's affections. Always had both he and his father put her in the middle of their fighting, their arguing, always relying on her and her wisdom to arbitrate, to keep them together as a family—to maintain the uneasy peace.

"A time of trial, nothing will remain the same."

"What, mother?"

"This Federation business. We've enough problems as it is."

"Have you told father what you think about it?"

"What I think is unimportant. Except about you."

"I know," he grinned suddenly. "What I need to do is find some nice young girl and settle down, right?"

Gwen smiled and nodded—too enthusiastically, Mike thought, but that was understandable.

10: THE GIRL

Rebecca Sing patted her burro on the rump and urged it forward. The beefaloe herd parted at her entry and she began singing, singing to soothe the unruly beasts. She pulled the lutar off her back and began caressing the strings. She liked the six-stringed lutar better than either of its parents, the fat lute and the thinner guitar. She felt safer among the beefaloe, for the local volves now had juicier targets.

She was tired of traveling and was determined to reach her destination soon; therefore, she had taken this shortcut pointed out to her by several of the Prince's vaqueros. Prince Michale, son of the King, owned these vast lands by right of some obscure hereditary title. More beefaloe than she had thought existed on the entire planet roamed the land. She understood the beefaloe were a strain bred from the sheepaloe to exist in dangerous areas—beefaloe could protect themselves from the rare snarves and packs of volves, where sheepaloe were docile and stupid creatures.

A bull dwarfed her and the burro and pawed the ground in front of her and snorted. He tossed his long horns, showing his displeasure. She continued to sing, low and throaty.

"I'm just as headstrong as you, so you'd best clear the trail," she told the bull as she finished her song.

Strangely, she felt herself smiling. The bull reminded her of the parting scene in Lonestar.

Jon, the smith's son, had thought her his for the taking; in fact, for over a year he had acted in a very possessive manner. And, therefore, none of the other young men would have anything to do with her. Jon's ever-looming presence intimidated them. Though she didn't truly dislike Jon, she found herself resenting him more and more and she felt herself boxed in, freedom somehow denied. He reminded her of the bull. Head down and charge. Overpower. Overwhelm with brute force, personality developed from his strength and large size. He had taken it for granted that they would marry. And she had been ready to marry, but realized Jon wasn't the one. There were some fine and gentle young men in Lonestar worthy of interest—yet none had challenged Jon for time with her. All of which confused her: she did not want to be the object of competition, she did not want a violent man to pay her attention, and yet it would take both to free her from Jon.

"You are leaving?" Jon had asked, bewildered. His thick black hair drooped across his shoulders and his giant left fist seemed to spasm.

"Yes. My brother does not return, now that he is enrolled in that fancy school."

"He does not need you. I do." Jon's voice boomed. Rebecca was surprised. Jon must have seen her determination to leave for he had never admitted to needing her. He wouldn't make a bad husband, she thought wistfully, but she did not want to tote and carry for him. It was just something she didn't want to do, she wasn't purposefully trying to break the mold.

Carefully, she explained that she'd promised her mother on the day she had died that she would care for her younger brother. "I told her I would watch over Kellen until he became a man," she finished. Kellen was now of adult age, but was he a man?

"You are carrying loyalty to a fault," Jon accused.

"No, it is my way. There are no other Sings left, that I am aware of, and I have a sworn duty." She didn't want to argue—he wouldn't understand the real reasons. Such as her yearning for new ideas and places and people. Could that be what affected Kellen? He'd changed so much recently and she hadn't grasped how deep the changes in him were until his absence gave her the distance she'd needed to assess him.

Jon brought her back. "But we are betrothed," he protested, and she thought she detected a trace of guilt in his voice.

"Are we now, Jon? Have we set a date? Have you formally asked me? Have you formally consulted and asked my family?"

"Your family is Kellen and he is in Crimson Sapphire. If he cared in the first place, he would have not left you alone."

Guilt of her own struck. The truth of his words was that she had not been able to control Kellen, not much younger than herself, sufficiently to keep him out of trouble. She even suspected that the Lonestar hierarchy had pushed Kellen into his role as emissary to the King to get rid of him. "Since he has not returned, that very fact probably means that my task in raising him is not yet complete." She was becoming weary.

"Take after your brother, do you not?" he sneered in the rejection. "In addition to his thumb drums and your lutar, you share the same affliction. Peace. Love. Forget yourself and your own needs. Preach the word, whatever the hell that is. Well, I tell you, every man on the planet is out for himself, the King included. And nobody's gonna listen to that crap Kellen spouts. Take what you can get when you can get it. That's the lesson of life. Beefaloe crap."

"Every man, Jon? What about women?" Her voice became dangerously low.

He ignored the warning signals. "Can I bear a child? Are there female padres? Think you to change life?"

"No, Jon, I . . ."

"Can women provide as well as men?"

"Jon, you infuriate me." She had found something on which to hang her anger. "That merely proves my point. Things change. Times change. At least it will be different in Crimson Sapphire."

"Will it?" he asked, obviously trying to keep the anger out of his own voice.

She hoped it would not be like Lonestar. But she was afraid Crimson Sapphire was only a larger, more cosmopolitan version. Her hope hung on a slender thread. The King had appointed only women as criminal judges. Rumor had it that TJ Shepherd had done so because women had more empathy, sympathy, compassion and all the other fancy terms the King chose to apply. But she suspected secretly that since women suffered more from violent crime, the King had chosen to put them on the judicial bench because they would be tougher to sway and mete out harsher judgments. After all, the King had a no-nonsense reputation as a ruler and administrator. She spoke not, for this was an old argument between them, but it had never before become so personal, always simply being hypothetical.

"This leads nowhere," she said, her voice flat.

She saw that he saw she wouldn't change her mind. "Goodbye, then, Rebecca Sing," he said, his voice low and resigned.

"Goodbye, Jon." She knew both could come up with no special words, even though she tried. And, because of this, she realized that her decision was a right one. Until it was proved wrong in Crimson Sapphire. If.

"You shall return?" he asked, sounding as if he were begging.

"I do not know."

"City life in the capital may scare you off."

"I do not frighten easily," she said kindly.

"Yes, yes I know."

And now here she was so very far from home, still determined, but apprehensive at the enormity of what she'd done. Her entire life altered, staked on guesses and speculation and hope. What *was* she doing giving up everything she knew, leaving all her friends and her family's home?

To find Kellen, of course, and yet she knew there was more, more bubbling just under the surface. . . .

The bull beefaloe seemed to catch her somber mood and snorted one last time and stepped aside as if he were a human making way for her.

Through the long grass she rode, a lithe-limbed young woman, blonde hair braided to the middle of her back, blue eyes squinting at the sun judging the time, pert nose not hiding the mouth which always seemed to be hunting a smile with warmth already in place, ready to latch onto the smile.

Was Kellen a fool? Or was she? Both had, she suddenly realized, a compulsion to give of self. She shook her head, she must find Kellen and watch over him, for surely he would land himself in a passel of trouble and not worry or bother about himself, but about others. He needed someone to care for him, someone to protect him from himself.

What would she do when she arrived in Crimson Sapphire? She fingered the gold Shepherd-imprinted coins in her pouch, half of which were legally Kellen's from the sale of their family farm.

She had committed herself. The gold felt heavy.

Suddenly, a whoop shattered the air and shouts, yelps, and whistles erupted across the silent range. A full twenty vaqueros on horseback spilled over a knoll on her right and raced toward her. One man with waxed handlebars splitting his face charged in front of the others.

He changed the angle of his approach, swept off his sombrero, and, as he passed her, leaned out and down and touched his lips to her cheek, a fleeting feeling highlighted by the stiffness of his mustache. It happened so fast that he was past her before the feelings registered.

Then, in a momentary flashback of the scene, Rebecca realized there was no threat.

For the man had worn the symbol of the Muster about his neck. Adopted from either The Finger of God—or the war assegai, no one knew.

She was safe.

The city of Crimson Sapphire was just ahead, off the plains, and on the other side of the forest.

11: TJ

"Forgive me, Padre, for I have sinned."

"You do not even know the meaning of the word." The Chief Padre put ice into his voice.

"Are you plotting against me? Would you take my life?" TJ made his voice just as hard. He fixed Roaland Cruz with a stony glare.

"If it were the Lord's will," Cruz replied evenly.

The admission surprised TJ and made him wonder if he was pursuing a wrong guess. "Is it?"

"I know not." Cruz shrugged.

TJ decided to try a different track. "Have your padres reported anyone confessing to attempting murder or hiring assassins?" He knew Cruz wouldn't answer, but his question established the gravity of the situation to the padre and put an unspoken threat out in the open.

"I could not say so if it were so. And if one did, the father-confessor would not tell it."

Like hell, TJ thought. He knew anything that could be of use to the padrehood would be passed up the line, particularly something of political importance to Cruz.

TJ had tightened his security. He wanted to show a sense of practical concern, one that would make potential and real adversaries think a long time before they challenged him, either openly or as they had been, in secret. He had allowed some of his famous anger to seep through publicly. He scowled about court and was harsh in judgments. At his direction, known criminals were being rounded up about the city and interrogated. He had little hope for success with this, but it was a fine show of royal strength and prerogative. Additionally, it flagged his determination to his enemies.

Padre Roaland Cruz stood before him. Camp slumped in a corner. TJ's guards stood outside the Chief Padre's receiving chambers. TJ had found it more effective to storm into the territory of others rather than order them into his presence at the palace. Not only did it impress people with his power, but showed his impatience and urgency. TJ folded his hands behind him and began pacing. Cruz' chambers were thoughtfully appointed—comfortable but bare. Obviously the Chief Padre did not wish to flaunt any wealth here where he greeted most visitors. Yet TJ knew Cruz had a taste for luxury, fine wines, and thoroughbred horses for breeding and racing. Unlike many of his padres, Cruz had no penchant for women. TJ regretted Cruz' vows of abstinence for it took away one possible handle to the Chief Padre. Even though celibacy was no longer required by the Church, many of the padres still practiced it. TJ looked at the simple cross attached to the wall. Then he glared at Cruz again, trying to make him nervous, silence speaking more than words. Cruz cleared his throat and TJ thought that it was lucky for Cruz that he had to wear those cumbersome brown robes since his legs were like parentheses. His drawn face was thin and clean shaven, topped by the regulation short hair.

"Perhaps, TJ," Cruz said, "there are some zealots who like not what you have done to the Church."

Was Cruz trying to misdirect his attention by admitting the possibility? "A hell of a lot of them," TJ said. "Though, as usual, they pay no attention."

"I've heard that speech before, TJ," Cruz said.

TJ ignored him. "Devil's balls. I conquer the whole planet, for all practical purposes, and you as Chief Padre in Crimson Sapphire inherit that mantle for all Catholics on Bear Ridge. No longer do you lord over one simple kingdom, now you have a whole planet of souls to play with." That is to say, thought TJ, you owe me.

Cruz looked exasperated. "What with all your bureaucratic levels in the ethnarchies and your constant governmental reorganizations, we hardly ever find the right officials to plead our case." He paused and rearranged his robes about his knees. "Also, mind you, that the padrehood in the outer ethnarchies is looked upon as suspiciously as are your bureaucrats. It is not an easy life for my padres when they're considered invaders, carpetbaggers."

TJ ignored this last—it was a recurring argument between them. "Take your case to the people. I will not interfere— but you'd best not interfere with the Muslims or Protestants. You can have all the atheists you can find."

"You, TJ, are you atheist?"

"No."

"You are drifting away . . ."

"Roaland, you know damn well I have no interest in confessing to you or your minions of padres." TJ cursed inwardly, knowing somehow Cruz had gotten them back to their old argument and distracted him from his purpose of coming here. Their discussions almost always ended with Cruz accusing him of killing indiscriminately and TJ shouting that Cruz and his Church had benefitted from the Consolidation wars. He was aware of the lapses in logic on both sides, and suspected Cruz was, too.

"Cut the beefaloe skin, Padre. I would like to know who is trying to kill me. And why. Perhaps some extremist group of padres? Rebels? Who?"

"None," Cruz said as if it were the last word.

"I warn you, Padre . . ."

"Warn me?" Cruz' face tightened and his eyes seemed to expand.

"Not only do I warn you, Padre, I threaten you or any of

your padres should you or they be involved. Also, you can put this in your canons: do not interfere in my plans for entry into the Federation."

Cruz began waving his arms in that specific manner that was noted across the land. Thousands made annual pilgrimages to Crimson Sapphire to attend his services. "Your Majesty, you overstep your bounds. You mind your state business and I shall mind the business of the Lord." He waved his arms, became conscious that he was doing so, and settled his hands on his hips. "The people are under my spiritual charge. *I* do not think the people of Bear Ridge are ready for your coming age. *We* are not ready. And I oppose what you are doing to gain technology and commerce with other planets. I shall oppose you legally where possible; I shall oppose you theologically at every step. The message shall go out to every padre and every flock."

TJ kept his face from reacting. He suspected Cruz had already done what he was promising to do. He found it tricky and dangerous to his rule to crowd the Church too much. Certainly he had the power—but how long would that power last if he simply had his way in everything? No, he had to work within the system, cajoling, tricking, deftly and diplomatically manipulating. Using as little of his royal power as he possibly could. Then Cruz surprised him.

"You intend to place, perhaps one day, a space field out on the plain, do you not? Where the wonderful farming soil is thirty feet deep?"

Taken aback at the change of subject, TJ nodded. "Yes, we can farm elsewhere."

"And where do the whorehouses go?" Cruz demanded. "And the gambling dens? And the moneychangers? And the beggars selling their sisters to the spacemen? Tell me where?"

"We have already got prostitution," TJ said, tone defensive.

"Yes, and for that I cannot dream what terrible punishment God will make your lot for eternity."

"Probably to sit and listen to religious services," TJ snapped.

"Flippant blasphemy." Cruz stabbed his finger at TJ's chest. "Just as naming the Muster medallion after the Finger of God. Placing God's name on a symbol for killing."

"Padre, you . . ." TJ started, then stopped. One of the mysteries of the Muster medallion was what the symbol on it referred to and meant. And TJ was content to allow speculation. For he knew none who suspected the answer would tell it. "Think what you like, Chief Padre." His voice was curt.

"As you will, Highness. You must excuse me, for I have to plan a crusade which just occurred to me."

TJ's eyes glinted. "Do not cross me, Cruz, for here *I* am the supreme authority. I judge that you have just made a threat. And I judge your crusade will be against Fed membership." He held up a large palm. "Do not interrupt me when I speak. For this is the one and only warning. Should you choose to go ahead with your plans, I shall amend the tax laws to include your Churches, their property, and your finances. Take about ten minutes. And the tax rate, since your income is, in effect, unearned, shall be ruinous." TJ found he could barely contain his anger—yet he knew it was wrong. He should have been more diplomatic with Cruz, conned him a little, given some ground for the Chief Padre's support.

Cruz' face expressed disbelief. "You wouldn't dare. It would end in a religious war none of us could afford."

TJ couldn't ignore the unmistaken challenge. "If so, the Church would have many martyrs to consecrate. Do you, Roaland Cruz, wish to be the cause of so many deaths?" Oddly, he recalled a statement from his reading of Earthe history. "Stalin once asked, 'How many divisions has the Pope?' "

Cruz ignored the comment. "I know you, Shepherd, and that you would do . . ."

"What you do not realize, Padre, is that if a religious war breaks out, we shall certainly not obtain the Federation Council seat. And I will have no ambitions left to me, and nothing else to do—save squelch your puny rebellion to ease my anger." He saw that Summer was now standing, body tensed. TJ forced himself to relax.

Cruz said, "Your position is understood, Majesty, and shall be taken under consideration."

TJ couldn't resist a last shot. "Could it be, Padre, that you envison a Church-run world with yourself at the helm?"

"It could be no worse. But that is not my intention."

"Good day then, Padre. Watch your step for there are many pitfalls along the road of power. And I am a mean pitfall." He did not wait for a response, but turned and strode out of the room. The jester scurried to catch up. Down the corridors they went, surrounded by guards and scattering lesser padres and acolytes from their path. TJ wondered how serious Cruz was. Cruz had always been right there at the periphery of the action, a dedicated man certainly, but an opportunist nonetheless. Both of them had always been careful not to overstep themselves, both aware of the no-win situation. Neither would personally win any power struggle regardless of who emerged victorious. Yet TJ had never seen Cruz so angry. He wished he himself had been able to control his temper better. But on the rare occasions he gave in to the impulse, he immediately felt better. It was difficult to be impartial, benign, gracious—kingly.

Outside, he climbed upon his stallion. The black pranced a little on his white-stockinged feet. TJ had found stallions always skittish, yet he must ride the most magnificent to be found. Image sometimes was everything. His guards hurried to catch up. The dozen men clattered on the flagstones to Bearpaw Avenue, a main thoroughfare through the city. Summer Camp rode a splotched mule in his accustomed position at TJ's left side. TJ was right-handed and Camp ambidextrous.

People waved and shouted and smiled. TJ forced himself to change roles and submerged his anger. Actually, he really liked this part of being King. Vanity? he wondered. Maybe. But he still enjoyed the feeling.

"TJ," Summer said in a voice designed to reach the King's ears only, "if you meant to stir the pot, you done it good. You've got one snarv-mad Chief Padre on your hands."

"Did you really think he would admit to being a part of some plot? No. A little prodding here and there and maybe the opposition's plan will be moved up, tried in haste next time. And thus be more vulnerable."

"Slow down a bit," Camp said, kicking his mule in the sides to urge the animal to keep up with the King. His floppy, long-tailed jester's hat blew in the wind and makeup concealed his appearance. "I don't know if these scare tactics will work. If these people, whoever they are, know what they are doing, we won't catch them this way. Especially if it is a deep plot to prevent our entry into the Fed."

"And if we don't find them this way, Summer, we'll know they are professional at least, and that they plan well. Which will be more than we know right now." TJ paused. Wearily, he said, "I fear that it may escalate. Suppose it is not one specific group but a coalition? Then the opposition powerbase would be spread out and thus more difficult to contend."

"Point taken, boss. Here's a big crowd. Smile."

"Got any candy for those kids?"

"In my saddlebags." Summer tossed rock candy to street urchins. Among the candy were coins of small denominations. Originally, he had instigated throwing candy and coins to children as a tactic to get them out of the way so the King's party could travel uninterrupted, but the practice had become custom—and Summer had thus insured that it did not appear to be a gesture of largess from a condescending King.

"In another generation, Summer, those kids will be in school learning how to install showers and work on weather satellites and not be on the street."

"You hope."

"I know." He felt a surge of confidence that wasn't really warranted. But his verbal battle with Cruz had sharpened his perceptions and given him a taste of action, passive though it had been.

"Hopefully your plans will work out."

TJ tugged on the reins to slow his mount. "Summer, you are trying to say something. Say it."

"Sure, boss. If the Chief Padre wasn't a part of a conspiracy against the crown before, he will be now."

"Cruz is smart, full of political savvy," TJ said. "He'd jump at the right opportunity regardless. But he's not going to expose himself, take chances. No, we can yell at each other all day—that won't change things except on the surface. However, we'd better watch him close. And he's not my problem. What I'm worrying about is how to discredit Tirano. That has me worried."

"He's a fool, TJ. He'll sink himself."

"It's not that easy, Summer. Look at it from the Fed's point of view. All things being equal, which would they choose—Bear Ridge or Two Tongues? Tirano and Two Tongues of course."

"Toss-up."

"Good thing *I'm* the King," TJ said. "The Fed can reap profits from Two Tongues we cannot match. That silly little mite dust. As if anybody needs an aphrodisiac. Anyway, the Fed simply slaps a tax on the dust and their budget is balanced for the next Fed fiscal year. They are not politically stupid. Surely they've had their eyes on Two Tongues since they rediscovered this system. We might even have been admitted to consideration just to make the selection of Two Tongues for the Council seat look legitimate and fair. Lord knows they've had plenty of time to evaluate. Why did they send such a young and inexperienced evaluator as Sharon Gold? And certainly they know Tirano and his peculiarities. So they don't care if Tirano is an ass or not, they care about the revenue he can bring and, consequently, the power. That expensive mite dust provides one fine powder base. Ironic isn't it?"

Summer didn't answer.

TJ concentrated on not colliding with Lieutenant Timmons in front of him. "What we need," he thought aloud, "is to come up with something from Bear Ridge that is appealing to the Fed and that would provide a comparable tax base."

"*I* might not be King," Summer said, "but I know there ain't any easy answers. What do we have? Sheepaloe hides? Beefaloe meat? Funny wood for crossbows? Super wool from sheepaloe? Those things don't match with energy weapons and synthetic fabrics."

"It doesn't necessarily have to be a product, Summer."

"Oh?"

"How are we on time?" TJ changed the subject.

"Close."

Ahead of them on Bearpaw Avenue, TJ saw the grandiose building that housed the Forty. Circular, with stone pillars, it sat upon a low hill where it seemed to lord over its surroundings. The Forty was the sitting body of the major nobles left in Crimson Sapphire. And they also spoke, as representatives, for the few remaining nobility outside of the capital city. TJ, as victor in the Consolidation wars, had stripped titles and property from nobles of vanquished countries and city-states who had opposed him. The nobility of Crimson Sapphire had fared better as a result of being on the winning side. And, TJ admitted, it would have been political suicide to eliminate them. But he had been minutely eroding their power on every occasion he could. And had made no nobles, given no titles.

They dismounted and the lieutenant and a squad of the palace guard went ahead to announce his arrival.

TJ, with Summer cavorting at his side, strode confidently up the wide marble stairs and down the corridor to the amphitheater where the nobles had gathered. He had called them into session this morning, allowing time only for notifi-

cation. TJ wanted the Forty off balance for this meeting. As
he entered, he put a scowl on his face and walked purposefully
down a ramp to the center of the large room. The other
squad of soldiers escorted him. The first squad was already
positioned around the upper level. Nobles stood quietly at
their places in a semicircle up the dozen levels of seating. TJ
arrived at the floor of the chamber and his guards split and
turned to face the crowd. TJ walked to the dais in the
center. The current president of the Forty, the Lord Mayor
of Montreal, knelt before him. Montreal was the closest city
to Crimson Sapphire and had been under Shepherd rule
before the Consolidation wars.

TJ paused, looked searchingly at the man at his feet, and
turned to look about the room. He said nothing. After he
judged the pause long enough to establish his dominance,
he indicated the president to rise. TJ did not give the sign
for the Forty to sit.

TJ fixed his gaze on the president's eyes. "Was it you,
Franz?"

The Lord Mayor of Montreal involuntarily stepped back.
TJ's words were the prearranged signal to his guards. The
squad at the top of the room cocked their crossbows. The
squad on the floor facing the nobles pulled their war assegais to the ready position. A little drama TJ had designed.

"No, Your Majesty," Franz said. He was a man of average height, given to wearing conservative dress. Since TJ
had changed the ground rules on the nobility, they had
become more business oriented, more involved in the dealings of their holdings, and thus less the deliberative body.
They still advised the King, yet he seldom sought their
advice. TJ knew his program for the nobility was working—
since they had stopped interfering with government so much
and started directing their own businesses, most of the nobility had become wealthier and their holdings had increased.
TJ was confident that as long as the profits held or rose, he
had effectively severed the nobility's authority and thus
decreased their power. Now he had only to deal with them
as a formality—or as merchants. Franz fidgeted and obviously felt he had to say something. "Does Your Majesty
suspect us of complicity in the assassination attempt?"

"I suspect everybody, Franz, you in particular. Would
you have my throne?"

"No, Sire, I . . ."

"Or would you rather have electricity and aircars—or

own the rights to some new technology?" He scanned the room. "What is it to be, Franz? Make your choice now. Do you want to try for my crown, or do you wish to be one who controls commerce to and from Bear Ridge? I suspect the landholders and industrialists in this room won't be able to count their profits." TJ saw that Franz was shaking off the intimidating effects of the Gyrenes.

"Our position is well known, Majesty, we are with you."

"Is it now?" TJ asked. Franz was obviously smart enough to see through TJ's anger. He continued on the principle of "kick 'em while they're down" and said, "Let the word go out, then, that those who oppose me shall be held to account, and swiftly removed. Their holdings liquidated and given away to middle level management people, holdings broken so that they could never again be identified as once great and large. I don't understand you Forty. There is an emergence of middle-class business people, farmers, men of vision who are growing with the times—and consequently encroaching on your profits. You should be tending business and protecting yourselves from this economic onslaught— not plotting and gabbing like old women here in these outdated rooms. And the only way you are going to beat your rising competition is to beat them under my rules. Keep ahead of competition. Get the new technological franchises. Will you remain here broken men, or will you be in the forefront of expansion? You, you Forty, think long and hard, for there is thin ground underneath you." TJ paused for effect. He knew the simplistic terms he used weren't all that true. The Forty could do away with him and still gain Federation entry. Yet he hammered his point in further. "Opposition, I can and will break. Including you. The only power base you actually retain is an economic one. And that, right now, is insufficient to overthrow me and my family." Abruptly he stopped and, hands on hips, glared around the room from face to face.

He knew what most of them were thinking. They should have thwarted him when they could, before he had consolidated what he had won in battle. They had laughed at his seemingly outrageous governmental reorganizations. They had laughed when he had abolished all previous national boundaries and drew arbitrary lines on maps to establish ethnarchies. And then he had appointed his own men, strangers to those ethnarchies, as province chiefs or ethnarchs. The geographical and demographical arbitrary boundaries, the nobility and former rulers had learned to their displeasure, totally changed the land. Different peoples were thrown together. Ethnic groups, religious groups, geographical groups all found themselves mixed economically and politically. Thus none could agree sufficiently with each other to form formal opposition to the King and his reorganization. Previous neighbor nations found themselves split in many ways, joined obscenely with portions of others which all managed to completely dissolve any regional loyalties. And with the new organization and the dreaded taxmen, TJ knew he had the odds designed in his favor. In the short few years since, he had insured against returning to the old ways.

TJ knew that they, the smart ones, were aware that this was his most devious and complete triumph. "Franz, you might think about retiring and letting your sons take over." Summer cartwheeled for emphasis. "I will have no opposition. And I will have the name of the one who hired the assassin. My wrath will descend on any group I think had a part in the plot. Pass the word."

"It shall be done, Majesty."

"Another thing." TJ changed the timbre of his voice to a more conversational tone. "This woman, the Federation envoy. I've told everyone involved to be completely open with her. Tell her anything she wants to know."

"Yes, Sire."

"Do so with temperance. For instance, she need not know about your dialogue here today." He scratched under his beard. "Nor of any skeletons buried. Nor of any opposition to our proposed Federation membership. Is that understood?"

TJ heard no dissenting voices—as he expected. Most of the nobles present would protect what little power and authority they retained. Undercutting them and their authority was neatly done, he admitted. Yet, the possibility that a disgruntled faction threatened him still existed. Some must wish to return to the old days before Consolidation, others simply wanted more power. TJ knew that historically the nobility had gradually taken over from monarchies and then succumbed themselves to emerging merchant classes. TJ had simply accelerated the process. But he held power for himself, always scheming to prevent any group from making him either a figurehead or unnecessary at all. A hidden reason he had so designed the confusing bureaucratic organization was to protect himself and the crown. He had built the system so that one-man rule was necessary. He did not fear a planet-wide revolt as the memories of the long Consolidation wars still lingered. And his changes came just slow enough to keep from causing unrest and trouble, and fast enough to keep his potential enemies off balance.

That is until the plunge for entrance into the Federation.

The people did not seem to dislike his rule either. For the moment they were safer since there was no war. Taxes were less, crime was down—a fairness doctrine seemed to rule the world. A sharp move, he thought, to appoint only women as criminal judges. Not only for the publicized reasons that women were more suited to the job and harsher on criminals and softer on victims, but the big plus for him was that the move endeared him to over fifty percent of the population. The smart ones had figured it out, but what could they do? It had become an acclaimed stroke of genius and enhanced his reputation. And further solidified his position. And, he grinned to himself, it worked. Women were proving to be better judges.

"So be it," he said calmly and walked up the ramp to exit.

A noble he passed looked up with a smile in his eye and winked. The symbol of the Muster swung loosely from his neckchain. TJ returned the gesture.

12: SUMMER

The King's next destination was no secret: the riverside locks for an inspection tour. It had officially been scheduled for this day at noon. The Howling Volv river ran from the mountains west to the sea. At Crimson Sapphire, engineers had built a series of gates and levees to funnel water into the city. As the river wound past the city and the palace and into the farmland, more gates were located for irrigation.

As they made their way through a particularly narrow street where a few people were the only onlookers, the shadows of the buildings pressed in upon them. This was an older section of the city, stone buildings lofting high with no pattern in their construction. The area had evolved into mainly warehouses and other storage facilities.

Summer Camp held his mule back, as outriders had to come closer to the King, and other soldiers moved forward to give the King room to ride.

Summer scanned rooftops and upper windows. "It is a mistake to take the most direct route," he said.

TJ shrugged. "It's the shortest—and time is expensive."

A cloud blotted the sun. Summer did not know much about science, but he always listened; and now he wondered why the Bear Ridge weather was what it was. According to Sharon Gold, none of the normal reasons for volatile weather were present: inordinate axial tilt, excessive sunspot activity, too many volcanic eruptions. Sharon had speculated on the effects of the two great ridges circling the planet, but had said she didn't know enough meteorology to specifically attribute the planet's erratic weather to these terrain abnormalities.

"Too quiet," Summer said aloud, echoing his inner unease. "Are you wearing your mail?" A spattering of rain hit him.

The squad leader, Lieutenant Timmons, rode calmly ahead of them.

"No."

"TJ, you . . ."

Summer heard the thunk and saw the shaft come out through the back of the King's shoulder. The clops of the horses' hooves seemed to continue.

"Cover!" he shouted and slapped the rump of the King's stallion with a stinging hand. The horse leapt forward, surprised. Summer goaded his mule to catch up. TJ lurched atop his mount. Summer stood in his stirrups searching the skyline.

Another bolt quickly followed and Summer saw its trajectory as it flashed out of the shadows from above and his jester's hat was off and he swung the two-foot length of the weighted end in an arc behind TJ and knocked the quarrel aside.

"Close up!" he yelled at the Gyrenes who were just now comprehending.

Uncontrolled, the King's stallion struck a post and the King fell off like a sack of grain. TJ hit the cobblestones and rolled only a little. Summer saw TJ's right hand had automatically grasped the shaft of the crossbow quarrel.

Summer stood his mule on its hind legs, stopping the animal with brute strength. Before the mule had regained its footing, he was out of the saddle and leaping for the still form of the King.

Blood spurted from the wound. TJ was either unconscious or dead. Summer knew TJ had maintained consciousness from far worse wounds. He didn't understand. Could the fall have knocked TJ out? Summer didn't remember the King hitting his head when he fell. Summer lifted TJ and he jammed the jester's hat into the wound, staunching the flow of blood from TJ's back. The entry point on the front left shoulder showed only a small leakage.

Gyrene horses clattered up. Lieutenant Timmons jumped from his horse and ran to the jester and the King. "My Lord!"

"Form a protective circle, man, there may be a follow-up attack." Summer's voice was commanding. His breath came quickly and he fought to control his own panic.

The lieutenant shouted orders. "First squad to the roofs." He pointed to a likely looking doorway. "Second squad, bodies between the King and all else." Summer admired the man's coolness and his precise directions.

The first squad began to move out and the second to encircle Summer and the King before Summer decided on a line of action. "Hold," Summer countermanded. The soldiers stopped immediately.

"You have command, sir," the lieutenant said.

"Timmons, look at the King. His lips are blue. We have no time to chase the assassin. We must get the King back to the palace and medical aid. Here, help me pull this bolt out."

"Should we?" asked the lieutenant as he bent to assist. Two squads of Gyrenes with weapons at ready folded around them shoulder to shoulder, blocking the light and casting shadows.

"I think it's poisoned," Summer said. "He'll have to bleed. That might remove some of the poison." But not enough, he knew. "Now!" The lieutenant broke off the fletched end and Summer pulled the quarrel through TJ's shoulder with a smooth and steady movement. He handed the bolt to a soldier. "Save that. Mount up," he commanded, voice rising. He was scared. More frightened than he could remember ever having been. He could think of nothing but TJ, not Gwen nor Michale nor Crimson Sapphire nor Bear Ridge nor the goddamn Fed nor their goddamn Council seat, not any goddamn thing but TJ.

Training came to his aid. A good soldier can turn his mind off when it comes time to do what is necessary, and then do it mechanically, swiftly, and efficiently. Then he can turn on his mind again.

With little conscious effort, Summer lifted the King, heavier and taller than he, and ran to his mule. The King's stallion was nowhere to be seen. The lieutenant ran with him, assisted Summer to mount and helped position the King. Summer swung the mule about and urged the animal to speed. While racing along the way, he managed to cradle TJ in front of him. He didn't want to sling him across the mule face down, not for dignity, but because that position might aggravate the bleeding. He kept his hat pressed against the exit wound allowing only a little bleeding.

"Lieutenant," he called as the officer caught up with him, "get one of your squads out front to clear the way."

"Yes, sir." The lieutenant signaled. Six men dashed ahead of the plunging group and formed a wedge stretching far in front.

The mule was a game one, thought Summer. Ears flopping, the animal had somehow caught the tension and was running full out. Summer thought about switching mounts with one of the Gyrenes, but didn't want to waste the time. He hoped the mule would last.

Around corners and up streets they dashed, clattering through markets and scattering people. The huge thoroughbreds of the soldiers made an effective shield, clearing the way. Summer did not think of the possible injuries they were causing.

Hoofbeats tattooed the roadway as they raced toward the palace. People stopped to stare, and unmistakable was the body of the King lolling in front of the bareheaded jester on the mule. The shock wave seemed to roll out in front of the hard riding men.

As usual, the gates of the palace were open and they sped through there for the main entrance to the front steps.

Summer did not stop, but rode his mule right up the wide stairs and into the great hall that served as the throne room. The Gyrenes followed. The roar of hoofbeats on the flagstones in the empty hall was deafening. Only slightly slowed, Summer guided the mule down a corridor to a ramp and shouted to the lieutenant, "Get Nora! Get the surgeon."

"Aye!" He signaled and his squads split up. "Second squad, guard the King, first squad, search for the surgeon." He turned his horse down another corridor and the last Summer saw was the Gyrenes scattering servants and administrative personnel. By now, the entire palace was in an uproar. Heads stuck out of doors and people ran down corridors shouting orders and questions.

Summer's mule died halfway up the second ramp. Summer kicked free and began running up the ramp, his King still in his arms, bleeding all over him and the floor.

A minute later, he was on the fourth floor, the King's chambers, and bursting through the master reception chamber. As he ran through, he saw that Queen Gwendlyon was hosting a tea party or something similar.

"Gwen, quickly now." He kicked open the door to the bedrooms and Gwen was running behind him.

"TJ!" Summer could tell from her voice she was fighting for control. She came up beside him and looked at the entry wound. "Is . . . is he. . . ?"

"I don't know, but it's worse in the back." Summer kicked open another door and went to the King's bed and laid him on his side. He ripped at sheets and jammed them against the wounds. "Gimme that pillow case, wrap it around these sheets. Tightly, now. Good."

Then she pushed Summer out of the way and peered underneath the makeshift bandages. "I've always dreamed it would end like this," she said. Her voice was flat. She ran her hands over the rest of TJ's body swiftly, then checked his breathing and propped open one eyelid. "He's alive. Barely."

"I've sent for Nora," Summer said.

"What happened?"

"A crossbow bolt from a rooftop. I suspect poison."

Gwen raised a decanter of water from a nearby table. She tried to force TJ to drink some. His lips and throat did not cooperate. He breathed harshly and his lips were turning purple. She jammed her thumb in between his teeth and poured the entire contents of the decanter into his mouth. He coughed and gagged, but the action caused some of the liquid to go down. Gwen pulled her thumb out and looked at the ragged gash made by clenching teeth. She wiped it on her gown unconsciously.

Just then crashing sounds came from the outer chambers and a horse slammed through the bedroom door. Timmons bent to hand down Nora from where he was carrying her on his horse. The horse was frothing like Summer's mule just before it had died. He addressed Summer. "Chambers clear and Gyrenes on guard. General Vero notified."

Summer nodded and the lieutenant dismounted and pushed his horse out backward.

"Nora, hurry," said Gwen.

"Is he alive?"

"Barely."

"My equipment," Nora snapped.

Timmons cursed and dragged a satchel off his pommel and brought it to her. "Sorry." He left and closed the door.

As Nora began to work, cleaning and inspecting, General Manuel Vero knocked softly and entered without waiting. His dark face blanked when he saw the King on the bed and Gwen and Nora working over him. He looked at Summer. "You have command. Your orders, sir?"

Summer turned to Gwen. "Let Nora work, Gwen. We've got to do this right, and right now." He knew the entire city of Crimson Sapphire would be afire with rumors. To maintain control, action must be taken immediately. And he knew Manny and Gwen knew it also.

Gwen didn't stop cutting TJ's clothes off as Nora worked. "Manuel," she said without looking up, "Summer speaks for me."

Nora glanced up, surprised, then returned to her work.

"Orders, Manny. Close the palace down. First line security. As many Gyrenes and palace personnel as can be spared to go off duty—and out of uniform—and spread through the city. Soothing and calming messages, that sort of thing—with wary eyes open. The Queen is in charge. As regent, while TJ is unconscious." He turned. "Nora, how long . . ."

"I do not know. Hours? Days?"

"Okay," Summer said, "it shall be as when Felicia had to rule when TJ's father was killed and he was on the Trek. Tell the herald to say that the King has been wounded and is recovering. I want the area of attack to be covered like stink on manure . . ."

"Already done."

"Good. No public dismay; outside this room, always optimistic, downplay the seriousness of the wound." He thought and made a decision. "Also, tell the herald that starting tomorrow, the Queen and Prince Michale will resume the King's official schedule as much as possible. The Queen is in active control. The rest of us do what we can."

"Aye, sir." Vero glanced at the Queen.

Gwen said, "A word from Summer is a word from me and TJ."

Summer actually felt the quiver in her tone, and could see the weight of the kingdom fall upon her as she realized the impact, especially since all she wanted to do, obviously, was comfort TJ. "It will be easier tomorrow, Gwen."

"Will it? I don't think so. Will you see to things? I'm not going to leave him now . . . now that he needs me." She looked startled by her own revelation.

Which echoed his own feelings precisely. And there was something he might have to do—and he could have no witnesses. He saw that Gwen saw his indecision. "Manny," she said, "you and Mike and Alfred run the store. I suspect if you give Alfred free reign, things will be all right. The man's an administrative genius, else TJ would never have picked him. Check with Summer on policy and the big things."

"It shall be done, and I'd best be doing," Vero said.

"Thank you," Gwen said and threw a blood-soaked tunic aside.

Summer turned and found Nora staring at the three of them as if not believing the conversation she'd just witnessed. He didn't pay her much attention. He was in an inner struggle of his own. Should he do it? It would be against TJ's expressed desires. But for his friend's life, he'd do anything. Then he realized. "Nora—stop staring and get to work." He doused a towel into a pitcher of water and began wiping off his makeup. Quickly, he stripped to his waist.

And the medallion that swung from his neck was the symbol of the Muster.

As Vero opened the door to leave, Lieutenant Timmons was standing there waiting. "Sir, we scratched a cheshire with the bolthead. The animal is dying." Vero glanced at Summer. Summer nodded acknowledgment and Gwen sighed. Vero closed the door and Nora shrugged as if to say she had been right and there was no need to kill a cheshire to prove it.

Summer stepped into the King's closet and selected a nondescript tunic and trousers. He tightened a broad belt around them to make the clothes fit better.

He returned to the bedside. "Nora, your silence on this matter and my position is required."

"Yes," she muttered, obviously unsure of that which occurred in the halls of power.

"What is your diagnosis?" Summer asked.

"He has lost too much blood. And the quarrel was poisoned."

"What kind?"

"I don't know."

"Have you an antidote?"

"For what? I don't know what poison was used, but I doubt I have anything to counteract it. Never have I seen symptoms like these."

"Do what you can."

"Obviously," she said. "For whatever use it might be."

"What?" Gwen demanded and Summer knew the Queen had caught on at the same time he did.

"He's dying," Nora said bitterly. "Only his tremendous constitution has kept him alive this long."

Gwen sank to her knees at TJ's side.

Summer stood and stared. He couldn't define his feelings. Just a complete emptiness. A frustration of things undone. The future gone like chalk erased from a board.

13: SHARON

Later, Sharon figured that at the moment the crossbow bolt pierced the shoulder of the King, she had just sat down in Prince Michale's spartan apartments.

A six-legged, two-tailed cheshire scrambled up and into her lap. The thought occurred to her that, in addition to roaches, there just might be another constant in the universe: something cuddly and cute installed in the ecosystem to control rodents. Did all rodent-eaters have to be cute? One at a time she idly caressed the cheshire's tails. She knew that the double tail was important in holding the animal's young while sleeping, but she didn't know exactly how.

The Prince was pouring her a cool drink. The King's son was an enigma, appearing to be almost the opposite of his father. Perhaps it was the influence of the gentle Gwen, Sharon speculated—or the over-protectiveness of the Queen Mother, Felicia. But he was an amazing combination of both his mother and his father. He did not have the harsh cut face that was the King's trademark, but the family resemblance was there. His soft brown eyes must have come from his mother as did his more oval face. Thick and curly hair hung casually over his forehead and he was clean shaven—she guessed in counterpoint to his father. His tunic and trousers were immaculately pressed.

And he wore no sword, nor had she ever seen him armed. Sharon looked around and did not see any weapon ready to hand. An enigma, all right.

He handed her a cold mug. She sipped. "Umm."

"Chocolate wine, very low alcohol, but high in calories. A specialty of a town far away called Lonestar."

"Lonestar? Isn't that where the young man with the thumb drums hails from?"

"Yes," said Michale, his face lighting up. "Plays beautifully. And quite an interesting fellow, I might add. I've had several conversations with him. Not a malicious bone in his body." He paused. "Now that we mention it, Lonestar is also the home of the court jester."

"An amazing man," Sharon reflected. "He must have the strength of a dozen men to do his job day after day."

The Prince gave her a sharp look she couldn't interpret. "Yes, he does have stamina," he said almost too casually.

The conversation lagged and, seeing that the Prince didn't wish to continue the small talk, Sharon said, "Forgive me, Prince Michale, but you seem to be the only one available right now. I have no wish to intrude, but I must complete my interview schedule before I review other matters on my checklist."

"That's quite all right, Sharon. May I call you Sharon?"

"Certainly, Your . . ."

"I'm Mike."

"Thank you. But I thought it was Mick?"

"To my father only."

His tone told her that she'd better follow another line of questioning. "May I turn the recorder on? You know what it is?"

"Sure, go ahead. I have nothing to hide."

"I didn't mean it that way . . . Mike. It will be transcribed later and placed into written format. It's easier this way."

"Should the Federation accept us, Sharon, I suppose I shall have to get used to electronic gadgetry."

"And more." She sipped her drink and found she wanted

to gulp it, but controlled the urge while wondering if Fed acceptance came, she could corner a small piece of the chocolate wine export business. She sighed inwardly. Politics already. Back to work, girl. "Mike, I'm after your perception of the planet. Of the kingdom. And your role."

"My role? I am the King's son."

"And you will succeed him?"

He shrugged. "Perhaps."

"Not of a certainty?"

"No. You have to be a Trekmaster to become King. It is an ancient tradition, one the people have come to expect. Especially in Crimson Sapphire. Their King has to be stronger and smarter than all others. Completing the Trek proves that."

The way he spoke of the Trek showed something of disapproval. "You don't approve?"

"It is not a thinking man's way. What good comes of it, I don't know. The survival rate is minuscule. Since there is nothing of real value over the ridges, not even wanderers of the wastelands attempt it. It remains a custom of Crimson Sapphire—and now, consequently, of the planet. Kind of a natural selection method of picking the next monarch." He smiled at some inner thought. "Those who attempt the Trek train for it vigorously."

"And you?"

"Some. I am more interested in other things."

"Suppose your father dies? Soon, I mean, before you've taken the Trek."

"I do not know."

"Let me ask the question differently. Suppose the Federation selects Bear Ridge and your father opts to occupy the Council seat himself and in person. Who would be King?"

"The successful returning Trekmaster. Or a regent until somebody lives through the Trek."

"I don't understand, Mike."

"Me neither, sometimes." He gave her a lopsided grin. "Ordinarily, the King and the Queen have numerous children and the males all take the Trek. Sometimes, one is strongest and smartest and makes it. The others die. Incidentally, this in itself is almost a blessing, for it precludes legitimate challenges to the throne. I suppose you could call it a custom that has evolved into a complicated selection process that actually works."

"But you are an only child." She tasted again the delicate

sweetness of the wine and wondered how to word her next statement diplomatically. "What happens if you take the Trek and don't come back?"

"Another will take my place."

"Who?"

"See here, Sharon. It's not as simple as I've made it sound. Because of the odds and because my mother cannot bear any more children, my father has sired children by other women. Women of noble birth, born and bred in Crimson Sapphire. 'Kinglets' he calls their offspring—as opposed to official Princes and Princesses, I guess. He thinks me having a bunch of half brothers and sisters panting after his crown will spur me on to greater achievements and make me train harder." He paused and his face was strained. "But such is not the case," he said as if he had to say so.

Sharon thought she saw part of his problem. A mother's son, maybe. Mike was well muscled, obviously a family trait, but his muscles and strength were not developed as you would expect from one constantly in physical training. A child raised as an only child, child of a much absent King, raised by a lonely Queen and only grandson to the Queen Mother. Always sheltered. Thus his character had been molded differently than his father's had. Where his father had been thrust into battle and decision making, Mike was expected to simply train and wait. And TJ was not one to share his power. Ah, she could see it, the conflict between father and son. And since he appeared to be a mother's son, obviously Mike resented his father's semi-official affairs—and that further added to the ever growing chasm between them. On the other hand, Sharon understood the attraction women must feel for TJ. He probably had his pick of the women of the kingdom. A growing awareness within her told her that Mike had some of the same attraction. But his was more quiet, gentle, and understanding. Not yet developed—and Mike probably didn't know he had it. But TJ durnwell knew he himself had it. It was a part of TJ's charisma, this attraction was, something he used to work his will, something he was so accustomed to it had integrated into his actions and his character. Was all this speculation part of her job? Back to business. And change the subject.

"Tell me about the Trek? What does it consist of?" She could slake her curiosity in this at least.

"What's to tell? All you have to do is climb Teddy Bear Ridge, somehow get across Devil's Dip Gorge and then

climb Big Bear Ridge and go down the other side to com-
mune with the Webbines. Then you have to bring back one
of those stones—the one which gave Crimson Sapphire its
name. You wear it if you want, on a ring or neck chain, or
you put it in a cabinet for display. The fact that you returned with the stone is significant. I sometimes wonder if
the giving of the stone isn't the Webbines' way of crowning
our King for us—sort of up to them to make the selection.
That's just something I wonder about sometimes, for you
can't find one on this side of the ridges."

"Why is it dangerous?"

"Treacherous terrain, man-killing snarves and other beasts,
the most godawful weather encountered anywhere, deadly,
seeping gases which sometimes ignite. Not just dangerous,
but damn near impossible."

If he thinks he's gonna scare me off, Sharon thought, he's
wrong. He's just sharpening my curiosity. "What are these
mysterious inhabitants, these Webbines, like?"

"Ask my father."

Your father won't talk about 'em, she almost verbalized
the thought. "Okay. Would you clear up a few things for
me?"

"Certainly." He seemed relieved to get away from the
subject.

"What is a kayoe?" She paused. "I think I know what a
nope is."

Mike grinned his special grin again. "Personally, I think
my father is bored with life. So he jokes a lot. Simple
cosmetics."

"Cosmetics?" What was Mike talking about?

"They are bureaucratic acronyms he's devised. NOPEs:
the letters stand for Number One Problem Entity. He uses
that a lot at staff meetings. It's goal oriented, sort of management by objectives. My father is a good troubleshooter,
I'll grant that. He establishes priorities and goals, lets the
right people work on them, and closely watches the big
problems himself. Kayoes are from K. O. or King's Orders.
This hasn't caught on as well yet. Cataloging. He issues an
order and the herald's administrative staff puts a number on
it, depending on type and area the order concerns, and
distributes the order to the right people. It's supposed to
work in place of certain laws and royal decrees."

Wrap a bitter pill in sugar, Sharon thought, and it goes

down easier. "And these ethnarchs see that the kayoes are carried out?"

"To a certain extent. Mostly. Except in military and tax matters."

So the King maintained the most powerful elements under his direct control. "In my nosing about, Mike, I have noticed that these ethnarchs are not native to the provinces they govern."

Mike nodded. "On purpose. You see, good old TJ has woven a fantastic web of checks and balances—but not on himself. He's invented a true Jeffersonian monarchy. There are many similarities between people on Bear Ridge—like language—but there are a lot more differences. He takes advantage of these differences to protect himself and the throne. There are still people who disapprove of him or would like revenge for his conquering of their territories. He reflects this in his appointment of ethnarchs to office. They are all bland, unknown people who are loyal to him alone. And they are excellent managers. They're selected also because they have no personal following—or charisma. They're assigned to provinces—I mean ethnarchies—different than their own to prevent them from quickly building a power base strong enough to oppose the crown. And many, not all, come from the despised tax courts or from within the Revenue Service itself."

"So they won't be loved enough to be followed into rebellion," Sharon thought aloud.

"Right."

"That's another thing I don't know if I fully understand. The King's use of the tax system." She understood all right, but she wanted to know what Mike thought of it.

"Some people call it abuse. Even I disagree sometimes with the harshness of his actions through the taxman. Once he coined the phrase, 'The taxman cometh,' and that implied threat has spread throughout the kingdom. But it works—for now. What he tries to do is to enforce his rule without the high-visibility presence of the military. It shows that he is ruthless—but cagey. If there is a riot in a parish, he slaps a higher tax on and hits them in their economics, so to speak. High crime rates, low school grade averages or attendance, failure to adhere to sanitary codes, stuff like that. It forces people to do for themselves, to meet standards. Or pay dearly. Nice threat. In the end, it is kind of a self-policing mechanism. Keeps the people busy and not idle."

"Does the Boston Tea Party mean anything to you?" Sharon asked.

He nodded. "Our heritage is North American. And we love our history—at least father does and thus so do the schools. The climate is not yet ripe for another episode of dumping tea. You see, old TJ, he is an advantage taker. He takes it when and where he can and in any fashion. Years and years of war, rape, pillage, plunder, peoples and lands torn apart, no certainties except more of the same. Then, all of a sudden, life is rosy and orderly. Sure, there is some inconvenience because of the taxman. But negligible compared to before TJ's planet-wide rule. I suppose when the people become unhappy with the Revenue Service, TJ will be one step ahead of them with some complex bureaucratic shakeup and a new system will emerge to replace the taxman."

Sharon thought that perhaps the single-mindedness with which TJ used his tax system indicated early on in his reign that he was already planning to civilize and modernize his world as much as possible—with Federation entry as the eventual goal. Well, it was a unique way of raising the planet-wide standard of living. And of orderly social change.

"And where does the extra money from all this taxing go?"

"Generally back into the ethnarchy. Some of it is used for welfare."

"Welfare? Your father doesn't seem the type."

"It is surprising, isn't it? And somewhat strange. The welfare is designed only for the very old or totally disabled who have no families to support them. You see, the King feels kind of responsible for the wars which generated many of these kinds of situations. But here's the really strange part: he puts these old folks to work."

"What?"

Mike smiled. "Not precisely as it sounds. He has a system whereby they earn their keep. They join together in local groups which periodically form to become 'think tanks.' They simply sit around and think and if they come up with any recommendations, they forward them to the palace, where my father or the herald reviews them. Some good ideas have come from this program. TJ provides bonuses for ideas he adopts."

Sharon thought. Another lever for TJ. She added in her mind. First the King bought the loyalty of most of the women by appointing only women as criminal judges. Now all the old folk, too? Plus, toss in the army and political appointees, and the people dedicated to him personally begin to add up in significant numbers. She wondered if the now mandatory schooling and government service equally endeared the young people to him? This last might not hold true, for she remembered her history—and her own rebellious youth. If Bear Ridge were accepted to the Federation, she wondered what kind of man she would be turning loose on the Federation.

"To hold the number of these welfare cases down," Mike continued, "taxes are lower on households keeping elderly or disabled."

There it was again, Sharon thought. TJ Shepherd using the taxes like the edge of a sharp sword, assuring his position and accomplishing his goals simultaneously. She'd have to be a trained pysch-analyst to figure him out in depth. She decided to ask if there were starving people, even though she knew the probable answer, when the unmistakable sounds of a horse galloping came from the corridor outside.

"Strange," Mike said and hurried to the door. Sharon followed a step behind.

The third floor corridor was a mass of confusion. Soldiers and servants stared and all talked and shouted at once. Trays and carts and paper littered the hall. A janitor was lying against a wall dazed, his bucket of soapy water sloshing around on the floor.

"What was that?" Sharon asked.

"I don't know," Mike answered, but he looked suddenly worried, no longer casual. He ran down the corridor toward a Gyrene. Sharon was right behind him. He grabbed the soldier. "What is it, man?"

"Oh . . . Prince. The King has been assassinated." Then he saw the look on Mike's face and added lamely, "At least that's what I heard."

"Jesus." Mike turned the man loose.

Sharon saw a blank look on his face. Then a series of expressions flickered across, too. Sharon could almost read him. First, realization, stark and naked. Second, personal: would he have to decide now whether to take the Trek or not? Then one of concern, for whom, Sharon couldn't tell.

"I must go to mother," he said to himself and started running. Sharon followed and had to run around a dead horse on the ramp leading to the landing above.

14: SUMMER

As Summer Camp stood at the foot of the bed watching Gwen and Nora trying to make the King comfortable, the door slammed open and Prince Michale ran in. The bedpost ornament Summer was holding snapped in his hand. The sudden crack froze the room and Summer looked down, realizing what he'd just done. The pressure within him to make his secret decision had transmitted to his hands.

Nora broke the tableau and raised TJ's wrist and began to take his pulse.

"Mother! It is true." Mike stopped in the middle of the room as if unsure of where to go next.

Gwen nodded.

"He's not dead yet," Summer whispered. He felt a sense of total frustration. "Mike, it was my job and I failed."

Mike didn't respond. His gaze was fastened on the King. Summer almost knew what he was thinking. As he watched the comatose man on the bed, a picture of the King guzzling sour mash, cursing, and polishing his own sword came unbidden to his mind. The person on the bed couldn't be that same man.

"*God,*" said Mike.

Summer took a deep breath. Quietly, he explained to Mike what had happened.

Mike nodded casually and Summer didn't understand the Prince's seemingly calm acceptance of the situation. Summer wondered whether Mike was thinking about the Trek and his obligations. Mike went over to the bed and put an arm around his mother's shoulders. "Let Nora work, Mother."

"Not much I can do," Nora snapped. "Get some fluids into him if possible."

The door was still open and Roaland Cruz walked in. "TJ?"

Summer jerked his head toward the bed and the Chief Padre made the sign of the cross. Then he looked again at Summer. Obviously, he'd never seen Summer out of his

makeup and jester's outfit. Summer followed Cruz' line of
sight and stuffed the Muster medallion into his tunic. "The
Last Rites, Padre."

Gwen sobbed and Mike tightened his arm around her.

The Chief Padre went to the bed and began chanting.

Alfred the herald and Sharon Gold appeared in the door.
Alfred crossed himself.

"Anything I can do?" Sharon asked in a small voice.

"Yes," Summer replied. "You can call in a Federation
ship with full medical facilities. A doctor and equipment."
His voice held the unmistakable ring of command and Sharon
looked at him as if seeing him for the first time. Summer
could see her mind reeling. First, the King lay there near
death. And now a court jester, a buffoon, was giving orders
as if he were the king.

All eyes went to the envoy. Her face blanched. She stammered. "I . . . I cannot."

"The hell with the rules, girl," Summer's face hardened.
"I no longer care about the Fed. Just get him some help and
do it quickly."

"I cannot," she repeated, voice strained almost to the
breaking point. Summer saw that it was a difficult thing for
her to say. "The rules. The laws. Any contact forbidden."

"And the Fed-sponsored conferences TJ attended?" Summer demanded.

"That's different. Information only." Summer admitted
to himself that she really did look as if she disagreed with
the policy. But she was doing her job. At least she's professional to the end, he thought.

"Damn their rules then!" Summer surprised himself with
the violence in his voice. And he knew he had made his
decision. "That's it, then. Everybody out. Gwen, you stay."

"What?" Mike said.

"I said out, Mike, and now." His voice was compelling.

Mike looked down at his mother.

She glanced at Summer then back to Mike. "Do as he
says."

Mike took another look at his father and turned and
walked out.

"I am sorry," Sharon said and followed Mike through the
door.

"Alfred," Summer said, "Manny Vero has the marching
orders." The herald nodded and left. "Nora," Summer said,
"you, too."

Surprise edged onto her drawn face. "Me, too?"

"Right now, you, too. But stay in the outer chambers. We may need you."

Nora shook her head and clucked her tongue as she left.

"Padre?" Summer interrupted the chanting. "Close the door on your way out."

"I have not finished yet."

"Do so later. Now please excuse us."

"Do not interfere with the work of God, man."

Summer took the Padre's elbow and firmly escorted him to the door. "I am sorry, Padre. But this must be. You may finish later." He turned to the sentry outside the door. "Have the officer of the watch double the guard here. No one enters until I say so. Understood?"

"Aye, sir."

Summer saw all those in the outer chamber watching him with curious eyes but ignored them as he closed the door.

Gwen was staring at him as if she didn't know him. "What's the mystery, Summer?" Her tone told him she trusted him but warned him that he'd better have a good reason for what he was doing.

Summer didn't answer but hurried to a recessed panel in a wooden wall and pressed a pattern. The panel swung outward and revealed a small room occupied by a table and a chair. On the table sat a black metal box. "This cost the kingdom the equivalent of one hundred thousand Fedcreds," he told Gwen. "It has its own internal power supply." Now that he'd made his decision, he did not hesitate. He punched the red button on the side of the box and a small red light lit atop the mechanism. He ignored the white button and its corresponding light. "Well, it works. I always wondered if it would." He opened a drawer in the table and pulled out a vial. "Another hundred thousand Fedcreds worth. A big no-no for us on backward planets to possess. TJ had to do some creative accounting with the books to hide the loss of all that gold." Gwen was just staring at him. He unscrewed the vial cap and heard the pop of released vacuum. He upended the vial and an ampoule dropped into his hand.

"What is that thing?" Gwen asked, indicating the box with the light.

"An emergency transponder. It calls a friend. If he's about, he'll come. A cool million Fedcreds worth of negotiable metal or gems. Costly and last resort. Somehow the cost doesn't seem significant right now."

"And that glass ball?"

"Something TJ bought for you, Gwen. When you were ill years back. But you pulled through before TJ thought it necessary to use this." He looked at the ampoule. "It is a life-maintainer. I don't know exactly what the space medics call it, but that is its function. If there are no medics or medical facilities, starships have these on board. There and other out of the way places without medical help at hand; asteroid miners have them. Of course, you have to be a citizen of the Federation to get one legally." He tried to keep the bitterness out of his voice. "As just now reaffirmed by Sharon Gold. At any rate, this thing slows down a person's metabolism. Like hibernation. Gives the injured or sick person time. A chance to hang on until help arrives or you can get him to a medic."

Now at the bed, Summer jammed the pointed end of the ampoule into TJ's neck and watched as it emptied itself. "Now we wait. As I remember, it will take effect in a few minutes."

Gwen still looked puzzled and walked to the table and examined the box.

"It sends a signal through a series of satellites and relay stations. The signal is going many different ways through different kinds of space on private channels. TJ could explain better, but that's the best I can do. It calls a man who has some medical equipment. A man who is going to be very rich for services—should he arrive in time."

Hope finally surfaced on her face. "Do you think TJ has a chance, Summer?"

"I don't know, Gwen. If a man named Fitzroy and his communications equipment picks up the signal and he comes, maybe. All quite contrary to Fed rules. But it takes a royal flush to beat four of a kind. If we're caught, we lose our chance at the Fed Council seat. But if I can help it, we won't lose TJ."

"I still don't understand all this, but thank you, Summer." Gwen tried to smile, but she failed. Summer knew the stark realization had finally settled over her. The crisis moment would be stretched out possibly for days. He hoped not. He didn't think TJ had that long. But TJ was the toughest man Summer had ever known. If anyone could survive, TJ would be the one.

As she stepped back to the bedside, Summer closed the

panel and went to the outer door. He opened it and told the sentry, "Send for General Vero immediately."

He didn't even look at the expectant faces outside. He closed the door and went to a writing table, wrote a message, signed it, and sealed it with wax.

Soon Manny Vero knocked and stepped inside.

"Manny," Summer waved the note, "I need six of your best and most trusted men for a critical mission."

"As important as security of the palace and the King?"

"More so."

"The six wear the symbol of the Muster then," Vero replied.

"Perfect. We are assured of their silence." Summer handed Vero the paper. "Have them take this. At once. Into the mountains behind the city on the other side of the river. It is a long journey. I've drawn a map on the outside for them to follow. Among the ridges there is a hidden plateau. The map shows it. Perhaps you have heard the King has a secret hideout?"

"The one where he supposedly keeps the artifacts from before the Rollback?" Vero nodded. "We've all heard those rumors. So it is true."

"That it is," Summer said. "Tunnels full of old junk, most scarcely recognizable. It is the location from which came the Shepherd family to Crimson Sapphire. Anyway, the men are to wait there. A shuttle craft from a ship may land, probably at night. Your men are to conceal the craft and bring back the pilot. Have them take an extra mount and Gyrene clothing—the man is big—so that he may come in disguise. His name is Jean-Claude Lafitte Fitzroy. When your men return with him, have them bring him directly to these chambers."

Obviously, Vero wanted to ask questions, but he said, "If it is to assist the King, I shall go myself."

"We need you here, Manny. This is only a prayer's chance anyway."

"Aye. My Lady, if you will excuse me, it shall be done."

As the door closed softly, Gwen said, "Damn the Federation and their insane policy. I vow right now to continue to seek the Council seat, no matter what happens to TJ." Then she yelped.

Summer had also heard TJ gurgle. It was as if a mental blow had staggered him. He saw Gwen had felt it, too. "At first there is an adrenaline-like surge that will go through him. Then he will appear to stop breathing." He hadn't wanted to say 'appear to die.' "But he will breathe occasionally."

Gwen stroked TJ's head. Then she rummaged through a bedside table and held up a handful of pages. "His Trekmaster Log entry. He's been working on it. He hadn't even asked me to read it yet. Some of the details he's never confided to me."

Summer wondered if TJ had included the episode in Devil's Dip Gorge. "I suspect that we shall have time to do some reading in the hours ahead."

15: THE PIRATE

"Special signal coming in," said the communicator.

"Decode and identify," said Jean-Claude Lafitte Fitzroy.

"Federation Navy scouts still out there, Skipper," said the navigator.

"Keep that asteroid rock between us, will you, Nav?"

"Roger. But they're gonna get an angle on us and then they got us line of sight."

"Signal decoded, boss," said the communicator.

"Do I need an appointment to find out, Comm? What is it?" Jean-Claude's voice took on a hint of anger.

"The Bear Ridge transponder," said Comm.

Jean-Claude looked across at Comm for visual confirmation.

"What about the Fed ships, boss? I project they're closing in," said Nav.

"Guns?" said Jean-Claude.

"Sir?" came the youngster's voice over the intercom.

"Can you blast that rock to give us a screen?"

"Yessir. Use an old missile, not energy. I've been wanting to find out if they work."

"Do it. Nav, punch in Bear Ridge. Let the ship decide the right moment to go translight. If we're lucky, the burst and debris will mask our trail."

The navigator's supple fingers flew over her control board. "Ready anytime. Suggest soonest."

"Noted. Guns? At your earliest convenience."

"Missile ops check good, arming sequence complete," said Gun's excited voice. "Launch."

"On target, " said Nav. "Bingo."

Jean-Claude was monitoring at his station. "Pretty; long time since I've seen that. Bye, Fed, better luck next time. Translight routine. Nav, watch our back trail. I don't think they can track us now, but you never know. The Fed Navy has some sharp people."

"Had, you mean," said Nav.

"Thanks, Nav," said Jean-Claude. He'd been an up and coming fast-burner in the Federation Navy himself—until they'd almost cashiered him. Captain of a NASCAR class Destroyer-Escort, the DE *Richard Petty*. But he'd taken too many chances. Then one day his ship had intercepted what they thought was a smuggler. But it turned out to be a space yacht undergoing a mutiny. On boarding, he and Nav had killed the mutineers. Meanwhile, Fleet had reprimanded him for exceeding his authority. The second officer on his own *Petty* had radioed that Fleet had recalled him and the *Petty*. Jean-Claude knew it was the end of his career. He and Nav had sat down on the yacht and worked it out. They radioed back that they were captured and being held hostage, went translight, changed the yacht's name to *Bobby Allison* and began a career of their own. The money was better, the opportunities for advancement nonexistent—but then he always hated authority. Comm signed on later. Guns was the third to occupy his position. He hoped by now he and Nav had been given up for dead—but he didn't think so. The Fed Navy was stuffy, formal, bureaucratically top heavy, and narrow-thinking. They weren't dummies though. If he and Nav ever retired, they'd need a powerful political sponsor to shield them.

"What's at Bear Ridge?" Guns asked, coming onto the bridge of the ship.

Jean-Claude grinned. "One million Fedcreds worth of gold or gems just for showing up. Ye reapeth what you soweth, I always say."

Nav snorted.

Jean-Claude went on. "Nav, there's our retirement money. We're gonna have to open our own bank to hold all the money. I suspect old TJ will need something or other we can provide at a suitably exorbitant price."

"What are you talking about, Skipper?" asked Guns.

"I haven't heard the whole story yet, either, boss," said Comm. "Though Nav told me a whopper I didn't really believe, once."

"The last one," said Jean-Claude, and went to a locker. He pulled out a bottle and four tumblers. He poured and handed one to each of the crew and sank back into his seat and sipped. "Chocolate wine. My last bottle. Gotta get more on our visit. Somehow, you can't synthesize this right."

"Great!" said Guns.

Nav was sniffing hers with a satisfied look on her face.

"Comes from Bear Ridge," said Jean-Claude. "Guns, you and Comm weren't with us then. Back when we were just getting started. Had to hunt up business. Checking out non-Fed planets. Bear Ridge at the time. Weirdest terrain you ever saw. Rotten weather, too. Had to be careful, on accounta the Fed, you know. They take offense when somebody breaks their rules. They want a monopoly—total control.

"Anyhow, we found a weak source of radioactivity and disguised ole *Bobby Allison* on their moon and took a shuttle down. There were seven of us, one left on watch aboard. We had too many crew then. Four is just right. Followed our instruments to this lonely plateau. Tunnels and caves in mountains nearby. Somebody had stacked old pre-Rollback artifacts in there. Some of those old mobile self-dampened nuclear power plants that still had some residual radioactivity which is what we picked up. Nobody around so we went down out of the mountains on foot.

"We found a patrol of soldiers out roaming about, swords and spears, can you believe that? We isolated one of the soldiers and he wouldn't talk. There are some tough sonofabitches on Bear Ridge. I was about to resort to drugs and was telling him about the benefits of the services we could offer—he had this strange medallion hanging from a thong around his neck—when he seemed to make a decision and talked almost freely. Said he'd bring our offer to his King's attention. Well, we had no way to contact the top dog, and this was as good a way as any. So we turned him loose and waited."

Nav laughed. "I about alternately froze or burned or blew away." She sipped her wine.

Jean-Claude nodded in agreement at the memory. "Me, too. After a few days, up rides this big, mean-looking fellow on a stallion and this other guy in a goddamn clown suit on a mule. A King and his court jester. Absolutely ridiculous.

Now you know my view on authority. I just flat don't like it . . ."

"Except when *you* are in command," said Nav.

"Different in a ship in space," Jean-Claude said. "So of course we didn't get along right there at first. Too many sparks. I suspect old TJ, that's Thomas Jefferson Shepherd, King of Crimson Sapphire and the planet of Bear Ridge, felt about the same. Pretty soon we were arguing, I don't know what about. Now you know I'm a big guy, beefy and slow-looking, but I got lightning reflexes and Navy hand-to-hand combat training."

Nav laughed again.

"Soon we had our hand weapons drawn and were ready to get the hell out of there. TJ was younger then, as I was, and jealous of his power and position. He really needed us then, but my mouth had gotten his dander up. His wife, the Queen, had some kind of internal female problems they couldn't deal with. It was probably why he took a chance and left a shaky kingdom to come meet with us. After finding out the history, I can understand what pressure the poor guy was under. Life is tough on Bear Ridge.

"Well, we almost came to blows when this clown guy pushed his way in between us and said, 'TJ, let me take him. It's my job.' The King shook his head and said to me, 'One on one?' I said sure, knowing I could beat him easily. I wanted to get down to business. I told the rest of our guys not to interfere."

Nav laughed out loud.

Jean-Claude squirmed at the memory. "He cold-cocked me before I could say 'go' and we got down to fighting. He didn't know any fancy tricks, but he was quicker'n greased owl snot and I couldn't nail him. We jockeyed around for position awhile and then went at it the old fashioned way, toe to toe, face to face, and he took everything I could hand him and was beginning to hurt me bad. Finally, he glanced over my shoulder, nodded, and finished me off without raising a sweat. As I went down, I saw that damned clown had decked all of our guys and had gathered their weapons. Ole TJ had maneuvered me so that I couldn't see what the hell was going on behind me. Our crew had been too engrossed in the fight to watch the clown." He shot a look at Nav. "That includes you, Nav."

She laughed again. "It was a super fight, I'll admit that. Wouldn't have believed it if I hadn't witnessed it personally.

Guns, never fight with anybody from Bear Ridge. Were I a mercenary commander, I'd take a thousand like that King and accept any assignment. And that jester, you couldn't even tell he was moving. I still get sore ribs when I remember."

"And then what happened?" asked Comm.

"We sort of hammered out a mutually beneficial arrangement," said Jean-Claude. "I told him what we could provide, but he was a cheapskate and didn't want to jeopardize his chances at future Fed entry. He bought the emergency transponder—which has two positions, incidentally. One for emergency, come right now, like we are doing. The other signal means routine non-emergency call, drop in when you're in the neighborhood. And he agreed to the million Fedcreds per emergency visit. He bought a couple other small items we happened to have, remember we were scrounging up business—relying more on future orders. But what he really wanted was medical attention for the Queen. No have. I felt really bad about that. Nav suggested the life-maintainer as a last resort. He bought that right off. And arranged for us to respond to his call should his wife be worse. I reckon she got better soon, because he never called us.

"But here's the biggie: when we talked, he wanted to know why we didn't carry a lot of medical equipment. I wondered too, because it's a lot less dangerous than running guns and stuff. So we did start in the medical business and as you know it's paid off. We ought to give ole TJ a commission."

"Should we alert our attorney at Fed Central to check our portfolio?" asked Nav.

Jean-Claude smiled. "We'll get paid in gold or jewels and we'll have to sell 'em before we can realize a profit. Hmmm. Maybe we can tack on a money-changing fee. Think TJ will go for that?"

"If he needs us bad enough," said Nav.

16: I:IMBAWE

He came out of the river near the outskirts of Crimson Sapphire and, changing configuration slightly, began walking along the road toward the palace. His webbed feet contoured to the hardpan and occasional cobblestone sections of the way.

I:imbawe could see that word of his approach preceded him. Humans stopped and stared. And grouped. Their single auras showed curiosity, some fear. Their group or joined auras reflected curiosity and a bit of daring when they formed crowds. Children showed more honest interest than adults so he adapted his aura to show them they had nothing to fear. But, as it was difficult trying to respond to so many children and people as he went farther, he had to color to neutral the effort was so great. Also, he had not the time to pursue this fascinating game. He could tell that his appearance was a singular event. Crowds grew as word spread. He reflected that humans must have some sort of quick communication of which he was unaware. An interesting concept for further study.

As he neared the palace, several warriors on horseback raced to him from the palace gates. The one-in-charge seemed not to know what to do; finally, he dismounted and his men followed his lead. They formed a pack behind him.

At the gates of the palace, he observed another gathering of officials. The foremost two were the paperman and the warrior-chief. They, also, did not seem to know what to do. He kept his aura neutral.

The warrior-chief stepped forward. "I am General Vero." I:imbawe sensed the danger just below this man's surface. His spirit was high with tension. "May I inquire as to your purpose?"

I:imbawe just watched him. He was deciding whether to transmit a soothing aura message when the other human, the paperman, stepped forward. "We represent His Majesty. I am Alfred, the Herald." He put a restraining hand on the warrior-chief.

I:imbawe acknowledged their presence with a pattern series which seemed to quell their suspicions. He stepped past them up the stairs and walked through the throne room. They followed him with the troops who had accompanied him. Many palace functionaries gathered along his route, making way and staring with awe. On the first ramp leading upward, a young man ran up. He had a pair of thumb drums attached to his wrist. I:imbawe knew there were few humans accomplished on the thumb drums and aura-evidenced immediate curiosity. Thumb drumming was one of the most intriguing and pleasant things about humans. Ah! The young man intercepted his aura message and . . . blanched and retreated. Something to be studied later.

On the second landing, the off-world woman rushed to the group surrounding him. She burned with interest also, but was more difficult to read as she was not native to his world, and thus not a part of the current scheme of things.

Fully as tall as the King, the Webbine strode off the final landing and into the chambers of the Trekmaster. He stopped to survey those present.

The son of the Trekmaster: worry. Yellow aura tinged with somber gold.

The mother of the Trekmaster: resentful. She had lost sons to the Trek, something for which she partially blamed his race.

The mate of the Trekmaster: concern for her life-mate *and* her son. I:imbawe began to understand the undercurrents. The son of the Trekmaster had much to decide.

Another . . . uncertain, and with intrigue . . . but then the entire spectrum was clouded by one inside the closed door . . .

An inner door opened and a human male stepped forward poised to kill, but with no weapon in his hands. Friend and accomplice of the Trekmaster: exuding danger signals so dark and powerful I:imbawe would always remember them for their unique content.

I:imbawe took on the respectful color of blue for it mimed the sky, the source of all life-support. The folds of his skin colored slightly, folds which he had expanded to hold oxygen should human-devoured air in this closed space not be acceptable. His eyes atop his head maintained forward vision but kept a careful observance of what occurred behind him. Membranes snaked over them rhythmically. He stretched the membranes between his finger-digits and his toe-digits. The number of humans gathered in one small area unsettled him and he tried not to show it, keeping his aura neutral and his skin blue—though he preferred the lagoon-green of the shallows off the eastern coast. The man who was ready to kill him exchanged signals with the warrior-chief and relaxed.

"Nothing to lose," killerman said. I:imbawe watched him control his violence, then he said, "Welcome," and waited expectantly.

I:imbawe reciprocated by changing his aura to reflect camaraderie. He sensed that this was a test and he must make plain his intentions. He was right, for the man relaxed even more and extended his arm to the room within and I:imbawe entered. The dangerman and the Trekmaster's mate followed.

I:imbawe went to the bed and looked down upon the Trekmaster. /Ah, 'tis true,/ he said-projected-whistled-sniffed-signed and thought.

The woman appeared startled. "Yes."

The killerman's aura struggled within itself. The human propensity for violence was amazing. They constantly in-flicted self-damage to their own species. On the other web, so, too, did snarves and volves. These aliens were indeed mysterious. Then he caught himself. He was stereotyping all humans from their history. Just as the oldest Webbines stereotyped themselves as total pacifistics, just like a bunch of ancient sea cows: dialogue and wishful thinking is all. And because of the humans, many of the old ones thought that their own history and racial makeup was simple and peaceful. Conceptually worth considering, but unrealistic. So he could understand the schisms within races. Earlier he had puffed himself up to the first level of inhalation and now, because of the fetid odor of illness, he fed off his stored oxygen. Soon, he would not look as bloated as he did now. He adjusted his aura to show the killerman his inten-tions were not harmful to the one he guarded.

/'Tis a shame,/ he indicated the Trekmaster lying there. /For what reason was this done?/

"We don't know," said the man.

/I am I:imbawe./

"I am Camp and this is Gwendlyon, wife of the Trek-master."

/I understand./ He thought./ Where is his stone?/

"The crimson sapphire?" asked the woman.

/Yes./

The woman hurried through the outer door. While they waited, I:imbawe studied the Trekmaster and wished that he were the stone-mate of the Trekmaster, not O:chacka. Shortly, the woman returned with the stone. He indicated that she place it on him. She did so, her aura whirling with uncertainty, lodging it on the Trekmaster's forehead with a cloth.

He studied the almost-corpse. /The physical being is near to dissolving back to the original molecules./ He carefully felt around the Trekmaster's aura. /Yet there is a spark within, one which refuses to accede to the final demands./ He fused some of his own aura to that of the Trekmaster. As he had already known, it was impossible to transfer any life-energy between his race and the humans. Unsuccessfully, it had been attempted in the past. He tried to nurse the spirit of the Trekmaster, but that also was of no use. He turned. /That is all. He dreams of things past and things which could be. Were he coherent, he would want you to know this thought which is the calm in the center of the storm in his mind: "I suspect the only death you ever accept is your own—and that only after the fact." It is a difficult thing to interpret./

"This is the purpose of your visit?" Camp asked.

/We watch. We listen. We observe. There are unstoppable events coming. Forces loosened that must proceed. A wave of higher proportions than before. To our knowledge, there is only one human capable of riding this wave to the finish: he who lies here at death's beckon. It has been collectively judged that this man's presence is necessary to maintain a proper balance of events. I am observing, taking measure. Information is required to make decisions, judgments. If there be chaos, we would know of it in advance and prepare. Life is not static, thus the variables must be monitored. I was closest, thus the task fell to me./ His skin deflated more as he consumed his stored oxygen.

Gwendlyon spoke. "May we offer you sustenance? Privacy to rest or dwell in?"

/I must return./

"The offer stands, for you, for any or all of your people." I:imbawe saw that she was unsure of protocol and was attempting to find a way to take advantage of his visit.

/Should the Trekmaster expire, who would take his place? Who would accomplish the Trek?/

"My son," she said and I:imbawe noted the pride expansion in her aura, the warmth of motherhood, the worry for the well-being of her offspring. "And perhaps other offspring of the Trekmaster." I:imbawe saw the disapproval of these other "offspring."

"You would meet him?" Camp asked.

/Affirm./ The killerman had some scheme he was working, thought I:imbawe.

Camp hastened to the door. "Prince Michale? If you will?"

The son walked in, followed closely by the off-world woman. Camp hesitated and then shrugged.

/The female, she is not native to here?/

"She is a visitor, from the human Federation," Gwendlyon said.

/Which means what?/

"It is an organization of humans, comprising many different planets."

It is much as we extrapolated, he thought. /And the young man would be the next Trekmaster?/ The son's aura seemed to fluctuate with static charges.

The son did not speak, but lifted his hands in a questioning manner.

/'Tis also our way of taking the measure of the man who would rule the humans on this world,/ I:imbawe stated emphatically. He saw that Camp had seen his opportunity.

"Perhaps," said Camp, "it would be possible for Michale to accompany you on your return?" Camp's aura flared hope.

The Prince's aura shone with sudden understanding.

/Can the young man swim upriver underwater under the mountains?/

"No." Camp's aura turned flat with disappointment.

The prince's aura glowed more constantly now, relief apparent.

/What you suggest flaunts tradition./

Camp smiled, "That it does. But the opportunity was there and," he pointed at the Trekmaster, "there may be no time to lose."

/I go now./

"Will you return sometime for a visit?" Gwendlyon asked, obviously still trying to capitalize, take advantage of his presence. He admired her for her tenacity. She didn't know how she could use him, but she would try. His translating the Trekmaster's thought had certainly made an impression on her.

/Perhaps,/ he indicated. It occurred to him that it required a great deal of diplomacy to deal with humans.

"Allow us, then, to escort you," Camp said.

/If you will./

"Mike," Camp said pointedly. "You and Manny and Alfred."

"And me!" the off-worlder demanded.

"Okay, Sharon," Camp said, and I:imbawe read the calculation in the killerman's aura. It was obvious that his own presence with the Prince would be a politically valuable occasion—for the return route Camp was outlining to them was not the shortest to the river. He would allow them their drama and follow them through the city. It would be interesting, something which he might be able to use when he contributed to judgments and opinions.

A party of soldiers from the palace led him and those accompanying him. The Prince occasionally pointed out some distinctive building or area. They were followed by a curious and growing throng. He marveled at the construction. These humans were builders, he realized, like some insects. He knew this comparison was not entirely fair, since humans did not have the natural protection that he did. Nor his people's most-of-the-time cooperative trait.

When he reached the fields, gladly did he allow his skin to mold into the colors surrounding him: the yellow of grain, the green of forest foilage, the hay-brown of dried grasses.

Here the off-world woman supplanted the others next to him. "May I talk to you?"

He reflected on her enthusiasm, youthful and female. Her aura was contradictory to those humans from Bear Ridge. At the same time it was more sophisticated, in an intellectual manner, but also naive in the ways of this planet: she did not yet quite fit. He thought that perhaps one day she would. There was adversity in her past, and thus he judged that she would fit in, eventually, with the human society here. He wondered why he had these thoughts, and then he knew he was stalling while something worked its way through his thought processes. Singling out her aura had begun the process. When he had entered the outer room from the Trekmaster and was cataloging auras, Camp's menacing aura had overwhelmed his senses and demanded all of his attention. There had been another dark aura present, at least he thought so, one which had merely blended with the others and with Camp's. He was sorry he hadn't been able to read more of this other dark aura at the time.

"Will you answer some questions?" she repeated.

/Perhaps./

"Is it possible I could visit your . . . Home Ground?"

For the first time among humans, he found something amusing. As a member of a staunchly male dominated society, he enjoyed the sensations involved with her suggestion. He allowed some green mirth to seep into his aura. /Perhaps you should accompany the young Prince on his journey./

He noted Michale's sudden intake of breath and immediate aura change: apprehension flooded the young Prince. Not fear, I:imbawe amended, but simple indecision. Too wide a gap for his father's son. Another interesting item for later speculation. Should the Prince attempt the Trek, I:imbawe determined to monitor him, if possible.

The girl was considering his communication. "My job may not permit it—and Mike might not want me." Her voice was low and barely discernible. He did not understand all the words of these humans, but he could interpret signals, mental intent, and other processes sufficiently to hold a dialogue. Others had studied humans more than he, and he had learned from them as had most of the male Webbiness. "Could arrangements be made, for later. . . ?"

He made a decision. Not for her sake, but for the future. This Federation business upon which the Trekmaster was embarked: extrapolations and projections strongly indicated an upheaval among humans, one way or the other. Thus, it would benefit his people to study an off-worlder. /Come over the mountains and the ridges and you will be greeted./

"But how? I . . ." Her aura solidified into deep determination.

They had reached the river, named The Howling Volv River by the humans. The large crowd stopped silently behind him. The Prince and the warriorman spoke together briefly. The offworld woman was burning to ask more.

I:imbawe forestalled ceremony by sliding into the cold water. For a moment he floated there, luxuriating in the icy mountain water. He breathed deeply, inflating his skin partially, molding it into a more aquadynamic surface unlike the ballooning he accomplished when on land or airborne.

Slowly he disappeared from their sight and began dancing about in the river currents, slithering upriver gracefully.

A human female wished to visit the Home Ground; a human male did not.

Strange, these aliens.

17: TJ, THE TREK

PREFACE: In the event of my death, I suggest my Trekmaster Log entries be read and screened by either Queen Gwendlyon or Delancy Camp before insertion into the formal Log. Additionally, in the interests of history and since I may be the last legitimate Trekmaster, I choose to make my entry more detailed than those already in the Log. (signed) Thomas Jefferson (Shepherd) Rex.

The Finger of God loomed over me and my horse was plumb tuckered out after the race across the great plain. So I turned him loose to fend for himself. He should stay hereabouts for a week or two, until he tires of that free life. The effort had taken the sting out of my father's death, though it remained with me. Certainly we got along, but . . . well, there never was much time for us to get to know each other. That and the competition between brothers.

My brothers, Theodore Roosevelt and Stonewall Jackson, I left far behind on the plain. Momentarily, I considered waiting for them and assaulting the ridges in a joint effort, but neither would stand for that idea—though there were no rules to go by. Also, I was in a hurry. The rough and tumble Crimson Sapphire soldiers needed a firm hand and some quick reorganization to improve their effectiveness. How confident I was before I even began to climb.

I never saw my brothers again.

For once, the weather was acceptable. It was early fall and the sun still shone hotly upon the plains. The higher I climbed on Teddy Bear Ridge, the colder it became. The going was not as difficult as legend would have us believe. Perhaps, I thought then, and wrongly so, the legend of the

Trek was a sham perpetuated by those who wielded power and did not wish to share it. Deliberate misstatement in the Trekmaster Log was not a trait I expected from my ancestors and their predecessors.

Halfway up Teddy Bear, I revised my opinion. Still in the shadow of the landmark I'd chosen, the Finger of God, I found myself unable to continue. A series of bluffs and overhanging lava formations blocked my way. My hands were lacerated and my knees bled. Crouched on a weather-smoothed boulder, I considered another route. Finally, I double coiled my rope and dropped down for about an hour until I discovered another passable route.

Once I almost decided to discard my sword as it was an encumbrance. Fortunately, I didn't. But the awkwardness of the weapon did start me thinking. That, combined with looking at the Finger of God all day, gave me food for thought—what else was there to do? Hence came the concept for the war assegai. The thought of the privations I'd read that Chaka Zulu had endured gave me some inspiration. The Finger of God was almost an exact replica of the assegai blade. A most striking peak. History once again came to my aid.

Eventually, I found a ragged canyon which seemed to split the side of the ridge and work its way vertically toward the top. I found it by following a slinker, one of those indigenous mountain scavengers. But I had not the claws to hold with nor the scales which could not be scraped, scratched, or lacerated like what was happening to me. It was he who warned me of the mountain snarv who lived in a hollow large enough to hold a palace. His tough meat and a run-off water pool gave me strength. His lair, while quite noxious, was a haven for sleep. No, never again did I think to discard my sword. The snarv skin also proved useful, for atop Teddy Bear Ridge the wind rose and the sun disappeared and rain turned to snow.

I wasted little time, save to search for my brothers below. I'd determined should I find either or both, I would lend a helping hand. But I couldn't see them, nor could I look far since I was perched on a saddle which climbed higher still to the Finger of God to the north and the way simply impassable to the south. Fighting the wind, I began descending Teddy Bear Ridge into Devil's Dip Gorge.

Soon, the shadow of Big Bear Ridge made climbing the

more difficult. On the other hand, I could use a doubled rope to assist my descent.

Devil's Dip itself was surprising. How could such exist when the sun nurtured it for short hours only? It would almost have to have been environmentally controlled. Bear Ridge weather is indeed a strange thing. Put me in mind of my mother's (Felicia Shepherd) tinkering with gardening. Thinking of her made me hungry for some of her special kobe beefaloe or okra gumbo.

Tall trees, some grass supporting small herbivores, slinkers feeding off the herbivores, cheshire or two, and snarves, many snarves. Evidence of volves, but snarves must have scared them out of this area.

The number of snarves surprised me. Since the number of lower order animals which the snarves must feed on was higher than expected, I guessed that they ran in packs and that the gorge was passable far north and far south. An interesting place to explore one day, should time allow. Perhaps there were passages through or under the ridges? Perhaps there were large herds of birds on which these beasts fed? Was the higher than normal amount of small plains animals here a result of man's using the plains, filling them with sheepaloe and beefaloe? Beats me.

I saw no sign of any Webbines.

I found a cave I could barricade and feasted on snarv meat because one had challenged my presence. Slinkers were not to my taste. And I didn't have the time to chase down and slaughter and smoke one or two of those little goat-like animals, the snobbi. I had brought several flintstones in case I had to hole up for a while and stock in food against the weather. Olde Earthe survival motto: Be prepared.

Rested and fed, after another day and night in the gorge, I began to climb Big Bear Ridge. I was determined to possess my own crimson sapphire or die trying. After a while, the dying part became more appealing. But I had learned on Teddy Bear Ridge. In the gorge, I'd cut up a snarv skin or two, and had leggings and wrappings for my hands and elbows. Lava was not so prevalent here.

There was one instance of a fairly steep slope, talus, I believe, and it looked to be easy. Appearances were deceptive. Halfway up, the entire surface of the slope began to slide down from my weight. And then the sword took on a new dimension of importance, for just as I was sliding off the cliff at the bottom of the slope, I managed to roll over, draw the sword, and stab it into the flowing rock debris. The point scraped along until it finally caught in a small fault somewhere beneath the loose rock. And some call it "The Widow-Maker." Not this day.

There I rested while I regained my strength—and there the rains caught me. Never have I spent a more miserable night, clinging to the hilt of a wavering sword, afraid to make any move lest I dislodge myself to an early and, as yet, unearned death. My feet scrabbled until they dug a pair of footholds at the lip of the ledge. At dawn, I worked my way across the ledge, cascading loose rock into Devil's Dip, until I reached the relative safety of an angular rock outcropping. Right there on a space smaller than my body, I fell asleep.

When I woke, the rain had quit and light showed through low clouds. But I couldn't see the top of Big Bear Ridge. A long way to go. I cursed myself and my father for making me take this counfounded Trek. He'd guided my training. He had been sorely pressed by our belligerent neighbors and must have realized his life expectancy was less than his predecessors in Crimson Sapphire. He had a fine grasp of the future, something to which I was now learning to dedicate myself. A lesson learned is a lesson not forgotten.

Hunger was overwhelming me when I found a series of cutbacks sort of swishing one way and then the other, but leading ever upward. I had to be about a third of the way up. That's when the pack of snarves came upon me. First came the slinker, scuttling the easy route in a panic. He didn't even see me. Unfortunately, he was going upward— and so were the snarves behind him and thus behind me. His panic alerted me for I knew well you can't hear an angry snarv until he wants you to. Three snarves ran around a rock face below me, saw me, and instantly changed their prey. I ran behind the slinker up the foot-wide path. Perhaps I could hold off the snarves; but then again perhaps I couldn't.

The path reached a ledge, a wide one, that reached back under an overhang.

And there stood another snarv. The slinker scooted around that one as his attention went immediately to me. The slinker disappeared into the darkness of the overhang, or fault or whatever it was. The snarv crouched.

No choice. I flung my new snarvskin cape in his face and followed with a quick sword stroke which disabled the beast.

I didn't have time to finish him for the first of the snarves chasing me came over the top of the ledge. I kicked a rock at him and backed up.

Suddenly, I felt dizzy. There was a strange taste on my tongue from the air. The other snarves were on the ledge— but curiously not attacking. The three ranged in front of me as if they were being cautious. The injured snarv dragged his body and left a trail of blood. Away from me. I looked around. The slinker lay behind me, not moving, but eyes rolling.

Three more snarves bounded up the trail and onto my ledge, joining their pack.

It came together then, as I recalled a Trekmaster Log entry. Whoever wrote it said something about gases or fires . . . I tried to remember, but my mind was fighting against me, patches of nothing edging into the corners of my brain and my vision. The hair on the nape of my neck rose and I finally heard the hiss of escaping gas. It was coming out of a small opening directly behind me and the now unconscious slinker.

My knees buckled.

I prayed for lightning to ignite the gas.

With a last effort, I groped around, found the slinker and dragged him out with me toward the pack of snarves. They watched. When the nausea began to recede and the snarves became bold again, I stopped, left the slinker, and retreated back into the gas flow about two of my body lengths. Here I scraped debris and dust from the ledge surface praying again for the right composition of rock. Then I scrambled off to the right watching the the snarves watch me until I was out of the gas flow.

The snarves had learned to be cautious of the gas. But the slinker was good bait. All they had to do was dart in and carry him off. They eyed me and then the slinker. Of course they took to the easier and more immediate meal. One snarv was bolder, but jealousy made the others follow him right away.

As they ran at the slinker, I leaped to my feet and threw a flintstone at the cleared rock on the ledge under the gas jet. It glanced off and I couldn't see a spark. I took my next-to-last flint, dried it on my tunic, and flung it also. The snarves were fighting over the slinker and dragging the poor creature off when the gas ignited with a whoosh. A straight flame lanced out and singed the rearmost snarves, and a small pocket of gas exploded. The concussion knocked me down but the force of it went out straight, rebounding off the rock wall, and knocked one snarv off the ledge and bowled the remaining ones over.

And extinguished the flame jet.

Smoldering snarves rolled and howled in the following deafening silence and ran off down the cutback. Two snarves lay either unconscious or dead on the ledge. A while later, my hearing returned. I ate a partially singed snarv haunch and cut a couple of slabs of meat for later. Right then I vowed I didn't need to see any more snarves a lot more than I didn't need to see a lot of other things. I think I understand what I just said. At the time, rationality was an elusive thing. I would have vowed the same about eating snarv meat, but snarv meat was becoming an acquired taste and when you're starving, well . . .

One night I was perched on some indefinable nubbin of rock, tired for I had to retrace my route many times that day dodging escaping gas. This tier of Big Bear Ridge must be riddled with faults and cracks and pockets of the stuff. As long as I was out in the wind, I was safe. In the distance, I could see several flames spurting out from the mountain's side. It was an unholy, unwordly experience. But they were all below me and I hoped I had passed most of the danger. If so, it meant that I was two-thirds of the way up Big Bear Ridge. The gorge swelled before me, dark and forbidding, and above me ran a great, upward leading crevice I planned to attack in the morning.

I was lying down and experiencing the transition between wakefulness and sleep when I felt something studying me. The Trek had sharpened my wits and perceptions considerably. At the time, I attributed it to survival instinct. Maybe it was. But I saw or heard nothing. Clouds had again covered the stars, but I thought I spied a blob, which is as good as I can describe it, floating out there, suspended above Devil's Dip. It was indistinct in the gloom. But I sensed some kind of intelligence. For a while I sat alert with my sword at ready, but the creature, if that be what it was, eventually glided off and I saw no more. However, the sensation of being observed persisted.

What could I do?

Nothing. So I did not waste time or effort doing so.

Soon I forgot how many days I had been upon this abominable Trek. No longer did I curse the Trek. No longer did I worry about the fate of my brothers. No longer did concerns of state and family intrude. I turned mechanical.

Just one handhold after another. One foothold after another. Hang patiently while rainstorm passes. Higher: blink against snow flurries. No part of my body escaped scrapes, lacerations, bruises, abuse and torture. My fingers swelled and only the cold helped hold down the swelling.

A lot of ice now. Holding on by an eyelash and when not enough purchase for that, by imagination.

An inevitable depression settled over me. I considered quitting and returning. Hadn't many of the original Trekmasters failed to make it past Teddy Bear Ridge? Past Devil's Dip? Only a few had reached the summit of Big Bear Ridge. And none that I recalled traveled all the way to sea level on the eastern side of the far ridge. Of course, the Log was sometimes vague and pages were missing. I prayed that I would find one of the mysterious inhabitants atop Big Bear Ridge, like some Trekmasters had. What would I do if I had to go *down* the other side of this monster I was climbing? If I did so, that would mean that eventually I'd have to repeat this whole damn process backward. All this told me I was not yet halfway to completion of the Trek and I felt more than halfway dead. Was it any wonder that my mood echoed the weather—drab, cold, dreary, gray?

I reflected I was doing a hell of a lot more praying on this Trek than I had done for many years. Roaland Cruz wouldn't believe it.

I'd begun clean shaven. I swore then, perhaps as my father before me, to retain my growing beard as a reminder of this insane task. Occasionally, thoughts of a besieged Crimson Sapphire crossed my mind and I felt helpless.

Hail beat at me just below the top of the ridge. Fist-sized ice balls glanced off me and my stinking snarv-hide cloak. Blood welled from where the hail struck. I was spread-eagled against a cliff face like some obscene Christ, fighting to maintain a tenuous grip when it came.

I knew I was dead, that I just hadn't died yet.

So I had nothing to lose. I shook one frozen hand free from its paralyzed grip and made a fist.

I shook my fist, defying the heavens, and swarmed up the rest of the way.

And I slipped, wrenching a leg painfully as I jammed it into a passing crack to save myself. I pulled myself back to the top with my hands and arms only.

As I wormed my way over the top onto a level place, my face struck the ribs of a human skeleton.

One of my predecessors had made it this far. The bones were wind-bleached and weather-etched. The story was easily told. A great crack ran laterally across the bridge of his skull. Her? Well, could have been. An expert could have told, but not me. Almost to the top, he or she must have fallen, as I did, recovered and continued, climbed over the parapet and died. Bled to death. Brain injury, who knows? The scope of the tragedy struck me. Others had made it less far than this one, yet had lived to reap the rewards.

I must have many sons for at least one to complete the Trek, I thought then.

On the contrary, was this any way for an intelligent, thinking man to gain command of a mighty nation? A hell of a way to weed out claimants to a throne. Couldn't there be a better method of selection? Right then I was disgusted more than anything.

But I remembered somebody's words, probably my mother's. "The Trek does not build character; it reveals it."

The hell with character, I thought. I wanted a warm bath, a cold drink, and a hot meal.

Suddenly, the sun came out and I realized I had made it to the top of Big Bear Ridge. The sun warmed my bones and life was again livable. Another peak, towering out of Big Bear Ridge, rose from the ridge to the north of the shoulder I was resting on. I walked as fast as I could on this miniature plateau. I hoped fervently to find a Webbine with a basketful of beefaloe liver and a bottle of good sour mash. I'd have traded a dozen crimson sapphires for that vision. But I had no luck.

Hours went by with the wind rising, finally howling, cutting through me like an icy executioner's blade. I remembered my recent defiance, though life was once again a dear thing, cursed my luck, and plunged over the side. Well, eased over, anyway, for the rope was fairly well frayed.

Compared to what I had been through, the climb down the eastern slope was a church picnic. The farther down I climbed, the better the weather became. It was as if some malevolent weather controlling spirit had turned benign. Hunger hurried me.

Finally the mountain simply turned into an easily negotiable slope, cut by canyons obviously dug by the streams of water pouring off the mountains.

The going was so much faster as to belie the effort I'd expended to this point. Eventually, the slope leveled off and I was walking through a glade-like forest I'd seen from above. The forest stretched for half a day's walk and, it had appeared from above, would go for many weeks' walk to the ocean. Which meant that there wasn't near the land area on this side of the ridges than on the human side. Interesting—if this fact foretold the population of Webbines. But since they dwelt as much in the ocean as on land, I could never vouch for total numbers of them.

A few forest slinkers, a lot of snobbis cropping the grass, and an occasional cheshire for rodent control were about.

No snarves. No volves.

All these creatures seemed tame so I could not force myself to slay one for food then. But many fruits grew on trees and bushes. Lesson learned: Never, after starvation, gorge on fruit. 'Nough said.

After that bout of illness, I drank some water and chewed on the local equivalent of grain and continued walking. Small patches of rain caressed me in direct counterpoint to the torrents which had assaulted me on the mountains.

While descending, I had seen a finger of the great ocean that snaked its way inland. And there I headed.

And there I found them.

I saw some in the distance as I crossed the veld. Not knowing what to do, I kept going. Nor did they approach until I reached the beach where the sea-finger lapped onto the land.

Then several greeted me; how I understood them, I didn't know. But they showed me grains and plants to eat so I could regain my strength. Sad to say, that first contact was somewhat anticlimactic as I was exhausted and fell asleep until the following day.

O:chacka became my unofficial companion. At least I think that's how his name is pronounced. Could be influenced by my recent thinking of ancient Earth's Chaka Zulu, and quite the opposite of the warlike Zulu, too. Or so I thought then. (To jump forward, ignoring proper chronological developments: You'd think these Webbines were all pious padre-candidates what with their solemn pronouncements, heavy thinking, logical arguments, patient and pedantic manners, and almost insufferable goodness. You'd think so. But. A snarv had found its way to this side and attacked a Webbine child: adults killed it with their minds somehow. A playful, but not mindful child: I could almost sense the mental force that went to the poor young Webbine and sent something into his mind, for his reactions were seen physically in chills and fever—and the Webbines appeared to be comfortable at any temperature. Hell, no wonder they all seemed to conform. I suspect I would conform, too, until I found a way to beat the system. At least I now understood why no snarves and volves were around on this side of the ridge—for long.)

/This place is our Home Ground,/ O:chacka explained. With strict attention, I had no trouble in communicating.

The Home Ground was an Eden-like area surrounding the finger of the sea. A central place where land and water trails met. Plentiful with land grown food. A training ground for youngsters. Adult Webbines teaching adolescents their philosophically based disciplines. They seemed to have an inborn grasp of mathematics and natural laws. Survival and cohabitation with nature appeared to be a basic instinct. Male dominated. Children stayed close to mothers until adolescence. (There are my judgments based on an admittedly small amount of unskilled observation.)

Surprisingly, for such a capable race, they seemed to have no racial or personal drive as we know it. Social or political or philosophical position was important—but living conditions and anything material was of little significance. They seemed to strive for inner accomplishment, whereas we strive for external or worldly accomplishment. My own guess is that you could characterize the Webbines by the quest of the answer to /Why?/ Humans, in contrast, it seems to me, ask "Why?", answer with "Because . . . " and take off from there for fun or profit or knowledge. Since I am not articulate in any of these sciences, I will stop my speculation here.

Except for one incident, which may explain what I was trying to say. One day O:chacka emerged from the sea and handed me a crimson sapphire.

/What will you do with it?/ he asked.

I thought. "Carry the damn thing back," I finally said, not able to come up with any fancy words or philosophical concepts to say "Use it to further my own ambitions."

They seemed to be a gentle people, filled with compassion and curiosity, and especially a thirst for learning. Such would not be bad for us and I determined then that learning should take a higher priority in Crimson Sapphire than it had to date. I would have learned more, save I spent a lot of time answering questions and explaining myself and the way we operated. During all this, it occurred to me that communication should be a science. Did not soldiers follow leaders who could best communicate with them? Were not most of humanity's historical problems a result of improper communication? So I invested time and effort into learning of these Webbines, how they talked, how they thought. Many hours did O:chacka and I converse and I got to where I could recognize certain auras (a skill which, when not used, atrophies quickly). But it did help to develop a certain sixth sense which has been of enormous benefit to my career and life to date . . . it helps to know if something or someone "feels" wrong. I suppose teenagers would call it "bad vibrations" or something. A heightened awareness might be a better way of putting it.

Yet overriding all was my constant worry about Crimson Sapphire and how it fared. Perhaps a more leisurely approach to the Trek, rather than a hell-for-leather emergency plunge immediately after the death of the current Trekmaster, would lead to better understanding of the Webbines and thus a more qualified monarch for Bear Ridge.

A lingering question: If the Webbines are such as I have characterized them, why then do they condone the continuance of the Trek? It would seem that a humble, peace loving, logical thinking race would not be a part of some killing exercise. Why allow so many lives, albeit human, to be lost in search of something that need not be found, and if found, could be gotten in some safer manner?

This I asked O:chacka and he could have been human in his answer. I've never heard such a convoluted series of off-kilter reasoning which never did answer the question. He would have made a fine bureaucrat. While I do not think there is a definite plot by the Webbines to influence the human community, I think perhaps they like the status of being a party to the selection process of the next Trekmaster and thus having some small part in the destiny and management of human society on their planet. I'm certain that, as premier statisticians, they realized the inevitability of humans on Bear Ridge uniting, sooner or later, and thus they have some conduit into that leadership. I only began to see their capability in subtlety, so if there were a plot, it would probably be unfathomable. I noted that each generation of Trekmasters seemed to reach farther toward their Home Ground that I finally attained. I had felt watched on the Trek. Yet I was not approached by any of them until I reached the Home Ground. And this I didn't understand: Webbines are not built for climbing. Much food for thought.

But I've long since determined that I have no time for deep philosophical questions. That I shall leave for others who are more suited. A terrific urge, once I was rested and had my jewel, overcame me to return to my world and resume where I left off. Come hell or high ridges, I was determined to live my life, find my destiny . . . this becomes too poetic. Suffice it to say, I learned as much as I could and departed when I thought I was ready to attack the way back.

I rewove ropes while we talked. These were longer and stronger and weighed less. And O:chacka pointed out a less difficult route, one which I might not have found.

Nonetheless, the ascent and descent of Big Bear Ridge was again exhausting.

Days later I was walking through Devil's Dip Gorge, retracing my footsteps to find the protection of the cave I'd used previously, starving, weak, scratched and bleeding from a couple of cuts, when a pack of volves discovered me. Twenty or so, unusual even for a pack of volves.

I was slow.

One heavy bastard knocked me down and was doing his best to chew off my arm and protect his kill from the attentions of his fellows. I didn't have time to wish for the as-yet-non-existent assegai, and the sword was too long to use well, so I pounded him on the head with my fist and the hilt of my sword. I'd be dead if he hadn't spent more effort saving me for himself from his packmates. These latter were darting in and nipping at him and me.

And they were flying over us. One of the advantages of four three-jointed legs is leaping ability. Height is another—where snarves are built close to the ground, volves are taller. And they are fast, fairly flying over the ground when they are in a hurry. All this and their sharp, downward streching claws were probably developed to counter the weight/strength advantage of their natural enemies, the snarves. Which probably accounts for their light weight, comparatively speaking to their size. Unlike the snarv, their hide is soft. But a volv is a tenacious beast which explains the old saying "volv ugly", referring to a bed companion. When you wake up next to her, you will chew off your arm to make sure you don't wake her. (Not a sexist joke, his/her are interchangeable.) Anyway, I'd seen volves fly over a plains snobbi on the dead run and rake four sets of claws across the animal's back.

So I managed to stick my sword into the air and gutted one while struggling with the first.

I thought it was a shame to die this way, Trek accomplished, a kingdom to run, and alone.

And then, suddenly and out of nowhere, came a shout. A youngster, maybe ten years younger than I, slender-strong, jumped into the fray. He was unarmed except for a great bundle of rope which seemed to weigh him down and almost cover his entire torso. He flew into the pack of volves like a whirling dervish, all arms, legs, and feet attacking quicker than I could follow. I heard volv bones break, skulls crack, beasts howl.

The diversion allowed me to gut the volv on top of me with my knife and scramble to my feet. My sword swung with renewed vigor. I tried using aura-control to drive the animals off, and was only partially successful. Or else the boy's onslaught and my resurgence unnerved them. I hacked about, sword blurring. Fur and flesh and hide flew. Damn volves were flying and leaping about like flies on carrion. This fact did make it easier to intercept them with my sword at shoulder level. And the kid was deadly with his feet at any height.

Shortly, only a half dozen or so were left, and these had cornered the boy and were bearing him to the ground. The coiled rope saved his life from their flaying claws. I decapitated two, kicked another off, and the rest fled.

But I missed one in my haste. He slammed into me from behind, and I dropped to one knee to brace the fall. I twisted and shoved the sword point down his cavernous throat, shearing off teeth under his short snout—strange for an animal with such a large overbite.

And heard a crack.

Unfortunately, my knee, in twisting position, had come down on the young man's right leg, and snapped a bone.

He didn't make a sound.

Exhausted, I sank to the ground beside the kid. I would have probably bled to death had he not bound my wounds then with cloth cut from my ragged tunic. He fed me water from a bladder and I drank. Still he did not mention his broken bone.

"I thank you for the rescue," I told him once I regained enough strength to speak.

"It was nothing," he replied haughtily. I could sense disappointment in his voice from his broken leg. But he was still a cocky bastard.

"What are you doing in this God-forgotten land?" I asked, rising wearily, and searching for sticks to use as a splint. As far as I knew, there were no settlements anywhere near Teddy Bear Ridge, much less here in the gorge. Most of what remained of humanity was spread along the western edge of the great plain through the farming and ranching lands to the sea. At the time, kingdoms and townships and city-states stretched from as far north as crops would grow to the bottom of this continent. There was one kingdom on another continent, several days' sailing to the west. But this latter, peopled by Asian-extracts, was seldom visited and they kept to themselves. They had a Filipino name for it and a Chinese name for it and a Japanese name for it; but some on this continent called it the Faroff Continent lands:

"It's my business," he said, bringing me back to the present. "But I suppose there is no harm in you knowing. I would surmount these ridges and become a Trekmaster."

Shocked, I asked, "You would rule Crimson Sapphire?"

"No. Last I heard, they already have a King. Perhaps I shall obtain one of those crimson sapphires and return to my own kingdom—Bexar."

I knew of it. It was a harsh, poor kingdom, the center of which was the city of Lonestar. As far as I recalled, its people were well respected, but not enough numbers to be counted in the growing continent-wide fighting. "Are you of a royal family?"

"Of course not," he said, "what's that got to do with it?"

On thinking about it, I had no answer. "So you would be a Trekmaster?"

"Yes, I already said that."

"You are rather young," I pointed out. I lined up stout branches and began to bind them on his leg.

"So? I didn't notice you complaining about my age when I pulled all those volves off you. Should I have waved my birth record at them? Besides, in Bexar we are men early."

"Still, a difficult journey." Yet here he was.

"And you?" he asked. "Your presence here?"

I felt uncomfortable with this cocksure youngster. I showed him my crimson sapphire. He said nothing, but his gaze went again to me as if taking my measure for the first time. "What is your name?"

"Delancy Camp." He thought for a moment. "And you must be one of the Shepherds?"

"Thomas Jefferson Shepherd. I have . . . had two brothers, perhaps . . . ?"

"No, I haven't seen them." He looked at his broken leg and I could see the disappointment in his eyes. He could not continue on his quest for a sapphire. He refused to give up, though, and told me he would go on.

"Look," I said. "*I* am not returning up Big Bear Ridge. I've had enough. And it's too dangerous for you to stay here in this gorge with a broken leg. I am leaving. Will you come with me?"

He looked up at the mammoth peak atop Big Bear Ridge. "You climb up old Forty-K there?"

"Across a shoulder of it."

He nodded appreciatively. "I'll go with you, then."

With both of our ropes and his skill, Teddy Bear Ridge was easier than I'd had it alone. With a broken leg, his climbing skill was greater than mine with two good legs. Though, in my own defense, the strenuous going of the past few weeks had severely weakened me and contributed to my slow pace. Together we made it, and not so surprisingly came to trust and depend on each other.

When we reached the foothills on the western side of Teddy Bear Ridge, he looked back. "I used to say my mother raised not a fool, bless her poor departed soul. But now, I'm not so sure."

"Come with me to Crimson Sapphire," I urged. "There you shall have honorable employment and a fine life."

"You think to buy me off? You would be the only living Trekmaster? You just don't want me to return and complete the Trek by myself. Perhaps one day I shall."

"Go then, damn it," I almost shouted. "Be gone with you."

"Nah. I can't, Thomas Jefferson Shepherd, for my pride is a great thing. I cannot allow the Trekmaster in my care to die of his wounds before he returns home triumphant and glorious." He tried not to smile. "Besides, the Trek has already been mastered this generation. Not much fun in being second, is there?"

"You'll play more havoc yet, Delancy Camp." I'd talked him out of taking the Trek—at least for now. But if and when I had my own sons, I would send them off to their deaths on the ridges. Well, it doesn't make sense to me, either.

18: GWEN

Gwen handed Summer the last page of TJ's Trekmaster Log entry.

"So now you know," he said.

"It doesn't surprise me." Unsuspected depths. The origin of the Summer-TJ bond now explained. With TJ barely breathing across the room, she looked at Summer with renewed respect. Gwen had been fully aware of the hidden aspects of the court jester—was he not her husband's closest friend and advisor? Had he not protected TJ for these many years? And was he not Mike's chief nonacademic instructor? Yet, he'd seemed to take on a new dimension since TJ had been shot—poisoned. The trouble was, Summer could not go fully public.

And she herself had refused to leave TJ's side. Felicia and Mike had carried the formal workload. And the pace was telling on Felicia—her face was gaunt and her eyes showed the strain. Gwen knew full well a mother's concern for her son. But Felicia would hold up. Gwen remembered the time when Felicia had had to govern the entire Kingdom alone. Until TJ and Summer came flying back from those awful ridges. One of her proudest memories was of a magnificent, torn, bloody, purposeful Thomas Jefferson Shepherd striding up the corridor in the throne room interrupting a formal court session and with Summer Camp limping along behind. He stopped in front of Felicia sitting on the throne as Queen-Regent, held out his hand, palm up, and displayed his crimson sapphire.

There had been no doubt who was in immediate command. Gwen was in awe of Felicia's royal performance. Instead of flying to him as a mother would, she'd stood and formally relinquished the throne. And arranged proper coronation ceremonies.

It was then that Gwen had known she was in love with TJ—probably along with every other woman in the great throne room that day. Yet in the patriarchal society of lords

131

and ladies, she was destined to marry whomever her father selected for her.

The abbreviated coronation ceremony lasted an hour. TJ then met with the Federation Exploratory Party. He spent most of the night in dialogue with them, and in the morning joined the army of Crimson Sapphire and went out to conquer a planet.

And Summer went with him.

"Well," she looked at Summer, "TJ always said you were fearless."

"I was younger then; now I'm scared."

"Me, too."

Gwen saw that the ordeal and having to be in this room was telling on Summer. He'd lost color and his voice was softer then ever.

The outside sentry knocked and Felicia entered.

"My son?"

"The same," Gwen answered.

Felicia went to the bed. "Nora Ahimsa has complained to me. Why is she not admitted to treat Thomas?"

Gwen glanced at Summer. He shrugged his answer. "Tell her, Summer."

Summer explained.

The Queen Mother said, "It figures. That is so like Thomas. I should have guessed. Never thought my son for so much of a schemer."

"Mother . . . how is Mike performing?"

"Fine, Gwen. As if he were born to the throne . . ."

Gwen caught the hesitation in Felicia's words. "But?"

"Down and dirty, Gwen, I'm too tired to be diplomatic. You—and I—have raised a young man who I think fears the Trek he might soon have to attempt."

"No," said Summer. He met Gwen's gaze. "Mike fears nothing but himself. He is young and unsure. I don't think it's the physical danger or effort, either. Something else, something within his inner core."

Gwen agreed to herself. Mike wasn't particularly interested in the arts of war or soldiering, but he did not ignore his training in these, either. She preferred to think of her son as gentle. And it had probably been her influence which caused this personality trait. She had done her best. What with TJ off to war for too many years to remember, it had all been up to her. And Felicia. Had they failed? Should they have been harsher on the young Mike as he grew up in his father's long but absent shadow? Would they all pay for the mistake, if mistake it was, with Mike's life when he failed on the Trek?

Felicia accepted a mug of chocolate wine from Summer. "You could be right, Summer. As I told Thomas and his brothers when they embarked on the Trek, the Trek doesn't build character, it reveals it. And so it was with Thomas. Perhaps the same will happen to Mike."

Gwen did not understand her own feelings. She agreed with Felicia's reasoning—but. Was it worth gambling Mike's life to find out? She surprised herself by saying, "Perhaps it is time to do away with the Trek and its traditions?"

"No," said Summer.

"No," said Felicia simultaneously. Felicia had paid for the Trek with two sons. Gwen suspected Felicia had had to embrace the Trek to reconcile her loss. "The kingdom needs a firm hand. That is a problem now. There are dissident elements always present, waiting for the right opportunity."

"That's true," Summer said. "I've heard the Padres are pushing. And the nobles are feeling their weight for the first time since TJ subordinated them to his system. And the trade unions are clamoring."

"And that ain't all, either," said Felicia. "Gwen, do you remember that young man, the one with the thumb drums?"

"Certainly."

"Well, he is preaching, lecturing, whatever you'd call it." Felicia hesitated.

"So? What is he saying, Mother?"

"Kellen Sing," Summer nodded. "My spies tell me the same thing. One man, one vote. Bear Ridge ought to be ruled by the people, for the people. Elected government, an ancient litany."

"He can't be serious," Gwen said.

"He is and he has Mike's ear, Gwen," Summer said gently.

Felicia nodded emphatically.

"Many of the students here in Crimson Sapphire are becoming ardent followers. But I'm not worried," Summer added.

Yet, Gwen finished silently for him. She didn't voice her own worry that the preachings of Kellen Sing might have the effect of reinforcing Mike's determination not to follow his father's footsteps, literal and figurative. Again she felt a

pang of guilt when she thought about Mike and his obligations to the kingdom and the people. Had she instilled the
proper virtues? If he failed, it would be her fault, her
responsibility. Even including TJ's "official affairs," Mike
was the most consistent sore point between her and her
husband. Who'd have ever thought, she wondered, that my
life led here, here to this moment worried about my son
while my husband lies dying within reach?

She remembered. Her father had pledged her to Tirano,
an alliance which would have linked both planets—and en-
riched her father greatly. And then along came TJ, the new
young King, bloody from battle, just as he had been on
returning from the Trek, sitting at a conference with Federation representatives and Tirano. He had overwhelmed her.
And her father could not spite the wishes of the King of
Crimson Sapphire. Gwen wondered if Tirano had ever married. Probably. On reflection, she thought that Tirano was
only looking for another kind of jewel, a female to show off.

Through all the problems, Gwen had never regretted
marrying TJ instead of Tirano.

19: TJ

Unbidden, it came to him, like a rock to clutch in stormy
seas, something in his mind which coalesced his thinking.
Thinking? Where? Somewhere.

The words: I suspect the only death you ever accept is
your own; and that only after the fact.

Before a battle he'd spoken those words to . . . Summer,
that was who.

Battle, always battle. His recall consisted of a series of
battles. In war. Against mountainous ridges. With recalcitrant peoples whose visions were not as farseeing as his.
With . . . Gwen . . . whose goals were not the exact same as
his. With Michale . . . who was not the same as the kid in
Devil's Dip, not a warrior prince, no matter how much he
dreamed/prayed/wanted Mick to be so.

The words had seemed to be sucked out of the quagmire

in his mind. A fuzzy warm feeling accompanied the theft, so he was not unduly angered at the invasion. The action brought him to a higher level of awareness, giving him, now, some minor internal control. Mind games he'd learned at the Home Ground came to his aid.

Control.

Another battle. Fight for control. Not normal to have no control. Drag up the forcefulness of old. Cling to it like that rock. Toss off anger at lack of control of physical being.

THINK!

Last remembered thought: diamond shaped flash, in and out of shadows, from above. Searing pain. Recall shape and . . . instant pain, relief of unconsciousness.

A handle: the shape. A crossbow bolt from above. An omen. A Finger of God lancing into him. Memory: The Finger of God. The Trek. Ah, this was more like it. History and fate intertwining. The Zulu assegai. The single weapon which had made the difference in the Consolidation wars. And consequently the symbol of the Muster. Certainly, homemade spears had abounded on . . . Bear Ridge . . . before his invention (reinvention?) of the assegai. There had been swords for close in-fighting, crossbows and the long bow for distance fighting. But, using his hoarded books, he'd come up with a strong alloy for the spear blade. He'd sheathed the blade to the hard, yowel wood shaft. Then manufactured them, actually mass produced the assegai. In battle, the assegai proved light and more effective than the sword for in-fighting. With his improvements, the assegai could and did parry sword thrusts. The spear shaft also gave the warrior a greater reach with the broad, razor-edged blade. And when thrown, was effective as a spear. All this gave his troops an advantage, and any advantage was necessary to the outnumbered . . . Crimson Sapphire army.

. . . the years of killing and fighting and battles had worn them down. Attrition was going to drag Crimson Sapphire under, finally, not lost battles or exhaustion of resources. He had hammered a coalition here, an alliance there, temporary things, actions designed to maximize his strength. Then came the realization that he/Crimson Sapphire would gradually be worn down until no one was left to fight.

Last desperate gamble: A final battle between the major participants in the continent-wide wars. First, cagily set it up: guerrillas, under Summer's command, harass enemy, infiltrate, kill off leaders. Wreak havoc. Second, forge real alliances, promise 'em anything. What the hell, they had tried to conquer Crimson Sapphire, hadn't they? Third, fake a coalition or two: Let spies tell, erroneously, two city-states and two kingdoms that each was allied to Crimson Sapphire secretly. Let 'em fight amongst themselves, get 'em out of combat arena, clean up what was left. Fourth: As always, insure the fighting takes place on someone else's land; decimation of antagonists' home ground aids in overcoming antagonists. Fifth: In all the confusion, attack attack attack strongest enemies. Diversions, tricks, lies, use terrain and superior troops. Lead battles proudly yourself. The final battle: Fake several of them into fighting amongst themselves, tricks and schemes working. Until they realize what you're doing and figure out your tactics and unite against you. Then just outfight 'em. When all is down to the final finality and the enemy appears to have won: Bring in Summer and his guerrillas from their flanks. The assegai makes the difference. One final glorious charge against overwhelming odds; a battle against combined enemies to be savored as an entity itself. Sixth: consolidate and mop up confused others. Not much fight left in anybody, including his own troops.

He remembered fondly that last battle. As the battle raged, three divisions had broken off from the fighting. He led one, Summer another, Manny Vero the third. The few who lived through that final assault on the enemy's leaders told the story. Shepherd, Camp, Vero, virtually alone, hacking and slashing up the hill, personally reaching the command position, blood lust coloring everything, hand-to-hand fighting with leaders and subalterns until all were slain and the three victorious. Below them, the tide turned and their forces won out. Shepherd, who had visions. Camp, the kid from the gorge. Vero, who had worked his way up through the ranks and hated nobility.

Each year since, the survivors of the final battle gather: The Muster. Adopt the Muster medallion. Generals, sergeants, padres, cooks, disabled war vets, vaqueros—all meet and reaffirm allegiance to each other—and to him. The initial reluctance to speak of their bloody battle led to rumors. The rumors led to speculation. Did the Muster medallion symbol refer to the war assegai? Or to the Finger of God? The two were inseparable. In addition, the annual secret gatherings enhanced the mystery of the Muster and those who wore the medallion. In time, he'd seen the possibilities of legend, and did not discourage rumor and gossip, laced with some fact, so that those who wore the Medallion became a sort of secret society. Nothing specifically formal other than the yearly reunion in the wilds and away from the public, but an inner pride kept them united. As a result, the general population gave those who wore the medallion much credit and honor.

"Just a bunch of tired, but lucky, warriors all growing old." Summer had said one time.

"So be it," TJ had replied. "They proved themselves, they lived through the years of the wars, they earned the legends surrounding them."

"We," Summer had said.

"Right." TJ had learned to use anything he could to enhance his position. God knew, consolidating a planet was difficult enough, use any tool. Like he used history. TJ doubted that any man on Bear Ridge was as militarily versed as he was, even before the Consolidation wars.

It had all begun with an assistant navigator on the "cattle ship" which brought the colonists to Bear Ridge in the first place. The first Bear Ridge Shepherd. Some called him the "Ragin' Cajun." One of the colonists' minor leaders had been a girl named Rebel. They fell in love and Shepherd had jumped ship.

The last the colonists had heard from human civilization was a garbled radio message from the already established colony on Two Tongues. They'd waited and waited. One result of the suddenness of the collapse had been the crash of a Pan-Asian warship on the far continent. But all they had known was that human civilization was in a major war between elements.

Then came the Rollback, for generations, until technology had lapsed on Bear Ridge without further support from Earthe. Humanity reverted to primitive agriculture. Survival struggle, that was all. Smart ones saved the sheepaloe. The genetic development of the sheepaloe had grown from something on Earthe called the "Cornucopia Project." One all-purpose food animal whose protective coat could be used to weave tough clothing. Another part of the Cornucopia Project also contributed to the ability of humans to colonize other worlds: amaranth. Amaranth, an ancient Earthe plant, was redesigned to provide protein, minerals, vitamins, and vegetable fiber. The engineers also bred into it weather and insect resistant properties. A man-tall plant which produced massive seed pods and heads, and could thrive on little water. The ag specialists had designed varieties of amaranth to fit conditions on each planet to be colonized.

It was a pity that social and political conventions did not keep up with scientific and engineering achievements. But thus it had been so for the history of mankind.

The Ragin' Cajun and Rebel Shepherd and a group of others had started a community in the mountains, trying to avoid the conflict which spilled over into the colony.

TJ always took a lesson from his first Bear Ridge ancestor. The Cajun had maintained the last operational power unit on the planet, guarding it and babying it jealously. Finally, before his death, he had seen that the connectors had deteriorated. Additionally, most of the equipment the unit powered was inoperative. No replacement parts. His last use of the power unit was to transfer all the computer data he had onto permaplas books—just printed everything he could onto these almost indestructible sheets and bound them by subject. Since then, bindings had worn and been replaced, but the knowledge printed on the sheets remained legible. Cajun had concentrated on subjects which would one day be of use to a technologically reverted people. History, science, math, ag, engineering, military science and history, and the like. Then one day the power unit could no longer function, and Cajun had punched the "DAMP/KILL" button that safed the nuclear unit.

Eventually, because the Shepherd clan in the mountains was too thin to continually regenerate itself, the Shepherds had moved down from the mountains—and brought their books with them. TJ had turned many of the books over to his scientists and professors for copying so students and researchers could use them.

Since he'd become King, TJ maintained standing rewards for pre-Rollback or colonization items. These, when found by his agents, he hid in the caves and tunnels of the original Shepherd settlement. There was nothing he could mechanically use, but the artifacts served to focus his attention, the past reminding him of a future, the past goading his ambitions. The almost "alien" artifacts somehow helped lift the parochial barriers in his mind. He developed and adapted new ideas such as periodic governmental reorganization, changing the role of women in the society. He didn't know whether to attribute his problem solving ability to the ancient artifacts or not, but they didn't hinder him. A mental crutch? No. A goad was better, a tantalizing glimpse of what could be.

Yes, studying history had paid.

Now he, Thomas . . . Jefferson . . . Shepherd, ruled the planet. Or most of the world, he amended. He did not consider the Webbines under his crown. And sometimes the Orientals on the Faroff Continent, which wasn't all that far by ship, only paid him lip service. He even found it difficult to keep track of who had the upper hand over there. Japanese, Filipinos, Chinese. Sometimes they called themselves the Greater Co-Prosperity Sphere, sometimes other things. He'd heard recently of a resurgence of a militant faction: the Huks. To minimize resistance and trouble, he'd broken his own rules and appointed an Ethnarch who had been born and raised Chinese on the Faroff Continent. They were a mean bunch over there anyway, had not contributed to the fighting during TJ's wars, so he had left them alone. Not much economics or profit in a place so far away and difficult to reach. And those Huks, they were wild. Named their cities like Killvolv, Killsnarv, Killman. He caught a wisp of mirth: an old joke to himself about bundling up all the Huks and dropping them on Tirano's ranch on Two Tongues. That would keep old Tyranosaurus Rex busy.

. . . that power hungry, bird-mouthed fool. A pure political animal, that one. 'Course, TJ admitted, I don't pass up political opportunity when it slaps me in the face either . . . one of the most satisfying acts of life: stealing Gwendlyon from Tirano. That's the way it all started out, but then it turned into something very serious, our relationship. Damn if events hadn't outrun my planning for once. But I never regretted it, not one minute . . . well, sometimes, but on the whole, our marriage has been satisfying and beneficial to the kingdom. Don't know why really, or where came the idea, but we almost lost each other when I went through my phase where I had all those affairs. Necessary, sure, but I coulda handled them with more secrecy and subtlety. A few very rocky years. Gwen had seemed to understand—or bore her burden quietly for the most part. She'd been having troubles, female troubles, after Mick's birth, and that's when I'd sought solace elsewhere.

When Nora said we'd have no more children, I rebelled, and continued with my affairs after having sworn off them. At least we maintained our royal dignity and let not a shard of our marital trouble show through the official veneer. And she'd stuck by me, first-class wife all the way. Not a sexist thing to mention, but a truism. Hell, I owe her for her patience and understanding . . .

. . . but life's a tradeoff sometimes, ain't it? She owes me for my patience and understanding. About Mick. And the way she raised my heir. Damn it, I wasn't *home* to contribute much to his development. Did she raise him to be a goddamn pansy to spite me? No, I don't think so. She had only one child, so she lavished love and affection on him— and I was gone for the most part. Perhaps, perhaps Gwen doesn't approve of all the necessary blood that gets spilled because of me. Well, God damn it all, neither do I. But there are more reasons for doing things in my position than pure ambition . . .

Where the hell is Summer? I need to get out and move, practice swords, ride a speeding horse, run with the recruits, burn some energy.

Summer? Gwen?

Where?

What the hell is going on? Strange. My anger overflows and I . . . can't . . . do . . . anything. . . .

Gwen?

20: GWEN

I shall marry Summer Camp, she thought suddenly.

Gwen eased her back. The pain there reminded her of pregnancy. Hours remained until dawn. Summer was off, somewhere in the palace, conferring with Alfred and General Vero. The days of worry had been long and discouraging. She tried to make herself more comfortable, could not, and rose to pour some of Summer's chocolate wine.

TJ is dying, I just know it.

She stood in front of the liquor cabinet staring at bottles of dark liquid.

The long night had been lonely with only TJ present and—how had the Webbine put it?—at death's beckon.

Fear had been creeping up on her for days. Now it overwhelmed her. She gulped the entire goblet of wine.

Fear of change, of circumstances no longer the same. Fear of responsibility to the kingdom. Fear for her son. Despair: TJ's death would lead directly to Mike's death on the Trek, she just knew it. She poured more wine and, on a whim, added sour mash to it.

She wondered what TJ would do in her place. He'd come up with some scheme all right. But he'd never been as down as she was right now. She envied his self-sufficiency. Oh, many times had he told her he could not cope without her. But his actions belied that. TJ could cope anywhere under any circumstances.

But TJ wasn't here now, not really. Here and now she was trying to rule a kingdom with a ragged coalition. Certainly Felicia and Mike and Alfred and Manny Vero were doing more than their part. She thought the wine-sour mash mixture tasted like a dead slinker, whatever that tasted like, so she pushed the goblet aside and filled a mug with some of Felicia's homemade citrus tea.

And Summer. Summer was wonderful, guiding everything and staying behind the scenes at the same time. He was into everything, making decisions and plans and running the day-to-day affairs that she wouldn't have even considered.

And there it was: A TJ-esque scheme, a grand one.

A coup!

Her mind worked furiously. She gulped the tea.

First I marry Summer. Then *he* could rule as regent, doing what he's doing now, but with a public profile. Which would consolidate power. And scare off those double-dealing nobles, and hold in check the power hungry padres. So far, so good. Marrying me, the Queen, would legitimatize his authority—and when it became known that he'd taken the Trek, albeit that he hadn't traveled as far as TJ over the ridges (none other had either, of course), the people would love him. A simple switch of a fake crimson sapphire for the real one as TJ's coffin was closed and lowered into the ground would give living proof of Summer's claim upon the throne. The best benefit: this plan would give Mike more time to ready himself for the Trek—or for Bear Ridge to gain Federation membership and thus hopefully discontinue the requirement for the Trek. And Summer. He was a good man, a dedicated man. He would step down when Mike was ready to take over.

Darn, TJ, I miss you already. She realized she was looking at him now without seeing him. She turned and poured
more wine into the dregs of her tea.

She rolled the plan around her tongue and her mind.
From every angle it looked good . . . or rather, the best of
all possible scenarios. It would require sacrifice on her part,
but the kingdom was worth it. And Mike's life.

A strong man in charge again!

The more she studied it, the more she appreciated the
nuances of the idea. TJ would have been proud of her . . .
whoops, would be proud of her. She did not love Delancy
Camp. She liked him. She believed that out of respect for
TJ and because it would be his duty, Summer would agree
to the idea. All men love power, would jump at the opportunity . . . if he didn't, she'd threaten to marry that old man
who led the nobles, the current president of the Forty.
That's all it would take to force Summer to marry her.
Felicia would see right through it, as would Summer. But
that was all right. It was for the good of the kingdom, both
would realize that immediately. And agree.

But Summer Camp? He was deadly, too deadly. He killed.

But not indiscriminately.

He was still a killer.

TJ killed also.

That's different.

Oh? How?

Uh . . . TJ didn't kill in cold blood.

You think. He agonizes in public, preaches he has to do
what he has to do. Words probably said by the first cave
man.

So? He used . . . uses . . . clichés and words to cover his
true feelings.

Are your true feelings showing now?

Yes, damn it. I don't know what to do. That plan is the
only thing I can come up with. Maybe Summer has some
idea.

Your plan is all predicated on protecting Mike. Keeping
him safe.

Yes

Maybe that's not the best way.

MIKE IS ALL I HAVE LEFT!

You're just desperate now. You've had no sleep. You're
burned out. Too much has happened too swiftly.

So? I have no choice.

Wanna bet? Why don't you ask *Mike* what he thinks?

No.

Weariness overcame her and she poured some of TJ's sour mash into the dregs of her tea and chocolate wine. She couldn't think any more. One thought comforted her: *Fighting with myself over my idea proves I am not afraid of responsibility, not afraid of what happens to me.*

Pride was becoming all. Was it? Yes, it was all she had left. That and a Summer-like dedication to doing what was right for her family and her kingdom.

This and her willingness to marry a killer like Summer Camp showed the depth of her commitment, and . . .

The door slammed open and Summer strode swiftly in and turned to wait. He had a purpose about him, so she decided to wait before broaching her plan. Then in walked a soldier she'd never seen before. He was big and broad and hairy. He pulled a strange case out of a sack and looked at her.

Manny Vero came in behind him and stepped in front of her, accidentally, tearing her gaze from the stranger's eyes.

Immediately she noticed the electric tension in Manny and Summer.

Hope?

"Gwen?" Summer said. "Ignoring custom, may I present Jean-Claude Lafitte Fitzroy?"

The man nodded casually and looked around.

She stood, the now-empty mug forgotten in her hand. Could it be?

"The Queen, Gwendlyon, Jean-Claude," Summer said.

"My pleasure, Ma'am." His voice was like a mountain waterfall. "Lemme at TJ." She was suddenly very sober.

"Right."

"I'll stand guard outside, Summer," Manny Vero volunteered.

"Good idea."

Gwen and Summer followed Fitzroy to the bedside. He looked at TJ and shook his head. "TJ looks like a bear in hibernation." He swept a small table clean and set his machine upon it. He opened one side and removed some tubing and some wires. He attached the wires to TJ's head and his chest. He pulled a protective sheath off one of the tubes and a sliver of metal or glass winked in the light. He lifted TJ's head and put his hand under TJ's neck so his head lay back at an angle. "Prop a pillow under there, Camp. Yeah, like that."

Before Gwen could object, Fitzroy had sprayed TJ's neck with something and was inserting the needle.

"Carotid," Fitzroy rumbled, "below the Y."

Gwen had to avert her eyes as he inserted tubing in several other parts of TJ's body.

"He looks bad, Camp. Poisoned quarrel, you say?"

"Yes."

Fitzroy fiddled with his machine. "This little beauty is something else, let me tell you. Cost a pot o' gold. But earns its keep. One man can carry it. Plug it into the blood system strategically, and turn it on. Them other wires, they're monitors—and will give us human heart rate electrical shock if we need it—not to mention electromagnetic treatment and stimulation. The box diagnoses foreign elements. Say. You reckon human chemical makeup is the same on Bear Ridge as elsewhere?" When neither Gwen nor Summer answered, he continued. "Oh, well, we ain't got a choice anyway. Humans should be humans. Once this thingamajig gets pumping, it'll run all his blood through its innards, filter the bad junk out, rebuild it, put in antibiotics, coagulants, vitamins, minerals, whatever is needed. Hope it works."

Gwen put her hand on Summer's arm and squeezed. "Summer?"

"I trust him, Gwen."

She relaxed a little. But then caught a strange undercurrent.

Fitzroy appraised her. She saw more intelligence in his eyes than she expected. "Don't worry, Lady. I ain't all that technically articulate, but the machine does all the work anyway. And I've used it plenty before."

She saw TJ's chest heave slightly. Blood began throbbing in his neck near where the tube was inserted. His breathing was becoming audible.

"What do we do now?" she asked. She straightened her dress self-consciously. Summer looked at her and she realized she was still holding his arm. His eyes had fastened on hers. Could he have guessed? Summer's done some amazing things, had surprised her more than once with his empathy. Could he read her idea of marrying him in her eyes? No, no way he could . . . could he?

"Wait," Fitzroy said, rescuing her. "It takes a while to process all that blood properly. And for the machine to do its job." He applied short strips of tape to the tubes where they met TJ's skin. "Everything's gotta be antiseptic, they tell me."

Flippant bastard! That's my husband's life you are toying with! A sudden thought occurred to her. She wondered if Fitzroy guessed Summer would kill him instantly should TJ die? She hadn't known it until now, but upon reflection, she knew in that case Fitzroy would never leave here alive.

And she'd considered marrying Summer?

She shook her head and walked away from the bed. Get hold of yourself, girl. You can't even control your thoughts. Your judgment is so far off where it should be that you can't even think straight.

Fitzroy was flipping switches, checking indicators on the side of his machine.

To cover her nervousness, Gwen poured three glasses of sour mash. Summer accepted and sipped.

Fitzroy tossed his down. "Rather have chocolate wine, if'n you don't mind, Ma'am. Anybody can brew up good sour mash."

She poured half a bottle into a large mug and Fitzroy thanked her with eyes beneath bushy brow. He sniffed and tasted. "Ah, well worth the trip. My crew expects a case or two of this, Summer. Call it an overcharge."

"First fix TJ," Summer directed.

Couldn't Fitzroy see the danger? Summer had relaxed some, but was still tense. She could feel random pyschic energy exude from him. But she knew Summer and his moods well, she could read him like . . . like a brother. Could Fitzroy?

Fitzroy hadn't paid her much attention. Now he was studying Summer over the rim of his mug. Which meant that he understood the stakes. Now she realized why Manny had decided to wait outside. Doubtless there were a number of additional Gyrenes outside waiting, waiting for a command.

Fitzroy understood, all right. Only his calculating eyes gave him away. He certainly didn't appear concerned. Quietly, he said, "Situation acknowledged, Camp. Remember, you are the one who called me."

Summer nodded and grinned at him, but there was no mirth in the gesture. Muscles were still bunched under his tunic. Gwen guessed that Fitzroy had some kind of modern weapon concealed on his person. Then she followed through on the thought and realized that he must have given his shipmates contingency instructions should he not return.

Why must men do this thing? Why? Where was trust? They were like two strange male snarves, ready to do battle because that's the way it was.

She moved swiftly, took Summer's arm. "You're tired, Summer. Come over here and sit down." She escorted him to a couch and forced him into it—obviously against his will. Then she went to Fitzroy and put her arm through his. All this time she'd kept her body between them. "Mr. Fitzroy *I* want to thank you for trying to save my husband. You have my gratitude." She turned to look at Summer. "My *long-term* gratitude."

Fitzroy looked down upon her with a new light of respect on his face. And smiled. She felt his arm relax, enough to tell her she'd won out for now. Summer slumped farther into the chair and managed a weak and real grin. "Me, too, Fitzroy."

"Now that's over, maybe we can get to work?" Fitzroy said and Gwen thought that she could get to like him. "Got a hot date with a navigator, Ma'am, and I should be hurrying." He checked digital readouts, dials, and lights. "Working."

Gwen could see blood pulsing through the transparent tubes.

Fitzroy dug into the bag again and came out with another small package. Roughly, he stripped covers and sheets off TJ. He lifted TJ and cut away bandages from his shoulder, sprayed something on the entry and exit wounds, wiped them down with a cloth, sprayed them again, and slapped flesh-colored, self-adhesive bandages over the wounds. "I'll leave you as many of these as I got. They have antiseptic and healants already impregnated in 'em." 'Less I miss my guess, you won't need many of 'em."

She went and sat next to Summer. She'd been trying to maintain a clinical attitude, but found she could not. Here it was, the big moment. TJ would live or die. It should be highlighted by drama, horns blaring, solemn pronouncements to waiting crowds. Drums rolling. A kingdom and a planet on knife's edge. But no. Jean-Claude was fussing with his machine. Summer lay back, seemingly unconcerned, and she sipped her sour mash. It occurred to her that she'd drunk more alcohol in the last few days than in weeks and months previously—and didn't even feel it. She allowed her head to rest momentarily against Summer's shoulder. He tensed and his body felt like stone until he relaxed. Then the contact became oddly sensual, a link cementing the closeness brought on in the last few days. How many days? She couldn't remember. Exhaustion. She snuggled into his strong maleness more and knew that if her crazy plan ever became fact, she would not regret marrying Summer Camp.

TJ's color began to look better. Hah! One of those technical terms, she thought. When Michale was a baby, she remembered once Felicia told her Mike looked pale and wasn't getting enough iron in this diet. She'd changed food a little and Mike's color had seemed to darken. This was sort of the same, wasn't it?

And TJ looked more relaxed now.

Fitzroy was studying indicators. "It's working."

She jumped on his words, standing to ask, "When will we know for sure?" Only a fleeting regret at breaking the bond with Summer. But a renewed strength. Exhaustion was held away for now.

"Couple of hours to make sure, but offhand, I'd say somebody better break out the keys to the bank."

A few hours after dawn, Felicia was spoon-feeding soup into TJ's mouth.

"Don't that beat all," Fitzroy said. "Twenty-five or thirty centuries of medical development since Christ was a corporal, and mothers still use chicken soup. I'll be damned."

"More than likely," Felicia said, "but I'll still be grateful to you."

"My accountant is gonna be grateful to you-all, too," he said.

Gwen's head throbbed, she couldn't think straight. She held her husband's hand and wouldn't let go. Should she tell him, maybe one day, about her plan to marry Summer Camp? He'd probably love it; it was his kind of scheme.

A soft knock came on the door and Manny Vero stepped inside and closed the door behind him.

Summer pointed at Fitzroy. "Jean-Claude, when the door opens, perhaps you should step away from line of sight?"

"Uh . . . oh, yeah, Camp. I forgot."

"That's what I came to say, Summer." Manny hadn't shaved, and Gwen thought that it was the first time she'd ever seen him with a beard shadow. "How it happened, I don't know. But the whole palace knows something is happening. Rumors, gossip, you name it. Place sounds like a giant insect with all the buzzing."

Summer shrugged. "Servants and soldiers and bureaucrats all have ESP for this sort of thing."

"That's not the worst of it, Summer. Sharon Gold is sitting outside, waiting patiently, and trying to convince Prince Michale to escort her in here."

Summer stood, alarm flashing across his face.

"How could she suspect?" Gwen demanded.

"I don't know, My Lady," Manny replied.

"We don't know she suspects anything," Summer said. "Nobody enters, Manny. We got to spirit Fitzroy outa here."

"Speaking of spirits, Camp, don't forget to round up a couple of cases of chocolate wine, too, and call the royal treasurer or whoever pays the bills."

Gwen felt TJ react. He couldn't speak yet, but he tried, and choked on some chicken soup.

"Thomas!" Felicia cautioned.

Summer said, "Jean-Claude, I might need to talk to you privately about the payment."

"Oh?" What seemed to Gwen about a pound of eyebrows lifted on Fitzroy's face.

"Yes," replied Summer.

"Does that mean. . . ?" Fitzroy asked.

Summer nodded.

Fitzroy grinned, finally understanding. "Boy, I really like doing business with you-all. You're spending money like Tirano."

TJ choked again and half rose. Gwen took a napkin and wiped his beard.

"Tirano?" Summer said.

Fitzroy shrugged. "Rumors only. 'Cept a lota new kinda aphrodisiac 'posed to be available for a high price."

"It figures," Summer said, "Tirano is probably trying to buy his way into the new seat on the Fed Council. Just like TJ thought, a lot of politics up there at Fed Central. He doesn't have the wherewithall to make it legitimately and on his own. Bear Ridge should get that seat."

"Hope not," Fitzroy said. He quickly added, "I don't wish to wreck this lucrative relationship I have here."

For the first time she could remember lately, Gwen saw Summer's expression change from the one of habitual gloom. "Consider, Jean-Claude, if TJ gets on the Fed Council, then you will have a powerful friend."

"Hey! That's right. I hadn't even thought of that. Wow! Maybe we can get something on Tirano that will disqualify him?" His voice was hopeful.

"On the other hand," Summer pointed out, "if *you* are found here, Bear Ridge will be disqualified."

"Point taken, judge, I'll lay low and clear the system like a ghost. Hot dog. I love profitable deals."

Gwen held the napkin under the spoon as Felicia put it to TJ's lips.

"That's it!" Gwen said. "Chicken soup."

Manny, Summer, Jean-Claude, Felicia, and even TJ looked at her strangely.

"Chicken soup," she explained. "Don't you understand? How the palace knows?"

Only bland gazes met hers.

"Why else would the Queen Mother walk into her son's chambers with a pot of chicken soup on a tray?"

21: I:IMBAWE

Just before dawn, the river-swimmer had climbed out of the Howling Volv, rippled his skins, and inflated his body. Internal biochem mechanisms separated and generated gases. Body heat climbed to assist. His folds of skin slowly expanded and stretched past what seemed the bursting point.

I:imbawe rose slowly into the air, and aligned himself. He floated up, taking opportunity of swirling winds, and soon he was hovering above the palace. He tuned his aura-reception more finely and began investigating. The Trekmaster's aura had changed from black to gray. And his energy field was stronger, reached farther.

Ah, 'twas a thing well done, he thought, much is to be said for technology in the case of humans. Of course, his people did not require such to repair damage.

He floated back to the river discharging gases so that when he reached the river, he touched the surface and sank beneath the waters. He reconfigured to aquadynamic and porpoised upstream.

22: MIKE

Mike didn't know which to concentrate on the most: his own incognito presence in Michale Shepherd Park, Kellen's obvious nervousness and chirruping, or the pretty young lady who was grabbing more of his attention than any girl recently.

Kellen Sing had invited Mike to hear him speak. Mike thought that almost every university student must be present in the park. Mike was surprised, for the crowds in the palace seemed to buzz and whisper, and even soldiers at ease laughed and talked quietly amongst themselves, but here young people were almost silent. Most sat quietly waiting for Kellen Sing to speak; they seemed to possess a sense of united purpose. A few spoke in normal voices, of sports, of politics, of Kellen. They were not an unruly crowd, Mike reflected. Why should that be surprising? Out of character, he decided. Could Kellen have that strong a hold over maybe two thousand people?

Mike saw a scattering of older citizens, those curious about the announced agenda. More padres than he would have thought. Soldiers wearing civilian garb and hats to conceal their military haircuts. But Mike recognized a few of General Vero's troops, if not personally, then by their bearing and behavior. Off duty and curious? Like hell.

Kellen worked his tongue, "Ahhh, bthbaa, badabada," and looked at Mike and grinned. "A little warm up. Can't disappoint the crowd with a faltering voice."

The girl still stood there.

When he'd walked up to Kellen, she had stood back and nodded to him. No obsequiousness. Of course, he was dressed like a young nobleman, foppish hat hanging low and shadowing his face well enough to prevent recognition save by someone who knew him well.

In front of them upon the stage, a student band struck up, strings seeking to unite the crowd before Kellen spoke. The "Slinking Snarves" were well known and Mike knew that they would have the crowd in a rousing and anticipative temper for Kellen.

"Ironic, no?" Kellen asked, apparently over his case of nerves.

"What?" Mike asked, still distracted by being a stranger among those of his own age. And by the girl. She was dressed as a man, unusual but not uncommon, wearing loose trousers and matching tunic, both very feminine green which augmented her eyes and accented her blonde hair. A double belt barely tightened her tunic low around her hips. She looked as if she belonged in the glade.

"Me speaking, right here in your park."

"Oh. Yes, I suppose so," For a public park, Mike had donated the land on the opposite side of Crimson Sapphire from the Howling Volv River and the fields. Lots of trees, underbrush cleared away, soft grasses, and a central clearing made it a perfect park. And by saying it was ironic, Kellen had confirmed that he was going to speak out against the King today.

Kellen gargled a sip of wine and grinned. "A big tax write off, no?"

"We don't pay taxes, we collect 'em," he snapped, quoting his father unintentionally.

"Well . . . excuse me, Prince."

The girl was watching him coolly.

"Aw, Kellen, I didn't mean to jump at you. This is the first chance I've had to relax since . . . well, since my father, you know." He didn't even admit to himself his relief that his father had lived through the assassination attempt. His own response wasn't something he wanted to explore right now. He had yet to make his mind up about a lot of things, the Trek and the crown not among the least.

"Yeah, Mike, I know. Look, I'm sorry, too. I know you don't take advantage of the people. Thanks for coming, okay?"

Ahead of them, the audience was settling down on the grass, clapping and humming along with the band.

"Hope the weather holds," Mike observed, not looking at Kellen but frankly appraising the girl. Her freckles were attractive. Her secret smile seemed to taunt him. Her blonde hair was splotched white and black in the sun and shadows from the trees.

"Perhaps I should have a padre give an invocation?" Kellen was definitely over his stage fright. And, obviously, he was quite outspoken these days.

A swarthy young man walked up and said, "It's about time, Kellen."

"Be right with you, Franco."

Mike tried to place Franco, but couldn't. Yet he was sure he'd seen him before. At least Kellen was respecting his wishes by not introducing him. It made him feel rather mysterious. He wondered if the girl thought he was mysterious. She might have heard his and Kellen's exchange about the taxes and guessed who he was. Nonetheless, it was exciting to think about impressing a girl on his own and not revealing he was Prince Michale. If it worked, it would be so much more to savor.

"Gotta go," Kellen said and moved away. He turned back and said, "Mike? Would you guard Rebecca for me while I speak?"

Mike thought Kellen was almost too casual about it.

"Sure." And he suffered disappointment. Kellen's words laid claim to her.

She smiled uncertainly, "Luck," she said to Kellen's retreating back.

Mike moved over to her. "I'm Mike."

"I am Rebecca Sing."

Kellen married? No, couldn't be. Then the family resemblance struck him now that he was closer. The freckles and hair had misled him.

"My pleasure," he said, spirits strangely rising.

"Thank you, Pr . . . er, Mike."

Damn it all! She knew who he was. No wonder she had stood back and smiled at his and Kellen's discourtesy of not introducing them to each other. Much experience at the art of being royalty came to his aid. "It is my misfortune for not making your acquaintance immediately, Rebecca."

She colored slightly.

"You are Kellen's sister?" He worried whether his voice showed not too much hope.

"Yes."

"Obviously recently arrived?"

"Yes. From Lonestar."

"Lonestar," he said thinking of Kellen and Summer Camp, "I have heard much of it."

"All good, I trust?" her voice held an internal melody that made him listen for tinkling bells in the background.

"From Camp, yes."

"Camp?"

"A friend," he covered. "But surely you don't wish to discuss hometowns. How long have you been here? Do you like Crimson Sapphire?" He drew her to a wide stump under an overhanging branch where they could hear Kellen and watch the reaction of the crowd.

They talked quietly until Kellen was introduced and the roar of the crowd was a single thing, a shared enthusiasm, a bonding of friends and strangers. Mike was amazed. Kellen was no messiah. He *was* a fantastic speaker and did have some solid logical and philosophical points to make, but this reception?

Then it occurred to him that it might not all be spontaneous. Having lived in open court all his life, he knew tricks could be done, people planted, favors arranged and collected. Yet there was a basic element of adoration for Kellen. Mike had held discussions with Kellen in private but was always amazed to hear him speak publicly. Kellen exerted some kind of influence over the audience; he could feel it.

Kellen smiled a little boy's smile and held his arms up and silence came immediately. Mike felt Kellen's . . . charisma? reach out and touch him personally. And Kellen had yet to speak a word.

Anticipation was a tangible thing in the glade.

"Bar Bear Ridge," Kellen said in a clear voice that carried even against a small wind which rose and died.

Kellen's opposition to Bear Ridge joining the Federation was becoming a trademark, a refrain, a rallying point. Mike knew it wasn't Kellen's main theme, but it served as an effective launching point.

Kellen began to caress his thumb drums and an eerie feeling shivered along Mike's spine, shaking his shoulders and causing him to stiffen his neck to fight it.

The melody beckoned, the music built a drama there in the park. Mike could feel it himself. When Kellen was ready to speak, he would have an audience who could be characterized as hypnotized.

Kellen's cadence became three strident tones and the crowd began to hum and then to chant along, "Bar Bear Ridge, Bar Bear Ridge."

Even passersby and soldiers were riveted to the performance.

It was a moment before the audience realized that Kellen was no longer playing his thumb drums. He stood quietly waiting. "Bar Bear Ridge" seemed to remain in his mind as a repetitive mantra.

"Mike?" Rebecca's voice held a warning.

"Huh? . . . Oh, yes?"

"It may not be my place, but considering your position . . ."

"I know what Kellen is going to say."

"Oh? Forgive my intrusion."

"Not at all. Thank you for your consideration." Then he thought that he sounded too pompous. "I've talked long hours with Kellen. I know what he thinks of my family." He didn't want to admit any more to this girl. He didn't want to seem against the regime of Thomas Jefferson Shepherd, but then again, he had an urge to share with Rebecca, not offend her.

Kellen nodded appreciatively for the silence. "What one person, one man, in the entire universe, has the lowest opinion of the people of Bear Ridge?"

Mike wondered what new gimmick opening Kellen had come up with. It was an interesting question until he saw where Kellen was leading.

"Who thinks the entire human population of Bear Ridge is stupid?" Kellen continued. "I'll tell you who. The one man who *does not* think the people of Bear Ridge capable of managing their own affairs. Our dictator."

Mike found himself holding his breath waiting for the crowd's reaction. But the young people in the crowd and, admittedly, some of the older people, were nodding silently in agreement. Others appeared too stunned to voice disagreement.

Kellen ran his hand over his drums, the sound a quiet hiss. "I quote the original Thomas Jefferson: 'It is not only your right, but your duty to overthrow an oppressive regime.'" Kellen paused. No one moved. Even the wind failed and leaves no longer rustled.

Mike glanced about worriedly. Free speech was one thing, but to speak openly of revolution? Albeit cleverly disguised by quoting father's namesake and idol? A blockbuster of an attention grabber. At least the soldiers in the crowd were not reacting—they simply sat and listened. Did they consider Kellen's words treason? More importantly, would his father? Doubtlessly, the soldiers were restrained by orders. And the Gyrenes were nothing if not disciplined. Perhaps Vero and Alfred hadn't expected Kellen to be so blatant in his criticism of the King.

Kellen was continuing to talk, quietly, occasionally accompanying himself on the thumb drums for effect. For a few moments he spoke on the merits of nonviolent protests. Mike thought it an attempt to ameliorate his revolutionary words. His historical references to Mohandas Ghandi, Jesus Christ, Martin Luther King, and others, made his arguments and served as transition to his next major point.

"Another thing that Thomas Jefferson said so many centuries ago. Speaking of the care of human life and happiness, he said it '. . . is the only legitimate object of good government.' Have any of you noticed that the care of human life and happiness has any place in the government of *Thomas Jefferson* Shepherd?" He paused, then added as if in afterthought, "Why can't the *Trekmaster* take a note from the Webbines he *ostensibly* trekked to meet and learn from? Their only concern is the care of life; a happiness in non-tech living." He immediately switched the subject to one of environmental concerns.

Mike thought Kellen's statements about the Webbines odd, but thought no more about it. Kellen went on to make the standard litany of complaints Mike had heard him speak of many times.

Mike noticed Rebecca's attention straying as she looked over the crowd. Had she heard it all before? Was she bored? Suddenly, it was important to him to know her position on what Kellen was saying. But he knew that he wouldn't find out because he didn't want to admit his own feelings. For all he knew, she disagreed violently with Kellen. A strange thought, he admitted, but a possibility. Family loyalty would tie her to Kellen, but she appeared to be a woman who thought her own thoughts and didn't need a man to tell her what to think. That was it, he decided. The thing that made her different. She was her own woman, even though fresh from the back country in Lonestar. Sharon Gold had that same quality, and she was from Fedcentral.

"Do we want to be a part of the Federation?" Kellen demanded. "Again, who wants it? Nobody asked me. Did they ask you?"

A quarter of the crowd shouted "No" in a ragged chorus.

"We haven't our own house in order and we are going off planet? Does it not seem possible that when technology arrives, we will become slaves for Shepherd riches?" Kellen paused, one of his effective speaking techniques.

Mike saw a look of distaste on Rebecca's face. She stirred

restlessly. She glanced at him and guiltily looked away. It struck him that she might be afraid for her brother. Or could she be wondering why he, Prince of the Realm, was not becoming angry? Could she think him a traitor to his family? No, he didn't think so, not specifically, for he was no furtive follower of Kellen, but an intellectual equal who agreed with many of Kellen's ideas, and disagreed with some. And obviously, Kellen had spoken of him to Rebecca.

Why, he wondered, was it becoming so important to him what Rebecca Sing thought of him?

". . . of profits," Kellen was saying. "Who will profit? On the other side of the city lies some good grain acreage—owned by the King. That is where the space port will go, I've heard . . ."

Damn, Mike thought. Shouldn't have told him that. Got to watch my mouth in Kellen's presence . . . but hadn't I thought the same thing about father and the landing area?

Kellen was speaking of nobles and land and technology and control of all new things from the Federation. Mike noticed more what Kellen didn't say than what he said.

He leaned toward Rebecca. "Kellen conveniently excludes the benefits of modern medicine."

Her mouth twitched and her hand went to her buttocks. "It was a long ride from Lonestar to Crimson Sapphire on a donkey. I would rather have spent the time differently."

His probe bore fruit. She was a logical thinking person. Common sense in a political setting wasn't something he'd expected to find. Another sudden realization hit him: Am I becoming as cynical as father?

"And the price?" Kellen demanded. "A toll. A cost. Not monies. In lives. In change. Instant change. For whose good? The rich cream at the top. The rest of us below stay the same."

A pair of soldiers on the outskirts of the crowd stood, hooted, and walked off. Mike caught a smile of satisfaction on Kellen's face as the episode merely reinforced his position.

To Rebecca, Mike said, "Your brother has forgotten another thing; the King allows free speech."

"My brother is quite hardheaded."

"Yeah." So am I, too, he thought. Just ask my father.

She smiled encouragingly at him. His rank had yet to impress her, and somehow, that irritated him. Was it so important for him to impress her anyway?

"How come your brother is doing this, saying these things?"

he asked. He had not been able to get Kellen to tell him in private, except for the reasons he was so eloquently expounding on the platform.

"I don't know," she said, "he was so much alone tending his flocks in the hills."

"Anger at your father not returning from the Consolidation wars?"

His knowledge obviously startled her. "You know?"

"It wasn't hard to discover. I've sources of information, of course."

She looked at him, smile no longer present, mouth tight, eyes seemingly critical.

Uh oh, he thought. Just because I fight with my father and don't necessarily love him doesn't mean others can't love their fathers. Damn. "You have my sorrow and regrets," he said.

"It wasn't your fault," she said wearily.

23: KELLEN

As he stepped from the speaker's platform, Kellen burned with anger.

He smiled and accepted congratulations and mentally whipped himself for his mistake. Surely Prince Michale had caught his error.

Maybe not. Mike might be familiar enough with the Webbines to miss the significance of what Kellen had said. A glance told him that Mike might well have been engrossed with Rebecca and failed to note his goof. At least that was going well. Get Mike and Rebecca together and that was one more attachment between Mike and him. More leverage.

The tricky part, he thought, came with gaining Mike's confidence originally. Mind-tricks would not suffice to bind them together in the long term, so he'd had to win over the Prince by friendship, by sharing goals, and genuine social-political concern. Too bad, too, for he liked Mike. But he was determined to use anyone, anything. Was he not using his own sister right this minute to attract Mike and keep him happy?

"Super, Kellen," Franco Valdez said and clasped Kellen around the shoulders.

"Yeah, sure, Franco," he said, still distracted.

Sure the Webbines value life and happiness and all that other stuff. But am I supposed to know that? Only a Trekmaster might know that—or the Trekmaster's immediate family, those who have cause to study the ways of the Webbines. And it certainly isn't in the curricula at Shepherd University. Shepherd Park, Shepherd University, Shepherd Avenue and Street, all those damned Shepherds!

A pert-nosed girl smiled an invitation. He nodded obligingly but didn't stop. No time for that.

He paused at a group near Rebecca and Mike. He strained to read what was happening. Mike's aura showed interest, concentration on Rebecca alone, and a high peak of anticipation. Rebecca's aura should be easier to read since she was his sister. It wasn't. You'd think we'd be more attuned, he thought. Yes, she was interested in Mike, but not as much as he was in her. Her aura was orange with caution.

He hadn't counted on that. He'd figured that Mike being Prince and heir to the throne would automatically sway Rebecca.

There! Mike was escorting Rebecca off, to a tavern for refreshment, Kellen garnered from the snatches of conversation he caught.

"When can we hear you again?" asked a townsman, not one of his regulars.

"It is yet to be arranged. But my friend Franco will be glad to notify you if . . ." Never pass up a chance to convert. Franco moved in to get the man's name. Might be good for a donation, too.

He excused himself and slipped off deeper into the park. In a while he found himself seated by a lake. He missed the time he'd spent alone in the hills. The emotional high of the occasion was wearing off and he felt reflective as he reviewed his performance. Well enough done, he thought. Words and concepts and ideas reinforced by Webbine aura-control techniques.

Charisma, they said he had.

Sure.

He had picked up no suspicion in Mike's aura. Mike wouldn't have been able to mask that in his aura. Nobody

present this day had been able to read auras—he always
checked. One thing that had puzzled him. The King, when
he had played the thumb drums in the palace, had not
appeared to have aura-control. But there was something
about Thomas Jefferson Shepherd that was tantamount to
aura-control and all that went with it. He possessed something more primal, more gut-level, less intellectual—an in-
nate quality which was perhaps the human equivalent of the
Webbine aura techniques. And that ability was probably
subconscious. Kellen termed TJ Shepherd's ability "basic
grasp" or subconscious ESP though he wasn't certain what
the King could or couldn't do. He'd seen no evidence of
overt aura-interference such as he himself had used here
today.

Because Shepherd was the Trekmaster and Kellen had
detected Shepherd's basic grasp, he had carefully controlled
his own aura efforts, kept his energy matrix neutral and
tried no tricks in the palace. Thus now he could speculate,
but not know.

One day he would, by God. As soon as he'd found that
his hate and burning anger helped him immensely in controlling his aura and using the energy matrix, he had vowed to
remain no longer a simple shepherd in the hills, but to
disrupt Shepherd and the kingdom of the Shepherds as
much as he could. Revenge, sure. But there was more. An
outlet for frustration and anger. A goal, a purpose, something to soothe his fevered mind when he thought about it.
Every time he thought about it, he became confused. Did
he want Shepherd to see the downfall of his kingdom before
he fell himself? Or did he want the King to fall first before
the kingdom fell?

"Off w' 'is 'ead," he thought and sensed his own aura
dangerously and pointedly gray. He curbed his mind.

Rebecca did not know that Thomas Jefferson (Shepherd)
Rex had beheaded their father. Personally been the one to
kill his mother's husband dead, dead as an aborted sheepaloe.
Dead as his mother's eyes when she heard. Dead as her life
after that. Dead as she was right now, from wilting at her
husband's death. Coreen Sing had been killed by the famed,
fucking Widow-Maker just as the King had killed her husband. Kellen knew of the beheading, Rebecca did not. One
of his secrets from her. Another from the village had been
at the battle and told Kellen about Shepherd and his sword

personally killing his father. And Kellen had personally seen his mother die—indirectly by the King's hand.

So what if their father had been on the wrong side in the wars? All Milvin had wanted was to support his poor family in time of strife in a war-torn land. Milvin had been mere fodder in front of Shepherd and his band of cutthroats. Kill kill kill. Just as he had killed the snarv in the palace on that fateful day.

Strangely, the snarv episode had made Kellen feel better about Milvin than he had in a long time. The King seemed quite competent with his sword, so perhaps Milvin had not suffered. But his mother had; she was dead for years before her heart actually stopped. And for that, Kellen would never forgive the King. Milvin had known what he was getting into. But mother? When Kellen was a child, she had healed his hurts with a touch. When she saw him, life came into her eyes. Between them had existed an empathy every bit as strong as if their auras were linked—which he now firmly believed had been the case.

And Kellen was surprised at his feelings when he'd heard the King was dying from an assassin's bolt. On one web, he enjoyed the obvious pain that the bolt and poison gave the King. And the agony of the King's family tasted sweet. On the other web, he was angry that the King's death had not been as a result of something he, Kellen, had done. He remembered what he'd thought at the time: Nice, but I wanted it to be me. But now that Shepherd was recovering, he could go back to his original plan.

So Thomas Jefferson Shepherd had killed Milvin Sing and, more significantly, Coreen Sing; so Kellen Sing had vowed revenge.

The lonely days and months and years alone in the mountains had given him a special self-awareness. He knew his intelligence and quick mental grasp were uncommon. His intellectual agility allowed him to pick up the Webbine thought techniques swiftly. He showed immediate talent and learned well.

His reverie was interrupted as the surface of the lake broke before him. A Webbine head appeared, eye membranes flickering, eyes restive. The Webbine sat up in the shallows and studied Kellen. Kellen smelled the reek of river plants the Webbine must have recently eaten.

Kellen quickly scanned the immediate area to detect if any humans were in the vicinity. None.

"O:omega," he acknowledged.

/Kellen Sing,/ replied O:omega.

"The event went well," Kellen reported.

/As I observed./

"From my point of view, the procedure worked."

/The link was effective./

"And unique, I'm sure." They'd linked auras, O:omega following Kellen's lead, to sway the audience in the park. Kellen wasn't certain whether they'd done it together or O:omega had merely augmented his own efforts.

O:omega. The renegade.

They were both alike, he reflected. Both wanting something outside of their own experience. Outside of their heritage and culture. Both shared a burning desire to change. A personal revolt against personal circumstances. And consequently revolt against the structures that held them in—he against Shepherd and his governmental suppression and O:omega against the strict Webbine society.

At first their anger had been sufficient, but each served to goad the other until they had made a pact. Two renegades against two nations.

Because of O:omega's stripe of nonconformity, the old Webbines in charge had branded him unfit for further training and had taken away his family tutor, O:chacka, and given his place to A:alpha. Apparently, this shunning had driven O:omega into a frenzy of revenge-dreaming.

O:omega had told Kellen, /Those old males who decide things act like webless old females. They sit and pass gas together. Dialogue is all they understand. They stagnate in their own wastes. They stifle new concepts./

"Oh?" Kellen had prompted.

O:omega related the incident where he had followed some tidbit of advice from a female and had been reprimanded. /Even outside my family the elders disapproved. So I began questioning, as we are wont to do, why females weren't more a part of the decision-making. More reprisals and ostracism followed./

Kellen suspected that the fault between O:omega and the Webbine hierarchy was more mutual than one-sided as O:omega painted. He even admitted the same in his own case. His caution had held his obsession in check and thus had shown him a higher goal than mere physical revenge on the King.

One thing scared him. The exposure and power he found

easy to come by and easier to build were changing him, changing his goals. He was discovering that he liked the power, the adulation of people, the ability to wield the sword of power. He fought to maintain his original purpose—the demise of the King—and he would. But what else might happen, he would take advantage of any position he carved for himself in the new world, the post-chaos world he was building.

Anarchy, with himself as the benefiter. A savior, a Ghandi? Certainly not out of the question.

He was intelligent enough to know that he had to work, to plot, to build before he could accomplish his goals. He had no delusions about that. The scope of his ambitions did not scare him. Hadn't the King himself united the whole world? Now all Kellen had to do was take it away from him, not nearly as difficult a task as Shepherd had done—but one which would prove Kellen Sing a better man than Shepherd.

After all, he had nothing to lose.

Except Rebecca.

And O:omega?

O:omega had told him once that their /personality quirks/ bonded them together. That Kellen would help him attack the static Webbine society.

They knew they had to overcome the humans on Bear Ridge first since the Webbines could read their intentions from afar.

Additionally, O:omega had broken taboo: he had unauthorized contact with a human.

It had been fortunate for them that O:omega was swimming downriver at the time of the visit of I:imbawe to the bed of the dying King. Could that Webbine elder have contributed to restoring Shepherd's health? No way to know.

O:omega speculated against it. But the visit had worried O:omega. He'd told Kellen, /Perhaps the elders are admitting that change is in the wind and the waves. They are now willing to become involved in human planetary matters./

"So?" Kellen had asked.

/The elders have extrapolated the future and they are taking an active interest after so much time merely monitoring? Come, my web-friend./

"Yeah, I understand." He thought he did until O:omega's next statement.

/Understand? I do not do so. For generations of humans,

the elders have been influencing the selection of the Trekmasters./

"What?"

/'Tis all I know. The elders maintain a closed group-consciousness about certain things and females and non-initiates are excluded./

24: TJ

TJ had sent for his crimson sapphire. At times, he needed its calming influence. And, he admitted, it was better than alcohol as a relaxant.

He seemed to need something every time he fought with Michale.

TJ was in his business office when Mick had come in the first thing this morning.

Mick had looked over his shoulder and had seen the written summary of all the reports on Kellen's speech and activities at the park yesterday afternoon.

"I knew it," Mick had said.

TJ pointed to the paper. "You were there."

"Are you accusing me of anything?" Mick asked.

"No. Stating a fact. Why didn't you tell me about it?"

"I returned late. And, you might note, here I am."

TJ ran his hand through his hair and then through his beard. This is going to be a bad day, he thought. "Okay. What about it, then?"

Mick slouched against his desk and indicated the report. "You already know."

"What was your function?"

"Function, father? Does everything have to have an administrative term applied to it?"

"You are evading my question."

"I was part of the audience, father. I just wanted to hear what Kellen had to say."

"And what do you think of what Sing said?"

"He's done his homework. A few new twists in his dialectic. Otherwise, his standard litany."

"You call treason and sedition a litany?" TJ demanded.

"Certainly, father, your reports show that Kellen covered himself well."

"Legally, perhaps, but what of his intentions?"

Mick evaded his eyes. TJ leaned back in his chair. "Well?"

Mick pushed off the desk and paced around to the front of it. "I don't know." His voice was strained.

"It's obvious he seeks to provoke an incident," TJ said.

"I don't deny that, father. But I think Kellen is basically . . ."

"Good?" TJ prompted.

"No. I've learned that there isn't much black and white, good and evil."

TJ nodded internally. The boy *is* learning something. "What is it, then?"

"He's trying to find something, maybe something within himself, something within the humanity of all of us. He cares about people. Everything he says is for the benefit of all the people—while the things he says cannot really benefit him, they can only hurt him."

"You don't know either," TJ accused.

"I can't articulate it precisely," Mick said.

"Me either," TJ agreed. "What would you recommend I do about Kellen Sing and his treason and sedition?"

"You will probably slap him in prison, father." Mick stopped directly in front of the desk and looked straight into TJ's eyes.

"I asked your opinion of what I should do." He fought to keep the anger from his voice.

"Leave him alone. That's what I think. He harms no one—now."

TJ leaned farther back and put his feet upon the desk. "If that's what you want, Mike, that's the way it will be." He saw the surprise in his son's eyes. He keyed it by using "Mike." He had decided to leave Kellen alone for now to see what would happen. To see if Kellen could lead him to other plotters. And most importantly, he'd decided to let Mick win one. To think his advice was taken seriously. I'll be snarved, he thought. I never thought I'd ever be in a situation where I had to allow sedition in order to please my son and get him on my side. Perhaps his association with Kellen Sing would help straighten him out. Mick's single concern should be the welfare of the kingdom.

He saw the expressions change on Mick's face. Perhaps the boy had outfigured him? Could be. Trapped by my own reputation, he thought sourly. Another of his management techniques that was becoming well-known: Do something out of character occasionally; keep 'em guessing. Shouldn't have tried to use it on my own son.

"I can guess why," Mick said.

"Don't read more into something than is already there," he said.

"I don't need warning, father. Really."

"You need to be cautious, Mick. Don't let this Sing sway you."

"He's not trying to sway me, we simply are . . . intellectually compatible and have a nice dialogue built between us."

Horse shit, TJ thought and said, "And the girl you left with?"

"Just somebody I met." Mick's voice sounded forced.

"Look son. I don't mess around in your love life, you know that. But be damn careful you aren't being used. You wouldn't be the first one who was subverted because of a woman." He paused. "Who was she?"

Mick simply looked at him. Without a word, he turned and walked out.

TJ rang for a secretary and sent for his crimson sapphire. He needed to calm himself and get his thoughts together for the upcoming meeting with Roaland Cruz.

Now as he waited, he glanced idly at the "incoming" stack of papers and the empty "out" box. He'd hamstrung himself. Built too much of an administrative structure. Bureaucracy seemed to be self-generating once started. A price he had to pay when he'd rather be out and active. He'd rather be a general than an administrator any day.

He answered Alfred's discreet knock. "Come in, Hark." Alfred brought the gold case in, set it down on his desk and left. TJ looked at the crimson sapphire he'd gotten from O:chacka. It lay on a satiny cloth that showed its colors well.

The thing fascinated him. Even though it gave him a feeling of serenity, somewhere down deep it gave him another feeling of uneasiness—and it shouldn't, for Heaven knew what he'd gone through to obtain the damn thing.

He lifted it and rubbed his fingers over it. Smooth. Though the light refractions seemed to show that it had different facets. When he held it, he felt a greater mental clarity—

perhaps a remembrance of Webbine ways? He thought his mind was sharper, quicker. He didn't know for certain, but would have wagered half his kingdom that those mental enhancement or mental augmentation feelings were merely tricks of his mind. What difference would a gem make in his thinking? How could a rock, a pretty rock, expand his mental horizons? Ridiculous. And perhaps because of this, he had a gut-level apprehension about the gem.

Most Trekmasters before him had worn their crimson sapphires on chains around their necks. Traditionally, the jewel should be worn in the formal crown, but those were uncomfortable and not worn all the time. His predecessors had preferred to have their crimson sapphires with them at all times. But because of his occasional uneasiness, TJ kept his on display in the throne room, either in a case or in a niche atop his throne. Sometimes, when holding court, he felt its presence. And it was amusing to watch reactions from those who went to look at it.

When a secretary brought the Chief Padre in, TJ was already in a better mood. He'd demanded Cruz' immediate presence to keep the man off guard.

"Your Majesty?" Cruz inquired as he walked in like a bird on his spindly legs.

"Roaland," he acknowledged. He saw the priest's eyes go straight to the crimson sapphire laying in its case.

"So that is your crimson sapphire," Cruz said. "I've never seen it up close."

TJ lifted it and tossed it casually to Cruz.

The Chief Padre juggled it a moment and then held it to the light. "It's like corundum," he mused. "The substance glows differently under varying light conditions." Then he hastily returned it to its case.

"Burn yourself, Padre?"

"I will have nothing to do with an object which can be construed as an icon."

"I'll be a wagging volv tongue. That's one you can't pin on me, Roaland."

"I admit that. You wished to see me?"

"Eighteen, Padre. That's how many of your . . . padres in Church garb that were counted at the Kellen Sing rally yesterday. An inordinate number, I say."

"So?"

"So contributing to sedition, albeit passively."

"As I recall, TJ, *your* first rule is freedom of speech."

"Everybody's got a cliché," he said. "Were they present at your direction?"

"I do not condone their actions, no. Nor do I disapprove. I remain neutral. My padres can do what they wish on their own time."

"The reason I wanted to see you, Padre: There is danger in associating with Kellen Sing's movement. Personal danger."

"You going to toss him in irons?"

"Not now."

"Ah, I see it now." Cruz moved near a chair. "May I sit down?" TJ nodded. Cruz continued, "You are using young Sing as bait. Get all the dissidents in bed with him and do away with them all at once."

One of TJ's intentions was to keep Cruz off balance. Perhaps his toughest political foe, the Church had more power than he wished to test at the moment. So he'd decided to keep Cruz on the defensive so the padre couldn't take the offense.

"My reasoning is none of your concern, Roaland. I merely caution you. Eighteen padres is a bit flagrant and does seem too coincidental an occurrence. Which leads me to believe that it was not coincidental. And only one man could issue such orders. You."

"It occurs to me that Ambassador Gold would take adverse note of your secular interference in religious matters."

"Is that called blackmail or extortion, Padre?"

"Pressure, I think, TJ. No more nor less than you are applying on us."

"Listen, Roaland. Just try to control your padres, will you? I've enough trouble as it is."

Cruz shrugged. "What can *I* do?"

"Keep *your* people away from dissidents like Sing."

"Those dissidents are your own fault, TJ. You have created them out of a placeless class. You reorganized the world too fast. There are people who don't fit anywhere—yet. And now . . ."

"There are always dissidents, Padre. I've dealt with 'em before and will again." He crossed his arms and sat straight.

". . . and now you want to create more classes of dissidents, more classless people who fit nowhere in your manufactured society. There is too much pressure on society now, trying to catch up with your whims and changes. Gaining Federation membership will accelerate this dangerously. Right now your taxmen are running around spying and raising taxes and lowering them here and there so fast and frequent no one can keep track of what they should be doing. Many old ways and many professions will be obsolete without normal evolution. I tell you outright, TJ, there will be trouble. You bring it upon yourself. Always there is some dissident group ready to take advantage of change and the resultant anarchy. Where does that put you?"

Will it never end? he thought. "I've heard that line enough times to choke a volcano. Students are spouting it and echoing Sing's words all over Crimson Sapphire. It's like a cancer here. I fear it will soon spread to other ethnarchies. And you, Chief Padre, have the gall to say that to me?"

"What do you mean?" Cruz asked, obviously taken aback by the vehemence in TJ's voice.

"I mean," said TJ, "that you forget your own roots, your own religious heritage. Just a minute." He fumbled around in a bottom drawer. "I came across something the other day and I've been saving it for you." He drew a permaplas sheet out and waved it at Cruz.

"Oh?"

"It's a speech by one of your . . . ah, predecessors." TJ cautioned himself to be diplomatic. "John-Paul the Ninth. Christmas message, 2085. I can just see the great man standing there in his balcony in The Vatican overlooking the crowds below. Do you know the speech?"

"No." Cruz' eyes showed interest, though. "The one who recommended a woman pope as his successor?"

TJ nodded. "You'll recall that John-Paul IX was the first North American pope. As a testament to the strength of his character and the power he held, note that single-handedly he was responsible for preventing Earthe-wide adoption of the metric system. Just because he didn't like it and had trouble doing the conversion mathematics in his head."

"So? What has this to do with. . .?"

"You are ignoring your heritage," TJ said. "You will recall that at the time Earthe was overflowing with people and that the Population Control Party had swept elections in most of the Consolidated countries."

"I do not recall, TJ, but nobody faults your knowledge of history. Please get on with it."

"A brilliant man," TJ grumbled, "ought to be remembered well. Lemme quote some from his speech." He searched the archaic English version of John-Paul's words for the proper place. "Ah. I quote. 'The meek shall inherit the

Earth. The strong, the bold, the smart, the fortunate will inherit the stars. The Lord went to too much trouble creating the Universe for man to ignore it.

" 'Let not the Population Control people overwhelm us, for it is our heritage to expand.

" 'How many geniuses in a million? One, perhaps. And if you preclude the birth of one billion people, how many geniuses have you killed or prevented? A thousand? Could not one thousand brilliant men and women contribute somehow to solving the problems of the world? Cheap energy and, consequently, cheap food. Could not one thousand geniuses together solve those basic problems? Or one of them alone come up with the answer?

" 'And the Population Control fanatics want to stop the birth of those one thousand geniuses?

" 'Thus I say let the people multiply. Let men of science and intelligence attack our problems and take us to the stars where the Lord intended we should be.'

"John-Paul IX said that, Roaland. And because of him, men went to the stars and here *we* are."

"Yes, here we are," Cruz responded dryly.

"Do I have to wave a flag in your face to get your attention, Roaland?"

"TJ, it is difficult to reconcile faith with reality at times. It is difficult to see the future clearly. I have made a judgment and shall stand by it. I remain opposed to Federation membership. It is too fast, too sudden. My concern is with and for the majority of my flock and I must do what I think best for them."

Somebody get a wheelbarrow and cart out all these clichés, TJ thought. "So I get no help from you? History shows you are wrong and you will not change your mind?"

"Your summary is correct, your assumptions incorrect."

So the hell what? TJ thought wearily.

He wondered if Roaland or anybody else opposed to Federation membership had gotten the idea to go straight to Sharon Gold. It would save them a lot of time, turn over a few rocks and find some of TJ's worms under those rocks.

But nothing anyone could report to Sharon would be a definite strike against his case for entry to the Fed—but a compilation of items might prejudice his case. Well, admittedly, he was trying to prejudice her in his favor. So it was up to Sharon to weed out the chaff from her information. Uh oh, he thought, Cruz has *me* thinking in clichés.

25: SHARON

Sharon was excited. It would be her first trip outside of the city of Crimson Sapphire.

Now she was waiting in Felicia Shepherd's private gardens. She would accompany the Queen Mother when the royal party formed.

Felicia's gardens were strange: many varieties of fruits and vegetables, some familiar, some unrecognizable.

"Pick 'em, cook 'em, and eat 'em is my motto," Felicia said. "The longer between the vine and the cooking pot, the more taste and nutrition you lose."

"My mother used to say something similar," Sharon said without thinking.

"Oh?" Felicia prompted.

Yeah, Sharon thought. Ma used to say, "The sooner you cook it and eat it, the sooner the evidence is gone; a perfect crime, you eat the evidence." But she didn't tell Felicia. Instead, Sharon said, "I was complimenting you to get on your good side."

"Humpf," said Felicia. "You're lobbying for one of my fresh garden salads," she said.

Sharon smiled. "Yep. Unabashedly. And I don't even understand all the ingredients."

Felicia indicated a small pool. "I'm experimenting lately with river plants. TJ says the Webbines eat a lot of them."

"Well, whatever you do, the food or something contributes to tremendous recuperative properties."

Felicia plucked a sprig of a mintlike plant and chewed on it. "The men of Bear Ridge are a hearty lot. My son is stronger than most. His willpower surely helped pull him through."

Sharon thought Felicia was a bit defensive about TJ's recovery.

Felicia kept talking, almost nervously. She managed a small laugh. She pointed to a clay pipe coming out of one wall of the garden. A bucket hung from the pipe and a large ball-joint valve was inset into the pipe with a handle to open and close it. "See that?"

"Yes, ma'am," Sharon decided to be more diplomatic with the old lady.

"That, my dear, is running water. You've heard my son complain about lack of indoor plumbing as one reason to join the Federation?"

"More than once."

"Yet in the palace we have bathrooms and running water and showers and baths and brass fixtures and toilets and lavatories?"

"Yes, thank goodness," Sharon said.

"It costs a lot of manhours to maintain, but since we're close to the river, Thomas has a system. Lot of rain catchers on the roof. When not enough rain, men and animals labor to pump water up to fill the reservoirs."

"I'd guessed at some kind of gravity feed and water tanks," Sharon said. "RHIP."

"What?"

"Rank Hath Its Privileges."

"Certainly, young lady, royalty does have some benefits." Felicia pointed vaguely into the mountains. "Thomas also has a crew way up there somewhere chopping hunks of ice and floating 'em down the river to the palace. There are some dank and dark corners under the palace where ice lasts a long time."

Sharon thought, Why is Felicia suddenly trying to talk my ear off? She'd changed the subject from the King's recovery. Suddenly, she asked, "Felicia, what is the order of succession? I understand it depends on Mike taking the Trek and all, but what about interim measures?" While she'd asked others this question before, she wanted to confirm what she'd found out and guessed.

Felicia seemed to relax a bit. "Well, you saw how it worked when Thomas was wounded."

"I did. But I still don't understand all I observed. The jester . . ."

"Oh, that was a special case. Thomas was still King. We all just filled in where we could. The people qualified to make decisions in different areas made them, that's all. And Mike and I did the official functions, things which could not be avoided."

"But, if . . ." Sharon didn't know how to ask Felicia a hypothetical question involving her son's death.

"I know what you're thinking," Felicia said. "Order of succession. Look you, honey. I'm tougher than appearances. Remember what I gave up for the kingdom."

Two sons and a husband, Sharon thought. "I'm sorry. And that was my question."

"After Thomas, Mike if he takes the Trek and returns, of course. If something happened, like on our outing today, Gwen first, then me, then Gwen's half sister. That's it for the royal family. Now you know one of TJ's basic fears—his kinglets don't count unless they make the Trek. And Thomas thinks that if we all go, then the kingdom would be better off if a power struggle occurred and the strongest survived to rule. Me, too. The Shepherds aren't the only ones capable of rule."

"Gwen's half sister?"

"Nora Ahimsa."

"She is a strange one," Sharon said.

"Anyone who deals with herbs and chemicals I don't understand can be termed strange," Felicia said.

"I knew she was the royal surgeon, but wasn't aware of her family relationship."

"It's not widely known. Her husband was the royal surgeon, and he died in the wars, so Thomas kept Nora on in his place. It was one way to keep her in the palace—besides her obvious skill. A fine acupuncturist, and holowhatchacallit, too." Felicia saw Sharon's look. "You've heard the palace scuttlebutt?" Sharon nodded. "Well," Felicia said defensively, "it was a short affair and might have produced another child with a more legitimate claim to the throne. But no such luck." Then Felicia Shepherd surprised Sharon. "Legitimate claim? Not a bad pun for an old lady." She giggled.

Sharon couldn't help but like the King's mother.

Felicia handed her a cherry tomato and Sharon nibbled on it. "Juicy," she nodded approval.

"Gotta find the right manure for the right plant."

Ugh. "Ahimsa. That's an odd name," Sharon finally caught the question she'd wanted to ask before.

"From ancient Hindu. Means something like 'All life is sacred,' you see. Kind of a name and a title."

"She is very skillful," Sharon prompted. "The King's recovery was miraculous."

Felicia frowned a warning.

Sharon decided to pass this time. "Wonder if it's time to leave yet?"

"I hope so," Felicia grumped. "All this talk of doctors and succession depresses me." She looked straight into Sharon's eyes and Sharon saw iron smelting in great fires. Felicia's voice was cold and level. "I am damn sick of people killing, and trying to kill, my family."

26: TJ

Dawn's Edge. From a rise, TJ studied the town he had created and then rode down into the dusty streets. The population was only a few thousand. A ranching community on the high plains. Far east of Crimson Sapphire toward the twin ridges, TJ had selected this site as the ranching headquarters for the royal herds—which were now Mick's responsibility and consequently now belonged to the Prince in title.

The savanna grass of the high plains made this the logical location for raising sheepaloe and offshoots like beefaloe. Millions of acres of land. TJ had in mind filling the land to the maximum with the various animals. Since the wars, he had pursued his program with little publicity. He guessed at an animal population of eighty or ninety thousand which was increasing all the time. Occasionally, blood lines from these herds were used to augment those herds closer to Crimson Sapphire.

It had occurred to him that population expansion would be one of the prime factors in the expansion of the Federation and thus require a lot of food they might not have room to grow. And his observations at the Federation conferences tended to confirm his early analysis. Was not Fedcentral a planet of people and government only? Sure, some agriculture. But you can only eat so much hydroponically produced food. A real steak in some places was worth pure gold. And with modern radiation-preservation techniques, the steak would be as fresh on Fedcentral as it was here in Dawn's Edge. He would certainly be ready for commerce with other

Fed planets . . . if Bear Ridge gained membership. He could see it now, laser slaughtering and butchering, radiation treatment to preserve the meat almost forever so no special handling would be necessary.

As they rode into town, he noticed Sharon Gold's look of disappointment. As a ranching center, Dawn's Edge had nothing special to show off. It was a dusty, dry town, built of lumber carried from the slopes of far off mountains and hill, thus making building expensive. He did see some homes made with clay. The adobe buildings would be better for dust protection yet had other drawbacks when the rains came in torrents. But adobe was cheaper.

TJ was fond of Dawn's Edge. As close as he could figure, he had established Dawn's Edge on the very spot that Joshua Jones and Chief Mathiew Bearpaw and their descendants had fought over and lived upon until the entire village moved to the current location of Crimson Sapphire.

His roots—and the heritage of a planet—lay here in the dry earth. He could feel history calling out to him. Even the permeating slaughterhouse reek contributed to the haunting echoes he felt.

After a formal meeting with the administrator and a status briefing, the royal party took a quick tour of Dawn's Edge.

Now they were in the slaughterhouse and TJ ran his finger along a meaty ridge. "Nice marbling," he said. The beefaloe carcass hung with many others. He was glad that this strain had been developed for he preferred beefaloe meat to that of the sheepaloe. Mike and Sharon and Felicia were with him—Gwen had opted for refreshments at the schoolhouse where the ceremonies were to be held. Camp and a soldier stood just within the doors to the slaughterhouse.

The administrator, a man named Chavez, was escorting the royal party. Chavez, a man of ordinary height and one arm (a wound from the Consolidation wars), was de facto mayor of Dawn's Edge. Since the royal family owned the lands and the animals, it was a Shepherd "company town" and thus exempt from being part of the nearest ethnarchy.

And since the concept was all TJ's and he had established Dawn's Edge in the location he had, named it, and since it was one of his fondest projects, he traveled to it at least once a year. The annual arrival of the royal party had evolved into an Event. TJ did not discourage this. People came from afar to observe the festivities, even those not company employed.

"It is close to time, Sire," Chavez said.

"All right." He usually made a speech.

It was a short walk through the town square to the schoolhouse. Each footfall raised dust. While the planet's wild weather did not neglect these high plains, it did rain less frequently here. TJ guessed this was due to the influence of the two great ridges farther to the east. The constant wind dried the land faster. Fortunate that the ecology of Bear Ridge had developed a nutritious grass which held the soil and that the original sheepaloe were able to digest.

TJ strode ahead and waved to the crowd in the square. Chavez had had the foresight to dampen the ground here and the dust was less bothersome. They cut behind another building and came to the front of the school without going through the crowd.

In front of the school an awning covered platform had been erected for the royal party. They stopped for introductions to minor functionaries and Sharon and his mother climbed the steps to the platform and joined Gwen.

"We have refreshments set up for you, Sire, inside the school," Chavez said. "It will be a while before the crowd quiets and I can make the introductions to bring you out."

"Fine," TJ said. "Prince Michale will make the remarks today."

"Certainly, Your Majesty . . ."

"Good. Mick, let's go inside and wait." TJ cut off Chavez so that he wouldn't say anything. Usually the King gave the address; but TJ had determined that since the lands were now officially Michale's, it was his place to do the talking. Additionally, TJ wanted to see firsthand how Mick handled himself formally. Mick hadn't wanted to speak, but TJ overrode his objections.

As TJ, Michale, and Summer approached the school, the captain of his accompanying guard stepped up. "The Gyrenes are in place, Sire. I shall wait outside and call you when Administrator Chavez is ready." TJ had surreptitiously checked the placement of his guards around the platform and was pleased.

"Thank you, Captain Timmons," TJ said. Timmons had been the lieutenant who had let the fateful party upon the recent assassination attempt. He'd been elevated to captain on Summer's recommendation. "Sharp kid. Follows orders

well. Executes precisely. Excellent soldier," Summer had
told TJ and Manny Vero when TJ had recovered and was
being briefed on events subsequent to his injury and unconsciousness. "And," Summer'd added, "you should have seen
the look on Nora's face when he carried her into your
chambers on his horse." TJ grinned at Nora's discomfort.

The school was of old lumber, dry as everything else in
Dawn's Edge. They entered through the double entry doors
and came into a long hallway that had doors along both
sides. Midway down the corridor, benches and a couple of
tables had been set up. A flagon of wine and pitcher of
water for him and Mick were on a table along with hand
basins. TJ went to a hand basin and began to wash off some
of the dust.

Summmer poured a glass of wine, tasted it, and made a
face. Mike paced nervously, obviously on edge a bit because
of his upcoming speech.

Timmons stepped outside and shut the doors for their
privacy. TJ glimpsed Chavez mounting the platform for his
introductory remarks. A few minutes, he thought.

He sat on a bench against a wooden wall. Place is a fire
trap, he thought. "Sit down and rest, Mick. A rule of
thumb—people introducing royalty like to talk a lot in doing
so." He eased his sword belt for more comfort sitting down.

Summer squatted against the opposite wall.

Mick took a drink from the table in the middle of the hall.

Feet scraping on the floor caused TJ to look down the
corridor.

"TJ!" Summer warned.

From open doors toward the end of the hall stepped six
men armed with loaded and cocked crossbows. They halted
and lifted their weapons as if they'd practiced the maneuver
many times.

"Down!" TJ said almost conversationally, and dropped to
one knee.

"Fire!" said one of the men simultaneously.

Mick kicked a table into the air.

Summer's jester hat flew out and, along with the table,
intercepted four of the bolts. Two others thudded into the
wall where TJ had been sitting.

Eagerness and overconfidence or else they'd have had us
on the first salvo, TJ thought as his hand grabbed under his
tunic. Out of the corner of his eye he saw Summer doing
likewise. No way for swords to combat crossbows at this

distance, and not enough time to reach the men before they reloaded.

Immediately, he had his weapon out and the "BRRRP" of his weapon beat Summer's by only an instant.

Deadly ice-needles crossed the air with the next salvo of six crossbow bolts.

Mick throwing himself against a wall to avoid the flight of arrows was the only sound in the strangely silent fight until the bolts began thunking into the wall and table that TJ dove under.

He rolled again and brought his weapon to bear on the far end of the hallway and pressed the firing stud. "BRRRP" exploded again, joining Summer's traverse across the corridor.

Only one man still stood and he and Summer cut the attacker down together. The man's exposed flesh looked like a pincushion. Bloody spots began to appear on him as blood seeped from tiny wounds. Water from the melting ice-needles blended with blood to spot and stain clothing and floor.

"Jean-Claude was well paid," TJ observed. The power pack in the weapon could only freeze twenty ice-needles per second from the water compartment and generate just enough compressed air to shoot those twenty. Each second. It had been enough. He figured a hundred ice-needles in five seconds. Two hundred between them. "Effective," TJ said and Summer nodded. "Though I'd have preferred to take them on in hand-to-hand combat."

"And you'd be dead right now, boss," Summer said as he rose. "As you would be if you hadn't rolled like a tumbling champion." TJ grinned to himself knowing a backhanded compliment like that one from Summer was unusual.

The doors behind them opened and TJ and Summer dropped to their knees, raised their weapons and aimed.

Captain Timmons stood in the doorway. "I thought I heard . . . Sweet Jesus, not again . . ." Then he had his sword out and was charging down the corridor.

Summer lifted a hand and Timmons stopped. "Close the door," Summer's voice commanded.

"Sir," Timmons said and rushed to the doors and closed them.

"We should promote him out of his field job," Summer said sardonically, "It'd be safer for you."

TJ noticed the look of horror on Mick's face as he stood against the wall. "Just a little something we bought, son . . ." he began to explain. Then he saw the bolt sticking out from Mick's tunic. "Uh oh," he said as he hurried to Mick's side.

"Missed me, father, " Mick said. "I'm pinned."

"Timmons," Summer said, "take the rooms along the right, I'll take left. I doubt anybody else is here, but we got to check."

"I'll alert my men, sir, and . . ."

"No," Summer said. "Let's move." They ran down the hallway ghosting in and out of rooms.

TJ ripped Mick's tunic away from the arrow, being extra careful in case of poison.

"Why won't Summer let Timmons call his troops?" Mick asked. "And what were those things you used?"

"I should have taken you into my confidence. These are," TJ held up his weapon, short and squarish, "ice-needle guns. And while they aren't as obvious as energy weapons, there are six men with ice-needle puncture marks all over their bodies. No one must know how we overcame them because Sharon Gold is out there and possession of these is a violation of Fed policy and we could be disqualified from membership this time."

"But it beats the hell out of being dead," Summer said as he and Timmons returned.

TJ put his weapon under his tunic. "A little action, eh? Gets your blood up, doesn't it, son? Makes you eat and drink heartier. Makes life sweeter. Makes me philosophize. Any suggestions, Summer?"

"We could probably hide the bodies and get away with it, after all you are the King. But we ain't gonna, in the minute or two left, do that thing and conceal all those needle holes all over the walls and ceiling. Only one answer."

"So I figure. It's going to be messy, Summer."

"Yeah."

Timmons was checking the bodies methodically to insure they were in fact dead. "All dead, Sire. But practically, I suspect someone is going to notice my absence from outside the door soon."

TJ decided. "Summer, we'll buy 'em a new school. It's not worth the price of this place to have Sharon Gold discover what happened here. And rumors get around, don't they?" He turned to Timmons who was searching the bodies. "Captain, your silence?"

Timmons looked hurt. "As always, Sire," He finished his

search and lifted bloody hands. In one hand was a large vial.
"Nothing, Sire, but this vial. Poison, I'll wager."

"A little drop will do you," Summer said. "The pattern
holds."

"Too much so," replied TJ. "While this event is not held
in secrecy, not a lot of people in Crimson Sapphire are
aware of it." He paused and Summer nodded at his speculation. "It begins to add up like an inside job. Somebody who
knows what I—or we—are going to do. Or at least has
access to the information."

Summer nodded again. "Reasonable. But the thought tastes
like sharp dung in my mouth."

Mick was looking at the three as if the close call and the
death of six men had not affected them a bit. TJ saw. "You
get used to it, son."

Summer turned to Timmons, "Find lamps. Splatter the
oil, especially here in the hall."

"Aye, sir."

TJ went to the doors and looked out. "Uh oh. They're
looking this way expectantly. They probably think Timmons
came in to get us. Not much time," he called.

Mick had regained his composure. "How do I explain this
torn tunic?"

"Or the charred bones in this building after it burns," TJ
added.

Summer and Timmons were splashing lamp fuel on the
walls.

TJ raised his voice so they could hear him. "We'll have to
admit to the attack. So that explains the burned bodies.
Lessee . . . they obviously fired the building to get at us as a
last resort, but we slew them anyway. Maybe a lamp was
knocked over during the fighting?" He strode to the nearest corpse, took out his sword and sliced into the dead man.

"My, God! Father!"

"You, too, Mick, quickly now."

Summer finished the last lamp. "Do what he says, Mike.
Do you think we four overcame six opponents by waving
our magic wands?"

"Oh." Michale pulled out his sword and carefully tinged
it red with blood from a pool on the floor.

"You, too, Timmons," Summer directer.

"Aye, sir."

"Mick, you got to have the stomach for this. Chop into
'em," TJ said. "Suppose somebody looks at the corpses.

Shouldn't they find blade marks?" He wasn't certain if burned bodies would show that—must depend on how burned the bodies were.

"I don't think . . ." Mick started to say.

"Never mind, I'll do it." TJ was slashing away at corpses as fast as he could swing his sword. Blood was splattered all over his clothing. "Won't hurt my reputation a bit," he said and enjoyed the look of horror on Mick's face. "You could use the publicity, too, Mick."

"Not me, father . . ."

"Have it your way, son, but you got to take advantage of everything that comes your way in life. Especially if you're going to run this damn planet one day. Don't ever miss a trick. Hurry, Summer."

"Done, TJ. Fire the place, Captain Timmons."

Timmons grinned. "With pleasure. Unfortunate these men are not still alive."

TJ wrinkled his nose at the smell of death and blood and fuel.

Timmons tossed a lighted lamp against a back wall and flame exploded with a whoosh.

Summer bent to a body and ran his hand across a bloody torso then smeared some blood on his jester's outfit.

"Might be out of character, Summer," TJ said.

"Even a jester would be expected to get involved more than normal when his salary is threatened," he said.

"Not to mention protecting the royal family," TJ said.

Flame was racing along the corridor pushing smoke ahead of it. The backed toward the door.

"Fire's catching nicely," TJ said.

Summer dodged flames. "*I* ain't waiting much longer."

"Yeah," said TJ and coughed. "Once we open the doors, the fire will really go. Everybody ready?" He didn't bother to look. "Keep your swords out, we want everybody to see the blood. Let's go—NOW!"

Thomas Jefferson Shepherd slammed through the double doors of the school house and both flew off their hinges. The other three followed quickly behind him. Smoke burst out with them. He knew the open doors would cause a bellows effect and accelerate the fire—he hoped before anybody could douse the flames.

A ripple went through the crowd as smoke and flames leapt into the sky. The front rows of people fell into an awed silence when they saw TJ and the others.

TJ saw Gwen and Felicia and Sharon rise. Gwen's face was too far to read, thank God. He stopped and turned to Timmons. "Captain," he said in his best commanding voice, the one that carried well, "have your men surround the building in case we failed to slay them all. Let no one in or out." He saw that Timmons understood. Firefighters would be hindered.

Timmons ran off.

Summer spoke in a low tone. "Poor guy has the worst luck on his shift."

27: SHARON

Sharon Gold watched with fascinated horror as the four men ran out of the burning school. Swathed in smoke, the King looked like some mythical god climbing out of the depths of hell. The sword in his hand seemed so natural, she hadn't noticed it right away.

Only when Mike and Captain Timmons, followed by the jester, came after TJ with their weapons drawn did she realize something was amiss. Yes, they all appeared to be unharmed.

Flames shot to the roof of the building. Sharon watched people react. As smoke poured out and then was swept away by the omnipresent wind, the crowd became spectators. Fortunately, no other buildings were near the school and thus the fire did not threaten to spread. After an initial few moments, the crowd quieted and simply watched. To all, it was obvious that matters were in hand.

Sharon had watched Gwen lurch to her feet with an oath. Gwen and Felicia had joined arms stoically. Sharon felt an empathy for them—both Mike and TJ always, nowadays, in danger.

Her eyes went to Mike, standing there talking to the jester. His sword has hanging loosely from his hand and was dripping blood. She saw his tunic was torn. Another sympathetic pang struck her as she remembered his abhorrence of violence.

The captain of the King's guard was organizing quickly. A

squad detached itself and formed a protective barrier around the viewing stand. They held their weapons at ready. A smart move, Sharon reflected, in case of a coordinated attack on the entire royal family.

The burning building was now past saving, though a few tried unsuccessfully with buckets of water and sand. With a shower of embers, the school caved in upon itself and at that point Sharon smelled the unmistakable stench of burning human flesh. The waft of breeze that brought her that smell also brought smoke and she coughed and gagged. Felicia turned and put her hand on Sharon's shoulder. Sharon nodded acknowledgment of Felicia's concern. She thought, not for the first time, that Bear Ridge bred some strong men and women.

While officials were reorganizing the festivities, the fire burned down to coals and charred lumber. The King insisted on continuing the ceremonies. During the intervening lull, Sharon managed to see Mike.

"Mike?"

He looked at her, eyes somehow tired for a young man, and managed a wry smile. "Some of it spills over, doesn't it?" He seemed to be maturing daily right in front of her eyes. She wasn't sure she liked this new change in him, this growth. She found herself with mixed feelings.

"It was another assassination attempt?" she asked.

"Yes."

She fingered his torn tunic and looked into his eyes and immediately averted her own, frightened that she'd shown too much concern.

"Pinned me to the wall, they did," Mike smiled ruefully.

"Certainly you must not make your speech, now," she said.

"On the contrary, I certainly shall." He seemed to be alive in some new way, the initial stage fright submerged by something new and different, something that made his eyes glow—yet his features were pale.

And later, after he had spoken to the people, she admitted that he had done a fine job. He was articulate and soft spoken—though he did seem to talk of the future in generalities. So he's becoming a politician, too, she thought cynically.

As the applause for Mike abated, the King rose and supplanted administrator Chavez at the speaker's rostrum. In short succinct sentences, he apologized for the circumstances that led to the loss of their school. He made a point of blaming no one locally for the attempt, so that no stigma would attach itself to Dawn's Edge. Then he spoke of the importance of the ranching effort.

He concluded his remarks, "I shall fund the building of a new school, immediately, in a different location. For that ground is soiled with blood and treachery. And blood and treachery are no grounds upon which to build the cornerstone of our society: a place of learning.

"Let the coals continue to glow until nothing is left but ashes. And then bury the remains and allow grasses to grow on the mound where once children learned and played. I would see the greenery abound on the ashes of what might have been. When I visit here I will see that greenery and remember that Dawn's Edge is a place of luck for me and the family Shepherd."

Sharon could not help but admire the consummate politician. And being from Fedcentral, she had seen some of the best. TJ Shepherd missed no opportunity.

During the fiesta that followed, Sharon wandered back to the smoking embers of the school. The smell of barbecuing beefaloe now obscured the stench of the razed school. But, apprehensively, she still breathed through her mouth and fancied she could taste singed flesh.

She tried to understand what had happened here. Why hadn't there been a greater hue and cry over another assassination attempt? Why had the effort to douse the flames been halfhearted and disorganized? Something wasn't making sense.

Another thing: Mike wasn't known for his fighting ability. Which left the King and Captain Timmons. Yet they had overcome six assailants in an obviously planned operation. And the jester, something strange there, too. Camp was becoming an enigma. She'd heard only whispers of rumors— no one in the palace ever wanted to talk and the subject wasn't one she could legitimately pursue. But she did remember the immediate aftermath of the previous assassination attempt and what the jester had done. Certainly he was no mere buffoon.

Then she recalled the incident of the snarv in the great throne room. The King had surely proved then that he was capable of protecting himself even at great odds. While thinking of that, she admitted that perhaps six assailants might not be sufficient to murder this King.

Gingerly she stepped forward among the ruins, some of

which still smoked. She avoided embers and the occasional licking flame. Something odd was urging her on. Risking glowing coals at her feet, she found it.

There—a roofing beam. A short section which had not burned. An oblique line of tiny holes, so standard in size and uniform in distance from each other that they almost had to be machine made. And she couldn't think of any reason to have such a finely calibrated machine, if there were such for construction materials, make these same holes. Nor were the holes in any apparent logical place. They simply started at the lower edge and continued along the beam at approximately a fifty degree angle and went to the upper edge.

A child with a toy? On a roofing beam? No way. Attachment point for something to hang from? Not that either. This speculation was getting her nowhere. It simply did not make sense.

"Ma'am?"

The words scared her from her reverie and she quickly turned about. "What is it?"

The Gyrene sergeant took her elbow patronizingly. "It is dangerous here for a lady, ma'am."

"All right." They didn't want her to see.

A cover up, of course. So what was it she shouldn't be allowed to see? She disengaged her arm and walked off from the sergeant. The answer came to her almost immediately. Part of her training included weapons familiarization. "WPNS FAM" read the entry on her training chart. A needle gun would fire its tiny metallic darts in such a line. But where was the evidence? If the King had used a proscribed weapon for self defense, and the school burned immediately thereafter, there had been no time to remove all the needles.

Except, she realized, in one of the new *ice*-needle guns. Untrained use of the ice-needle gun could result in a stich-like line of holes in a roof beam.

Across the way she saw Mike looking at her. His half-smile she took to be an invitation and headed for the group of people around him.

As she wound through the crowd, she shook her head at this intrigue. When she'd been assigned the Bear Ridge project, she had thought it would be a straightforward assignment. But now, it began to look as if she were caught up in something she did not understand. Nor could she be excepted to put it all together and figure out exactly what was happening. Damnitall! She was just supposed to be an observer, a note-taker, a checklist filler-outer, a criteria matcher. And give an informed opinion to the Council. But what if she were fighting forces on that same Council? Could there be interference from a part or all of the Council? From Marxists? From Free Traders?

And what was Thomas Jefferson Shepherd hiding?

Then she made a decision.

For the time being, she would ignore the fact she had discovered. Not only because she had found no hard evidence, but frankly because she didn't want to see the King killed. Although the attempts on his life appeared to be in conjunction with his drive for Federation membership. Something to ponder.

She found herself uncontrollably becoming involved with the fate of the King and his family.

She admired him and he intrigued her. Was it a terrible thing for him to have such lofty dreams? It was unusual for a fighting man such as he to have seemingly conflicting personal traits. Was it normal for such a competent soldier, a war leader, to have the kind of grasp of the future that TJ did? She didn't think so. And, she admitted, he'd shown streaks of administrative genius in his organization of governmental functions.

A startling realization hit her then: In the Federation, the managers, the supervisors, the administrators were all there for various reasons—none of which were management ability. Yet on Bear Ridge, TJ Shepherd was in his position, not only because he had fought his way to the top, but because he could maintain his position through effective managerial ability. He could *manage*. He could *supervise*. He could *administer*. Conclusion: should the Federation grant him a Council seat, the Federation had best be willing to suffer the consequences. The enormity of her thought frightened her and then she dismissed the thought with a laugh. She giggled to herself. The Council could use somebody with a modicum of managerial talents.

She'd just do her job as assigned. That was the only thing to do.

28: KELLEN

Kellen Sing sipped a light ale at a table against the back wall.

The Poet's Corner had become a student gathering place. Tonight was dedicated, not to poetry or singing or instruments, but to Kellen Sing and his advocates.

Right now, Franco Valdez was speaking. Kellen's turn would come soon. The place was crowded and occasionally a subdued murmur ran through the patrons. Valdez was speaking persuasively on the environmental impact of new technology when the Federation and their ships came.

Valdez had been easy to recruit. Kellen had found him shortly after the incident with the King on the King's birthday. And Kellen had immediately gained a convert—plus a nucleus of about one hundred other conservationists who followed Valdez. It had not been difficult to persuade Valdez and, consequently, his group to join him in Crimson Sapphire and aid in his cause.

Franco concluded his remarks to scattered applause. Kellen thought then that maybe the King had turned loose something he could not control in education and free speech. The young men and women in Shepherd University were the first who had matriculated through most of the system to get that far. And those who were in the university had become a class of people, of students, educated out of their time and place. Kellen had recognized that fact and didn't think that either the King or his cronies had figured it out yet. So Kellen was there to take advantage of the disenfranchised, so to speak, young men and women. And with his Webbine aura techniques to augment his arguments, he always swayed them.

He rose to go to the slightly raised floor in front to speak. He passed a table of padres and managed to broadcast on the spectrum a message of concern, one calculated to attract the churchmen.

As he stood waiting for the applause to die, he manipulated his way through skeptical auras. He beamed confidence and good will. Not only did it make strangers more pliable and open to his suggestions, but it reinforced his influence on his converts.

He launched into his "education and prejudice" talk, the one where he admired the King for the opportunities of education and slammed the monarch for intending to turn those so educated into lackeys for off-worlders. And Prejudice. The King was prejudiced against his own people in favor of those already in the Federation. This last argument was weak in foundation, but good fodder for his ardent followers.

He'd found gatherings like this to be very good practice. He was well versed in aura influence in one-on-one situations. But handling a number of people simultaneously required timing and practice and luck. And some were strong individuals and not easily influenced. Weak personalities simply begged him to make his subtle suggestions—not in specifics, but in emotions. Care, concern, love, hate. He manipulated all these to his benefit.

He decided he'd talked long enough and concluded. Instead of going back to his table to join Valdez and other close advisors, he left through the rear door to use the outside facilities. When he'd finished and was walking back to *The Poet's Corner,* a robed figure intercepted him. He'd been preoccupied and hadn't noticed the approach of the man's furtive aura.

"Kellen Sing," the voice said. Kellen determined the speaker to be a padre.

"Yes?"

"This way please."

"Why should I?" he asked mildly. He read no danger from the padre's aura.

"A few moments only to meet someone."

Kellen read the importance of this meeting in the man's projections and decided he had nothing to lose. "All right."

A five-minute walk and the priest led him into a small chapel along a side street. The place was bleak and poorly lighted. His guide disappeared and he saw another robed figure on a front pew. The sound of the outside chapel doors closing startled him. Kellen, more apprehensive now but still finding no danger present, walked down the aisle.

He stopped center aisle, knelt, made the sign of the cross, and looked at the Chief Padre. "You wished to see me,

Padre?" He was careful to insure his voice held no hint of subservience.

"Yes." Roaland Cruz indicated the bench beside him. "Sit down."

Kellen studied the man with intensity, delicately feeling out the padre's aura and trying to mold it to favor him.

"Are you of the faith?"

"Did I not just show such?"

"Actions can be meant to deceive."

"Then you must take me for what I seem," Kellen said. It was difficult to find the key to the Chief Padre. One of the problems with influencing people, he'd discovered, was that the older they were, the more difficult the task. Combine age with the strong will of one whose personal drive was such that he had reached the peak of his profession, like the Chief Padre, and the task of influencing was almost impossible. Until, Kellen amended, I become more proficient.

Kellen guessed why Cruz wanted to see him. He willed his aura to encourage Cruz to talk. Lengthen the time and perhaps he would have more success in influencing the padre. And might even learn more, he added to himself.

"Have you complicity," the padre asked, aura tentative, "in the murder attempts on the King?"

Kellen wondered irrationally why the Chief Padre couldn't speak in more simple terms. "No." He added a small compulsion to his aura that told Cruz he, Kellen, was speaking the truth. Might as well start building a rapport at a basic level, he thought.

Cruz paused, then obviously chose his words carefully. "You could, ah, do better than you are, young man. You could gain, shall we say, a more stable platform from which to pursue your goals."

Kellen read right through him. Obviously, the older man wanted his support which would include the following he'd already developed.

"I'll be frank with you," Cruz was saying, "we'd use you to an extent. You've become a powerful force with the young people and the Church is not appealing as much as it should to that younger generation. Thanks to the King and his liberalism."

Kellen had been working on an effort to increase the padre's urge to talk. He concentrated on that compulsion. "Why?"

Cruz seemed to jump on the opportunity. "Why? Besides

the King's blasphemy and vulgarisms? Besides his ignoring the Church and steering away from our precepts? Besides his diminishment of the Church's authority? Besides his authoritarian one-man rule which excludes the Church from its traditional role—in both society and government?" Cruz seemed to realize what he was saying and fell silent.

"Padre, do you suggest an alliance?" Kellen realized just by his presence, the Chief Padre had given him a boost of credibility. It gave him something concrete to show of his success, more than just applauding students.

Cruz appeared surprised. "An alliance? With you? I hadn't thought of it in those terms. Your support, perhaps."

"For you to regain power?"

"No, my son, for the Church to regain its proper place. And to return to the fold some of my padres who have strayed to your cause."

"Ah. Now I see." He could observe the frustration seeming to boil from the padre's aura. Obviously, the padre was being besieged on both sides. Officially by the King and his bureaucratic minions, and now by the power of the people, the young people. Obviously, the Church had not changed rapidly enough after the Consolidation wars to maintain its status quo.

Kellen saw Cruz reappraise him. He knew what the padre was thinking. Not just some punk, loud-mouthed kid. No. He was seeing, now, a confident young man, one who seemed to be guiding this conversation contrary to his initial purposes.

Cruz seemed to revise his thinking. "Your following is strong and loyal. That my people inform me. You speak of things people can grasp, not theological things, but everyday things. And it would seem that we have common goals. Especially the goal of rejecting membership into the Federation. Certainly we could use the medical advances, for instance, but not the overwhelming amount of technology and changes the King is going to turn loose upon us. And so far your words do not suggest conflict with the Church. I submit that the two are not mutually exclusive and separate . . ."

Kellen had influenced the padre more than he thought. "You think we can do each other good?"

"To put it baldly. We would evaluate your abilities and train you in our facilities, Kellen; I doubt you would have any trouble in becoming a full padre."

Kellen had to admire the older man. All the padre wanted

to do was buy him off, in any way possible, and get him under his own Church-structured control. And, perhaps because of Kellen's own tinkering, the padre had not been very subtle in the offer. He did not speak.

Cruz said, "I sense you do not wish to become a part of the religious orders. Very well, something else can be arranged. A high administrative position within the Church. A secular one, so to speak."

Kellen considered the offer. It was tempting and would give him a broader power base. But it wasn't what he wanted, nor did it take the route he had planned. The possibility of totally subverting the Chief Padre to his own purposes during the obvious close association occurred to him. But there were too many drawbacks, most of them involving the highly structured orgainization of the Church. Any position he held would open him to minute scrutiny. He'd be vulnerable. One thing he'd learned was that when it came to religion, people were not very logical thinking or amenable to change. Could that be what the Church's problem was now?

So he said, "No," and made his aura as calm and soothing as he could. Much of his technique involved having people react to him as he wanted them to, not always influencing them.

Cruz sighed. "You know, I once was, and suppose I still am to a degree, an avid student of human nature. It was that ability that opened doors to my present position. However, I think I'm losing touch with my talent."

Kellen thought that Cruz, at that moment, was simply a tired old man.

Well, he'd sort of won that confrontation. But it had drained him. Suppose he were to struggle mentally with a stronger and younger man?

29: SUMMER

"Your appearance belies your profession, jester," Kellen Sing said. "But then, upon the King's injuries, strange rumors about your position and actions were whispered."

"People love to talk," Summer said, voice tight. "Your innocuous appearance at the King's birthday festivities belies your current profession."

"I am a student, and I express my opinions."

Mike stirred uncomfortably. They all stood after Mike had formally introduced Summer and Kellen in the corridor of the Shepherd University. Summer had ostensibly accompanied Mike on an errand—but his actual purpose was to take the measure of Kellen Sing firsthand.

"If you will excuse me," Mike said, "I must confer with the headmaster." Summer thought they ought to change his title from the traditional headmaster to something more authoritative, prestigious. "Kellen, would you show Summer around for a bit?"

"Certainly, I will give Señor Camp a quick tour."

Summer nodded, wondering at the formal use of the title señor. He felt an instant antagonism growing between him and Kellen.

As they walked the halls, Summer grimly noted the constant greetings and words or respect with which students and instructors addressed Kellen. He thought that had he worn his jester's costume that no one would have paid him any attention, just Kellen.

He wondered if some radical professor had influenced Kellen. He resolved to find out.

Kellen interrupted his thinking. He stopped in front of a square building. "Food and drink inside if you need refreshment. Maybe we could discuss what you really want."

"Ah, you see through me." Students waved at Kellen and Summer found it continually distracting.

"Not really, " Kellen said. "But our meeting was rather contrived. Am I under some sort of surveillance now?"

"No."

They went inside and got some hot herbal teal and returned outdoors to sit on one of the many benches. Automatically, Summer checked the sky for the possibility of a quick rain.

At first they were silent. Kellen seemed to be concentrating on something and it made Summer feel uncomfortable. Kellen shrugged finally and said, "Shall we get on with it?"

Summer dropped his indifferent expression and put some iron into his voice. "So be it. The question is why."

"Why?"

"You heard me. Why?"

Kellen blew over his steaming cup. "Why not?"

"Don't play your word games with me, Kellen Sing. I'll say it flatly. The King befriended you. Rewarded you. Now you return his favors by publicly denouncing him. You seemed to be aiming to thwart him in his desires for Federation membership. And many of your words are designed to preclude his continuing rule. Why?"

Sing sighed. "It has come to that, has it? I owe the King; therefore, I also owe him my strong support. And thus I must cease speaking what I think is right. I'm supposed to forget the truth that he is a dictator and is suppressing the people."

"Save that line for your friends, Sing." Summer stopped and breathed deeply. He was trying to dislike Kellen Sing and found it difficult.

Kellen seemed to concentrate and his eyes grew larger. Summer wavered in his determination to wring the truth from the young man. But to drop his purpose of coming here today went against his strong will. He seemed to be waging an inner battle with himself. Then a lifelong tradition of toughness, that fabric that had been woven into his character through adversity and experience, took control and he felt himself bursting through some sort of barrier and returned to pursue the conversation. Maybe he'd be a little easier on Kellen. The young man was a likeable chap anyway, no need to go through an inquisition.

Kellen shook off some mood and smiled benevolently. "Sr. Camp, it is not my intention to violently overthrow the monarchy. I merely ask questions. I only want to know why things are as they are. It is something they encourage here at this university."

"They encourage sedition?" Summer asked, anger once again strengthening his purpose.

"Not at all," Kellen said, showing his own anger. "Here I have learned that the smart man asks 'Why?' and seeks to find the answers."

Summer shook his head. "That's not the same thing as publicly opposing the King."

"I seek only the truth . . ."

"The truth as you see it," Summer interrupted. Kellen and his inane preaching were feeding his anger.

"The truth is that each man and woman should be his or her own master."

"Fine. Leave it at that."

"But a Shepherd is their master, now."

"Your words border on treason, Sing."

"I invoke freedom of speech."

Summer admitted TJ had gotten carried away when he gave blanket freedom of speech. "Your mother is a whore and let's run inside that building and shout 'fire,' all right? Freedom of speech implies discretion."

Kellen brushed an insect away from his forehead. "You leave my mother out of this. Was not freedom an avowed goal of the King's Consolidation wars? Wasn't it?"

"Well, sort of. . ."

"And how many people were killed in the name of freedom?" Kellen demanded. "And how many lives were shattered because of it?" Kellen's voice had turned bitter.

Summer recognized the despair being the words and began to understand. He felt sorrow for Kellen Sing and others like him of his generation whose lives had been torn by the wars.

"I don't want your pity, Camp." the young man snapped at him, and Summer wondered if Kellen could read minds.

Summer saw he would get no further with Kellen and this disturbed him. The unrest Kellen was causing could be squashed at any time. But Summer was concerned with an additional dimension of the Kellen Sing problem: Mike. Mike was thick with Kellen and Summer had wanted, to evaluate the extent of Kellen's power—or was it influence?—on Mike and on others in the university. He'd hoped to find something he could use to act as a wedge between Mike and Kellen. The trouble was that any action taken against Kellen might have a reverse effect on Mike, further straining the relationship between him and TJ. Finally, Summer had hoped to find the Kellen Sing phenomenon a short-lived fad on the university campus. Unfortunately, this was not the case—though he'd guessed such from reading reports before he ever came.

He wondered why he kept thinking of Sing in the more familiar address of Kellen?

He decided to throw Kellen off balance. "Kellen," his voice was low and did not carry, "do not attempt to use your friendship with the Prince as a shield. Or to your advantage."

"A warning, Sr. Camp?"

"More than a warning. A threat." Summer admitted to himself that the Kellen Sing problem might need to be taken care of even at the expense of Mike's friendship. Even at the expense of further widening the rift between the King and the Prince.

Kellen's eyes had narrowed and he locked onto Summer's eyes. Pressure between them built into a solid thing, but Summer had already overcome whatever force of will Kellen was trying to burn into him and found it not difficult to ignore this time. He smiled at Kellen and wondered what the young man was trying to do. Hypnosis?

Kellen tore his eyes away first.

Summer grinned at Kellen's discomfort. The renowned charisma had no effect on him. "A little advice, Sing. Stay in the shallows where there are no dangerous creatures."

"What?" Kellen almost recoiled and Summer did not understand his reaction.

"Oh, Kellen, there you are," came a lilting female voice.

Freckles. And braided blonde hair. She stood in front of them, eyes searching. She was dressed in loose trousers and a tunic, somehow very feminine. She smiled curiously at Summer. "Hello."

Summer rose quickly to his feet.

"My sister, Camp. Rebecca, this is Sr. Camp." Kellen sounded distracted.

"Summer," he said automatically, extending his hand.

"Oh?" She took his hand. "The name has a certain ring to it, it does."

"Thank you," Summer said, wondering what to say next, and how to prolong the hand contact.

"You don't look like an instructor or professor here," she said gauging the width of his shoulders.

"No. I . . . er, work at the palace."

"He's a friend of Mike's" Kellen said.

"Oh," said Rebecca Sing, "I remember Mike saying something about somebody named Camp being from Lonestar just like we are."

"I left at a very young age to seek fame and fortune."

"And did you find it, Summer Camp?"

"I . . ."

Kellen interrupted, using words like a hammer. "He is the court jester."

Rebecca didn't seem to notice Kellen's tone. "That must be very interesting." Then she noticed that he still held her hand and pulled it away. Summer felt awkward.

"If you will excuse us, Sr. Camp?" Kellen's manner said the discussion was over.

"Kellen, do not be rude," Rebecca chided.

"He is a spy for the King," Kellen replied, trying to humiliate Summer.

"Oh? That must be interesting, too. I thought . . . oops. I have intruded." She sat down abruptly.

Summer said, "Rebecca Sing, I assure you I am not on business for the King. I am down here on my own account so that I might understand . . . but that is neither here nor there. I must go. Kellen Sing, remember our conversation. Rebecca Sing, perhaps I shall see you later?" Summer had tried to make this last a statement but, unfortunately, it came out as a question.

"No," Kellen said sharply.

She tossed her head. "Pooh, Kellen, I don't think Summer Camp is a spy at all. Why if the King wanted to spy on you, all he'd have to do would be to ask Mike, isn't that correct?"

"No."

Kellen was becoming surly, so Summer nodded as pleasantly as he could to Rebecca and walked off.

Shortly, he found the headmaster's office. Alexander Levkas was a gaunt, middle-aged man who went to extremes to effect the professorial image. He and Mike were speaking of a program in animal husbandry when Summer was ushered into the office.

"I'm about ready to leave," Mike said.

"A question first, Prince Michale. Professor Levkas, I'd like to see what you have in Kellen Sing's file and I'd like for you to give a progress report on him."

"Who is this man, Prince Michale?" Levkas demanded.

Summer kept his expression the same. He returned Mike's glance.

"He is a palace aide," Mike told the headmaster. "I'd recommend cooperation." And he conspicuously failed to introduce Summer.

Levkas sighed. "I know what is in the file. Simply grades and attendance figures, that sort of thing. His grades are all excellent. He is a superior student who has great mental faculties. His ability to absorb data is astronomical. He is a good student."

Summer waited, but Levkas apparently had nothing else to say. "Does he push his political views on this campus?"

Levkas raised his hands. "Not any more than he does in the city. But to answer your question, students talk. Kellen Sing has many friends, I won't deny that."

"Supporters?" Summer asked.

"I don't know. I don't categorize students by their extra-curricular endeavors."

"A final question, Dr. Levkas. Is the Kellen Sing phenomenon epidemic on your campus?"

"No, it is not, sir. It is more than likely a passing fad, like the adulation a winning handball team garners."

Summer didn't know whether to believe Levkas or not—and he was inclined to think that perhaps somehow Kellen Sing had recruited the headmaster to his cause.

30: I:IMBAWE

Fools! Gasbags! A race was dying and all they do is con-verse. No action. No wonder they drove O:omega out.

O:chacka ought to know better, for was he not the one linked to the Trekmaster through the /crimson sapphire/?

I:imbawe was disgusted. He sat in the glade with the older elders, all adult males. In a nearby pond, two new-born were learning to splash along the surface with their webs. Their auras were innocent and gleeful.

The auras of all the elders were guarded and neutral. Naturally. Only A:alpha resting nearby failed to hide his excitement. A:alpha was not invited to the meet; however, his mentor, O:chacka, had bade him stay nearby. Since it was a continuing topic, the meet was open and A:alpha could participate if called upon.

/Events race to culmination, then?/ repeated O:chacka.

/Projections remain true,/ I:imbawe said: /As your ward, A:alpha, is acclaimed a budding genius in projection, perchance he can verify? If his proficiency is as stated?/

/'Tis a fact,/ O:chacka said. /A:alpha's calculations confirm age-old predictions./ He checked for aural disagreement and I:imbawe leaked a shade more confidence into his own aura. /His prognostications fit, though the formulations were different and thus gave more credibility to his projections./

I:imbawe knew they would discuss methodology for a while. He wanted to delete that part of the dialogue and get to the action phase: What could they do about the problem?

Too many centuries ago, the Webbines had realized the potential problem represented by the humans. The problem became blatantly obvious when the humans were abandoned by their own kind, almost died out, reverted to primitive, and began rebuilding their civilization from that new start. And flourished.

The Webbine calculators had determined through study that *any* outcome would be disastrous for the Webbines. The first possibility was that the humans would continue to grow upon Bear Ridge and eventually require the use of the entire planet, thus condemning the Webbines.

The second possibility was that the other humans on other worlds would regenerate their populations as the ones on Bear Ridge were doing and population pressure would make it only a matter of time before Bear Ridge was rediscovered and again become the recipient for human population overflow elsewhere.

This realization brought the Webbines to the point where they had only two options. The first was immediately discarded: change themselves and their way of life sufficiently to live and thrive on human terms and in the human environment. Through the centuries the elders had rejected this as unthinkable. As they did now. The fools! Time changes, times change, why not Webbines?

The Webbines' other option had two possible trails: one, kill the humans—if possible; two, change the humans to benefit the Webbines' needs. Killing the humans had been discounted because they didn't know if they could kill all the humans, and secondly, they were certain that Bear Ridge would be rediscovered by other humans—was it not foretold? —and the problem resumed.

Which left one way to go: change the humans, and do it sufficiently before the Bear Ridge humans reunited with other humans from the stars.

So changing the humans became a matter of racial survival for the Webbines, though some still would discuss it into the afterlife. I:imbawe admitted that it was not a very well coordinated plan nor was it comprehensive. More like several failed experiments, and a partially successful one or two.

The goal: to make the humans more like the Webbines philosophically so that when the final moment came, the Bear Ridge humans would have more in common with the Webbines than the off-world humans and thus the slow-reproducing Webbines could be saved. It had occurred to I:imbawe that the humans, even though gaining domination, might do their best to maintain the integrity of the Webbine race, give them a "reservation" and keep them there like tame animals. But he knew humans better than most Webbines and did not bring this possibility up for discussion.

I:imbawe checked the progress of the meet. Nothing. N:tasse, he who was primarily responsible for the expulsion of O:omega, was still challenging the validity of the latest prognostications. Old females!

After years of observation, the Webbine elders had determined that to change humans would be a long, involved process and adopted the Trek as one of the vehicles to accomplish this change. They had encouraged the Trek and used it. The Trek weeded out weaklings, so that only the strong survived—the strong as defined by the fact that these humans adapted faster and more effectively to the ecosystem of Bear Ridge and thus had similar interests to the Webbines.

The Trek gave the Webbines a strong human leader on which to work their changes.

First they bonded Trekmasters to the Webbines through the "crimson sapphire." The stone, the jewel, was born, developed, and expelled from the body of a Webbine. It began as a precipitation of certain mineral salts which condensed on any one of several microscopic nuclei and grew from there, inside the filtering-organ, the one with many metabolic functions. Coral polyp and certain river plants accelerated development of the crimson sapphire. However, since it took a long time to grow crimson sapphires, generally only aged males passed them. Time and diet contributed to this.

One of the first Trekmasters had liked the "pretty bauble" and when he had held the crimson sapphire, it was discovered that the jewel augmented that Trekmaster's mental abilities. It served also as a bridge between that Trekmaster and any Webbine, and a particularly strong bridge evolved between the human who held the stone and the specific Webbine who had grown and passed the stone. I:imbawe wished he had been the one to give the current Trekmaster a stone, and not old, deluded O:chacka. So the strongest empathy now existed between O:chacka and Shepherd. The biggest problem here was confirmed by I:imbawe on his recent visit to the Trekmaster. Shepherd did not wear his crimson sapphire. He displayed it. So the catalytic and empathic power of the jewel was wasted most of the time. And so was the possible Webbine influence over the Trekmaster.

The use of the stones was more or less successful. Another experiment had yet to be proved out, and was already discontinued—though one instance of success was shown in the Trekmaster's first son.

In order to accomplish their goals, they had decided to circumvent and accelerate the natural selection process. The Webbine goal of developing a human more like Webbines than humans was based on biology. Genetic fitness. And genetic fitness presupposed increased personal survival ability which in turn dictated stronger reproduction traits (and more reproduction) which in turn passed on the increased survival and reproduction genetic codes to descendants, direct and indirect, all expanding the gene pool.

So the Webbines had attempted to tamper with the genetic traits of one of the early Shepherds. But the genetic sequences of the four human building blocks turned out to be too difficult for the Webbine-induced virus to manipulate. So the project was discontinued. (Even though I:imbawe had discovered one outcome of the tampering: the Trekmaster's son had webbing between his toes and was temperamentally more like the Webbines than any of his ancestors.)

Nonetheless the attempt to circumvent the natural selection process was deemed a failure. I:imbawe admitted the concept a good one: develop a superior version of a human

who was more like Webbines philosophically than like other
humans. By being stronger and smarter, these humans would
be able to dominate non-Bear Ridge humans, after a sufficient period of expansion, and at the same time be web-
brothers to the Webbines. And if not controllable, at least
they would have common attitudes and goals. It was the
Webbines' only hope of survival.

For a while it appeared that the process was working on
Shepherd, the current Trekmaster. He was larger than most
humans, and he'd gone through a period of sexual hyperac-
tivity specifically to increase the number of sons, which
functioned to increase the number of the strong Trekmaster-
sired breed of humans.

But something worked and something did not work. Perhaps it worked on Thomas Jefferson Shepherd for a while
only because his wife was no longer able to mother his
children. Shepherd might have worn his crimson sapphire
for a while and been subject to O:chacka's subtle urgings.
One the other web, the Trekmaster did seem to overcome
the influence of the crimson sapphire and terminated his
siring of many more sons—"kinglets" he called them. I:imbawe
did not understand human humor nor did he think he ever
would.

One prime item I:imbawe had noticed: that there *was* a
difference between Bear Ridge humans and the off-world
woman he'd observed at Shepherd's palace. But in his central thinking section, he knew full well that the difference
was probably more due to humanity adapting to the Bear
Ridge ecosystem than any Webbine machinations. Also, he
admitted, the Shepherd family might well have a strong
survival trait already built into its genetic code. Had not
several of them completed the Trek? No one family had so
dominated the Trek in the past. Now this Trekmaster had
conquered not only the obstacles on the Trek, but *all* the
other humans in the world.

There was a mathematical relationship there, one for
figuring, a glimmering . . .

N:tasse was finally tiring of being a bore and making a
nuisance of himself.

The formulae I:imbawe was running through told him
that race can exceed the commands of its own genetics.
Where did that thought come from? He had stolen it from
the Trekmaster when he snooped in his aura-mind at the
palace. And the Trekmaster had—stolen?—no, not the

term, "read," that was it, "read" that fact and retained it in upper memory. Strange.

Again I:imbawe regretted not being the stone-mate of this Trekmaster.

I:imbawe's attention was wrenched back to the glade.

O:chacka was saying, /. . . A:alpha differs from other projectors in that he admits a small possibility that the danger can be harnessed. . ./

N:tasse managed to make his aura sneer. /A theoretical possibility, but child's dreams, nonetheless; therefore, not germane to our discussion./

O:chacka glowed anger. /Perhaps it is time for young blood among the elders./

Ah, thought I:imbawe. That's more like the O:chacka of our youth.

/O:chacka,/ said N:tasse, /the schism between us is growing. I say the old ways are better left untampered. Your voice has, lately, ignored this logic./

O:chacka's aura bristled, rippling through a spectrum of colors. /Your ways have already deprived us of the brilliant O:omega. Not only do we seldom reproduce, but even less often do we produce one such as O:omega./

I:imbawe felt A:alpha's aura from the pond shrink in jealousy.

N:tasse retorted immediately. /No one in your family has ever been wrong./

/Hold!/ interceded V:hoy. /Perhaps you both should meld auras to lessen this enmity./

K:lent further interrupted. /Disregard all of this. Is it not said that dissent has an argumentive value of its own? If we were all of one mind, would we need be here discussing?/

/Perhaps I can summarize?/ came the soothing aura-voice of X:tol. /N:tasse wishes to take strong measures against the humans. O:chacka wishes to study further but is swayed by his student, A:alpha, who wishes more active involvement. Others back one faction or the other. And I:imbawe does not speak./

I:imbawe sighed visibly. He felt too old. This meeting merely reinforced his opinion that his people were stagnated. The possible human-changed environment with which they were faced became a thing to be desired, then, because of one basic factor: it was different. He realized then, that whatever happened, the humans were necessary, the force, the catalyst that would change the Webbines. He knew now that the humans were more dynamic and thus had initiated the sought change in the Webbines while these oldsters were talking of changing humans.

He could only hope it was not the death of his race. Something O:omega once said (before his expulsion) had made I:imbawe think that their people should have concentrated on their own genetic codes to develop manipulative digits, perhaps like human fingers, that would change the course of their future history. The Webbines should have begun investigating changing themselves eons ago.

He could not say what he thought. He'd have to be diplomatic. /This current Trekmaster whom I visited possesses a drive, a vision, one that matches our people's in scope, though not in final result. He is the key, I acknowledge. His crisis is upon him and his machinations in the near future will be the determining factors for both his people and, complimentarily, ours./ He paused and decided to strengthen what he'd said. /I say this: our destinies, his people and ours, rest upon this Trekmaster./

/Blasphemy!/broadcast N:tasse.

A change is needed, thought I:imbawe. Suddenly, he decided. /I hearby relinquish my position among the elders and formally deed it to A:alpha./

A stunned silence followed. Auras rippled and clashed and melded. A:alpha was not even matured, much less an elder.

I:imbawe knew he would retain his power, his voice, but at least would no longer have to deal with these old females. He'd really put A:alpha right in the incipient volcano. Well, that's what youngsters are for. /A:alpha,/he broadcast, /I recommend you expand your diet to include more river greens and coral. You must accelerate growth of your crimson sapphire. Should circumstances dictate you—and your talents—to become stone-mate to a Trekmaster earlier than estimated, you should be prepared./

I:imbawe saw the calculating look of O:chacka, the shocked aura just now regaining its shape and color. O:chacka was beginning to color agreement.

Perhaps a new faction had come into being here today. Perhaps a new way of thinking.

I:imbawe hoped it wasn't too late.

1: TJ

Slopping bloody drippings across the tablecloth, TJ placed a large slab of almost raw meat on Sharon's plate.

She swallowed and said, "Could I have a portion that's been cooked, please?"

"He always does that," Felicia said. "Don't let him get to you, my dear. He eats like that; we don't have to."

"I like it so rare that I want the beefaloe to remember my name when he wakes up." TJ looked at Gwen who pointed to the well-done end of the roast.

They were in the family's small, informal dining room, Mike passed Sharon a bowl of river-grown vegetables.

"Just like a bunch of Webbines—no meat," TJ said. "After I came back from the Trek, it took me a while to start eating meat again. And this isn't a bad cut, it it?" He sliced his own and tried it. "Fresh from the ranch at Dawn's Edge. I swear the beefaloe and sheepaloe meat tastes better since Mick took over control." He knew Sharon had something she wanted to discuss, but she wasn't talking yet. She'd perked up when he'd mentioned the Webbines. Could that be it? He wondered what the Webbines would be like if they ate meat. Probably decrease their life span. But might make them more ambitious. They sure as hell needed some kind of boost.

Sharon must have read his mind. "You know, TJ, that is one area we must discuss at length."

"I know."

"And resolve."

"Nothing to resolve," he said, "but. . ."

"For admission to the Federation . . ." she began.

"God, those words will be inscribed on my tombstone I've heard them so many times."

". . . this is a very critical area. Federation criteria must be completely met and the program approved by the Federation totally before membership can be granted." She turned a forkful of river greens in a 360-degree circle, looking at it, shrugged, and put it in her mouth.

TJ was silent.

"What would the Federation like to do with the Webbines?" Gwen asked.

"In short, insure their survivability."

"They don't need help," TJ said, voice tight.

"Father," said Mick, "they show no signs of technological progress."

"You might damn well find out one of these days first-hand what kind of progress they show or don't show." TJ was angry with himself for the outburst.

Mick sat back and glowered at him.

Sharon spoke quickly, obviously to fill the void. "Better decisions could be made after intense study."

"Sounds just like benevolent patronage," he said uncomfortably. The subject was one he wished to avoid for he had not been able to come up with a plan to incorporate the Webbines into his own long-range goals after acceptance to the Fed. Which made him uncomfortable since he'd about decided that there was nothing he could do for them except protect them from outside influences. Did he really want to keep them on their side of the ridges and never the twain shall meet? He freely admitted their society was stagnant and needed an occasional boost to get them out of their rut. But—the big "but"—who was he, or any other human for that matter, to determine this? Especially a bunch of jerks from Fedcentral who'd never seen an intelligent non-human before. He didn't want to discuss this with Sharon or with anybody because he had no answer. He felt he had regained his composure and smiled. "Why can't we accord the Webbines the courtesy of selecting their own destiny?"

"Well, of course," Sharon managed through a mouthful of sheepaloe cheese.

Mick nodded approvingly and TJ admitted he might have accidentally made a point with his son.

Sharon sipped some wine. "I still don't believe chocolate wine. More of a liqueur . . ."

"Royal distributors sell more wines than liqueurs," Mike said with another smile. "Merchandising."

She nodded. "But back to the Webbines. The problem must be resolved. TJ, how do you reconcile your entry into the Federation with the Webbine problem?"

"I don't have to." He thought he was on safe ground.

"If Bear Ridge gets into the Federation, you are going to leap forward technologically. That will change the face of this planet, now and later. Perhaps not physically, but the character of humanity and atmosphere and all sorts of things will change. The change will eventually affect the Webbines."

"Sharon, I am not King of the Webbines. I have no control, no say in their affairs, no influence."

"Your entry into the Federation and the Webbines maintaining their status quo appear to me contradictory." She sounded angry with his intransigence.

He said carefully, "They can work out their own problems. If we change, if the planet changes, the Webbines are smart enough to adapt to the changed environment. I don't want to sound casual about their fate, but on the other web . . . hand . . . I do not wish to place any more odds against our gaining Fed membership. Can you not see my position, Sharon? My personal druthers are to leave 'em alone and let them go their own way, just like I'd expect from them if they were in my place. I don't want to sacrifice them for Bear Ridge to become a member of the Federation. But I do want Bear Ridge to belong to the Fed. I'm not exactly in a quandary, but I ain't out of the woods either." He dabbed at his chin with a napkin.

"How many Webbines are there?" Sharon asked.

Not enough, he thought. "Nobody knows; not many. A few thousand at least. Their reproduction is slow, not anything like the human rate."

Sharon looked as if she were going to pounce. "So. There you are. They don't have a large gene pool to continue the species. Federation policy is to preserve any form of life which may be endangered. And by any criteria, the Webbines will be grossly affected."

I knew it, he thought. Get a scientist near something like the Webbines and they can't leave well enough alone. No matter what they say now, they will swarm all over the Webbines. No matter how many fancy terms Sharon uses or her own personal opinion, some clowns from the Fed will come here and mess up the Webbines worse than any gradual change our technological evolution will make. Unless, he amended, the Webbines have a powerful friend on the Council. "Don't judge their gene pool by what you see on the surface," TJ said. "I'm no biologist. I just know they need lots of room. They don't need to be penned up like a herd of prize sheepaloe for public inspection. I think they can survive without our interference."

"Land which you can or can't provide, TJ. Where is their agriculture? Do they trade? What?"

"So what? They have enough land now."

"Statistical data shows . . ."

"The hell with . . ." he started.

"Father . . ." Mick said warningly.

"TJ . . ." Gwen cautioned.

He grinned and looked at Felicia. "Mother, you used to be first in correcting me."

"You used to need correcting a lot more than you do now." she said.

He winked at her, knowing her for an ally in this discussion. She knew his problem. Was he ready to sacrifice the Webbines for his own ambitions? And that's what Fed membership would mean. But wasn't change already in the wind? Irrevocable change?

He saw that they had made Sharon feel like an outsider. Well, that's what she was, wasn't she? To change the subject, he asked, "Sharon, I trust they have prepared you for the royal ball tomorrow night?" He used the ubiquitous "they" so that he wouldn't have to ask Mick or somebody to be her escort—on second thought—"Mick?"

Mick's eyes met his. "Yes?"

TJ remembered the strange girl reports had shown Mick with in the Shepherd Park during Sing's oration or whatever the hell the kid called his harangues. "Would you escort Sharon to the ball tomorrow night?"

Sharon scowled momentarily and her eyes locked with Mick's for an instant. Had Mick already asked Sharon? Had Mick made other plans? Well, from the way he had said it, Mick didn't have much choice without a major and embarrassing confrontation.

"Yes, sir," Mick said simply and TJ couldn't read anything into his words or expression.

"Thomas," his mother said, "you are not worried about the planned riot tomorrow night?"

"What planned riot?" Sharon asked.

"Demonstration," Mick corrected stiffly.

Ah, so that's where Mick had planned to be.

"Nah, mum," TJ said. "I'm going to the ball and let others handle policing and law enforcement."

"You're not going to disrupt the demonstration by force," Mick demanded.

He looked at his son for a moment without speaking and thought he ought to just have Kellen Sing arrested and hanged. That would remove the problem.

"What riot, what demonstration?" Sharon asked again.

TJ tore his gaze from Mick's. To Sharon, he said, "The young man, Kellen Sing, has a quote nonviolent demonstration end quote planned for tomorrow evening. It is supposed to occur simultaneous with the royal ball. Some kind of symbology involved that I don't care to take the time to understand."

"Will there be trouble?" Sharon asked.

"No," TJ said and grinned as evilly as he could. Not good politics, but he had to let go once in a while. The unexpressed threat lay thick in the room. Maybe Mick would take a message to Kellen to call off the "demonstration."

32: REBECCA

"Kellen, don't do this!" Rebecca said again. She wished it would storm and rain. But the fast approaching dusk showed no hint of that occurrence.

"The sun sets on Bear Ridge," Kellen intoned to the crowd. "Let us light the way."

"Kellen," her voice was more urgent. What Kellen intended had a high element of danger in it. All about them torches and candles sprang to life. Kellen had timed the march to begin at dusk and arrive at the palace during the height of the royal ball.

"We light our own way," Kellen chanted. "We seek Truth. Nor do we allow others to force their lights on us."

Young people nearby chorused, "Light the way, light the way." And the crowd farther away took up the chant.

Kellen began forcing his way to the front of the crowd where he would lead the march on the palace. He tentatively caressed his thumb drums in cadence with the "Light the way" chant.

Rebecca caught his arm. "Remember Mike's warning," she hissed in his ear. "He's your friend, Kellen; you're doing him a disservice."

He paused and removed her hand from his arm. "Don't you think the King has spies and runners throughout this crowd to keep him advised of what we're doing? There are too many innocent people here for him to risk any action. Do not worry, Rebecca." He thumbed his drums with renewed vigor, building tempo.

Rebecca stood her ground as the crowd followed Kellen and flowed around her. She shook her head in disgust. She guessed there were over a thousand people following Kellen on this fool's mission. Not all were fellow students either. Some local townfolk had joined has effort. Plus plenty of padres, she noted. She wished for the good old days when the Church was apolitical—maybe it still was outside Crimson Sapphire. But these padres had a strong determination about them. They were some of Kellen's hard-core followers. Perhaps his most dependable followers besides the environmentalists

People stopped near her, the front of the procession not getting underway fast enough. Rebecca feared that this march would provoke some response from the King. And, she admitted, she wouldn't blame the King either. She didn't understand Kellen repaying the King's kindness with this ultimate slap in the face. Nor did she know if she approved of Kellen's activities. She had a basic dislike for radicals of any persuasion. But she felt helpless, unable to sway him; somehow, her influence over him had waned significantly. He used to listen to her advice. He used to be mild mannered, thoughtful, introspective.

But now? He was different in some way she couldn't identify. He now possessed an inner drive, a compulsion. She saw no good coming from his actions. If nothing else, she was a realist. All things considered, the King had done a decent job while on the throne. While he did have some shortcomings, she doubted anyone else could have accomplished what he had in the time he had. She was a firm believer in the old adage, "If it ain't broke, don't fix it." There were more important things than removing Thomas Jefferson Shepherd from power.

Yet she was still loyal to her brother. His words seemed on fire at times—but when she examined them for content, she found little. She knew there was a lot she must reconcile to herself before she could become an ardent Kellen Sing follower.

The marchers began moving out again, strings of people joined with a common bond. The rear bunches were passing her now. In a few blocks they would join with Shepherd Boulevard—or was it Avenue? She had to agree with Kellen that there were too many things named Shepherd here in Crimson Sapphire and that made for confusion.

Kellen's drums were no longer audible. Those near her were chanting "Bar Bear Ridge." She sighed and followed the last people. At Shepherd Street—Avenue—she would go left as they went right to follow the thoroughfare straight to the palace. Others began following the march. The curious, she thought. The morbid who hoped to see blood shed.

Suddenly, it occurred to her to wonder if Kellen were not in fact trying to provoke the King into some act of retaliation he could use as an incident. Did Kellen wish to become a martyr? It wasn't like him, no, but. . . ?

Or was Kellen's purpose to gain attention for his cause? A show of strength perhaps, with notice of more to come?

She found she knew her brother less than she thought.

She hurried along and noticed the procession was growing as men and women joined other marchers. As they wound their way through the city, onlookers sometimes cheered, sometimes booed and hissed. But the marchers shouted down these hecklers and Rebecca sensed a nasty mood building. Which led her to another thought: could other, more violent elements have infiltrated the march to use it for their own purposes? She fervently hoped Kellen knew what he was doing.

The march reached the main boulevard and turned right. Rebecca gave in to her inner voice and followed. She halted on a rise and viewed the entire procession. Kellen was certainly upsetting commerce and travel this night. A shower of rotten fruits and vegetables flew from a group of whores on an upper balcony.

No one noticed.

And then apprehension leapt into her throat. The crowd had swelled. Her original estimate of one thousand was no longer good, it was almost double that. As she watched, steely-eyed men slipped from the sidewalks and alleys to mingle with the marchers and take over the rear echelon. Was she the only one to notice? They carried no weapons, certainly, but all seemed the same: all were dressed as civilians, but possessed similar haircuts, an economy of motion, a repeated cadence when walking. Most carried stout walking sticks.

"Oh, my God," Rebecca Sing whispered to herself. Something dreadful was going to happen.

The front of the procession was now approaching the palace, only minutes away. She had to warn Kellen. There was a solid line of torches and candles across the avenue where she guessed the front of the column to be. Even from here, she could tell the palace was more well lit than usual this evening—probably for the ball. An air of gaiety seemed to emanate from the palace. She fancied she could hear the music, but knew she couldn't.

She began running. As her feet slapped the pavement, a strong breeze momentarily whipped in her face stringing her hair out behind her.

She wore a wraparound skirt over short pants this night, and the skirt was cumbersome in which to run. While the shorts were acceptable attire in which to lounge around the countryside or home, she didn't think they were appropriate to wear in the city. Nonetheless, she removed her skirt and threw it over her shoulder, tying it quickly like a cape. She began running again, sandals creaking and complaining about the unaccustomed activity.

She wove her way through the rear of the march, seeing some student protestors glancing fearfully about themselves as if not understanding the position in which they found themselves. Tall, strong men loomed out of the night and became the outlying part of the procession, effectively bottling the original marchers in.

She ran on, stumbled against a rock-hard body.

"Here, ma'am, let me help you."

She stared in horror at his easy confidence while he pulled her gently to her feet. "Ma'am" he'd called her. Students, Kellen's main following, were not like that. And Valdez' group—they were a ragged bunch. Nor was that man a padre.

She feared violence, but could not reconcile violence with the soft-spoken soldier dressed in civilian garb.

She ran faster, apprehension crawling over her scalp. The roadway was clogged with people now, and she had to dodge between and around them. She pushed her way on, breath coming in short, hard gasps—more from worry than exertion at this point.

The avenue narrowed as the gates to the palace rose ahead. She could no longer force her way through the throngs of people. She pleaded, but to no avail. People weren't listening. Those in her way couldn't move any more than she could, just maintain a simple shuffling gait along with the rest of the marchers.

She worked her way to the outer edge of the crowd and found both sides of the avenue enclosed by retaining walls.

She pushed against a man, "Help me, please!" she demanded. "My brother . . ."

Then she realized he was another of *them*.

"Yes, ma'am," he said maddeningly. Then he picked her up and put her on top of the wall. Did he think he was helping her to escape?

Not unmindful of his gaze up at her legs, she turned and fled along the flat top of the wall toward the front of the procession. She held her arms out for balance and seemed to fly along just above the crowd.

She could see well ahead of her and saw the leading edge of the procession flow in between the massive palace gates, gates she'd never seen closed. Near the front, the crowd was moving slower and more people watched her curiously. She wanted to shout at them, but her breathing wouldn't let her.

She still hadn't reached Kellen, and he must have gone inside with the first of the column. She just knew she wouldn't be in time.

She heard Kellen's drums now, echoing the crowd's chant "Light the way."

The wall tapered down to road level at the great palace gates. Marchers were streaming in past the gates. She took the plunge into the crowd, forcing her way through.

Urgency grabbed her. "Kellen!" she shouted involuntarily.

Some in the procession took up her words as a chant. "Kellen! Kellen! Kellen!" replaced "Light the way."

She groaned in frustration. Then she noticed there were no soldiers inside the palace gates. Save for the marchers, the whole great courtyard was deserted. She heard Kellen's drums echoing hollowly against a far wall where people had not filled the empty space yet. The drums and chants bounced off lofty walls. She felt as if she were in a giant prison yard.

She didn't think that the courtyard could hold all the people in the procession. People still streamed in through the gates forcing her and those in front of her forward against their will.

Then she saw it and knew. Not exactly what, but something.

There were no doors open anywhere. Windows facing the courtyard were shuttered and obviously barred from the inside. Again the prison image leapt into her mind.

She couldn't go back, the inexorable movement of the crowd behind her pushed her ahead. People were spreading out, flowing into corners and against walls to escape the pressure from the rear. Soon the courtyard would be jammed with people.

People near her began complaining about the surge of bodies still rolling through the gates like an unstoppable tide.

While she had a chance, she made for a friendly looking wall. She found a small door inset in the wall under a balcony and tried it. No luck. But in front of the door was a decorative stone snarv with a vine covering it. She climbed this figure and found her knees about level with the heads of those below her. She could finally see well. She couldn't locate Kellen.

She watched helplessly while she got control of her breathing. She saw some of Kellen's followers beating upon the massive doors of the throne room. Soon the press of bodies would prevent even this activity.

At the massive gates, she saw the rear of the crowd being forced in. In torch light and star light she watched as hundreds of civilian-dressed soldiers forced those ahead of them relentlessly into the courtyard.

"Kellen!" she shouted, searching for him, knowing he would not hear her.

"Well, I'll be damned," came a voice from above her. Suddenly, a supple, but strong, pair of hands grasped her arms and she felt herself rising into the air. Torch light shed an eerie glow about the courtyard, yet when she landed on her feet on the balcony, she could barely distinguish anything up here in the shadows.

"Hi, Freckles," said a voice she recognized.

"Summer Camp?"

"In person."

"You can let me go now, Mr. Camp."

"Oh. Oops. Call me Summer."

She was able to make him out now. He wore formal clothing which could not conceal the barely restrained strength in his limbs. There was somebody else up here in the shadows with them.

"Summer . . . can't you do something?"

"We *are* doing something."

"But . . ."

"I rescued you, didn't I?"

"But I wasn't . . . oh, never mind. But, please, they, those people down below, they mean nothing by this. Don't let them be harmed." She was afraid her voice sounded pleading.

"Why should we harm them?" he asked.

The crowd had been milling below, but with the addition of more people there was no room left to move about in and so movement was limited to shifting in place.

"They . . . that is, my brother . . ."

"Your brother will not be harmed." His voice took on an edge she wasn't prepared for. What was he doing here? Kellen had jokingly said he was a spy for the King. Also that he was a friend of Mike's and the court jester. She did not know which to believe. "Save by his own actions," Summer amended. "Manny, we got to do something soon."

"Interesting spectacle," said the other shadow.

Manny? Who was Manny?

As if reading her mind, Summer said, "May I introduce General Manuel Vero? Manny, this young lady is Rebecca Sing."

"Good evening, ma'am."

Rebecca was bewildered. This jester, this Summer Camp addressed the military commander by his first name?

A great clang came as the mammoth courtyard gates slammed shut behind the last of the crowd.

"What are you going to do?" she demanded.

"Why, nothing. They came uninvited, so they must accept the little hospitality we have to offer," Summer Camp replied.

She could almost feel Kellen's humiliation. No, she corrected herself. The old Kellen would be humiliated. The new Kellen? She sensed a calming influence from him, amplified by the gentle thumbing of his drums. He was trying to avert disaster.

Occasional screams burst out as people found their torches and candles were lethal weapons in such close confines. Gradually, these were thrown to the ground and stomped out. The courtyard darkened perceptively.

Then she realized something. Other light sources in the courtyard had disappeared. Upper windows had been closed. Torches extinguished. A cloud mass moved over the stars.

The crowd silenced suddenly as their realizations matched hers. It was like a calm before a storm. A waft of music from the royal ball escaped into the night as if to remind the marchers of their insignificance.

Uncertainty swept through the crowd and a rumbling of nervousness began. Kellen's drums increased in loudness to compensate, a soothing rhythm reaching out. If anybody could maintain order, he could. She'd seen him in action too much lately to doubt his ability. But could even he control this crowd?

Panic was only seconds away. She smelled it on the air.

"Summer Camp. General Vero. If you strip these people of their pride, you have lost them forever."

"Some humility won't hurt," Vero observed.

The rumble of the crowd increased, drowning out Kellen's drums. Screams and shouts broke his rhythm. People began shoving and shouting.

"Reckon all your men are free, Manny?"

"Most fell out before entering the gates."

"I agree with Freckles here," said Summer Camp. "We've nothing to gain now, and if some should get hurt, we shall lose."

"It is not an easy business, is it?"

"No, Manny, it's not."

"Decision time," Vero's voice said.

"See, Rebecca," Summer said, "there are some sluice gates in the far wall," His shadow-arm pointed. "Taps water from The Howling Volv. We open the sluice gates occasionally to clean out the courtyard—lots of horses ride through here, you see."

"You wouldn't!"

"Do not fear, the water wouldn't get more than ankle high. But I don't think we'll do that."

"What will you do?"

"See, once upon a time, man brought to this planet sheepaloe for food and clothing. Horses and donkeys for beasts of burden. And, inadvertently, a thing called a skunk. A smelly little animal which was brought for rodent control—and the few remaining in the highlands have redeveloped certain glands which exude an odor which even snarves and volves find unpalatable."

"Skunks?"

"Sure. Cute little furry creatures."

"I'm not from that far out in the sticks, Summer Camp."

"He has a tendency to lecture, given the opportunity," Vero said.

"Thing is, the taint from a panicked skunk will remain for a few days." Summer chuckled.

And Rebecca saw it for what it was. There would be no injuries, no retribution—just a lesson. She laughed. She saw Summer's teeth gleam in the faint light.

"Good," he said. "Manny, we better do it before they panic too much more down there and somebody gets hurt. Doubtless, they'll blame the King."

"Done," said Vero and a light flared briefly.

"I suggest a strategic withdrawal," Summer said. He grasped Rebecca's arm and guided her inside off the balcony.

Vero stepped in behind them and shut the door and placed a bar across the inside. "We'll open the gates in about five minutes. They won't waste any time getting back to the city."

They walked through the room, some kind of office, and into a lighted corridor.

Rebecca became conscious of her bare legs and swept her skirt off her shoulders. As she adjusted it around her waist, she saw Summer Camp watching her. Men staring at her, especially her legs, wasn't a new experience; but with Summer it was a new feeling.

"Camp, you have no class," Vero said.

"Wanna dance, Becky?" Summer asked her.

The royal ball? "I'm not dressed properly. And most people call me Rebecca."

"Come along, you will stun the whole crowd. Keep all the attention off me."

"Well . . ."

"You'll knock their eyes out."

She wondered if she would see Mike. Then it struck her that Summer Camp was a brave man—being seen in the palace of Thomas Jefferson Shepherd with Rebecca Sing, the sister of Kellen Sing. The spirit of adventure reached out and grabbed her. "Let's go dance, jester, or whatever you are."

Later, tired from dancing and full of the King's food, she had time to reflect. No one had paid any attention to them. It was as if they didn't know who Summer Camp was. Like he was just another minor duke or successful merchant. He danced marvelously, his body fluid and completely under control at all times. His balance and grace were unlike any she'd ever encountered. Yes, he was a strange man. Maybe he was a spy.

There were perhaps four hundred people in the ballroom now and, she reflected, just like anywhere else, the main occupation was talking. Groups formed and dissolved like sand bars in a river. Refreshments were located against a wall. A central space was for dancing.

They had just reentered the ballroom from an adjoining room where servants served liquor and a heavier fare of food.

Summer nudged her and pointed. "You asked. There he is."

Mike was in the center of the dance floor, a strange woman dressed in a glittering golden jumpsuit draped all over him.

"Sharon Gold," Summer explained, "from Fedcentral."

"She's the one?"

"Yep. All eyes have been on her all night, Becky."

"Rebecca."

"Sure. But she's gotten the attention. I don't know if she likes it, though. It's as if she was the central exhibit here tonight, the purpose of the occasion."

Rebecca felt a surge of sympathy for the strange woman. She'd heard others talking about the woman this evening.

"Uh oh," Summer said, and drew her into a shadow against a wall and slightly behind a pillar.

"What?" she asked.

"Company, Freckles."

Then Thomas Jefferson Shepherd was standing in front of her, looming over them both. His uniform glistered, red sash contrasting the formal white. His eyes were curious, but she didn't think they were as piercing as Summer's. She thought of Mike. How unlike father and son were.

His voice seemed rough to her—but that might have been only because of his reputation. "Well, Summer. Is this the nice girl we were speaking of the other day?"

Summer colored slightly. "No, er, yes. I mean, she is a nice girl, but . . ."

The King grinned and held out his hand. "While Summer is stumbling over his tongue, perhaps we should introduce ourselves?"

He was charming, she decided.

Summer said, "Boss, this is Becky Sing."

"Rebecca," she corrected before she remembered herself.

His eyebrows raised. "Any relation to. . . ?"

"Sister," Summer said.

"Well, young lady, I will say one thing," the King spoke with a hidden smile. "You are a lot more pleasing to look at than your brother."

She found herself holding his hand and couldn't remember if she'd bent and kissed it or simply shook hands. The King was attractive—for somebody as tall and . . . craggy as he was. "Thank you, Sire . . . I think," she said. He was taller than Mike and had sharper features. His eyes were practiced and sure. Where Mike was soft, the King was hard. She noted the thickening around his middle and thought it made him look more solid.

"You'll do," he said, and released her hand. "Would you take a message from me to your brother?"

Suddenly, his eyes no longer smiled. Beside her, Summer stiffened.

"I . . . uh . . . of course, Your Majesty."

"Tell him if he lays off for a while, I will let him in on an official state secret."

She didn't understand.

"A simple trade," the King said. "My mother informs me that juice of the tomato removes the taint of the skunk quickly and effectively."

"Oh." She thought for a moment. "Perhaps I will make your offer—in a day or two."

The King smiled, winked, and wandered away into the crowd. Summer put his arm through hers and led her out from behind the pillar.

"Are you ashamed of me, Summer Camp?"

"What? Oh, certainly not, Becky. It's . . . it's . . . hell. I just don't advertise my attachment to the King."

"Oh." But she still didn't understand. "You *are* a spy."

"No. Er, I . . ."

"Summer," came Mike's voice from behind. They turned to meet him.

Mike said, "I just wondered how it went tonight . . . Rebecca!"

"Good evening, Mike." She could see his shock.

"Guess I don't have to make introductions," Summer observed.

"Not at all." Mike had her hand and was looking into her eyes. "Kellen didn't listen to me, did he?"

"No. But he paid," Rebecca said and smiled.

"Ah, the devious mind of Summer Camp," Mike said.

"It all went according to plan, Mike. I was informed a little while ago that the courtyard is now clear and airing out."

"Well, hello! Anybody home?" came a strange voice. The woman in the glittering jumpsuit was standing next to Mike.

Mike dropped her hand and turned toward the woman. "Sharon." It was a statement. "May I present Rebecca Sing? Rebecca, this is Ambassador Sharon Gold of the Federation."

Rebecca was surprised. Sharon Gold was about her own age.

The Ambassador stuck out her hand and said, "Pretty stuffy introduction, Mike. Rebecca? I'm Sharon. I've met Kellen. Your brother?"

"Yes."

"I can see the resemblance. A truly unique musician." Sharon Gold looked at Summer. "You, I know barely. You threw me out of a bedroom once."

Summer colored again. He stammered, "What she says is misleading, Becky. It wasn't my bedroom."

"Right," said Sharon.

"Oops. I mean, it was the King's bedroom."

Sharon was smiling at Summer's discomfort, yet there was a bit of competition between them.

"When the King was ill," Summer finished lamely.

"Ah," Rebecca said, "you-all aren't just trying to tease a country girl."

"No," said Summer pointedly.

Rebecca thought then that there were undercurrents here she didn't understand.

Mike seemed to be enjoying himself. "Actually, the last time these two spoke formally, Summer was shouting and screaming at Sharon."

Summer said, "Make that 'speaking in an authoritative manner.' Trying to obtain medical assistance."

Mike grinned mischievously. "Summer? May I dance with Rebecca? Surely you and Sharon can talk while we're gone." Before Summer could answer, Mike drew Rebecca off.

As they danced, Rebecca occasionally glimpsed Summer and Sharon standing stiffly together, probably not speaking.

"I didn't know you would be here," Mike said tentatively.

"Me, either," she responded and told him an annotated version of the events.

"Thank God Summer heard you."

"Oh, I don't know. It would have been uncomfortable for a few days, but I would have gotten over it."

"You would have had a lot of company."

She smiled. "It is nice to be here and not soaking in a cold river."

Mike did not move as smoothly as Summer, yet he seemed more polished. His conversation was practiced, but occasionally naive and he showed a strange vulnerability for being the Prince of the Realm. He seemed somehow conscious of himself, very different from the supremely confident Summer Camp.

After the dance, Mike said, "Well, got to get back to work now." If she read him right, without saying so, he'd told her that he would rather be with her than Sharon, and that he might even have been at the march with her if he hadn't had royal obligations. Did that mean he was interested in her? For that matter, was Summer interested in her? Summer had rescued her from a smelly fate if nothing else. And he hadn't had any reason to bring her to this royal ball—but he had.

A long way from Lonestar, she thought.

She had a lot to think about.

33: TJ

When Summer came into his office, his anger had been building for hours. TJ told his secretary, "Close the door on your way out and no interruptions."

As the secretary closed the door, Summer slumped onto a chair and tugged uncomfortably on his jester's collar.

"What's the reaction?" TJ was afraid his impatience was showing.

"Not all good," Summer said. "It's like we stirred up a stingbee's nest. Oh, the people got a good laugh at Sing's expense—but there is a lot of skunk taint in the city today—

everywhere. Homes, offices, businesses. Mass this morning hit an all-time low in attendance. We might have given them a rallying point."

"That's what Kellen Sing has been looking for," TJ said thoughtfully. "But we allowed that factor in our calculated gamble last night." He grinned. "I thought it was just plain fun. Wish I could have seen 'em retreating down Shepherd Boulevard."

"Avenue, isn't it?"

"Whatever. But the smart ones will know. We could have snuffed the entire movement like a weak candle last night. Hope they got the message. Why are young people so contrary?"

"You were the same at that age, TJ. You simply had different outlets for your frustrations. You ended up with an entire planet to rule because of your rebelling."

"Ah. Youth. I remember it fondly. I recall you weren't exactly a Sunday School teacher yourself."

"My point is that perhaps we humiliated 'em too much last night."

"I don't care, Summer. I'm losing my patience. And I'm dead serious. I'm about done with Sing and his crew. Fun is over. They're beginning to bother me real serious."

"Then you ain't gonna like what I have to tell you next."

TJ waited without speaking.

"Early this morning. A clandestine meeting. That group of ex-attorneys we've been watching. They call themselves Attorneys for Civil Liberties United."

"Aff clue?"

"AfCLU. Right. With Kellen Sing."

"They deserve each other. The smell of the skunk probably did not mask the smell of the lawyer." He knew, even though he had outlawed the practice of law, that he could exaggerate like that only with a few people. Kings were supposed to be diplomatic. "At any rate, somebody's getting serious. Bankrolling, you reckon?"

"That's the only answer, TJ. Plus they're looking for allies. I see Kellen becoming a focal point. Add to the dissidents he's generating lately the lawyers, the unconverted nobility, and some unhappy padres—you are getting a formidable opposition."

"You left out the ecologists or environmentalists or whatever they call themselves today."

"Yeah. It occurs to me that these various groups have

something in common: pit Kellen Sing against you, pick up the pieces afterward."

TJ sat back and thought. It all added up. Before, his enemies were scattered and disorganized. But with the press for Fed entry and the sudden appearance of Kellen Sing and his movement, things seemed to have polarized and the issures were no longer cloudy. Well, it had to happen sometime. "I didn't think Fed entry would tear the planet apart," he said slowly.

"It hasn't. You have tunnel vision. You see only the focus of everything here in Crimson Sapphire. People elsewhere might not have the same opinions."

"Can't they see what I'm trying to do?" TJ demanded.

Summer held up his palms. "Don't take it out on me, TJ. I'm on your side."

"Yeah, I know. Sorry. I'm thinking about squashing 'em flat." I'm not keeping this a monarchy for nothing, he thought.

"Heavy-handedness," Summer said, "and brute force will only alienate. Which might be worthy of comment by Sharon Gold."

"Democracy is not a criteria for admission to the Federation."

"No, but they look closely at repressive regimes." Summer waved his hat. "I know. I know. How does that explain Tirano and Two Tongues? Don't ask me. Politics."

"Point taken. I think we could get away with the tough tactics, but it would be wise not to test those political waters." But he admitted to himself that Kellen Sing was getting out of hand. They hadn't expected the numbers that had turned out last night to follow Sing. He had to do something.

But how about Mick? Any action against Sing, and Mick would hold it against me, he thought. Mick was at some kind of turning point, that he sensed. He wouldn't handle Mick delicately, he decided, but diplomatically. Treat him as an equal. Respect his wishes—no matter how distasteful they were. On the other hand, he thought, I don't want to turn this kingdom, this planet, over to a goddamn wimp.

"We have to handle it right, Summer; this might be the eye-opener Mick needs."

"If you can do all that without offending Mike and keep all those others off your back, you are a better juggler than I will ever be."

"I'm working on it."

"If you salvage Michale," Summer said pointedly, "you ought to be the court magician, not the King."

"Harassment," he decided.

"Cut off Sing's schooling?" Summer asked.

"No. That would show that I go back on my word. Not a chance. Besides, as long as he attends classes, he can't be out recruiting dissidents and preaching against me. And we can watch him better at the university."

"There will be confrontations." Summer warned.

"Yeah. Speaking of consorting with the enemy. About your choice of women—though I must admit she is good looking . . ."

"Things weren't the way they appeared," Summer said sharply.

"A bit protective today, aren't you?"

Summer scowled.

TJ probed some more. "A bit of competition between you and Mick there."

Summer's face clouded. "I am not pursuing her."

"She *is* charming. Can't blame you if you are."

He knew now that Rebecca Sing was the mysterious girl Mick had been seen with at Shepherd Park. He chose to regard these developments as auspicious in his son's life. Mick seemed somewhat jealous that Summer had brought Rebecca to the ball last night. This kind of thing would strengthen his character, make him more a man of reason and decision.

Conversely, the prospect of conflict between Mick and Summer saddened him. And that he could not reconcile.

34: KELLEN

As he walked into the cloakroom that Professor Innsbruk called an office, Kellen hoped that the odor of the skunk was finally off him. He knew that he would still smell it for days, whether or not it remained physically.

Innsbruk looked up and grimaced. His aura warned Kellen to be alert.

"Kellen, I called you in for it seems your work has been substandard lately."

"Has it, now?" There was a falseness about Innsbruk's aura. It took Kellen a few moments to figure out what was happening.

"It has been decided," Innsbruk said using the safe, academic passive voice, "that to make up for falling behind, you should conduct several of the seminars yourself. Because you have it in you to be a fine student and perhaps later an instructor, you should enjoy these assignments. They will require much research and preparation on your part, but . . ."

"On what subjects, Professor?"

"Various. It has been suggested that you could maybe start with man's relationship to the land of Bear Ridge. The evolution of humanity hereon. Benefits of engineering and scientific breakthrough. That sort of thing."

Kellen fine-tuned his aura-control and concentrated on Innsbruk. "Is this your idea, or . . . ?"

Innsbruk colored embarrassingly, and stared at a map on the wall. He cleared his throat. "I, er, don't disagree, Kellen, with what you say or do . . ." He brightened. "Don't fret over this, Kellen. I shall assist you with your preparations."

"Thanks, thanks a lot."

Innsbruk beamed. "I knew you'd understand."

Franco Valdez had become Kellen's de facto administrative aide. Kellen thought of him more as a handy tool. Franco did what he was told, and did it quickly. He managed the necessary day-to-day coordination of Kellen's movement. Kellen knew as long as he controlled Valdez, he could trust him implicitly. Every so often, he reinforced Valdez' opinion of him with aura control techniques. Of course, it wasn't really necessary—Franco was a natural follower. He'd be off chasing some other cause if Kellen hadn't intercepted him.

"I was engaged in arranging your turn at the park for a speech this weekend," Valdez was saying, "with the park manager. I told him it would be a large rally and to give us plenty of time at the speaking area. Usually he's real cooperative since he gets a rake-off from concessionaires. But everything has changed. We have to get a permit now. So I went to the city admin center to get this permit and they ask me how many people will attend. I say I don't know, maybe two or three thousand. And you know what they told me?"

"I can guess."

"For any gathering over fifty people, the permit costs a gold piece for every one hundred people."

"Expensive." He grinned. "We're getting to them, Franco."

"Sure. But where are we going to get the money? They want it in advance."

Kellen said thoughtfully, "And if we hold a demonstration without a permit they will take strong measures."

"Exactly." Valdez looked like Kellen had taken the weight of responsibility off his shoulders.

"Well, we aren't ready for open defiance—yet. Remembering the skunk trick, they might just have something similar left in their arsenal. I would like you to run over to those lawyers . . ."

"AfCLU," Franco smiled. "I'll see if they want to live up to their words. But it's still a lot of money."

"Yeah, Franco, but it works to our advantage. If the disgruntled attorneys give us that much money without complaining too much, it bonds them to us."

"Kellen," Valdez reported sadly. "We've been tricked. I got the money, no sweat. The people at the admin center took it for the permit and checked some books. Then they said there would be a forty percent windfall tax on the money since it was something called 'unearned income' and they had the money already and I couldn't get it back."

Kellen groaned to himself. Why must I deal with fools?

"Then I started complaining and they started charging me fees for organizations of more than ten people and registering our organization. So finally, I could afford a permit for only five hundred people, not the two or three thousand."

"A benefit, though, Franco. Think about it. We are now registered nice and legal. Perhaps it was worth it."

"Good thinking, Kellen. But I didn't tell you the bad news. There is a monthly fee to maintain that status."

"Exorbitant?"

"Yes."

Kellen thought furiously. "This is what we'll do. We will have the five hundred people. But the park is free. People can picnic. Others can be vendors. Someone could hold a tournament—say one where the contestants would sit and be quiet for the longest time. Trite, but you get the point."

"Some of *our* padres could conduct open and silent prayer sessions, they wouldn't dare mess with that."

"Good, Franco." Kellen wondered if what he'd learned from O:omega included some foresight. He shivered. His mind's eye saw violence and blood.

Kellen had long since moved into a student dormitory at the university. On the final day of the week, several students made allegations of theft. So all students were forced to remain on campus and were personally searched. This took hours. Then doctors checked for signs of the pox—some students had ostensibly come down with the disease. Kellen began to understand.

That night, there were four fire drills in the student housing. No one slept much at all.

The next morning, Kellen dragged himself to the park early to see Franco and insure the preparations were going smoothly.

When Franco saw him, he ran to him shouting and pointing. Kellen did not need Franco's report to know things weren't going according to plan.

A traveling circus had set up in the middle of the park. In the other large area of the park, a group of genuine vaqueros were holding an impromptu rodeo.

Valdez mopped his brow. His aura showed discouragement. "The park manager told me the public notices were up in plenty of time. So we missed the deadline and forfeited our fees."

And this is only the first of it, Kellen thought. Well, he'd known it wouldn't be easy. Anger began building and he wished he could confer with O:omega.

Valdez interrupted. "And the lodgings where me and the other Ecofriends stay?"

"Yes?"

"Public health officials closed them this morning."

"It mounts, right with my anger," Kellen said.

"What will we do, Kellen?" Valdez was like a household pet, waiting for the answer, not able to reason deeply himself.

"A little escalation, Thomas Jefferson Shepherd? Then you shall have it."

"What, Kellen?"

"Nothing, Franco. We shall persevere."

35: REBECCA

How would she get through the palace security and staff?

She couldn't just walk in and demand to see Summer Camp. Or could she?

She took a deep breath and walked through the palace gates. The sentries looked her over closely, but did not interfere.

At the main entrance to the palace itself, the very same great doors to the throne room that had been barred shut a few days ago trapping Kellen and his followers were open.

A sentry moved to stop her. "May I be of service?" he asked with the frank, appraising eyes she was used to.

"I would very much like to talk to . . . Mr. Camp."

The sentry stiffened. "Are you expected?" he asked more formally.

"No, but I think he'll see me." Why wasn't she going to Mike instead? Certainly Mike had more influence than Summer Camp. But she knew the answer.

The sentry said, "Follow me, please," and led her to another set of doors to an administrative reception area and pointed to a receptionist and turned and left without another word.

The clerk was disinterested. "Whom do you wish to see, again?" he asked.

"Mr. Camp."

"Purpose of your visit?"

"Personal." She wouldn't say more.

He raised an eyelid at her. "I don't know a Camp."

"Well, I do," she said, anger beginning to build. "And he works here."

"What section?"

"For the King."

"Lady, we all work for the King." He turned to a woman at an adjacent counter. "You know a Camp?"

The woman shook her head.

226

Her frustration grew and she stamped her foot and turned angrily.

"Ah, Miss Sing," a familiar voice spoke. "Applying for a position on the staff?"

She found the author of the voice. General Vero stood there dressed in a uniform, plain in comparison with the one he had worn the night of the ball. She thought him quite handsome and dashing for an older man. "No, I have come to see Mr. Camp and I don't seem to be getting anywhere."

A smile glinted at the corner of his eye and she blushed, remembering the night of the ball. Vero was a man who missed nothing.

"Well," he said, "I'm headed that way, come along with me. You must forgive the slowness of bureaucracy." As they walked, he continued, "The King, in his infinite wisdom, has chosen a system which seems to choke us at times. But other times it acts as an effective filter."

Finally they arrived at the guarded suite of offices which obviously belonged to the King. She had a fleeting thought of being interrogated by the King and his piercing eyes about her brother's activities. Apprehension gripped her. Somehow, she had gotten the idea that this palace didn't operate in that fashion.

They went through an outer busy office and into an inner one with its own sentries. No one stopped her with Vero. They merely snapped to attention for him.

Only one man was in this inner office, but several doors opened off this room. Vero went to what she guessed was the King's secretary. "Bossman and his flunky inside?"

"Yes, sir, you can go on in."

Rebecca was horrified when Vero smiled and stuck his head through the King's office door and said loudly, "Hey Camp, you got a personal visitor out here." Vero seemed to derive a pleasure from baiting Summer—but the other night they had been equals. She didn't think she'd ever understand the organization here. "Hurry up, Camp," Vero said, "she's gonna turn into a pumpkin."

Summer must be truly important, she decided, to be in with the King. Did he have a desk in there or was he just reporting or whatever it is they do?

Then he stepped through the door and she had to laugh. She knew it was him by his step, height, carriage, and smile. His face was covered with flour-white makeup, his eyelids painted thickly with maroon eye shadow. Green shadow was layered beneath his eyes. His clothing consisted of a single outfit, tailored to look bulky, but which in fact flowed around him. It was covered with black and white blocks with an overlay of red stripes. It was so ridiculous, so out of character from what she knew of him that she laughed again.

His red painted mouth drooped initially then went up in a smile. "Freckles!"

Then she saw it. He had freckles painted all over his face.

"You came to see me?" he asked. When she nodded, he said enigmatically, "Not Mike?"

"Correct."

He led her into what appeared to be a VIP waiting room. "Coffee, juice, tea? Wine?" He indicated a table full of refreshments.

"Tea sounds fine."

"Me, too." He poured two steaming cups and led her to a pair of chairs on either side of a low table.

As they sat, he removed his tassled hat. They were silent, as if in a contest. While she gathered her thoughts, she remarked to herself that it was strange, but pleasing, that he was a man who had no urge or need to break a silence.

"Summer . . . this is difficult for me. I've come to ask your aid."

"Kellen?"

"Yes. He means well. And there is no criminal bone in his body. I think, though, the . . . ah, pressure which the Ki . . . rather which is being applied to him, is beginning to show."

"The 'pressure' is not only being applied to him," Summer said, "but to others. His accomplices."

Summer's use of the word "accomplices" startled her and gave her the first inkling that perhaps she should have gone to Mike instead. "I care not for the welfare of his friends or associates," she said, making her point. "I came to ask you to intercede with the King on Kellen's behalf."

"You want me to speak his case with the King?"

"Yes."

"Why me? Why not Mike?"

"I thought about it. Perhaps it is that you seemed more attuned with the circle of power here. Perhaps it is that Mike and Kellen . . . well, they seem so alike in thinking and temperament and ideas." She didn't want to say out loud, "If Mike could do something, he already would have."

Summer's eyes showed understanding. "What can I do?"

"Ask the King to be lenient. Kellen is just a boy."

"As old as Mike who could be King in the space of time it takes a bolt to fly or a sword to strike."

"Granted, Summer," she said forcefully. "But Kellen is my brother."

"Ah," he grinned to try to defuse the situation. "A motherly attitude. I see it now."

She refused to be sidetracked. "I raised Kellen some and am beginning to see what a terrible job I did."

"You can't be all that much older . . ."

"You are dodging the question, Mr. Camp."

"Dampen that fire, Freckles. I'd like to help, but my hands are tied."

"Please try," she said, wondering at herself for losing her temper. She knew her voice was louder than usual.

He looked angry. "Becky, you know damn well that I am one of the architects of the pressure on Kellen. Hell, the other night you saw my role . . ."

"You don't have to yell at me, *Mister* Camp."

"*Me* shouting? Look, you, my first duty is to the King. Then the realm, then the planet. Kellen Sing ain't on my list."

She stood suddenly, right knee banging the edge of the table and slopping tea upon it. "I should have known."

He rose with her. "Let me suggest that you talk to Kellen instead of me. Ask *him* to drop this insane cause of his. Or campaign or whatever the hell he calls it. They broach treason and sedition. Anyone can look at what they're doing now and see that their so-called 'nonviolent' advocacy is going to be short-lived. The next stage is going to be rough." He paused. "If things get that far."

Even though her anger overflowed, she wondered if Summer were trying to give her a subtle message.

Some of the fire left his eyes, but he pointed his finger at her and said in a husky voice, "Others are beginning to use Kellen Sing and his movement. For their own purposes. Do you deny that?" At the end, his voice was almost a challenge.

"Deny it? I don't have to deny anything." She glanced around wildly for escape.

The door swung open and the secretary stood there. "The King is leaving now."

"I'll be right there," Summer said. "Look, Beck . . ."

"Call me Rebecca—or better yet, don't call me anything

at all." She couldn't believe her own loss of control. She saw him pick up his jester's hat and heard the strange thunk when the weighted end struck the table.

She couldn't think of a thing more to say, turned and stormed out past the secretary who was still standing open-mouthed in the doorway. In the office, she strode purposefully for the door past the sentries and brushed against someone in her anger, muttered something, and slammed out the other door into the outer office ignoring the astonished stares of office workers.

Only later did she realize she had run into the King and pushed him aside.

36: SUMMER

The King's sword flashed at him. He tilted his head and the blade cleft the air next to his ear. He thrust and the King blocked the point, turning it neatly and followed through with a kick which knocked him off his feet.

Summer recovered and kept rolling, scissoring his legs and bringing the King into the dust beside him.

"Tricky devil," the King spat dust.

"You used your feet first," Summer pointed out.

TJ climbed to his feet and groaned. "I'm getting old. Another round?"

"Do you think your stamina will allow it?" he asked, rising also.

"We'll see," TJ said conversationally and lunged. He was using a practice sword, not Widow-Maker. "My shoulder seems to be performing well without much pain."

Summer skipped aside swiftly and they settled down to parrying. "You realize once we're part of the Fed that swords and all they mean will become obsolete?"

"Not for me. Keeps my eyes straight, my muscles toned, my timing perfect . . . ouch." TJ stared at the cut.

"More or less," Summer said.

TJ whirled his sword until it glittered in the sunlight. "What did Miss Sing want?"

Summer scrambled backward, not about to face the Widow-Maker's mate when whirling. "For me to plead with you to go easy on her brother."

"I couldn't help but notice she left mad," TJ dropped his sword momentarily.

Summer grinned sheepishly, kicked at TJ's sword hand which was no longer there and found himself backing from another frontal attack. "I told her I had to do my duty as I saw it."

TJ parried and leaped above a low swing. "Does she know you are primarily responsible for the dirty tricks?"

"Vaguely."

"Doesn't matter. Let me tell you what I'm inclined to do." TJ stepped back and motioned for a rest. "I'm inclined to jail the son of a bitch."

"On what charges?" Summer was surprised at the inner conflict that was raging within him.

"Treason. Sedition. Malicious misbehavior. Spitting on the road. I don't care. Unrest is beginning to spread. His new phase, this 'nonviolent civil disobedience' at times becomes violent."

"If you lock him up—well, think of the effect it'll have on Sharon Gold. On the people. On Mike."

"Summer, I know it. But my authority is being challenged. I don't like it. He becomes stronger every day, making it more difficult to deal with him when we finally do. It occurs to me we might have made a mistake by not cutting him down right away."

"I think we should give him time to burn out. People aren't stupid, they'll figger out what he's doing."

"Hell, *I* can't figure that out, Summer, and I get reports daily. I can't understand his motives—any that I apply to him just don't fit. Even the dead father bit. It doesn't fit precisely."

"You used to say, TJ, life ain't a bunch of uniform compartments."

"Sounds like something I used to say." TJ slumped onto a bench.

Summer looked down at TJ, feeling pressures he didn't want to admit, pulling him from different directions. He didn't hate Kellen, he kind of liked the kid's spunk. But he was fully on TJ's side. Then put Becky—Rebecca—into the equation and clouds boiled. "Maybe Kellen will lead us to something," he said finally, and saw that TJ recognized the weakness of the statement. "We could have him watched day and night."

TJ swabbed his face with a towel and tossed it to Summer. He sighed. "Too late for that. He quit the university this morning and went underground. His movements are now concealed. Oh, he'll surface when he has to for exposure, but we don't know where he's based now."

At Rebecca's rooms? Summer wondered. He also wondered if his meeting with Rebecca had resulted in Kellen's hiding out. He said, "Surely, things will be okay, TJ." Weak, he cursed at himself.

"So that's the way it is, is it?" TJ asked with his eyes locked onto Summer's.

"Yeah," Summer said and wanted to add something else, but couldn't

"All right then. It's on your back, Delancy Camp. Give him some new rope to hang himself. But *you* have the responsibility. Let's cut the crap. Talk him out of it if you can. We got to get on with conning this young lady from the Fed. Time we don't have much of. Kellen Sing is interfering with my plans. I personally give you time, how much, I don't know—ten, fifteen days. Depends. Then I take drastic action." He trust his beard forward. "Final action."

Summer only looked at the King. Anger and frustration were building within him and he didn't know why he had almost defied his King and his friend. He thought of Becky. "Another round?" he demanded roughly.

TJ rose. "I'm calling it quits for today."

"If you run into Mike, send him down." Summer began slicing at the practice stake.

"I don't do errands," the King said and bawled for a soldier to carry the message. "Tell him to bring his sword," TJ finished.

The soldier trotted out of the isolated courtyard followed by the King and Summer set his sword on a bench and began leaping and kicking the practice stake. The thick cords of wrapped rope withstood his assault but he continued until he no longer thought about a freckled face. He stopped when Mike arrived.

Mike flung off his cloak, drew his sword, took four cuts at the practice post slicing deeply, and cursed.

There's a lot of frustration going around, Summer thought. Maybe TJ's right, something must be done soon. He cut off a nostalgic yearning for the old days, knowing these new days were as good or better. Or at least safer. "Trouble?"

"Why do I have to prove myself to him?"

Soon they were faced off and Mike came at him swinging a murderous figure eight. Mike's fury continued. Soon Summer got the practice post between them. "Keep that up and you'll be a swordmaster soon—not much expertise, but one hell of an attack." Mike had shown unexpected talent. But in battle you couldn't always depend on anger to drive you. You had to be calm and think a lot.

"Coward."

"Look, Mike, keep the point up—and angle it so that it points directly into your opponent's eyes. That way he can't gauge your intentions as well as he might. It also serves to ruin distance perception. Also, there is a psychological advantage: the point threatens directly more than the blade."

"Sure. Now come away from that post and let me show you how, old man."

They parried and thrust for a few moments. Summer could have disarmed Mike several times, but chose not to so that Mike would gain confidence. After a while, Summer said, "Now who feels older?"

"Me," Mike said without shame, but added a smile.

"Let's talk for a minute, Mike. About your friend Kellen."

"Oh?" Mike put the point of his sword into the ground and leaned on it.

Summer winced. "If Kellen doesn't pull in his horns soon, your father is going to squash him, and if he's lucky, he'll see daylight again before he dies."

Mike shot a surprised look at Summer. "I thought you were on his side?"

"I am," Summer said, knowing his exasperation was going to show soon. "If we can stop Kellen, then TJ wins."

"Why come to me?"

"You know why, Mike. You're friends, I guess. You can talk to him, I can't. I tried, remember? And you both see some things sort of the same way."

Mike spat. "I don't really approve of his new civil disobedience. And I'm not about to get between him and my father in this instance. I'm not in bed with Kellen, Summer. Is that what you insinuate?"

"Gee, I don't know." Summer's words had already been thought out and he hoped they didn't sound calculating. "You've changed lately. You are changing. We don't talk as much as we used to. We hardly practice like this together any more."

"I blame my father. I blame the stupid goddamn Federation and his asinine fixation on membership. I don't really know what to think. I wish I'd never heard of the Federation. I wish I'd never heard of the Trek. I flat plainly don't know what to think."

Mike had everything, Summer thought. Power, money, looks, youth, authority—and very little responsibility until recently. Although Mike didn't seem to realize it, TJ was edging him into control of all the Shepherd commercial enterprises—such as the vineyards, the ranches, the liquor monopolies. Preparing him for the future. But Mike needed something more; in that respect he was like his father. Mike had no overpowering ambition, no specific item of interest to pursue, to put his feet upon and climb to his place in life.

"Maybe you need to find a nice girl and settle down," Summer said and was surprised at his own words.

"For a while I thought I had," Mike said with hooded eyes. "And was exploring the possibility. But the rumor mill has it that I have stiff competition."

"Oh, shit."

"Yeah. See you later," Mike said and pulled his sword from the ground splattering Summer's legs with dirt.

Summer wanted to say he didn't know. That it wasn't intentional. That Becky had walked out on him before he could even talk to her, that there was nothing between them. But again words wouldn't come. Emotions clashed in his mind. Instead, he ran after Mike. "Talk to Kellen? Please? The flash point is near."

"Tell him yourself."

Summer stopped and watched Mike's retreating back. First, I blew it with Becky. Then I blew it with TJ. Now, I blew it with Mike. Three in a row. Maybe my luck will change.

He saw that old relationships were changing, new ones forming. Times were changing. Was the Federation really worth it? Was his dedication to TJ and TJ's dream flagging?

37: THE SPY

Tirano's spy moved back into the shadows. It had been easy. With enough money, you could buy anything—including arson. The grain storage warehouse, belonging to the royal family, would be demolished in minutes, long before any effective firefighting could be organized.

And shortly, if not already, a similar incident would occur on the far side of the city.

A fine day's work. The spy hurried off, face covered by a hood and nondescript cloak. It had been an eventful week. The meeting with those bloodthirsty Hukbalahaps from Far-off Continent had been fruitful to say the least. The spy had guaranteed the Huks that the King was too occupied to retaliate. And that the King didn't care about Faroff enough to bother with a little rebellion in a place which had no economic value to the kingdom. Of course, the Huks' representative indicated that they would seek their own assurances in their own way. The spy shuddered, thinking how wild those Huks were. Don't trust them at all. Had to reveal my identity to the representative, though. If TJ captures him or one of the Huk leaders, I'll have to assure they are killed before interrogation. Although that's probably a moot point as I've never heard of a Huk being captured—alive. Fanatics, all of them.

The spy categorized, and probably unfairly, the Oriental offshoots in Faroff, by their types. The Japanese and the Chinese were always battling for economic superiority with each other. The Filipino descendants were the manpower—until the Huk movement gained momentum. Before the Consolidation wars, the Huks had gained supremacy and enslaved the Chinese and Japanese. When TJ won the wars and consolidated the planet, he'd installed a Chinese Eth-narch who continued to rule—and the Chinese gained as-cendancy over the others—to their displeasure. Now the Japanese wanted to rule economically with something called the Greater Co-Prosperity Economic Sphere, but the Chinese were holding on, fighting off both of their ancient antagonists politically. It wouldn't take much to ignite that mess. And, to finish the stereotypes, none of the three groups could get along with the others in the long run. TJ would say "History repeats itself, no?"

All the spy had to do was sniff about in the King's intelligence files, open to most of the upper cadre in the palace, and find the right people. TJ had made a mistake when he combined the three previously antagonistic lands into one ethnarchy. His bureaucratic bumbling hadn't paid off on this one.

Horses' hooves on flagstones warned the spy who slunk into an alley as the squad of soldiers raced by to the growing warehouse fire. One more group of soldiers not available for aiding in police duties for the Kellen Sing demonstration in the center of the city which was planned for right now. Supposedly, Sing's new program of nonviolent civil disobedience. Well, a few coins and a few thugs would change that. Hire a few louts to stir up trouble—wouldn't be the first time. Kellen Sing and his group of neophyte idiots were providing a fine springboard for chaos and anarchy. Exploitation was easy. Disguised, spread the money. The hirelings, if captured and questioned, would have no answers. And no way to lead questions back to me. Just like the assassin who almost killed TJ. The most difficult part had been to weaken the chain links on the snarv-cart chain-collar for the King's birthday celebration. As I'd figured, the threat of all the people in the throne room had antagonized the snarv enough for it to exert sufficient strength to burst loose. The possibility that the snarv might have slain many in the crowd? Even better—scare people away from TJ and his high-handed, noncaring throne.

The only real personal threat so far had been when one thug had thought to take all the spy's money and forfeit the job. But the spy had a poison needle ready, tip between forefinger and middle finger. I had to reconcile murder then for the first time—but even before then I knew I found death exciting. The soldiers are past, now I can go observe Kellen Sing's demonstration. From afar, of course.

Too bad Kellen Sing is unapproachable. I know he won't be bought off and that he would be unmanageable if so. The kingdom is beginning to crumble and Kellen Sing is the matchpoint. But, admittedly, there *is* something different about Kellen Sing, something ungiving, some unknown drive—else why would he continue his foolish efforts against TJ. Especially with the growing violence that I've paid for? A fool child.

But fortunately, pressures from Kellen and other events are mounting on the King and his rule. Should I arrange Kellen's death? That would lead to a great deal more violence and, thus, reciprocation from the palace and, in turn, more violence. A never ending spiral. But Kellen was such a magnetic personality that, if he died, his movement would eventually wither without him. And now I need his movement to cover my efforts. But it was something to consult with Tirano on. Kellen Sing is still ripe for the picking— what better vehicle to use for chaos and anarchy—and revenge?

The spy decided to return to the palace. No use getting involved in violence and risking exposure.

38: SHARON

There was no hint of danger.

Sharon was accompanying the royal party on another excursion, this time one more interesting. Upon the west coast lay the Pima Ethnarchy where they were visiting the city of Westbygodvirginia (Westginny for short, she learned. Being from Olde Earthe herself, she thought: Boy, you can tell this planet was pioneered by Norteamericanos. Maybe when all this is settled we can get a geodetic survey satellite in here permanently, map and locate everything and make them rename all these tacky-named places.) Here the King was pursuing some technological advances of his own.

Actually, the trip, she was sure, was for her benefit—for at the last moment the King had begged out and sent Mike in his place. She suspected he wanted to take some action in Crimson Sapphire without her presence. Something in response to Kellen Sing's new "creative nonviolence?"

TJ'd been so proud of those efforts in Westginny, so she'd agreed to the trip.

So, after a few days' ride, here they were. As usual, Gwen and Felicia had come along.

"Westginny is cold because a polar current streams down from the north and parallels the coast here," Mike was telling her.

She was sweating as if she'd just run a forty-K marathon. "You can't prove it by me."

He grinned like a little boy and faked pushing her into the bubbling mud below.

This day she'd seen steam vents, mudpots, geysers, and three small magma outlets which, fortunately, only spewed smelly gas and heat on the landside. Oceanside, one lava river flowed into the ocean, providing a constant steam plume. But underneath, she fancied she could feel a continuous rumbling. She hoped an eruption would not occur while she was here. Obviously, the people who lived here were not afraid of any imminent volcanic explosion; but Sharon wasn't convinced that their warning system—cages full of animals called slinkers, for God's sake—was adequate.

Some of the royal engineers were trying to harness steam and scalding water to produce things like milled lumber and heat-treated metal consumer goods in volume. Since the project had just begun, they weren't very far along. They'd already succeeded in devising systems to dry fish and sea salt.

But Westginny had existed long before TJ began his projects—for in the natural warm valleys nearby grew some of the best produce on the planet. It was obvious why Felicia had come along.

Felicia had told her that most dwellings here were heated naturally through harnessed steam—or steam-heated water piped through their buildings.

Right now they were on a volcanic ridge overlooking the sea to the west.

Sharon shivered. A gray overcast hung hungrily in the sky like a predator. On one side of the ridge lay mudpits, some bubbling, others roiling, still others perfect for "therapeutic" bathing. Gwen and Felicia were below in one of these latter. Sharon turned and followed Mike down a path into a grotto. The path was worn, all else a sharp lava maze. Recent, geologically speaking, she thought. She saw Mike check the soldiers who'd accompanied them. They were deployed discreetly on the inland side of this place. Apparently, they didn't fear anything from the ocean side.

Major "Tough Luck" Timmons was in charge of the escort. Because of attempts on the King while Timmons was leading the soldiers, he was getting a reputation around the palace. The word on Timmons was almost schizophrenic, Sharon thought. People kept trying to kill the King during his shifts, but because of Timmons' military efficiency, he kept getting spot promotions. He was what, in the Federation's military, was called a "fast-burner." She kind of liked Tim. She'd sought him out discreetly, stalked him like a hunting cat on its prey, and captured him. Of course, Tim didn't know it yet. She'd subtly been working on him to find out what really had happened at Dawn's Edge when the school had burned down. But Tim thought she was sincerely interested in him. She hadn't been, but now?

She couldn't help but side with him against the palace rumor-mill. The gossip about his rapid promotions hurt him; he obviously cared what people thought about him. Yet he remained fiercely loyal to the King. So he was defensive about his quick rise in the ranks, and especially touchy about the King being vulnerable while under his ostensible protection. Sharon had found his emotional clash appealing and had let him think he'd talked her into dining with him. She'd realized, that, accidentally, she had provided him with a coup against the gossips: Tim was the only one who had escorted her anywhere socially. (Mike apparently didn't count.) So, while she had not encouraged further social engagements with him, she had not discouraged them either. No matter how obliquely she'd addressed the subject, he wouldn't talk about the events inside the burning school. He'd deftly avoided her attempts.

And, damnit, he was the only man on the whole damn planet who had looked at her frankly as a woman (except for TJ!) and not as some strange freak. She didn't count traditional male calculating, undressing looks.

At the bottom of the trail was an overhang, just inside the grotto. It was about ten meters above the pool within. Wisps of steam rose from the pool into the cool air. They stood on the lip of the overhang and Mike motioned her for silence. For a moment, she couldn't understand the sound and then she saw it: a far away hissing and millions of tiny droplets.

"I see now," she said. "The magma heats underground water way below somewhere, the steam escapes into a recess back there," she pointed into the dark part of the cavern, "and the steam condenses on the ceiling of the grotto and drips into the pool."

"Exactly," he said, kicked his boots off, stripped his tunic and trousers down to bathing shorts he already was wearing and dived off the overhang.

In seconds, he surfaced, splashed, and whooped. The sounds echoed slightly in the cavern. He turned on his back and kicked a plume of water powerfully. His strength surprised her. In fact, his physique surprised her. He always appeared so deceptively slender. Were his clothes designed to hide his muscles? Mike certainly wasn't as solid, as massive, as TJ. Nor did Mike have that rugged attractiveness (yet) which TJ had and used like a tool. But he darn sure wasn't a kid. She'd have to run his and her different solar system ages through her wristcomp data base, but she knew they were roughly the same age. She wondered if Mike made his appearance thus on purpose.

"C'mon in, scaredy-slinker," he shouted. She stripped, as he had done, to her bathing suit and got his immediate attention. Nothing sexist in his look at all—just male-female attraction. She smiled.

It felt good to not be so much an outsider any more.

She unsnapped her wristcomp and dropped it on top of her clothing. Her wristcomp was good for short range communication, running her data base, time, recorded reminders, weather conditions, monitoring body functions like temp and metab indices, and something she had told no one on Bear Ridge: it could be set to explode or be used as an energy weapon. One of the command function tabs would disengage and stretch a silk-thin filament which attached to a ring on her forefinger. The power wasn't much, but could regenerate (like an ice-needle gun!) every second, and shoot short energy bursts where she pointed her finger. While it was no quick-draw weapon, she'd practiced sufficiently to arm herself within two seconds. The disguise factor more than made up for the slowness of getting the weapon into operation.

She paused on the lip of the overhang, more because of the chill breath of breeze which had wafted over her shoulders and onto the back of her neck than enjoyment of Mike's now appraising look at her in her tasteful two-piece suit. She possessed other, more enticing, swimming suits—but her position required a degree of conservative dress.

Her flesh broke out into bumps of warning.

"Hurry up!" Mike urged.

She glanced around, unsure of herself. Where was Tim? She stepped away from the diving overhang and ran lightly up the trail to the ridge separating the grotto from the mudpits.

"That's funny," she said aloud. Felicia and Gwen weren't there anymore. And where were the soldiers? Some of them should have been visible from her vantage point. Falling gravel startled her and she turned. And looked up. Along the top of the entrance to the cavernous grotto squatted twenty-five or thirty men, lean, hard men with slight Oriental features. Most were grinning, bows and crossbows held loosely in their hands. All had machetes—and some of those glistened like wet rust. Blood, she realized.

She jerked her head back around searching for Felicia and Gwen. Nothing. The men leered and grinned.

The wristcomp!

She spun and ran for her clothes and her weapon.

One of the men dropped from the lip of the cavern and landed in front of her. Casually, he leaned on his machete, obviously keeping her from Mike's weapons which lay atop his clothes right next to hers.

She stopped and edged around him. She could make no false moves. She stepped onto the overhang. "Mike?"

He came swimming out of the shadows and stopped, treading water.

She felt more presences. Three more men appeared at her back.

One of them, short, with unruly black hair, and a face which reminded her of an olive background on a video terminal, said, "Prince Michale, would you come up here?"

Mike obviously had no choice. He climbed out, dripping water, eyes alert. In a moment he had scrambled up the rocky path to where they stood. Sharon saw his body tense.

"Prince," said the short man, "I came to extend to you and your party an invitation . . ."

"We decline," Mike's voice cut him off. "Please, go about . . . drop the please. Go about your business and leave us."

Sharon was surprised at the level of command in Mike's tone. If he was scared or nervous, you'd never know it. *Something is drastically wrong and Mike is trying to bluff our way out.*

"Leave us!" Mike's voice reminded her of TJ in a rage.

"I'm afraid that is not possible," the man told him. "Your mother and grandmother have already joined us."

"Who are you?"

"Taruc."

"Commander Luis." Mike's voice went flat, dead. "Huk-balahap."

"Ah, it would seem that I am not unknown in the royal court."

Men were going through their clothing. They took Mike's sword and a knife she hadn't known he possessed. From her jumpsuit pockets, they took mechanical pens and an electronic pen she used with her data base. A man was inspecting her wristcomp which had the ornamental cover over its face.

"Give me my bracelet," she demanded and stepped forward and snatched her wristcomp from the man's hand. Surprise was on her side. She stepped back, snapping her wristcomp onto her wrist. The man reached out for her and she pivoted and shot a heel into his knee. He went down, his companions laughing.

"Enough," said Commander Luis. "Call Yoji."

A man trotted up the trail and out of sight.

She hoped they had forgotten about her wristcomp—and apparently they had. Should she use the weapon? No, not yet. They had Felicia and Gwen. Wait and see.

Over the ridge came a giant of a man, head shaved, only a pigtail hanging from the top and back of his head, wearing a loin cloth and some kind of eye shadow. Samurai. The word came unbidden to her mind. Traditional samurai. A Filipino Huc, Taruc, following the ancient Japanese code of Bushido with his Japanese servant? Ridiculous, she thought. Yet here they were.

Yoji was so large that she didn't at first notice the burden he carried. Yoji's nostrils flared as he carelessly dumped the body at Commander Luis' feet. Three arrows impaled the torso and there were many machete wounds. The body was flaccid and pale from loss of blood, overlaid with the gruesome wounds and blood.

Mike gasped and then she recognized him.

"Tim!" she fell to her knees beside him. "Tim." She put her hands on his bloody shoulders and shook him.

"A lesson, Prince Michale. Resistance is futile," Luis Taruc said. "He was a brave man, he killed two men by hand after he had lost his weapons. Not many men can best a Huk one-on-one, much less at greater odds."

Sharon caressed Tim's forehead and brushed his hair away from his eyes. She closed his lids, hoping they'd stay closed, erasing the look of failure on his face. "Tough-Luck" Timmons finally got his. Yeah.

They dragged her to her feet and Mike had to help her dress, his cold, wet touch reminding her of a corpse.

In a stupor she followed orders and soon found herself on a black sand beach boarding a long boat on the cold, cold, ocean. Gwen and Felicia, still muddy, were in another boat already meters out from shore, quiet, stone-still, faces drawn.

A ray of logic and sanity broke into her mind as she unconsciously licked the back of her hand—which she saw had some of Tim's blood on it. She kept licking.

Her instructions came clearly to her: "Don't get involved, don't take sides. Just observe."

Like fucking hell.

A cold drizzle began to fall.

39: TJ

"They *said* Gwen and the others were all right," Summer told him for maybe the thirtieth time. It occurred to TJ that Summer was as worried as he was.

Gwen. Mother. Mick. Sharon. Gone. Captured.

Evening was coming and they stood on a hill overlooking the Chinese capital of the Faroff lands. Nihaoma. According to the Huks' messenger, the Huks occupied Nihaoma now.

The Huk messenger had come to the palace only moments after the messenger from the Ethnarch of Pima.

A simple trade, he'd proposed. The Prince, the Queen, the Queen Mother, and Fed representative. For autonomy. The King was to agree that the Huks rule a subjugated Chinese and Japanese peoples and not interfere. He assured TJ that the hostages were being treated well.

"What's to keep me from agreeing and then come in with my army once the hostages are free?" he asked.

"We propose to keep, in good quarters of course, two of the hostages—your choice of the two. And you can change the hostages at any time, so long as we have two." The man smiled.

The smile had died as secretaries and papers scattered all over the office when TJ'd jerked him from his feet and slammed him across the room against the wall. His knife had been sliding into the man's right eye when Summer pulled him away.

Later, the man had died while undergoing medical treatment to revive him from the injuries inflicted by the King's questioning. Fanatics, TJ thought. Son of a bitch wouldn't say anything until Manny had worked on him for a while. He shook his head. Huks were tough foes, fanatics who had no need of logic and reason. The Huk had managed to give a more underlying reason for the kidnapping. The Huks figured that TJ had too many problems in Crimson Sapphire to leave or dedicate any military to fighting the Huks. They'd been led to believe that he was holding onto power by a thin thread and couldn't devote any manpower to them for fear that his whole kingdom would fall. They also believed that the kingdom was falling. That it was only a matter of time. Well, they were mistaken. Badly.

In an hour, he and Summer and a select group of Gyrenes were mounted and ready to ride.

TJ leaned down from his horse and spoke quietly to Manny Vero. "Manny, if we don't make it, that leaves Nora as the last member of the royal family. I'm not convinced of her ability to rule wisely. I put it square on your shoulders. Do what you think is best for the kingdom. If necessary, dethrone her, lock her up. Send off my other offspring." He meant the kinglets. "If none of them make it, you still got the reins."

"Sir," Manny had said, voice dead, "if you do not return, I will kill every man on the Faroff Continent."

"If you think you must," TJ said, knowing Manny wouldn't do so. Although his loyalty to him and Gwen and Felicia and Mike was unquestioned—now TJ knew the magnitude. "You give Timmons and his men heroes' burials, hear? And plenty of soldiers in the streets, all the time, showing a presence. Maybe the people won't hear about what's happened over in Westginny."

"They already have," Manny said.

"My God, how?"

"I don't know, Sire. Perhaps in the same way the Huks knew about Mike and Gwen and all going bathing."

"There's that." He thought for a moment. "Well, if Kellen Sing or someone attempts to take advantage of my absence, arrest him. Do what's necessary. Maybe Nora can arrange for him to get whatever virus is going around."

"I'll take care of it, Sire."

Taking extra horses, they went, faster than any other return messenger, to the coast. Half the army was to follow after proper arrangements could be made. At the coast, they took ships to a panhandle of Faroff sticking out into the ocean. There, they raced up the coast until they reached Nihaoma.

"The problem," he told Summer, "is to rescue the hostages. And a hundred or so soldiers might just tip our hand."

Summer nodded. "Just you and me again?"

TJ looked at Summer. "Thanks." He remembered the battle which gave birth to the yearly Muster. They could pull it off. But this time they had four important lives in their hands, lives they were not ready to sacrifice.

Two farmers and a trader were being held, as they had seen the small band from Crimson Sapphire. TJ didn't want his opponents to know about the soldiers, so he and Summer waylaid another merchantman. He was told to go into Nihaoma, find this Commander Luis and tell him that the King would ride in that night to personally negotiate. And that he would come with only one other man. The important thing was for Luis Taruc to have the hostages present so that TJ could verify that they were unharmed.

A bargain Taruc couldn't deny. The King alone? It was like TJ would walk into a trap of his own making.

But the plan would insure that all the Huk leadership would be present—for who could miss such an opportunity?

The soldiers would sneak close under the cover of night, and await TJ's signal—or evidence of combat.

The meeting place was to be the Ethnarch's court, the location where the merchant said the Huks had settled.

In an hour it was dark and they rode into Nihaoma. No one stopped them. TJ reflected on the city. The predominantly Chinese city certainly was in love with angles. And colors. But he had no eye for architecture. Strangely he felt no tension. A fleeting regret that were they in the Fed, he wouldn't have had so many days hard ride and the short trip

246 James B. Johnson

by sea. Then it occurred to him that he could probably have
requested Federation assistance in rescuing their ambassador—
just find Sharon's radio. Was the whole thing blown now?
Would he, even if successful tonight, lose his bid for Federation membership? Clearly, if Sharon Gold were present in
the chamber tonight, and he and Summer used their ice-
needle guns, then she could arbitrarily disqualify Bear Ridge
from Fed entry. She probably wasn't any too goddamn
happy about being a prisoner and a hostage, either. Maybe
she'd already decided to abort her checklist.

Nothing he could do about it in any case. He was already
committed. And no man threatened Thomas Jefferson Shepherd through his family.

While the streets certainly weren't deserted, they were
quiet. Occasionally, a man in the streets would indicate the
way to go even though it was a straight line to the Ethnarch's building. He hoped the Huks hadn't had sufficient
time to gather a force. He'd counted on surprise and his
quick trip here to Nihaoma to keep them off balance.

"The biggest problem as I see it," Summer said, "is to
make sure we have a good line of fire without hitting the
hostages."

"We'll see."

Presently they came to the Ethnarch's court and administrative building. It was a tall building with towers and swoop-
ing roofs. They dismounted and started up a series of wide
stone steps. A dozen silent Huk soldiers fell in behind them.

The court wasn't as big as his throne room in Crimson
Sapphire, but it was much more decorated. Fancy carpets
and woven wall hangings, treated and stained wood. Big
enough to hold a soccer game in. A thought that this Ethnarch might be garnering riches by using his position struck
TJ. It could be one of the reasons the Huks rebelled. No
matter.

The soldiers weren't really soldiers; they reminded him of
guerrilla fighters in the field. No uniformity of clothing or
military bearing and behavior. Yet, they were disciplined.
TJ estimated maybe a hundred present, scattered randomly
throughout the room.

As they walked down the aisle, the large entry doors were
slammed and barred. The Huks were taking no chances that
he had brought a force with him.

At the end of the parquet-floored aisle, a raised platform
sat, apparently for the Ethnarch's throne. In front of the

platform was a line of crossbow-armed Huks, situated an arm's length from each other. Twelve, he saw. On the platform were several men and against the wall behind them were the hostages.

His eyes immediately sought Gwen. She was pale but her chin was up. She didn't appear to be harmed and a look of relief shot through her eyes only to be replaced by concern. He had to admit that what he and Summer were doing looked foolish.

Felicia was wearing a satisfied grin, but appeared weary. She trusted his trickery more than any one else in the world.

Mike was shaking his head in disbelief. Obviously, he couldn't believe his father had been dumb enough to walk into this trap, to commit suicide.

Sharon Gold was grim, but her face showed she was alert. She was uncharacteristically rolling up the sleeve on her jumpsuit, exposing her wristcomp.

TJ and Summer stopped just short of the line of crossbow-armed Huks.

A short man stepped forward, ran his hands through his messy hair.

"Taruc?" TJ demanded.

"I am Commander Luis, yes."

"Release the four prisoners now and I give you your lives."

"You and a clown threaten us?"

"My army even now surrounds this city. No man will escape alive."

"You bluff, King."

TJ shrugged casually. "I got here swiftly, did I not? Before your representative or a messenger possibly could have. Think about it."

Taruc barked a short laugh. "If what you say is true, then I have two more hostages. If they kill some of us anyway, those of us who live will go back into the jungles from whence we came. We shall not live as slaves to these thieving Chinese."

"Where is Zhou Xuegei, my Ethnarch?"

"Dead."

"Unfortunate," TJ said.

"You blabber much. Are you stalling for some reason?"

TJ let a death's head smile across his features. "And if I am?"

"Then you are dead, Señor Shepherd. Without any Shepherds," his head jerked toward the four hostages, "the kingdom will be a little too busy to bother with this poor place. We shall determine our own destiny for a change."

He sounded just like Kellen Sing! And just like I sound when I talk about the Federation! Is the whole world crazy?

TJ felt Summer tense and edge away from him. Summer knew the play acting was about over.

Taruc snapped his fingers. "Yoji! Forgive me, Shepherd, but I have heard how great a warrior you are and I would test your mettle."

A giant Japanese with a braided topknot of hair hanging over the back of his head stepped from an alcove. He carried a double-edged sword with a two-handed hilt.

Now TJ understood why he hadn't been disarmed.

Yoji lumbered up to TJ and bowed.

TJ glanced at Summer. "I wish Jean-Claude were here. He'd enjoy this."

Summer nodded, having gotten the message and stepped aside, giving the two combatants room, but also moving to position himself and await TJ's signal.

TJ casually drew Widow-Maker, palm and fingers automatically finding the right grooves. He bowed to Yoji who seemed to tower over him. As he came out of the formal bow, he spun and lashed a heel into Yoji's midsection. It felt like stone.

He kept spinning because Yoji swung his mammoth sword at TJ's lashing leg.

Finally, their swords struck, TJ's in protection from a wide swing. He danced about taking Yoji's measure and scattering the guards directly in front of the platform. He could see the Huk leaders leaning forward in anticipation. He fended off another onslaught clumsily, not wanting Yoji to know the extent of his skill. He kept Yoji's back to the platform and worked them back and forth.

He couldn't help but notice Sharon Gold who seemed to be standing taller, ready for some play of her own. Gwen and Felicia scanned the other entrances to the court room, obviously looking for what they thought was succor. Mike was watching the battle and glancing at Summer for some kind of hint. But Sharon had a deadly determination on her face.

He tripped on purpose and rolled away from a slash of Yoji's sword. He saw that the other Huks in the room were gathered in a semicircle to watch.

Everything was almost perfect.

He scrambled to his feet and let Yoji drive him backward toward the platform. With the back of his legs against the platform, he made his decision. Obviously, the most immediate danger would come from the dozen or so crossbows and that's where Summer would concentrate his efforts first.

So, TJ had to make his move and get out of the line of fire and somehow occupy those on the platform before they could grab the hostages.

He engaged Yoji in a fierce exchange, waited for his opening, found it, kicked Yoji's sword arm aside, sliced into Yoji's neck, almost severing it, and dropped on his butt, jerking his sword from Yoji's thick neck. Then he spun, rolled on the floor, and lashed out with his sword.

As he slashed into several now stampeding legs, he heard the hum of Summer's ice-needle gun and saw Yoji finally collapse, head lolling at an obscene angle.

The dead silence erupted into a place of hell-noises, screams from dying and wounded. Many of the leaders were down from his floor-level sword sweep and he killed one man with a thrown sword as he rose. He kicked another in the groin while he pulled his ice-needle gun from beneath his tunic.

"BRRRP" went his weapon as he traversed those who were in the bunch in front of him.

He turned and froze, stunned from the action. Mike was rolling on the floor with one Huk while Gwen and Felicia scrambled for weapons, but the rest on the platform were dead.

Except Sharon and Commander Luis.

He was cowering against the throne, mouth slobbering and almost lying across the arm rests.

Sharon Gold stood over him pointing her finger at him. "This is for Tim, you bastard." Her finger seemed to twitch and glow at the tip and she lifted her hand from Taruc's crotch to his head. Taruc's scream was primordial fear. A black line appeared and TJ heard the sizzle of burned flesh. Then he grabbed himself and whirled.

A quick glance showed Summer had accounted for ten of the twelve crossbowmen and TJ finished off the other two as they fired at Summer.

Summer nimbly dodged the bolts and turned his weapon on the now advancing crowd of Huks.

TJ did the same. The second-long burst cut down the

front waves of charging enemy. He kept his thumb on the firing stud and hoped that the water would last.

Another glance told him that Sharon and Mike were now fighting at the edge of the crowd together, protecting each other, Mike with a sword and Sharon with her energy weapon.

The strange sounds coming from the ice-needle guns seemed to scare the Huks and disrupt their natural fanaticism. TJ was killing them faster than he could count them. And so was Summer. The barred doors trapped many and TJ ran after them, concentrating his fire on the mass of bodies. He didn't want to think whether this was right or not. But he continued on, determined to make an example by killing as many Huks as he could. The more he killed now, the less his troops would have to hunt down—if the Hukbalahaps continued to be a problem. Summer was giving his attention to those Huks trying to escape through other, smaller exits.

Then his ice-needle gun quit. He'd kept the firing stud pressed since he'd started. The weapon felt hot in his hand.

The four remaining live Huks in front of him realized what had happened and turned on him. He crushed an Adam's apple with a stiff-fingered blow before falling back from two swinging swords and a machete. He ducked and threw a body at the three, feeling as he did a sliver of melting ice stab his palm. He snatched a machete and tore into the three. One man turned and ran, and TJ split the other two and killed them before they could reposition themselves. He threw his machete at the retreating one and looked to see if Summer needed help.

Summer's arms and legs were whirling and dealing death. His ice-needle gun must have quit, too.

TJ ran over to the melee and broke a neck from behind. Mike ran up with Widow-Maker and started slashing away.

In a moment, there were no Huks.

"Any of them escape?" he panted.

"A couple," Summer said, "but maybe our troops are in position by now."

"It's not like you have to conceal the ice-needle weapons from Sharon, now," Mike said.

Sharon walked up. "You have to shoot an ice-needle gun in bursts of five seconds or less; else the coils overheat and burn out."

"They're ruined?" TJ asked. Summer had only bought two under his guidance. He should have purchased enough for an army. But that would have been too dangerous. And now these two were gone. One of the drawbacks of hi-tech, he thought.

"Useless," she said and looked at the dead in the room. She shook her head sadly. "It doesn't matter. I won't refer to your possession of hi-tech weapons." She was quiet for a moment. "Too many brave men dead. Why?"

40: TIRANO

TIME BECOMING RIPE. SITUATION DETERIORATING TO OUR ADVANTAGE. KELLEN SING'S FOLLOWING GROWING. SOME MINOR UNREST IN CRIMSON SAPPHIRE. REBELLION IN FAROFF ETHNARCHY PUT DOWN WITH MUCH BLOOD. REQUIRED ARMY MANEUVERS FOR FEDERATION REP REVIEW DUE SOON.

Tirano read the now uncoded message on the screen of his clandestine console. It was a mixed version of Yaqui and Serbo-Croat, which probably none but one or two Federation scholars and their computers could figure out. Since Bear Ridge had been settled by North Americans and Two Tongues primarily by Europeans, the combination of the two was possible. Tirano suspected his spy was a scholar—or had some distant Yaqui blood.

He tapped out his reply, checked it, then punched the transmit button.

PLANS MOVING AHEAD RAPIDLY. DO YOUR PART, REWARD HIGH. REFERENCE SING: IS IT POSSIBLE HIS EARLY DEMISE COULD BE ATTRIBUTED TO SHEPHERD? MIGHT HASTEN REVOLT. OR WOULD SING'S DEATH END THE MOVEMENT?

He waited for the response. He knew the spy had already thought out the possibilities and wondered what the recommendation would be. He was thankful for the spy's personal grudge against Shepherd. The revenge factor and the promise of leadership position after Shepherd's death should be plenty to hold the spy's loyalty.

EITHER/OR. IF SING IS DEAD, HIS MOVEMENT

WILL DIE. HE HAS SOME SORT OF PERSONAL MAG-NETISM THAT ATTRACTS FOLLOWERS. PERHAPS SOME INITIAL RIOTING AT HIS DEATH, BUT I SUG-GEST HE IS MORE VALUABLE TO US RIGHT NOW OPPOSING SHEPHERD REIGN AND FOSTERING UN-REST. AM SURPRISED THE KING HAS ALLOWED THIS MUCH OPPOSITION. REMIND YOU THAT SEV-ERAL ATTEMPTS ON LIFE OF KING TOTAL FAIL-URE. SECURITY AT MAX. I CAN PERSONALLY GET TO HIM, BUT WOULD REVEAL SELF. FAILURE WOULD BE FATAL. DO NOT CHOOSE TO DO SO AT ANY RATE. REMOVAL OF KING NO LONGER RECOMMENDED ANYWAY. SINCE INVASION PLANS REVOLVE AROUND ARMY MANEUVERS, THESE MANEUVERS MIGHT BE CANCELED WHILE NEXT IN LINE CONSOLIDATES POWER.

An idea occurred to Tirano, and his response was immediate.

IF SHEPHERD KILLED OR KIDNAPPED, SUCCES-SOR MAY DISCONTINUE EFFORTS TO JOIN FED-ERATION. REPLY.

He preferred this electronic written communication. Speed-of-light transmissions were fast enough. The slight delays gave him time to think in between messages. He guessed the hi-tech boys of the Fed could unscramble any-thing his small machine could scramble. Now, using writing only, he could blame these communications on some dissi-dent element. His Bear Ridge representative had been in-structed never to refer to him personally.

POSITION OF PRINCE KNOWN TO BE ANTI-FED. HOWEVER, ON PREVIOUS ASSASSINATION AT-TEMPT WHEN THE KING WAS IN HIS COMA, IMME-DIATE FAMILY PROVED MORE POWERFUL AND SECRETIVE THAN I ANTICIPATED, AND NONE MOVED TO WITHDRAW FED APPLICATION. ALSO SOME ODD PEOPLE MADE DECISIONS AND TOOK CONTROL. LIKE THE COURT JESTER, THE QUEEN MOTHER, THE COURT HERALD. ALL ACTING WITH AUTHORITY OF NEXT IN LINE, QUEEN AND PRINCE. I HAVE NOT BEEN ABLE TO BREAK INTO THIS TIGHT INNER CIRCLE AND CANNOT COUNT ON THEM TO WITHDRAW FED APPLICATION IN CASE OF SHEPHERD'S DEATH. ALMOST IMPOSSIBLE TO KILL ENOUGH SHEPHERDS TO GET DOWN TO ME.

TRIED THAT WITH THE HUKS AND IT FAILED. SO
HAVE DISCONTINUED THOUGHTS IN THAT AREA.
THE MORE I THINK ABOUT IT, THE MORE I URGE
RECONSIDERATION OF REMOVAL OF TJ SHEP-
HERD. RECOMMEND SHEPHERD AND SING BE AL-
LOWED TO CANCEL EACH OTHER OUT—THOUGH
KING STILL ALL-POWERFUL AND CAN SQUASH
SING ANY TIME AND AM UNCERTAIN WHY HE
HAS NOT YET DONE SO. UNLESS YOU HAVE BET-
TER SUGGESTION, WILL LET SITUATION BOIL AND
CONTINUE TO CONTRIBUTE TO UNREST. AM
AFRAID SHOULD ANYTHING UNTOWARD HAPPEN,
THE SITUATIONAL EQUATION WILL CHANGE
FROM WHAT WE'VE PLANNED ON. SOMETHING
TO CONSIDER: JUST PRIOR TO YOUR ARRIVAL,
KILL SING WHICH MIGHT PRECIPITATE RIOTS AND
CONFUSION AT EXACTLY THE RIGHT TIME. AD-
DITIONALLY, AT THAT TIME THE ARMY WILL BE
GONE FAR AFIELD ON THOSE MANEUVERS—TOO
FAR TO BE RECALLED IN TIME TO THWART US.

Tirano thought about the spy's proposal. Let Sing and
Shepherd bleed each other and he'd pick up the pieces. It
was all in the timing. That gimp-legged captain was about
ready with the transports. Tirano's personally selected invasion force was at the peak of skill in training and ready.

And he himself was ready. Though he didn't call them by
their names, greed and revenge were a good part of his
reasons to invade Bear Ridge. But there were more reasons,
not the least of which were boredom and ambition. He was
ready to move into the Federation's governing body. And
he was bored with the low-tech life on Two Tongues when
there was more to be had. The original idea had been born
of greed and revenge, but had mutated now. He felt more
alive than ever before while he was planning the invasion
and directing the spy's activities. Playing this game, the
trickery, the planning, the anticipation—all had become self-
supporting reasons for continuing. There was also the thrill
of evading Federation regulations, outsmarting them, so to
speak—and meanwhile playing the under-the-table political
games. He grinned, pleased with himself. This was fun. A
whole helluva lot more fun than worrisome domestic problems always clamoring for his attention.

He decided.

CONCUR. PLANS AS PREVIOUSLY SCHEDULED.

254 James B. Johnson

CONTINUE DISRUPTION ACTIVITIES. DISCONTINUE
ATTEMPTS ON SHEPHERD. IF POSSIBLE, PLACE AN
AGENT WITH SING. WHEN INVASION IMMINENT,
REMOVE SING BLOODILY AND BRUTALLY AND
PLACE BLAME ON SHEPHERD AND FAMILY. COM-
PILE LIST OF THOSE IN PALACE TO BE ELIMI-
NATED IMMEDIATELY WE TAKE OVER.

The answer was slow in coming.

HAVE ALREADY COMPLETED LIST. QUESTION
IS DISPOSITION OF ENVOY GOLD. ANY INSTRUC-
TIONS?

He hadn't yet decided upon Gold's fate. If she were left
alive, then she could put a crimp in his plans. But he would
present the Federation with a fait accompli and there was
nothing she could do about it. The Fed would know soon
enough he had invaded Bear Ridge and taken charge.

On the other hand, should something happen to her,
Shepherd would be blamed for failure to protect and other
diplomatic garbage. But if she were to die or disappear,
then the Federation might launch an immediate investigation,
thereby interfering with his plans. All he needed was a Federation fleet circling Bear Ridge when he appeared with a squad-
ron of troop transports loaded down with soldiers from Two
Tongues. Her death wouldn't do . . . but there was one thing.

IMPORTANT GOLD NOT—REPEAT—NOT BE
HARMED. SHE OBVIOUSLY HAS COMM GEAR WITH
INSTANT ACCESS TO FED NAVY. DEVISE PLAN FOR
DESTRUCTION OF THIS EQUIPMENT AT PROPER
MOMENT—NOT TOO SOON TO GIVE US AWAY,
NOR TOO LATE FOR HER TO NOTIFY ANYONE OF
INVASION. END.

41: MIKE

Mike landed on his shoulder and rolled in the dust. He
thought about lying there and resting.

"Up and at 'em," Gil said. Gilbert Haynes Trevan was
Mike's hand-to-hand combat instructor (Summer couldn't

do it all), his half brother as a kinglet, and a direct descendant of Mark Trevan who was one of the original Trekmasters before the Shepherds came out of the mountains.

Gil continued to taunt. "You'll be eating my dust on the trail up the ridges, too. Are you practicing to eat my dust?"

Mike rose silently. "Not yet." Was the Trek worth all this? Did he really want to go out into the wilds and surmount insurmountable mountains and ridges just to be king? The question was becoming, Did he really want to be king? Being king had been his goal, not his personal ambition. He didn't think he had any personal ambition. Maybe to write, to study, to . . . fix stuff that was wrong. His father had the authority to fix stuff that was wrong and he failed to do so. What TJ thought was wrong, he fixed with armies and swords and force and blood. That wasn't the way. Do it with reason, with logic, with love and kindness. Which led him back to the beginning of the full circle. His ambition could only be fulfilled by ascending the throne and running things his way. He would be a scholar-king, not a philosopher-king like he'd thought. Nor would he be a—what would you call Thomas Jefferson Shepherd? A killer-king? A warrior-king? Either.

Anger filled him again. Earlier this morning, his father had shouted at him. "You tell your girlfriend's brother that he's at the end of his rope. Period. You control your friend, Mick, or else."

"I have no control," Mike had said, making a conscious effort to control himself. Summer had cowered in a corner in his clown's suit.

Summer. Summer and Rebecca. Mike's inner conflict seethed like an ulcer breaking open.

"Hey!" Gil screamed.

Mike looked up to see Gil's right foot poised over his throat.

Anger boiled over. Suddenly, Mike lashed his legs out, tripped Gil, butted him in the midsection in a surprise move, and had his thumbs in Gil's eyes before Gil could react. He found his knee pressing hard on Gil's sternum. Why was he acting this way? The outburst was so unlike him.

He relaxed and rolled off Gil and sat next to him. As Gil sat up, Mike said, "Why are you helping me? I'm competition when the time comes to take the Trek."

"Yup. You're beginning to figure things out. Boy, you

clobbered me a good one there." He rubbed his ribcage. Gil
was the acknowledged best of all the kinglets. His mother,
the daughter of a noble slain in battle, married a wealthy
merchant after Gil was born—so he retained the name Trevan.
The merchant prospered even more after the marriage. The
King took care of his own, and raising a son of the King
insured prosperity. Mike thought that his father had invented a new classification of offspring, something between
legitimate and illegitimate.

"Gil, why are you going to take the Trek?"

Sweat ran off Gil and dropped into the dust. "Why? It's
what I've trained to do. I never really thought about it. I
don't have to, you know. It's expected, but *I* don't have to
go through that."

"More than likely you won't live through it."

"Ah, Mike. But if I do, I will be King of Crimson
Sapphire—and now the kingdom, the planet, and maybe
even be on the Federation Council."

"You've got father's ambitions." His voice was accusing.

Gil's face fell. "What else have I got?" he whispered.
"His name? A position of authority like you have? No. I'm
a goddamn kinglet, a half-bastard, grown from a seed sown
in lust, raised for one purpose: to die for my kingdom. What
the purple fuck do you think I've got?"

Mike recoiled. He thought about it. "It's not really fair to
you, is it?"

"Not a fuckin' bit, Prince. But you know what? I like me.
I like what I am. I'm proud to be TJ's son. I'm tough.
People point at me behind my back like they used to when
we were children and they would whisper. I know what
they're saying. But none can stay in the ring with me. And
now that I am old enough, I have some power. I am assured
of wealth and want for nothing. I just have to be ready to
die."

"Me, too, Gil."

Gil studied Mike. "There's that between us, isn't there?
We're both sitting here waiting for TJ to die so we can climb
some mountains and die ourselves. Ain't that a dumb fuckin'
system?"

Mike nodded, although he knew there was a little bit
more to the Trek than that. He suspected, depending on
circumstances, that meeting the Webbines and receiving the
crimson sapphire was more than simple ceremony. "The
system is so dumb, I haven't decided if I will go yet."

"If? You are a bigger fool than you claim to be. You got to earn your position in life, halfbrother. I've learned that the hard way. Maybe the system ain't so dumb. Maybe father will figger a way around it, what with this Federation thing. Is that what you're counting on?"

"No." Mike's mind went off on a tangent. Gil complained that he wasn't a legitimate prince, living the life of royalty in the palace. But he didn't have to live with TJ Shepherd. Gil hadn't seen a court room in Nihaoma littered with corpses. He didn't see his father slashing into dead corpses in Dawn's Edge. He didn't have to stand with his father on execution day and tell the executioner to kill people and stand there and watch it done. Nor did Gil have to put up with the King running every facet of his life, threatening him and cajoling him and goading him. . . .

His anger mounted.

Fury blinded him. Franco Valdez blocked the foot of the stairs in a smoky tavern. Mike's cloak dripped from a sudden rain,

"Is Kellen up there or not, Valdez?"

"Well, uh, he's, uh, kinda busy, Mike, you know?"

"Prince Michale to you," Mike snapped and did not register any of his normal regret when he caught himself acting haughty. "Out of my way."

Valdez' eyes went wide. "Sir, Kellen doesn't want to be disturbed."

Mike grasped Franco's shoulder with a grip learned from Gil and applied pressure. Pain leaped across Valdez' face and his head jerked as Mike moved him aside. Mike brushed past him and took the steps two at a time.

He slammed the door open and surveyed those in the room. Mike recognized an ex-attorney, two padres, and didn't know the four others.

Kellen rose. "Mike? What is it? We'll be through in a little while and I'll come down and talk to you. Franco should have told you."

Mike saw that he'd interrupted some sort of planning session. He realized that neither Kellen nor any of these men took him seriously. Was that his problem? No one except Kellen had risen on his entry. Suddenly, he didn't like any of these people. His anger rose. He shook rain off his cloak unmindful that it wet two men nearby.

"Everybody out, I want to talk with you, Kellen." His voice cracked with anger.

All looked to Kellen for instructions.

"I didn't say later, I said *now*." Mike put some of the famous Shepherd fire into his voice.

The men stood uncertainly and Mike grabbed a padre as he had grasped Franco Valdez and pushed him toward the door. The others quickly followed.

"What's wrong, Mike?" Kellen said, closing the door. Kellen's eyes seemed to grow larger and his gaze bore down on Mike. He recoiled slightly and went back to his seat an uncertain man.

"Kellen, I have to know your plans."

"Why?"

"My father gave me an ultimatum to give you. Quit all this or else. I have to know what you plan so that I can assure myself you will not physically harm the kingdom." That didn't sound right, but Kellen got the message. "I need to be certain you aren't going to become any more violent, that you aren't going to get innocent people involved. I need some assurances, Kellen."

"You have them, Mike. Just more of the same." His voice rang false to Mike and he could tell Kellen was trying to appeal to him in that special way of his. His anger was like a wall between them.

"And those men in here? You need them for peaceful demonstrations?"

"Well, you know, the movement needs allies, and. . ."

Kellen kept talking, voice soothing. But Mike realized that all he'd even been was an ally, one who was an information source in the palace. He saw confidence returning to Kellen's face. He knew Kellen thought he was swaying him with his persuasive talent. Mike was surprised by the clarity of his own thoughts.

Kellen's been using me, he thought. And the strange thing is that I still believe in most of what Kellen stands for. But does Kellen?

"Kellen," he interrupted. "Do something for me. Get rid of those padres and lawyers and eco-freaks. Go back to the park by yourself. You don't need them. Back to the old days. Do it for yourself and for me, your friend."

Kellen looked speculatively at him. "I can't," he whispered and Mike wondered at the compulsion to tell the truth. He could have lied. Was his own anger so strong now? Or did Kellen realize Mike was really his friend?

A change appeared to take place in Kellen and for the first time Mike was aware that Kellen's anger was building, too. "Join me, Mike." Kellen sounded like he had gravel in his throat he was so serious.

"No, Kellen, you join me. Let us make history. Let us use compromise, diplomacy, love, and kindness."

"No. I am my own man."

Mike saw that he himself was the man he had thought Kellen originally was. And he could do nothing about it. The whole thing was more frustrating than anything in his life had been. He put his hand on Kellen's shoulders. "You have my father's warning. You are still my friend. If you need help, send Franco or Rebecca. I'll do what I can. I don't abandon friends."

"Friends, shit. Get out of my sight, Shepherd. And stay away from Rebecca."

Mike had to restrain himself from striking Kellen. "No."

"You have taken my mother and my father. Will you take my sister from me also?" Kellen spat at him, the globule landing on his shoulder. "I'd rather see her rut in the street with whores than be with you."

Mike reached out and grabbed Kellen's shirt into a bunch and lifted him off his feet and brought their faces close together. He was surprised how easy it was. "Don't talk like that, Kellen. Rebecca is special. You shall not interfere, understand?"

Kellen seemed to lose all his composure. "Franco!" he screamed.

Mike shoved Kellen away roughly. How could he have been so wrong about Kellen?

Am I the only man of civilized principle in the world?

He was no closer to the answer when he rode into the palace stables. His anger and frustration had grown so that he had a difficult time controlling them.

He was just in time to see Summer Camp and Rebecca Sing riding off.

"I thought Rebecca was mad at Summer," he mumbled aloud.

He figured that made him a three-time loser today. He considered getting drunk, but decided to break the good news to his father. At least that would give him some pleasure. Tell the king that Kellen was probably going to escalate his activities. Father would die of apoplexy.

He ran through the royal family's entrance and up ramps to his parents' suite. He found them together, just emerging from a steaming bath. He looked at them as if he'd never seen them before. His mother seemed older than he recalled her being, smile marks from the corners of her mouth up her cheeks etched deeper than ever. She wore a towel wrapped around her like a toga. His father showed signs of strain about his face, even where his beard couldn't hide them. His shoulders and arms and torso still rippled with tremendous strength—Mike knew he could never match the man in those terms. His father was wrapping a towel about his waist. Had they both changed so much? Or had he?

"Mike," his mother said.

"Mick," his father said.

"Stop calling me that!"

He followed them into a sitting room and accepted the sour mash his father poured for all three of them. Ordinarily, his mother drank only wine.

"Father," he blurted, "how can you sit here and drink while the city is burning down?"

TJ sat on a lounge. "You exaggerate to make a point. What is it?"

Mike had a difficult time justifying to himself why he had approached the subject thusly.

"What would you have me do, Mick, slaughter people?"

"No. Stop the violence. Use force."

"*You* say that? Prince Michale, the well known pacifist?"

"Innocent people suffer."

"And perhaps these innocent people will tire of this foolishness and take action to prevent it from happening."

Mike understood. The violence was affecting innocent people, and his father was looking for a backlash against Kellen Sing and those who caused trouble in his name. If the King took military action against the dissidents, then he, too, would lose. The publicity and backlash would be directed at him. He would be retreating from his avowed "open government" to an oppressive regime. And he might lose points with Sharon. Which all led Mike to the inevitable conclusion. "You must give it up, father, this crazy obsession of yours to join the Federation."

Gwen was still standing and glanced at Mike. When he

tried to meet her gaze, she averted her eyes and turned to pour herself another sour mash.

"Isn't it obvious," Mike continued in the face of TJ's silence, "that these people are not yet ready?"

"*I* am ready, and that's all that counts."

"For more power. That's all you care about, father. Don't the dead and injured have a place in your feelings? Don't you feel responsible for what's going on out there?"

"Certainly, and I was responsible for tens of thousands of dead people during the Consolidation—yet that paid off, too." He drained his drink. "Besides, I've shown 'em the way, now, and they must take the first step themselves."

"Horseshit!" Mike surprised himself with his own vehemence. "I gave Kellen your message and he told me to go to hell and that he'd send a stronger message later."

"Oh?" TJ's eyebrows shot up.

"And it appears to me that he has more high-powered allies than ever before."

His father nodded knowingly. "That confirms some reports."

"Why can't we all share a common goal?" he pleaded. "I just don't understand." Some of his bitterness at Kellen overflowed again. "I don't understand why my father either ignites the whole mess or stands idly by and watches it all crumble. What's to be gained in either case?"

"Mick, a lot of times my hands are tied." His father looked tired, as if he hadn't had any rest in months.

"Oh?" His voice held disgust. "Are you sparing Kellen because his sister is running around with your real son, Summer Camp?"

Without sensing the motion, Mike found his father's fist stopping a finger's breadth from his mouth. He hadn't even seen him rise.

"Thomas!" Gwen said in her voice that was calculated to show displeasure.

TJ put his finger in front of Mike's eyes. "I'll tell you one goddamn thing, son, I've been on Summer's ass a lot more that I've been on yours about this whole Kellen Sing thing. It's time you grew up and saw how the beefaloe eats the cabbage."

"Horseshit." Mike didn't believe it.

"Watch your mouth in front of your mother, boy."

"Words of wisdom from the Profane King," Mike shot out. TJ never followed any of the rules he laid down.

"Hold on, you two," Gwen interrupted. "I do not wish to

be in the middle of this argument. Nor do I wish to be placed in a position of choosing between you. Mike, you know how I would choose and I fear losing you."

Mother! his mind screamed. Not you, too! Of them all, you always stood by me. The one person I could always count on. Don't turn against me and side with that brutal tyrant.

TJ tried to calm him. "Look, son, I've gone over every possiblity, and the current route we're taking seems the best for now."

Mike was now in control of himself, an icy inner calm smothering all emotions. "There is one alternative you've overlooked, father."

"No. None."

"Me," Mike went on as if lecturing.

From the look of horror upon her face, Mike saw that his mother knew immediately.

"In what respect?" TJ asked, still not understanding. He looked sharply at Gwen as she dropped her glass unnoticed.

"The Trek, father, I shall take the Trek."

TJ had been leaning forward. Now he stood back, sat down, slumped against a cushion. "You're crazy."

"No. I am sane. Everyone else is crazy. And that, in itself, is crazy."

"You'll never live through it, Mick. Your training isn't complete." His words turned brutal. "You are neither skilled enough, nor tough enough."

"I'm going."

"No," cried Gwen weakly, face pallid with shock.

His father looked like he always did when he got tricky. "You know, Mick, that when the word gets out that you're on your way, all the kinglets will bust a gut to catch you and return first with a crimson sapphire."

"And I suppose you favor Gil?"

"No. Listen, you. For too many years too many Shepherds have been dying for Crimson Sapphire and now for Bear Ridge. That is one goddamn tradition that is fact. I intend for Shepherds to rule for a long time."

Selfish power, Mike said to himself. "Let your bastards come, father. I don't care." Blood was pounding through his head faster than he could handle, making it difficult to think properly. Yet his resolve remained.

Gwen sank down on the floor, her face in her hands.

TJ's words came to him so low he had to strain to hear

them. "When you return, assuming you do, you will have a real live king to face. What are your intentions?"

"I shall challenge you. The situation is not without precedent."

His mother sobbed. Ordinarily, it would have torn at his heart. But not today, not after all this.

TJ was looking at Gwen with a combination of fondness and grief. He rose, stepped to her, lifted her, and laid her on the couch. Then he went to the counter and made himself another drink. He held the bottle up to Mike who declined with a shake of his head.

"Mike," his father said pointedly after glancing at Gwen again. "I've decided to do away with the Trek. Put my personal prestige on the line. Be a plus with Sharon Gold. We get in the Fed, we'll have air transport and the Trek will be history, anyway. You just be patient and stall a bit longer."

And lose my chance? Now that I'm committed? After all the indecision about taking the Trek or not. Nope. "I shall go. It's the only solution."

He saw a new respect dawn in his father's eyes. TJ finally realized that he wasn't just taking the Trek for his own benefit, to grab power for himself—but to stand for his principles, to gamble his own life for his beliefs and hopes for the people of the world.

"Goodbye, father," he said quickly. "I shall return with my gem." He moved to the couch where his mother was watching him intently beneath her wrist which lay across her forehead. He reached down and touched her hair, said nothing, turned, and walked out.

On the way to his quarters, he sent a servant to the royal chef with orders to prepare field rations, with plenty of jerky, and to do so immediately. Another servant was dispatched to the hostler to prepare a mount, a spare, and a pack mule for the rations and equipment.

He knew how much different equipment and food he would need, but also knew from reading the Trekmaster's Log that he would not be able to carry much up the ridges.

In his apartments, he quickly got his sword, crossbow, knives, gloves, leather boots, and traveling clothes.

Finished, he stormed through the halls to the royal family's entrance, scattering people.

Before he knew it, he'd bounced off Sharon Gold, knocking her to the floor.

"Mike! What's wrong?"

He helped her to her feet. "I'm leaving."

He could tell she knew instinctively. "The Trek?"

"Yes."

"Your father?" Her question was more solicitous than he would have liked.

"He is well."

"Oh."

"Yeah."

She grabbed his arm as he started off again. "Mike. Don't go. You've been through too much already. This world is changing. Perhaps soon there will be a new society here, one in which this Trek won't be necessary."

"No. That's the point, Sharon. It is necessary and it's necessary right now."

"I see." She wouldn't meet his eyes. He resumed walking and she kept hold of his arm. She whispered, after looking around to see if anyone could hear her. "I have a weapon, an energy weapon, you could take with you . . ."

"No."

"All right." She seemed to accept his decision, both of them. "Be careful, please?"

"I will."

Her eyes were cloudy and he couldn't interpret her expression. "Fortune be with you, Mike Shepherd."

He smiled, more to the world than to her, for he was a man with the weight of the world off his shoulders for the first time in a long, long time. He exuded confidence, a trick he'd somehow learned from Kellen Sing. For now, he was in total command of his own situation and others around him.

The hostler and his helpers had seen Mike waiting and led two horses and a mule out. Kitchen servants were tying the rations onto the mule. Mike noted the hostler had put his traveling kit aboard. He handed the hostler his weapons to secure.

Sharon was still standing beside him as if she couldn't decide what to do.

As the hostler tightened the last cinch, Summer Camp and Rebecca Sing rode up in a clatter of hooves and laughter.

Rebecca saw him first. "Hi, Mike!"

Summer pulled to a stop and stared at him speculatively.

To Rebecca, Mike said, "I thought you and Summer had a big fight. Did you make up already?"

Rebecca colored and made to get down. "We did . . . but you assume a relationship," she said and he stepped forward to help her off her horse. "I can dismount myself," she snapped. "Anyway, I'll ride with whomever I please."

Mike glanced guiltily at Sharon who was staring at him.

Summer crooked a leg over his saddle horn and calmly asked, "Going for a trip, Mike?" Damn that Camp, always in command, always in control.

"Yeah."

"It finally blew up, didn't it?" Summer asked. Without waiting for an answer, he continued, "Somehow, I always thought this is the way it would end." He looked truly sorry.

Rebecca's face fell and uncertainty replaced anger. "What is it?"

Sharon was looking at Summer who was dressed like a nondescript civilian rider. "Mike is going to take the Trek."

Rebecca's hand went to her mouth to cover the sudden intake of breath. Her eyes wildly sought his for confirmation. He nodded.

"Mike," Summer's voice was urgent, compelling. "You check with the boss on this? I have to know."

Mike nodded. Summer had guessed right and wasn't concerned that TJ was dead, the only other reason Mike could be taking the Trek.

Summer slid lightly to the ground. Rebecca stood back next to Sharon and they seemed to lean against each other.

Quietly, Summer said, "If you would continue this foolishness, how about if I ride along with you?"

"No." Mike found that he was controlling his sustained rage rather well. He wanted to shout at Summer that he was so much like TJ. but . . .

"Listen, then," Summer whispered hoarsely, "did TJ brief you?"

What did Summer mean? "I didn't give him a chance."

"Okay," Summer's voice was still low, but Mike saw Rebecca and Sharon edge forward to listen, too. "From Dawn's Edge, get a vaquero to show you the trail to Teddy Bear Ridge where the Finger of God is. Climb the ridge just to the south of the Finger of God. When you get to Devil's Dip Gorge, beware of packs of snarves and volves in the gorge and somewhat up Big Bear Ridge. The midsection of Big Bear Ridge is combed with natural gas outlets. Beware. Above there, the weather is horrible. Cold, winds, snow, hail, you name it. Be prepared with clothing. Kneepads can be made from snarv skins, and they are better than those made from volves or slinkers. Don't worry about carrying water—rain and snow and ice will suffice. Don't pass up birds' nests and slinker holes. You can survive if you think everything through. At Dawn's Edge, get plenty of rope. Wrap it around you, it will provide some protection. And you will need all you can carry." Summer paused. "And opposite the Finger of God on Big Bear Ridge is a peak appropriately named Forty-K. Make for the south shoulder and you will find passages cutting through the saddle of the shoulder."

"How do you know all this?" Mike demanded. All three were looking at Summer.

He shrugged, hesitated, and said, "TJ told me."

"I don't believe it."

"Well some of it anyway. But that's not your concern now, Mike. Remember what I've told you."

"I will." Mike wondered if any other taking the Trek had gotten advance information. But then, why else was he always in training? He laughed and seemed to frighten Rebecca and Sharon.

He swung onto his mount and tied the reins of the spare to his saddle horn. The mule was already tied to the spare horse.

He surveyed the three standing below, eyes sweeping them, beaming his newfound confidence. He raised his right hand and pointed between Summer's eyes. "Keep the kingdom safe, Summer Camp, for I might have need of it on my return."

He kicked his horse into motion and began the Trek.

42: TJ

Thomas Jefferson Shepherd didn't know what to think. His son had gone off on the Trek, probably to his death; however, his son had finally made him proud by taking that very same action.

Summer came into his office, interrupting his thoughts.

"Sorry I'm late, boss, but I've been out counting the number of kinglets riding out of Crimson Sapphire. The number of eligible young men here has drastically fallen."

I don't need reminding, TJ thought. "Oh?" he said.

"You know what amazes me?" Summer asked.

"What?"

"We don't even have electronic communications yet—if we ever will—and yet the word gets out. The entire city is buzzing with it." He hesitated.

"And?" TJ prompted.

"And the specualtion is that because of your current troubles, Mike is going to challenge you for the throne. It's the only conclusion that makes any sense to them."

"We'll see, then. What do the oddsmakers say?"

Summer looked at the floor. "The smart money is on Gil Trevan. A hundred to one."

TJ sighed, releasing tension. "No need to be embarrassed. Gil is my son, too."

"One to be proud of," Summer said.

"You are coming close to patronizing me, Summer."

Summer lifted his head and looked TJ straight in the eye. "How am I supposed to address a friend who will probably never see any of his sons again?"

TJ slumped back. "That is something I'm finding very difficult to reconcile. I don't know if I can overcome it." He tugged at his beard. "You know, I was so angry last night I didn't even think of it. But this morning I realized that Mike and his actions have precipitated all those young men out to die. And I share responsiblity." And all the mothers who will cry for lost sons, he added silently, who will comfort them? Some ancient traditions which says the sons of the king shall try to climb mountains and die?

Summer raised his eyebrows.

TJ lifted a hand. "Enough. I've been responsible before, and my actions daily are life and death to somebody. Now it's struck home, right in my own family. I'll deal with it myself in my own way and in my own time." He saw he'd hurt Summer and tried to smile his way out of it unsuccessfully. Summer would understand. "What are the odds on Mike?"

"Two hundred to one."

"Fools know nothing of the Trek. I would increase the odds on both Gil and Mike."

"The rest are an even one thousand to one," Summer said. "The two girls that went are fifteen hundred to one. They don't want to discourage betting."

"If the others have any sense they'll go out into the plains for a couple of weeks and break a leg or an arm and return heroes," TJ grumbled. "Alive."

"Ah, TJ. There is more. No oddsmakers will accept bets on Mike to win a challenge should he return with a crimson sapphire."

"Smart. But it is a cloudy issue. What will Mike do?"

Summer shrugged.

"Well, I can deal with it at the time," TJ said. But could he, really?

"Suppose, TJ, Gil is the one. What will *he* do?"

"Valid question. My opinion? Gil will do nothing. He will walk down the aisle of the royal court, swear fealty to me, and wait for me to die before he ascends the throne. He is strong and street smart, which sets him above most of the others. He'd have nothing to gain by challenging me." An idea had been bubbling within him since Mike had left. "Look, Summer. There's nothing that says Mike can't have a little under-the-table help . . ."

Summer dropped onto the couch. "I already tried, TJ. I knew you'd approve if I went with him. He would have nothing to do with it."

Damn. "He's probably too far away now to catch up to?"

"That's about it."

"Mike intimated that Kellen Sing is going to escalate. And I'm not convinced that there is a growing backlash against him. He seems to win people over, not alienate them. What I'd like you to do is a little snooping, find out if what Mike said is true, the extent of it, whatever you can."

"And then?"

"Give me your recommendation as to what you think I ought to do." TJ was aware that he had given a deadline sometime recently, but would ignore it depending on what Summer suggested.

"Sure thing. Might even run into a lady friend."

"Ah, there's that." TJ forced a smile. "I don't need you this morning. You can go ahead and do those things."

After Summer left, TJ thought about Summer. Had the possible romance between Summer and Rebecca Sing generated jealously in Mike? He remembered his younger days. Young men would do more for women that they would for their nations. Ain't love wonderful? Of course, sex is genetic, patriotism isn't. Uh, oh. Write that down. Another TJ-ism. Wonder if there is a competition between Summer and Mike for Rebecca Sing? Both seem to like her and seek her out.

Is my loyalty to Summer and Mike keeping me from imprisoning their girlfriend's brother? If so, it ain't like me. But right now I don't wish to examine anything in my inner soul. I might not like what I find. How am I going to face Gwen? I've thought about how I feel. *I* have more than one child, one offspring. Gwen has only one, and that one I've somehow pressured into taking the Trek which is the same thing as a death sentence. And Gwen knows it. She hasn't spoken two words since Mike left. But her loyalty to Crimson Sapphire and the kingdom hasn't wavered. Though the dam may be cracking, if this morning was any indication. I'd bet she'd trade the Federation and the kingdom for the well-being of her child. Both Gwen and Felicia were in seclusion today. Well, he had to put on the Shepherd front of business as usual. All three were prisoners of pride and habit, he reflected.

If Mike returned, what would his reaction be? Would he claim the throne immediately and thus cause a father-son battle to the death? Maybe I could just abdicate in favor of Mike, he thought. Save face all around. But how about the Federation?

For once TJ was at a loss to plan ahead. He suspected that Mike wouldn't be a bad king at all—if his kingdom were happy with few dissident elements and with its economy rolling. And if he scrubbed some of those idealistic ideas out of his mind . . . .

The knock on the door was sharp, crisp, military.

TJ groaned. "Come in, Manny."

Manny Vero entered with an armful of papers and maps. "Sire, I have the final plans for the exercise for Ambassador Gold's review."

TJ saw that Manny was going out of his way to be proper, not mentioning Mike's seeming defection. Typical of Manny to react that way.

"You drew up the plans yourself?"

"Yes, Sire."

"Well, let's look at them." TJ knew he wouldn't make any changes in Vero's plans. After all, the exercise was a test of Vero's leadership and planning potential.

To meet Federation entrance requirements, there had to be an on-site evaluation of a planet's military. In this case it was the army. The purpose of the evaluation was to gauge the strength, the effectiveness, officers' abilities, strategic and tactical capabilities, organization, and all the other military managerial terms. The objective and subjective information would be fed into the Federation's computers. Should a general Fed conscription be necessary, each planet would be required to furnish whatever the computers determined was a proper share. Also, it gave the Fed bureaucrats some idea of what they had to plan as far as transition training, from the swords and crossbows of Bear Ridge to energy weapons. At least this was their public reasoning, TJ knew. But it was more subtle than that: If the Federation itself did the arming and training, they would be able to establish more control than if he himself armed and trained his own soldiers in modern warfare techniques and equipment. Training his Bear Ridge army would surprise a lot of Fed officials!

Another reason for the evaluation was that each member planet had certain quotas to fill in the Federation Navy, and the Fedcentral administrative bureaucracy. This insured no one people could take control of the Federation.

The location of the maneuvers had been selected: the Plains of Burial, three weeks ride south of Crimson Sapphire where many battles had been fought, and only a short ride from where the battle that gave rise to the Muster occurred. Since Crimson Sapphire was not centrally located upon the continent, they'd selected the Plains of Burial because it was easier to reach for the scattered elements of the army. TJ had assigned units of his army to the different ethnarchs, figuring if rebellion happened, it would be easier to put down an uprising than to defend Crimson Sapphire with a larger army. And in most ethnarchies, the army served the police function.

So the army in Crimson Sapphire would join its counterparts in the south, leaving the Gyrenes as the only military units at the capital.

TJ knew thus was Tirano's military evaluated on Two Tongues, and thus would his own be.

43: MIKE

Dawn's Edge was a blurred memory as he scrambled up a steep slope on his hands and feet. At least he didn't have to climb right now—but the awkward effort gave him severe lower-back pains. He reached a mostly-buried boulder and thankfully sat on it. He sipped from his water bladder conservatively and surveyed the distance he'd come. He groaned. Only about a third of the way up the western slope of Teddy Bear Ridge and it seemed like he'd lived his whole life on the damn thing. Sorry, mother, I know "seems like" should be "seems."

The sun cast the shadow of the Finger of God down upon the valley where he'd left his horses and mule. Even in the clear mountain air, things down there were no longer in sharp focus. He chewed on some jerky.

The serenity of his surroundings made him forget; it took a conscious effort to retrieve the anger that had kept him going. Solitude, distance, the draining physical effort had all conspired to leach away the burning anger that was his fuel.

But he felt surprisingly fine, astounded that his body was peaking, coping well with the energy output. In fact, he never felt better. He hoped it wasn't a false feeling.

By nightfall, he had still not reached the top of Teddy Bear Ridge. As he climbed through great slabs of rock, he realized a new respect for his father and the previous Trekmasters. With little trouble so far, he was confident he could take his place alongside them.

Then, while nestling into a hollow for the night, he disturbed a stingbee nest. As soon as his knee broke through the light, clay crust of the innocuous looking rock, and he heard the deadly humming of their wings, he knew.

Chased by the fist-sized insects, he scrambled and slid down through rock slabs that dwarfed him. He hated retracing his steps, but downward was the fastest way of escaping the enraged stingbees. Somehow one stung him on the left thigh through his clothing before they gave up chasing him. Be-

271

fore he found an alternative place to spend the night, the wound had swollen to a knot every bit as large as the stingbee itself.

He shifted his legs to ease the pain. Why had he gone off half-ready? He could've waited until Fed membership and flown over these goddamn mountains. If Fed membership, he amended. He found himself always saying if, just like his father and mother—probably playing to some atavistic superstition. On reviewing his motives, he knew that he had to complete the Trek legitimately, and do so now. His sense of purpose remained strong.

Another thought struck him: his mother. A fine son he was to do this thing to her. Chewing on the jerky he already hated, he hoped she would understand.

As if to test him, a rainstorm blew up and pelted him through most of the night. He nursed his anger to keep himself warm.

At the first sign of light in the morning, he was off again. He spent two hours moving laterally to avoid a sheer rock face. As he traveled slowly, one foothold and one handhold at a time, he kept wondering why he was doing what he was doing.

She would understand.

She. She had been with Summer, riding and looking full of fun. Yet she had shown shock and worry when she realized he was taking the Trek. He'd detected sadness and perhaps tears in her eyes. Was it empathy? Understanding? Genuine concern? He didn't know. He leaped a slim crevice and found a series of rock formations leading upward. He followed.

Sharon had understood, had even been supportive. Of course, she was probably doing so out of a vicarious pleasure for when he returned and told her about the Webbines. He resolved to tell her everything he could remember—unlike his father who refused to discuss them.

At midafternoon, he was perhaps an hour below the top of Teddy Bear Ridge at this point, just before it rose to the slopes of the Finger of God a bit to the north.

Determined to gain the summit this day, he was lying back with closed eyes when a cascade of gravel roused him from his stupor.

Even surprised, he was slow to gain his senses.

Midway between him and the top of Teddy Bear Ridge, Gilbert Haynes Trevan dangled from an overhang by one arm. Rope was wrapped around his midsection, but he obviously disdained its use right now.

"Sorry to wake you, Mike," Gil shouted, "but my hand slipped." He laughed in the silence.

Mike watched with amazement as Gil reached his free arm over the lip of rock and easily swung himself up and out of sight. Mike doubted his own ability to climb that particular section and knew he'd have to find an alternative route.

"Gil," Mike screamed and a chimney somehow echoed his voice, "take the south slope of the peak Forty-K on the next ridge." Then he stopped and wondered what compulsion had made him call out his only advantage.

A faint sound answered him and he wasn't sure whether Gil had heard or not.

"Why did I give up my only advantage?" he wondered aloud. Then the strangeness of the coincidence struck him. With all the mountains and different trails to begin the Trek, how had Gil crossed his path?

When he thought about it, the answer was obvious. Gil had figured, and rightly so, that Mike had inside information on routes. So all Gil had done was to catch up with him anywhere between Crimson Sapphire and Dawn's Edge—or for that matter bribe someone who'd see Mike come through Dawn's Edge first. Then Gil had simply stayed out of sight and shadowed him.

But obviously, Gil had tired of Mike's pace, and decided to go ahead himself.

"That scoundrel." Mike smiled and appreciated Gil's resourcefulness.

He felt an urge to jump up and continue hastily, to keep Gil in sight, and beat him. But a voice from his training came to him. Summer'd said, "A battle does not make a war. Sometimes it is necessary to not rush into battle. Fresh troops, fed and rested, are worth more than time. A soldier knows to eat and sleep when he can."

Resigned, Mike settled back and took a sip of water and treated himself to an amaranth cake. It made him feel enormously better. He suspected the fact that he wasn't alone on the mountain also contributed to his cheerfulness.

In a few minutes, he rubbed the knot on his thigh, realized it was going down, and rose to resume his climb.

Even paralleling the top of the ridge to the south for a while, he managed to reach the top in a relatively short time.

The late afternoon showed clouds settling into Devil's Dip Gorge. He looked back toward the west and could see a long way onto the plains. He realized that one day the plains would throng with people and was sad at a loss he couldn't specifically identify.

Finally, he got the courage to look directly to the east across the gorge from his position. He raised his head, neck stretching, as his eyes followed the height of Forty-K.

"My Lord, what have I done?" He felt like a child and wanted to sit down and cry.

Big Bear Ridge, not to mention Forty-K, was there. A solid wall across the face of the world. He generously estimated that where he stood atop Teddy Bear Ridge, his position was approximately halfway up Big Bear Ridge, maybe only a third.

The enormity of his task overwhelmed him and he sank to his knees.

"What *have* I done?"

He realized if he hadn't stormed out of the palace intent on his own problems and not thinking about the difficulties of the Trek, he could have queried his father on routes and dangers. Summer's hurried instructions had been helpful, but he now would have preferred the details he knew his father would give him—even though he'd vowed to return and challenge his father. Again he wondered how Summer had known what to tell him.

Unbidden to his mind came words TJ had told him at least a thousand times, in the same monotonous voice: "Don't forget the Seven P Principle: proper prior planning prevents piss poor performance."

There was one thing he could do: he could follow Gil now, knowing Gil would select the quickest and safest route and perhaps save Mike some time.

He hurried to the north to where he estimated Gil must have climbed over. The crest of Teddy Bear Ridge was better going than the western slope. Part of the way was open and flat, not like the mountain top scene he'd pictured. Once or twice, spires went up and he had to climb around them, but soon he found scuff marks in some gravel which the wind had not yet had time to smooth. Carefully, he scanned the slope downward into the gorge, but could not find Gil. That evening was coming soon caused shadows that seemed to move. Then he saw a ledge that ran across the steep eastern face of Teddy Bear Ridge and he knew that would be a good target for Gil—and himself—to spend the night on. He didn't want to be atop the ridge at nightfall. He had to lean into the wind now as it was.

Perhaps he could spot Gil in the morning light.

The ledge below, he estimated, was about half the length of his rope, maybe less. He anticipated climbing down to be easier since he could use his rope to much better effect. Soon he found a compliant boulder, looped his rope around it, and walked down to the ledge. He cast loose one end of the rope and pulled it through until it fell past him into the chasm below.

It was his first experience with vertigo and acrophobia. He was winding his rope between hand and elbow when it snaked past him. As it bottomed out, it seemed to tug him to the lip of the ledge and he inadvertently followed its length with his eyes. He couldn't find the end which disappeared into the shadows, but the bottom of the gorge wasn't visible and his throat closed and dizziness overcame him.

He staggered back on the ledge and jammed himself against the rock wall. He slid to a sitting position. It took him until dark to regain the strength to pull the remainder of the rope back to the ledge.

Exhaustion put him to sleep and in the morning he climbed down an hour before he took the time to eat. He had to wait a while for the sun to come closer overhead to light the farther depths of the gorge.

Once he thought he saw movement and supposed it might be Gil, but wasn't certain.

His hands were developing calluses and he was glad he'd worn his leather climbing boots. He learned quickly that his feet were the most important part of his body now.

The ease of descent made him careless. It had taken so long to climb the other side, he seemed to by flying down this side. Find a sturdy point to loop his rope around, insure there was somewhere within the length of half of the rope to land, and drop down.

Once, he thought he could climb down without the rope, and fell three body lengths before catching himself on a jutting rock. The collision knocked the wind out of him and it was then he knew absolutely that he was in a life and death struggle. After that, he used his rope more often.

By noon the next day, he had not yet descended to the floor of the gorge between the two ridges and knew he was in trouble.

Blood seeped from a cheek wound where he had hugged a cliff face even using his teeth to retain his purchase. He had either a broken rib or a tremendous bruise on his right side. He squeezed his eyes closed to shut out the pain but that didn't work. He wondered where Gil was and that gave him some energy. Why hadn't Gil offered to help him? Perhaps together they could have made it easier—and in the process forged a new alliance with which to rule the kingdom.

He fell asleep on a ledge a rope's length above the floor of the gorge, his last common sense telling him that it was safer here. Hadn't Summer said something about volves and snarves?

At noon, he was wakened by a pack of mewling monkey-birds. The furry little creatures scuttled above him on the rockface and he dodged their defecations.

In no time, he was standing on the solid ground of Devil's Dip Gorge. He estimated that the bottom of the gorge received no more than three or four hours of direct sunlight.

While there were trees, they seemed slim, and extremely tall. The branches were wider than seemed possible. The brush was scruffy and much of it wasn't leafy. Sunlight determined the vegetation here.

He wandered aimlessly toward the base of the far ridge. It was farther than he would have thought. When he emerged, hours later, from the brush, Big Bear Ridge towered over him like eternity.

He groaned.

Teddy Bear Ridge seemed a child's tree house compared to this monster.

Suddenly, he shouted, "Gil! Gil!"

He listened to the whine of the wind through the gorge.

The answering silence was broken by the howl of volves.

Between him and the foothills at the base of Big Bear Ridge were patches of dried grass reaching to his knees. Quickly he wound some of the grass around a stick for a torch. Then he gathered several armfuls and stacked them in front of a cave which had been dug out of a steep hill by water runoff. If the volves found him, he was prepared.

He heard them in the distance. Did they smell his scent? He couldn't tell if this were possible since the wind was swirling swiftly from random directions. Surely this would confound the volves.

Their howls faded eventually. Mike knew he was temporarily safe when a small herd of snobbi, the goatlike herbivore, appeared at the edge of the brush and began digging for the roots of live grass.

Right then, Mike wished he had brought a long bow or crossbow. But he'd decided that the awkwardness and weight would be worse than the possible benefits of carrying them, so he'd cached them with his packs where he'd left his mounts. He was pretty good with a sling. Soon he had several rocks and was whirling his sling around his head.

He launched two rocks before they figured out what was happening. Only one of the missiles landed, and that cracked against the leg of one of the snobbis. The herd broke back into the brush, the wounded one limping heavily.

Mike ran after it, following it by the sound of its blundering passage through the brush. In a few moments, the snobbi broke alone into a clearing and staggered across, followed closely by Mike. Mike was amazed at the speed of the animal which was barely using its left front leg. But he reveled in the glory of running, of stretching his legs after so many days of riding and cramped climbing. His ribs pained less than he would have thought. Soon he caught the creature and killed it with his short sword, hanging it to bleed before gutting and cleaning it. He determined to use the hide.

He worked quickly, concerned that the odor of blood would attract predators.

He covered the entrails and bloody ground with sand, and hurried toward the foothills again. When he emerged from the thicket, he thought he smelled smoke.

Gil? Another of his half brothers?

He followed his nose during a lull in the wind and found a sand-doused fire at the base of a hill.

Gil.

Gil had done what he himself planned. Yet Gil had come and gone already. Bones and bits of hide indicated Gil had slaughtered a volv or two, and maybe a snarv. Scavengers had cleaned up the remains.

Mike marked the location in his mind, assuming Gil had begun ascending Big Bear Ridge at that point. Then he returned to the makeshift camp he'd established earlier. He cut thorny brush and circled his hiding hole with it, confident it would discourage even the meanest snarv or volv pack. To be absolutely certain, though, he stacked piles of dried grass around, too, that he could ignite for protection.

Back against the hill, and under an overhang, he built a

fire and cooked a snobbi haunch. He'd smoke the rest of the meat to carry with him.

While the meat cooked, he found a stream, bathed as long as he dared, filled his water bladder, and returned to his camp. He gathered more wood, determined to have a fire all night.

He grinned at the things he now considered luxuries. If Sharon could only see him now!

At dark, he built his fire high and stood looking up at Big Bear Ridge. His fire was a calculated challenge to Gil. Gil would be able to see his fire from above and know that he had made it this far. The firelight served as a beacon, one which linked him with Gil in an odd camaraderie.

Good food and being clean made him jubilant. "Hell, I can finish the Trek, no sweat," he told the darkness.

Above him, far above him, he saw the wink of flame and thought it was Gil answering his fire until he remembered about the natural gas outlets.

He decided to stay here for a day or two, eat, rest, regain strength. He'd show Gil. Gil should have done the same. Poor judgment, Gil.

On the second day following, he began his ascent of Big Bear Ridge. He started where he estimated Gil had and was rewarded by sighting a cheshire and its young crouched in a tree on the initial slope. The cheshire tucked its young against her with her double tail. Mike waved cheerily at them, acknowledging their traditional good luck factor. He remembered Sharon liking his pet cheshire and determined to get her one which was young enough to be bonded to her.

Occasionally, he found chalk arrows indicating the route Gil had taken. The marks on rocks and walls began at a limestone outcropping where he estimated Gil must have been spending the night when he'd lighted his beacon fire.

So Gil was showing him the way he'd found. Why?

Did Gil share the same sense of camaraderie he had? Could Gil be paying him back for his shouted advice to try the southern shoulder of Forty-K? What was Gil's motive? Of course, they were brothers and Gil had contributed to his training for years now. Mike thought about it and finally guessed that even though on the surface Gil and he were competitors, they had shared too much.

As the days passed, Mike found at least two marked passages he could not negotiate and wondered if Gil were

testing him or . . . was the whole thing a challenge by Gil?
A contest within a contest?

He couldn't resolve it.

He continued to climb.

He found a long slope, one which would occupy him for a
day and save much time over the rocky terrain he was
following. Why hadn't Gil gone that way? He rested and
studied, and the movement which momentarily lifted his
spirits turned out to be snarves. He continued his way,
avoiding the easy slope.

Occasionally, he thought he'd lost Gil's trail, but choosing
the logical routes, he found other marks. On one of these
occasions, he found a human skeleton, clothes and flesh
gone. He was stepping toward it beneath a large formation
when he stopped and sniffed the air. Gas? The skeleton lay
crumpled unnaturally—if skeletons can be crumpled naturally, he amended—suggesting something other than violent
death. A rusting knife was partially concealed by a hip
bone.

Mike wondered how many such skeletons there were on
these mountains. He admitted what he was doing was pretty
stupid.

Then he realized that his anger was gone, that driving
force which had goaded him this far. Oh, he was still mad at
his father and fully intended to challenge him for the throne.
But the heat of anger had left him. He understood Kellen
and Rebecca and Summer. He even understood Thomas
Jefferson Shepherd; he didn't agree with TJ, but he thought
he understood. The kingdom still needs a new ruler, he
thought, one with compassion and foresight, one more concerned with the people than things out of the monarch's
control.

He thought all this through while huddling in some shale
in the shelter of an overhang avoiding the brunt of a
rainstorm.

"Okay, Mike Shepherd," he said, "if all that be the case
then why are you continuing this God-exempted Trek?"

He couldn't put it in words, but he knew his original
purpose remained. Also, he suspected, he was learning what
other Trekkers had learned: that the Trek takes on a life of
its own. It had become an overwhelming obstacle to be
conquered. Though he had thought it all along, now he
really knew it: he had the ability to complete the Trek. And
this wonderful fact buoyed him, amazed him. His pride

grew and his confidence skyrocketed. He knew exhilaration for the first time. An accomplishment to prove he was a man, a man of strength and endurance and especially will.

He vowed to be different. He knew that many Trekmasters before him had continued the beards they had grown on the Trek. He took his knife out and wet it in the rain and patiently scraped at his face. Good thing he'd brought a sharpening stone.

The following day he was climbing through a lava field when he realized he hadn't seen a mark from Gil lately. He stopped to look around and saw nothing. He wondered at the lava. Though each of the ridges seemed to have some lava, Teddy Bear Ridge had by far the larger amount. He wished he hadn't ignored the archeology professor. But he did wonder at the seemingly contradictory geological forma-tions: lava and rock, natural gas escaping from within a huge ridge where it had no real right to be. Sure, he could make a far-out guess why some of these things were here together on the ridges, but that wasn't the same thing as knowing.

Suddenly, he realized that his current position was higher than the crest of Teddy Bear Ridge. He was actually looking down upon it. And he realized that the haze he was seeing far to the south could be from an active volcano.

Where was Gil?

His now experienced eye told him that the immediate going ahead would be the most difficult yet. But it had to be done.

The next day he was making headway only slowly. Futility attacked him, the lack of progress contributing to it. His anger returned.

He gave the face of Big Bear Ridge the face of Thomas Jefferson (Shepherd) Rex. He refused to let the damn thing dominate him the way his father had dominated him. When that paled in significance, he began climbing over Kellen Sing's body, step by step. He was past Kellen's traitorous body and tossing his rope over TJ's chin again when he thought to give it all up. He sat down heavily on a wind-rounded stone and felt wetness beneath him. He looked down and saw blood dripping down the stone. His buttock had been pierced by some rock spear.

He sat on it for an hour to stop the bleeding. When it was time to go on, he pulled the last snobbi skin from his pack and cut knee and elbow pads. The hide hadn't cured, although he'd stretched it out every night. He knew the rock would scrape the remaining fat and squeeze the animal's oils out of the skin. He scraped some of the rancid fat off and smeared it on the wound of his buttock.

He chewed smoked snobbi wishing he had smoked it longer and wishing he had some ale and amaranth cakes.

He began climbing again. Does life consist only of climbing? Why am I doing this? Where are my dreams? I can think of only this face of Big Bear Ridge, nothing else. What happened to my purpose, to my dreams? I don't care about people, Crimson Sapphire, Bear Ridge, the Federation, nothing.

His whole world had shrunk to survival on the western side of the massive ridge.

Until he found Gil's markings again. And lost them again. And saw a flash of metal in the sunlight.

Stupidly, he looked at his hands and knees, not recognizing the bloody things as part of his own body. A flash of metal? Oh, yeah, over there. The steep slope, not a cliff face.

He made his way to that point, the last few minutes scrambling on all fours through loose rock. He slipped, losing two paces for each three he took. Another cliff face loomed over him and a sudden gust of wind blew sand in his eyes. He pawed them clean and scampered the last few feet, crouching on smoother rock.

A sword lay at his feet. A sword showing no signs of weathering. It simply lay there in the sand and rock. He didn't understand. It just lay there, like some war-sign outpost of civilization. The sign told him that there was more to his world than survival on the face of the ridge.

A cold wind chilled him.

He had seen that sword before.

On Gil.

He was suddenly very thirsty. Gusting thunderstorms had missed him recently and his water bladder was almost empty. He did not drink.

"Gil?" he whispered.

Nothing.

"Gil?" he said, voice cracking from disuse.

"Gil!" he was shouting now, screaming with the wind, against the wind, screaming through cupped hands. He took Gil's sword and banged it on the rock. The metallic clank might carry farther than his voice.

Then he heard it. A quirk of wind swirled about him and he heard the moan. He looked about, found nothing. He saw the cliff face in front of him had a fault in front of it, between the face and the rock slope. Cautiously, he leaned forward and saw that the fault came to a vee not far below— probably etched there by rain runoff.

Gil lay lodged there, at the bottom of the vee. Unconscious. Mike scrambled down the fault. Gil moaned again.

Kneeling at Gil's head, Mike held his water bladder to Gil's mouth. Gil swallowed automatically, thirstily. Mike smelled Gil's wastes. From all indications, Gil had been here at least a day, maybe two. Lying here in a coma or unconscious.

A cold dread climbed Mike's spine. Empathy for Gil wiped out the thought that it could be him lying here.

Then Mike saw the abnormal form in which Gil's torso was twisted. His legs were askew beneath him.

Gil's back was broken.

Mike could only stare stupidly. He wanted to say something, anything, but he couldn't.

He straightened Gil's legs out in front of him and sensed more than saw on his half brother's unshaven face an easing of tension.

Gil opened his eyes.

He croaked and Mike gave him some more water.

"Two days. Maybe a year. I've laid here. Christ."

Mike gave him more water, glancing involuntarily into the sky hoping for rain. But rain would have drowned Gil.

Perhaps that would have been better. He jerked his attention back to Gil. He pulled a piece of snobbi out of his pack and offered it to Gil.

Gil did not take it.

"Save it. Not hungry. Mike." He tried to move. "Thought I could climb that cliff."

It was then that Mike knew that Gil was paralyzed below the neck.

"Yeah. I can't move." Gil read his mind with a mad clarity. "Why the fuck do you think I ain't pulled out my knife and done the deed?"

"Oh."

"Now I know why I marked my passage." Gil coughed and his eyes closed.

Mike thought he had fallen back into unconsciousness. "*Why* did you do that thing?" he demanded.

Gil didn't answer, but Mike thought he knew the answer to his own question. A combination of companionship, loyalty, curiosity, fear of the unknown. A compulsion to share, between equals, the alien terrain. An acknowledgment that this was a separate world from the rest of Bear Ridge and a desire to share the experience. A lessening of competition due to respect for a brother and the brother's tenacity. Mike realized that everything in life couldn't be placed on two lists, good or bad, black or white. There was only gray.

He avoided thinking what he knew must come shortly by smoothing Gil's hair back off his forehead. "You were right tricky, Gil. Couple of times you almost fooled me."

Gil's mouth stretched into what he probably thought was a grin, but to Mike it was a grimace. "Knew you'd figger 'em out, old son. Coupla misdirects to keep you thinking."

Mike thought about crying, but couldn't. There were no tears in him—but he wanted them, he wanted them badly. Was this Trek making him inhuman? But he knew he cared, more than he ever cared before. What happened to all the answers I used to have? he wondered.

Gil's eyes opened again. "Let's see if you got what it takes to be King of Crimson Sapphire and Bear Ridge, Michale Shepherd."

The speech drained him and Mike gave him the last of his water.

"Stop stalling. You have no choice." Gil's voice rasped, grating on Mike's soul.

"No . . ." Mike began, but knew he had to do it.

"Swiftly, Mike, for the love of God. I feel no pain, only regret."

"You were the best of us, Gil . . ."

"Not any more. But you can make it, I know you can." He tried to roll his head, but it only shook a little.

Mike's legs ached from kneeling. "You did fine, Gil, you could have . . ." He realized what he was saying and stopped.

"Sure. Let's grow up together, here and now, Mike."

I won't let them forget your name, Mike thought, cautioning himself to not patronize Gilbert Haynes Trevan. "You gave it one hell of a try, Gil."

"Yeah."

Mike locked his eyes with Gil's and drew his razor-sharp knife. With one hand he stroked Gil's brow and with the other hand he slid the knife into Gil's chest. Blood spurted and Mike withdrew the knife and struck again, fearful that even though Gil was paralyzed, that he would feel the pain.

A sign escaped Gil's lips and his body convulsed. His head slumped to one side. His teeth chattered and then were still.

Mike withdrew the knife.

Ordinarily, he would have termed his next gesture barbarian, but now it seemed natural, like a christening, a mandatory bonding of Gilbert Haynes Trevan to Michale Shepherd.

The Prince of Crimson Sapphire put his still dripping knife into his mouth and tasted Gil's blood.

"Now we are one, brother," he said matter-of-factly. "Together we shall assault the mountain."

He settled himself with Gil's head in his lap and tried to weep. But he couldn't.

44: SUMMER

When Summer arrived at TJ's office, he was ready for a restful afternoon since nothing formal was scheduled.

TJ was reading and lifted another piece of paper and waved it at Summer. "This will belie Sing's new reputation as a mystic and a visionary," he said.

Summer reached for it and sat in a corner chair to read.

Since Mike had left for the ridges, Summer had increased his surveillance of Kellen Sing and his activities. He'd added new and younger agents with instructions to get as close to the power center as possible. One particularly bright young woman had managed to become close to Franco Valdez, Sing's coordinator. Additionally, Summer had other agents spend money and promise more for information among the criminal underground. While this latter was not rigidly organized, if anything big came along, he'd know about it. He'd thought about organizing crime, as TJ had done recently in the Faroff Continent for information and control.

TJ had provided a lot of gold to start a Chinese Triad since he couldn't seem to control the government, and his aim was to combat the Hukbalahaps. But Summer had decided that a crime syndicate, even under his control, would be more trouble than the benefits produced.

TJ waved another sheet at him and he rose and retrieved it. The two were composites of messengers' reports: Summer couldn't afford to be seen with any of the agents he'd recently hired.

He read.

"Violence lurks," TJ said. "You'd think a true visionary could predict it."

"And we'll be to blame."

"That's true, maybe. But it may knock some sense into fools who follow Kellen Sing." TJ made a shrugging gesture.

The reports showed that Kellen Sing was to hold a large rally at the park this noon. And someone had spent a lot of money on hoodlums and jobless to incite a riot among Kellen's followers. Violence was guaranteed.

"At least he's paying exorbitant fees for all of this," TJ grumped. "Whatever lumps he gets, he deserves."

"Uh oh."

"Uh oh, what?" TJ asked.

Summer was already rising. "Noon?"

"Right about now, Summer. What's wrong?"

"Rebecca. She planned to go today." He was already out the door when he heard TJ call for the Officer of the Day. TJ would send soldiers to help him, but it would take a while. Time he didn't have.

As he ran down palace corridors, he tore at his bulky clothes, tried to wipe makeup from his face with his sleeves.

He flew out the rear entrance of the palace heading toward the stables. A mounted sentry was just entering the courtyard. With a leap, Summer dislodged the soldier and was turning the horse around when the soldier hit the ground.

He kicked the horse to a gallop, swatting its haunches with the weighted end of his jester's cap.

When he went through the main gates of the palace, visitors and sentries alike jumped aside. At a dead run, the horse's hooves echoed like an entire squad on the flagstones of Shepherd Avenue.

He cursed himself for failing to take the time to arm himself—though he did have the ever-present dagger strapped to his thigh.

He saw people stop to watch a half-dressed clown whipping his horse to greater speed ignoring all traffic courtesy.

He reflected grimly that lately there wasn't much left to his disguise.

Would he be in time?

Once his horse brushed a cart and knocked it over. He urged the horse on, leaped a retaining wall, and cut through a field angling for the park area. He took all the shortcuts he knew through alleys, streets, and property. He was thankful the Crimson Sapphire was such an open city, not one built up on every piece of ground.

Before he reached the park, he heard the noise and saw the first strings of people escaping the rioting.

It had already started.

Choosing caution before haste, he slid to a stop at the rear of the booths and stalls that fronted the tree-filled park. The horse was breathing in nasty-sounding gulps, but Summer paid no attention.

The main speaking area was in a clearing in the center of the trees—trees, tall with low branches and leaves, which effectively contained the riot for now.

"This is 'creative nonviolence'?" Summer said aloud as fighting spilled through the trees. A ragged crowd of forty or fifty burst through and began looting merchants' stalls of fruits and vegetables and turning over booths. Fighting spread. Farmers retreated. Pottery crashed. One booth went up in flames immediately, but he knew there was little likelihood the fire would spread.

Where was Rebecca?

In the center of things, of course. The answer was not comforting.

He slipped through between two farmers' stalls and found a man with a cloak assaulting the proprietor of an amaranth and sluice-berry cake stand.

Summer chopped the man behind the neck and had his cloak off him before he fell. He wrapped the cloak around himself and ran for the center of the park. He ignored the screams of the innocent and saw that the riot had become self-generating.

There was some fighting all through the trees as he ran dodging groups of struggling people, avoiding confrontations. He smelled fear and crushed vegetation.

He brust through a group, stiff-arming a youth in his way. When he was clear again, rocks flew around him, being thrown from different places, not intentionally at him, but at others.

Where was Becky?

He knew panic, then, for there was a great melee in the clearing as he reached it. He passed a woman bleeding from the mouth; with locked fingers he stabbed a thug in the throat who was kicking a padre.

He selected an avenue between people and an ankle-deep stream to make his way into the center of the fighting. An occasional tree provided an oasis away from the fighting.

Toward the far side of the clearing, he thought he saw a knot of concentrated fighting and he made his way toward that.

Would he be in time?

45: KELLEN

"Kellen! Do something!"

"I'm trying," he said.

Rebecca stood beside him staring at the erupting violence. It had started on all three sides of his audience even before he had begun speaking.

"It's not my fault. This wasn't planned. Damn that Shepherd."

"He wouldn't," she said and stepped back against him to avoid a flying rock.

Kellen concentrated on his aura. He forced peaceful thoughts and love and kindness to pervade the air about him. But his pounding heart and constricted throat seemed to interfere with his control. *O:omega, where are you when I need you?* Kellen knew he was in the river, probably downriver from the amaranth fields. Rarely these days did O:omega come into the city.

He knew his aura-control efforts were failing. Even Franco and his group of eco-freaks were ganging up on people, ostensibly trying to stop the fighting, but reveling in the fact that together they overpowered any opposition. Initially, the group had made a move to surround Kellen and Rebecca and Franco, but they had been engaged by another group and had followed that group when the attackers fell back.

Now Kellen and Rebecca were without organized protection.

He began strumming his thumb drums. The sound failed to pierce the din.

By now Kellen could tell this was not a spontaneous outbreak of violence. It had been planned.

"Shepherd, you shall pay," he vowed as he saw friends and allies turning against each other.

Four new members of his following broke free of the crowds and approached him, ignoring other fighting. A handful of others he did not recognize joined them.

He read their intentions ann projected his aura toward theirs. The milling throngs of fighting, cursing, injured, and excited people made any aura reading difficult, but he read danger in the auras of those approaching. His own excitement and the perilous intentions of these men rendered his aura-control ineffective.

He tried to call Franco and couldn't.

Even without training, Rebecca noticed their danger. "Kellen!"

He panicked, turned to run, and became entangled with Rebecca. When they'd sorted themselves out, the men had circled them. He fought for self-control. At least go down with your head held high, he told himself. And Rebecca, you got her into this, protect her.

"We have a message for you, Sing," said a muscular man with shaggy hair and dirty hands. The man swung from low down and punched Kellen in the kidney.

Kellen felt immediate, searing pain, felt the air go out of his lungs, felt himself fall to the ground spasming against the pain.

The man began kicking him viciously in the stomach, in the kidneys, in the back as he squirmed to evade the brutal onslaught.

Rebecca jumped at the man with a pounding fist and before others dragged her off and held her, scratched a jagged streak along his forehead to his left ear.

Free, the man jumped on Kellen's chest with both feet. "This will teach you to fuck with the system." He scrambled off and motioned to the others.

Two of them lifted Kellen to his feet. Kellen knew he

would never breathe again, but his aching lungs sucked in air and the movement inflamed his chest. He had air.

The leader began slamming heavy fists into him.

With one swelling eye, Kellen saw Rebecca try to break loose and run to him. She fought and clawed and kicked and spun, but wasn't able to escape. They weren't seeming to hurt her. In a detached portion of his mind, Kellen wondered about this. Did they have orders to spare her because they knew she was known to socialize with Camp and Mike? A man backhanded Rebecca and Kellen thought then that no one had guessed Rebecca would be with him; she hadn't been lately, and thus they hadn't issued any orders about her. It would be just like Shepherd not to bother considering women when he ordered violent retribution.

One of his captors wasn't paying attention and Kellen was able to jerk his arm from the man. But all he did was fall with the man on the other side still holding his left arm. Kellen couldn't move. He could see, though, and saw what concerned his attackers: the fight had turned deadly. Swords and knives were out and being used. He heard the clash of metal. And the cries of wounded.

The leader kicked at Kellen's groin and drew his own sword. Kellen thought that if they wanted to kill him, they wouldn't have wasted time beating him up. But when he heard Rebecca gasp in pain, the thought did little to console him.

He smelled dirt and grass as his ear jammed into the turf. He tried to project a calming aura to help Rebecca, but couldn't concentrate. What could he do?

Suddenly, two men in front of him flew into the air. A man in a swirling cloak was moving so fast Kellen's mind couldn't follow his actions. The whirling figure was grabbing the men clustered about Rebecca and throwing them aside, breaking bones wherever he could—arms, necks, shoulders, legs—with deft, strong motions that took only fractions of seconds.

Camp!

And he looked like an ogre from hell as the cloak slipped from him. Face paint smeared and half off, clown suit ripped and torn—not from any hand or weapons laid on him, but from the wide, sharp, and deadly movements of his body.

Kellen thought he'd never have imagined so many different methods of killing and disabling without weapons.

Rebecca was staggering free now, staring at Camp in

disbelief. He read her aura and she, too, thought Camp was the devil's avenger.

A chop to the throat. An eye hanging from a slender tendon. A broken neck.

I was right! Kellen's mind screamed. The jester is a killer. A trained killing machine. Why aren't I grateful? Why is Camp here if Shepherd instigated the violence? And then the answer leaped at him: the whole situation was designed so that Camp could rescue him and Rebecca. He'd known the King was cunning, but he hadn't thought the man would resort to this depth of trickery.

The last man fell to a bone-crushing palm which jammed his nose inward, killing him instantly.

Then Kellen saw Camp's hands go into a blur and a thrown knife fell at his feet and a crossbow quarrel was deflected.

46: SUMMER

Never before had he been as vulnerable.

Until now.

They'd been assaulting Rebecca.

Two more men charged out of the struggling crowd and ran at them. From his belt, he pulled out his weighted jester's cap and swung it for momentum. The lead man brandished a sword and Summer ducked under the first swing, straightened swiftly and smashed the man's skull with the weight. Number two had to step aside to get around his companion and Summer leaped into the air lashing out with his foot. His heel crushed the man's temple.

A compulsion overwhelmed him. Must get Rebecca to safety. This sudden vulnerability scared him. Unlike him and Kellen and TJ, Rebecca was an innocent in this drama.

He looked around and saw Rebecca slumped to one knee and staring at the bloody mess that was her brother. Summer wondered if TJ had troops here yet. Not enough time yet, he decided. He saw smoke toward the farmer's market. Though the space about them was temporarily cleared, save for the bodies of the dead and wounded, he saw menace from the surrounding crowd. Kellen's followers were now turned against him, too. They thought the dead were their own.

Stones and sticks flew, the crowd surged toward them.

He couldn't tell friend from enemy.

Decision was action. He lifted Rebecca into his arms.

He looked down at Kellen. "Save yourself," he said in a normal tone, "I recommend the trees." At any rate, he didn't care whether Kellen reached safety or not.

Rebecca was groggy and obviously unable to move well by herself. He ran for the trees, lashing out with his feet at opposition. He ignored the pain as a staff slammed into his thigh. He kept running.

The trees momentarily concealed them from pursuit and Summer swung onto a low branch and began scrambling higher, aiming for a stout limb which led to another tree. He ran lightly along it until it bent from their weight. He leaped and grasped another limb and continued his swinging motion, one hand holding Rebecca and the other the limb, and let go even as that limb snapped. They fell forward and down until Summer could hook a leg over a broad branch. He locked his other ankle over the ankle of the supporting leg.

Rebecca gasped as they hung upside down, still swinging residually.

"Hang on, Becky. We'll be out of this in a minute."

Her legs were locked around his hips now, and her arms around his neck. An awkward position while hanging upside down, he reflected.

He powered them up and onto the branch and then into a fork in the tree. She hung onto him as he climbed higher. Finally, he stopped when he found a comfortable webbing of branches and limbs. Thick foliage blocked their view of the ground and screened most of the noise out. He thought them safe.

He felt her cheek against his throat and gently disengaged her hands and noticed, surprisingly, that her eyes were open.

"Most people call me Rebecca," she said into his ear.

"Any exceptions?" he asked.

"Now there is."

47: MIKE

Mike wondered what Rebecca was doing and pulled on his boots. They were worn and holed. His feet were swollen.

He stood and cascaded rocks and gravel down into the fault. It didn't take long to cover the body of Gilbert Haynes Trevan. He wedged Gil's sword into a crack in the rock above Gil's head. He could do no more.

For a moment he stood there and rain began to fall, a warm and invigorating rain. He drank runoff from the rocks. He washed himself. He filled his water bladder.

Through the rest of the day he climbed. No longer was he bitter or angry. He climbed with a single-minded concentration that excluded all other thoughts.

Once he scrambled up rock shelving until his lower legs ached. On the next day he hung onto a scrub bush by his teeth while he rearranged his footing and handholds. That night he didn't remember whether he'd slept the night before at all. He could tell that the face of the mountain was changing. It was cold more often than not. Icy winds attacked the tatters of his clothing.

When he awoke in the morning, a light dusting of snow had just fallen. It made climbing all the more difficult—and then he found why Summer had told him to take the south shoulder of Forty-K: the shoulder served as the local summit for Big Bear Ridge and, instead of climbing to it, all he had to do was trudge up a snow packed slope.

Which took him two days.

But if he fell here, he'd simply freeze—not fall to his death.

The shoulder of Forty-K wasn't flat. He found a protected pass where the snow only reached to his knees and followed this to the eastern side of Big Bear Ridge.

Far in the distance, he saw the shore and the ocean, a sight he never thought he'd see. From the ocean to the hills at the base of the ridge spread a lush landscape, calming and lulling him, seeming to invite him like a womb.

While the way down the eastern side of Big Bear Ridge was the least difficult passage he'd yet encountered, it was still sufficiently dangerous to end his Trek should he misstep. He took a chance by tying Gil's rope to his own and doubled the distance he could drop where the situation called for dropping. The height did not bother him.

His mind was beginning to pull itself together with the comparative ease of travel. He was weak from hunger. Rain fed his thirst. He recalled that fasting was supposed to be good for the soul, that it cleansed the mind of impurities. He laughed because he didn't think he had a soul that was Michale Shepherd. That person was gone.

Or was he?

"Might be good for the soul," he said to a ball of lichen, "but it isn't good for the stomach."

The closer to ground level he came, the more he remembered the easy self-confidence he'd recently gained. He also realized his strength had endured.

And so had his sense of purpose.

The angle of decline decreased and the slope became easy. He had to fight to keep from running downhill. Then he came to a position where he traveled on the foothills and not on the ridge itself.

When he emerged from the small series of tree-lined hills, he found himself in a green valley, like one at the bottom of a canyon.

Immediately he felt a sense of comfort and well-being. From beside the stream rose a Webbine, one smaller than I:imbawe who'd visited the palace.

/Welcome,/ the Webbine said-whistled-signed-thought. /I am known as A:alpha. I will guide you to the Home Ground./

He wasn't surprised. He nodded. "I'm Mike, er, Michale. Michale Shepherd."

/ 'Tis a fact you are the son of the current Trekmaster?/

"Yes."

/We knew that the Trekmaster was ill and that he was recovering. For what reason do you take the Trek?/

He was weak from hunger. "Right now, I'm not sure." His voice was hoarse from disuse. Then his sense of purpose came back. Should he tell the truth? That he was unsatisfied with his father's rule and wished to supplant him? A simple answer that hadn't seemed so simple before he began this insane adventure.

/Perhaps you shall discover the answer here,/ A:alpha's

aura-sound-gestures said enigmatically. /For you are now Trekmaster./

That's right! Mike's mind screamed. You are a Trekmaster. Nobody can take that away from you. You achieved a distinction only a few humans in the history of Bear Ridge have attained. Sonuvaduke. How about that? He smiled wearily.

The following day he had rested and eaten. He was sitting on a moss covered rock next to the inlet A:alpha assured him led to the sea and having an informal conversation with several of the Webbines. He'd met O:chacka, I:imbawe again, X:tol, B:bsle and others. He was just getting used to their conversing gestures and becoming comfortable with the Webbines themselves—occasional smells, reminiscent of newly uncovered mud, rotting vegetation, and sulfur to name only a few, wafted through the glade. He knew he must accustom his senses to the alien nature of the Webbines and their habitat.

Some of their skins hung in folds, others were stretched tight. And the changing colors! He was having a devil of a time keeping straight the Webbines he'd met because of their changing skin color as they moved—or even, perhaps, changing by whim alone. He figured a system of keeping track of them by position; so he was busy watching all the ones he was supposed to know as they moved about.

Mike himself was refreshed, not completely physically recovered, but mentally a cloud had lifted. His awareness had changed between the western side of Big Bear Ridge where he'd left Gil's body, returning from survival and mental disorientation to the world as he knew it—or was learning it anew. He sensed opportunity within him. He was glad he was alive.

He was a Trekmaster. The impossible goal. But, strangely, his soon to be increased standing in the human community did not impress him much.

He'd conquered Teddy Bear Ridge, Devil's Dip Gorge, and Big Bear Ridge. Within himself he had conquered something also, something he couldn't identify right then.

Had his father felt thus? Had the other Trekmasters? Now he understood a little more about his father, about TJ's approach to life. After this experience, all else seemed inconsequential. As the old saying his father used a lot went, "All else is gravy." Life looked up, was there for the taking. No problem seemed as significant as it had once been.

He wondered about Rebecca and how she was doing, then shied away from thinking about those people and those problems. He was here, now, and had no influence over them. He'd face them later upon his return.

If he lived through the return trip.

Anyway, he acknowledged that he had changed.

A:alpha and others took turns sitting within arm's reach of him, concentrating.

After a couple of hours of one-on-one conversation, and during a dialogue with A:alpha, he sensed a bond growing between them. With A:alpha he felt more relaxed than with the others. There was a sort of emotional or psychological kinship he could just about put his finger on. As time went on, he sensed/saw a hazy outline around A:alpha, centering on his mind, emanating . . . colors? emotions? feelings? Yes, that was it. It reflected A:alpha's essence; it presupposed a higher level of communication and awareness, one tinged with thicker emotive tensions than he'd ever before encountered. It seemed to radiate. Once he concentrated on it, it gave him a totally new sensory experience, one which staggered him with its impact. His self-awareness was peaking, allowing him to expand his mind and sense these things.

Then he noticed less distinct outlines around all the Webbines. By now he'd observed that the Webbines had almost 360-degree vision from each eye and he guessed that the brain which could handle the disparate visual patterns the Webbines received would develop aura-control in the evolutionary process.

A:alpha was urging him on with obvious anticipation. /You have discovered auras./ It was a statement, not a question.

"Do I have one also?" Mike asked.

/'Tis a fact. An alien aura, to be sure, but one nonetheless./ A:alpha touched Mike's arm. /*We* have never attempted to instruct a Trekmaster in aura-technique before. The elders, this time, think it necessary. There can be no missed communication between us. Also, there is much to learn about you and your inner workings; time erodes faster than a beach during a storm./

Mike caught some of their concern, then, for their future. It gave him much to think about. "I have much to learn."

/'Tis true,/ said A:alpha, obviously misunderstanding,

/though possibly melding and the higher arts of aura-control are physiologically beyond your capabilities./

Mike did not correct him. He knew eventual disposition of the Webbines in an increasingly civilized human world was another problem his father was wrestling with.

"My father? Thomas Jefferson Shepherd, the current Trekmaster? Does he know aura-control?" After he asked, it occurred to him the question sounded stupid.

/We know who he is,/ O:chacka interrupted. /He is my stone-mate. He picked up a rudimentary understanding of aura-techniques. He had no time to develop his latent talent. Nor do I think he would have done so as quickly as you have. You are much more emotionally attuned to us than he is./

Of course, Mike thought, TJ had had a kingdom beset by warring neighbors and had to speed back to become king and take the wars to them.

"Why me?"

/You have an inborn empathy that allows us to communicate better,/ O:chacka continued. /Change is coming. A bridge of understanding must be built. You are the closest human to us, physiologically and mentally, and you have the empathy; thus the task is accordingly simpler for us and for you./

Mike began to understand some things he had never questioned. He dangled his bare feet in the seawater of the inlet. "Oh, no!" he said as his gaze fastened on his toes, and the webbing between them.

/Mike! Do not surmise too swiftly!/ A:alpha cautioned.

"Oh?"

/A discontinued experiment,/ O:chacka said, and went on to explain.

I am a product of two races? Mike wondered to himself. A staggering revelation.

O:chacka and A:alpha fused their auras with his to reassure him. Then something passed so quickly between them he could not follow.

A:alpha dove into the inlet and disappeared. O:chacka continued to soothe Mike.

In a few minutes, A:alpha reappeared. He climbed back out of the water and opened his webbed "hand" and held it to Mike.

Amidst a green slime and some blood sat a crimson sapphire.

/We are stone-mates,/ A:alpha said, and collapsed as if he'd gone through some draining physical experience.

Mike took the gem. "Geez." He didn't know what to say. Then another emotional impact struck him and he had no need to speak. He felt as if one with A:alpha, and he no longer regretted and cursed the Webbines for interfering with his physical makeup.

He stretched his toes in the water.

After the newness of the bond with A:alpha wore off, he looked at his crimson sapphire. Like his father's, it could show different colors. But it was small, not even half the size of TJ's. He looked a query at A:alpha with whom he felt comfortable enough now to ask the possibly embarrassing question—or perhaps the discourteous question.

/'Tis true, Mike. It is not fully developed. It comes from within my body, and I have not sufficient years to develop one the size an elder could produce./

"Oh," Mike indicated neutrally. He now knew where the crimson sapphires came from and could extrapolate, from his recent experience, that the gem also functioned as some sort of catalyst between them, a bonding agent perhaps, linking him and A:alpha in some ethereal fashion.

In the following days, he increased his abilities to read auras and to project his own. At the time, he was lounging with A:alpha in the shallows of the inlet. A:alpha was ingesting an occasional seaweed. He began to see a little of the Webbines' concern about humans and their eventual impact upon the Webbines—that was it!

Kellen!

The answer shouted at him. It had been there all the time. Kellen's concentration, his intensity, his charisma, his ability to sway people. "I'll be damned," he said aloud.

/Your aura rainbows, Mike./

Before he thought to be cautious, he was explaining Kellen Sing and his theory about Webbine influence. Too late, he thought that they might already know, that Kellen could be the result of a Webbine plot—but O:chacka and I:imbawe then speculated openly on O:omega and his anti-Webbine behavior.

/We drove him out, and he was brilliant,/ I:imbawe told him.

Mike noticed A:alpha's aura bristle. The small Webbine made a farting sound with his mouth. He saw that within auras he could read that there were no falsehoods. He suspected that the Webbines could conceal thoughts and attitudes from their auras, but was certain the Webbines were not collectively behind Kellen Sing. What would he do about Kellen when (and if) he returned? What difference did it make anyway? None.

I:imbawe asked him about Sharon and the Federation and Mike began explaining. Suddenly, the glade was full of Webbines and their peculiar noises and smells—but all paid him strict attention. Their questions went on till well past dark. They communicated with each other, also; sometimes he could follow, other times on a level beyond his experience—especially the elders.

During one of these lulls when the elders were conversing among themselves, Mike realized that this conversation was reminding him that the kingdom of the Shepherds was in danger, in flames now perhaps, because of his father, his father's obsession with the Federation, and Kellen Sing and the renegade O:omega. He had a responsibility and he was not living up to that responsibility by sitting here.

What would his position be when he returned? A lot to think about. At that moment, he knew he'd have to return soon. And make a few decisions.

But he had one thing, one considerable thing, going in his favor now: he was a Trekmaster.

He must take his rightful place, whatever that was, and help shape the destiny of his people. A racial imperative? he wondered, or just another Shepherd with an obsession?

He'd withdrawn and been thinking to himself, so he missed most of what went on around him.

/'Tis settled then,/ said I:imbawe. /A:alpha will accompany you back to your home./

48: TIRANO

The Birdking of Two Tongues stood in the receiving room of his suite on the troopship and screamed at Captain Shawn.

"I don't give a beggar's goddamn about shipboard routine. Screw your procedures. I want Two Tongues time."

"Your Majesty, I ordered this shipboard time for your own benefit. It occurred to me that instituting Bear Ridge cycles now would acclimate you and your troops sooner."

"Well, we never discussed it." Tirano frowned. Maybe Shawn was right. Even though minor, he didn't want any glitch in his planning. It made him uneasy.

Shawn was speaking now of navigational matter, assuring him that they would arrive at Bear Ridge on the target day. Something about not going translight. Tirano hoped his troops were adjusting. He wanted them ready when they got to Bear Ridge. ". . . get us there at the exact time."

"Like I wanted. Good." Tirano didn't even want to understand the navigational machinations and hadn't thought of approaching Bear Ridge in anything other than a straight line from Two Tongues. When he had his Federation Council seat would be soon enough to learn terminology. He'd selected the Bear Ridge day and time of landing, derived from information transmitted by his spy, and instructed Shawn to insure the Federation Navy wouldn't notice their passage.

He reached to a counter and lifted the glass container of mite dust. "Yours, Shawn. You will be rich," he said, and thought, You can buy all the little boys you want, you fucking faggot—if I give you your payment. "Now about the energy weapons. I must arrange training for my personnel."

"Other than the ships' normal compliment, there are none . . . Sire."

"But, I thought we agreed?"

"No, sir. We didn't. I couldn't give you any." His tone told Tirano that he didn't trust him, that he didn't trust Tirano's troops to be so armed. If they were hi-tech armed,

Shawn probably guessed, and rightly so, that Tirano would double-cross him and take personal command of all the ships—after landing, and thus not have to pay the agreed mite-dust. Not only would he be the emperor of two planets, actually the entire solar system, but he'd have his own fleet, too.

"It was my judgment," Shawn continued, "that large arms sales would attract unwanted attention and jeopardize this venture."

Diplomatically put, Tirano thought. What Shawn hadn't said was that Tirano's troops, armed with percussion weapons, should be more than a match for soldiers armed with crossbows and swords. "Okay, okay." He had felt obligated to his sense of trickery to try to bluff Shawn into obtaining the weaponry. He'd already been told he wouldn't get hi-tech weapons by his contacts at the Council. They were probably afraid he would practice genocide on Bear Ridge. Nah. He never practiced anything. "Just get us there."

Shawn left. Tirano was glad he wore trousers. He was tired of the sexoff pervert staring at his shaved legs.

He considered whether to message his spy or his backers at Federation. He decided against the latter. They probably didn't want to know anything he had to tell them. But they damned well better be ready to recognize his rule on Bear Ridge and to admit him to the Federation immediately.

Not even his closest advisors knew of these backers at the Federation. Nor did his spy in Shepherd's court know of them. Although others at Federation Central might suspect: some mite-dust had made its way into the Federation system. And certain Federation regulations had thus been relaxed for him. He needed the money for his invasion of Bear Ridge and to spend on bureaucrats and administrators at Fedcentral. The Council needed to be aware of his financial position—money smoothes anything, even Federation entry. So his already powerful contacts would assist him in his bid for the seat over Shepherd's bid for the same Council seat.

All for power.

He kicked a bulkhead in anger. He even had a newly discovered reason for hating Shepherd more than he already did and it also increased the necessity for invading Bear Ridge. An embarrassing reason. One he guessed to be true and leaked to him only to goad him on.

Those on the Council were jealous of their power and partisan politics were always the order of the day.

He'd learned that the Federation assholes in charge had run computer profiles on him and Shepherd. These profiles showed, while both Tirano and Shepherd were ambitious, that Shepherd was more aggressive, more likely to attain power.

It really hurt Tirano's pride. It angered him that they did not fear him more than they feared Thomas Jefferson goddamn Shepherd. It had been the final factor in his decision to invade.

He'd show the assholes. What did they know? Power hungry megalomaniacs who had lackeys like frigging Shawn? What did that say about them?

So with one bold stroke, he was going to rid the universe of Shepherd—make that all the Shepherds—and steal both a planet and the new Federation Council seat.

Something then occurred to him that hurt his pride more: the assholes at Fedcentral were using him as a *surrrogate* to rid themselves of Shepherd and his threat to their power. Their own stupid goddamn rules had handcuffed them.

But Tirano would win and show the bastards who was more clever.

He went to the miniature console Shawn had installed for him. He suspected Shawn had a duplicate somewhere and would intercept his message—but no way he could decode it. Serbo-Croat crossed with Yaqui? Nah. Tirano was an expert at languages; already he had mastered the Americanish spoken on Bear Ridge. He wondered how the Webbines' language was structured and became excited when he thought about translation *and* transliteration (if applicable).

He tapped out his message.

EN ROUTE. INSTIGATE PLAN.

Tirano laughed, anticipation building pleasure. Old TJ would think he'd won. No more spontaneous outbreaks of violence (unless they'd gone too far and were now self-sustaining) and TJ would feel safe in dispatching his army far, far away from Crimson Sapphire for the Federation required maneuvers.

Because he felt so good, he added uncharacteristically, LET'S LULL THIS BABY TO SLEEP.

He also was enjoying the irony of landing right in Shepherd's own amaranth fields where Shepherd intended to put his landing field if he won the right to do so.

302 *James B. Johnson*

He recalled an earlier conversation with Shawn as they were planning the invasion.

"You mean we just land your troop ships right there in the fields? That isn't the way the Federation Navy does it."

"Sure," Shawn said, "the Federation Navy lands its troops in smaller vessels because the large troop ships would be tracked and blasted while screaming through the atmosphere. But for us to do so, we'd have to obtain the smaller vessels and store 'em somewhere or drag 'em with us. But we have one invasion force going to one landing site. If we got power enough to go translight, we can set her down and lift off." He'd licked a finger and run it over one heavily painted eyebrow. "It's not like they can shoot us out of the sky, Majesty."

Well, here they were on the way to Bear Ridge.

The invasion was on!

Revenge would be his. Gwendlyon would be his.

He only wished that Shepherd and Gwendlyon had had a daughter so that he could use her instead of Gwen as the instrument of his revenge and, more importantly, the statement of his power on Bear Ridge. As it was, the wimp son and all of TJ's illegitimates were off killing themselves, saving him the trouble.

And the spy. He'd made promises to his agent. He had taken advantage of the spy's hatred. Perhaps he should have arranged for more than one spy, the other a different source of information and to check on the primary agent. But time had been short and he'd seen the spy's disillusionment and capitalized on it. Just as TJ had used a Fed-sponsored conference on Two Tongues against him to pull the "bird shit" episode, Tirano had used a similar Fed conference on Bear Ridge to locate and enlist his agent and deliver the illicit comm gear.

He'd even promised the spy the crown, for conceivably the spy could claim the throne by the stupid rules they had on Bear Ridge. If he followed this through, it would legitimatize his takeover. They could call it coup d'etat; instead of his troops mounting an invasion, they could call his presence military aid requested by the legitimate government to help suppress a rebellion. While this twisted legalistic doctrine was all fine and good for the lawyers, it wasn't his way.

For one thing, he didn't trust the spy's ability to govern and follow his orders exactly. For another reason, he kind of liked the idea of being the feudal emperor of both planets, and thus the solar system.

Additionally, the spy could tell of his duplicity, of his planning the invasion for a long time, and he didn't particularly want his plotting exposed—even though it would be obvious he had to plot to take over Bear Ridge.

He also thought that if the spy could work against Shepherd, the spy could work against him. He didn't trust a traitor. Once a traitor, always a traitor. The stain remained.

No, he'd kill off the spy immediately. Right after he no longer had use for the information the spy could provide.

Anyway, he certainly didn't trust someone near him who was so familiar with poisons. He shivered.

END. he typed and hit the transmit button.

Yeah, it'll all end soon, TJ, he smiled. Right there beginning in your amaranth patch.

49: REBECCA

Rebecca rode with Summer Camp through the amaranth fields. She didn't know why she was riding with him. They hadn't spoken in a while. She was still furious at herself for succumbing to his charms—in a tree, yet!—after he had rescued her.

They hadn't spoken since he'd asked her about Kellen.

"I don't know about Kellen. I don't care about Kellen," she'd snapped. She wouldn't have had these problems if she'd married Jon, the blacksmith's son.

Now there was an uneasy silence between them. He doubtlessly was wondering why he'd asked her for a ride today.

Well, so was she. The hell with all men. She knew that she was reacting to her own circumstances. Besides her anger with herself, she'd fought with Kellen and they'd fallen out.

Kellen was out of control, obsessively pursuing some obscure goal of anarchy.

Well, she'd had enough of him. And of his freaky friends. Time had separated Kellen from her. Their parents' death had affected them each differently. She'd finally reconciled herself to the fact that their parents were dead. Kellen obviously had not. And was probably a vendetta against the King; after all, Milvin had died in some battle against Crimson Sapphire and Coreen of a broken heart thereafter. And Kellen had been Momma's boy.

Rebecca had tried to contribute to his upbringing, but that was rather difficult with him off in the hills most of the time.

Now, Kellen was like a stranger. And she was sick of him and his whining about the King. Why couldn't he do something constructive?

Mike. Was he still alive? When he'd lifted her off her horse just before he'd departed on the Trek, his eyes had been like twin volcanoes, his grip strong with unsuppressed inner tension which had leapt into her.

"Where *are* we going?" she demanded.

"To see the last of the sluice-berries," he said. "Look, Becky, I'm sorry about . . ."

"What do you mean the last of the sluice-berries?" she asked, not wanting to think about Kellen or Summer or Mike any more.

They were riding along perimeters of amaranth plots. She estimated they were grouped in ten-acre plots, separated by large irrigation ditches.

"We're harvesting the sluice-berries now," Summer said. "And it's too late to start another crop before we're admitted to the Federation. The King is already planning a landing zone right here."

"Oh. I understand a lot."

Summer managed a dry laugh. "These berries are picked in a unique manner." He pointed to their left at an irrigation ditch. The amaranth plot was on the right. "We grow the berries on the edges of the irrigation ditches." He paused as they had to ride single file to cross a culvert.

When he caught up with her again, he said, "We have all these irrigation ditches and the berries criss-crossing all the fields. So we open the sluices," he pointed obscurely again, "over at The Howling Volv River, and flood the ditches. Got to be careful not to let too much river in, it would flood the amaranth fields. We keep the irrigation lines to the amaranth closed. Water flows through all the fields to an outlet on the river."

"So?" she prompted and then saw the answer. Pickers

were going through the waist-high bushes picking the berries and tossing them into the irrigation ditches. "They float down to the outlet on the river where people pick them right up."

"Correct. And we don't have to carry 'em. That's where the drying warehouse is located. We just screen across the irrigation exit to the river and we have them all. It's even designed into the outlet mechanism. We've got it built so that we can slow or hasten the exit flow. Or even stop it, for that matter, if the berries start backing up. And a set of signals to tell the engineers who are letting in the river water upriver to stop their flow so they don't flood the fields."

They had stopped their horses and were watching four men and three women go quickly through the bushes and drop the sluice-berries into the flowing ditch. A boy and a girl, twins, were splashing in the shallows, paralleling the pickers and brushing the floating berries toward the center of the ditch. Two older children followed, wading in the middle of the ditch, with long, floating poles, gathering the sluice-berries and pushing them ahead.

"Why are you showing me this?" she asked.

He looked apprehensive. "Why? I couldn't think of any other reason to see you." He looked away. "I hardly have any time to myself; you know that."

"Oh." She knew she was being unfair to him. She remembered the relief she'd felt, the strength of his arms and body. It had all been so simple until the riot in the park.

Yet she didn't want to admit that a person who had plotted and acted against her brother could be a serious suitor. Why did she have a hard time saying the word "love?" Could she love Summer Camp? Or maybe the real question was did she love Summer Camp?

"Any word from Mike?" she asked.

"No." His voice was hard.

She realized her mistake right away. "I'm sorry." I've been cruel, she thought. Well, say it, then, she told herself. "That was cruel."

His face was resigned. "I care, too, Becky."

"Rebecca."

"Oh." He stepped down and picked a handful of sluice-berries and handed her some. "He's my friend, too, *Rebecca*. I watched him grow up. I spent a hell of a lot of manhours training him." His look was a challenge.

"I know. I'm sorry." She tried to be as meek as she could

to make up for her error. She saw it helped a little. "It must be hard on you."

"Yeah. Not to mention family."

"Yes?" she prompted, curious.

He shrugged. She knew he seldom talked about the King and the Shepherd family. He was very close-mouthed about most things. He ate another handful of berries.

"Summer, will Mike make it? Live through the Trek, I mean."

His face fell. "I know it's important to you. I don't know the answer. The odds are against any man. The Trek has killed most who've tried it. The only thing I can offer is that Mike is his father's son."

She grasped at the straw he offered. "There's that." She dismounted and they walked together leading their horses.

"Rebecca, how hurt would you be if Mike didn't come back?"

She saw that he was embarrassed. So he, too, had a difficult time admitting his feelings.

"Plenty," she said.

His head seemed to droop, but she knew it hadn't. He was always too proud. "Would you be inconsolable?" He didn't look at her.

It was a question she'd been avoiding herself. She cared about Summer. She'd stood up for him in front of Kellen who had accused her of loving a killer, a butcher, the King's executioner, an assassin. That had been the start of their final falling out.

So Summer killed sometimes. It was part of . . . the world. Maybe the world would change.

But his killing only served to highlight the difference between him and Mike, gentle Mike, Mike who wanted to change the world for the better. Maybe even gentle to a fault.

She kept finding herself comparing the two. Did she have to make a choice? Neither had indicated they were ready for a long term commitment—though by his question whether or not she would be inconsolable, Summer had hinted. Was it time for her to stop having fun and face up? The country girl goes to the city and has a ball, and now has to pay her dues? Is that what it is coming down to?

She had two apparent suitors. One a prince, and ostensibly the next king of the entire world. A gentle and thinking man. At times an angry young man. The other? A clown. A jester. A man of physical strength and ability, probably unmatched in the world (except the King, maybe). A man of power, enormous power, perhaps even more powerful than the top military officer in the world.

At another time, the comparisons of the two men would amuse her. Some women would kill to have her problems.

Maybe she'd never have to make a choice.

Summer was looking at her now, expecting an answer. He knew damn well she was physically attracted to him. Hadn't her behavior in the park showed that?

She stopped and her horse bumped into her.

"I would live through the experience, if that's your question, Summer. But be aware that your question is unfair. I am a woman. I have my own mind. *I am obligated to no one,* for no one has declared himself to me. So while I may enjoy the occasional social engagement, I don't think that social engagement should commit me to anything."

"Oh." He stroked his horse between the eyes.

She turned and strode off, at first dragging her mount along.

Just exactly what were her feelings?

She was angry at Summer for assuming.

She was angry at Mike for running off on the Trek and maybe killing himself.

She was angry at Kellen for being Kellen.

She was angry at herself for not knowing her own mind.

She felt caught up in a whirlwind, something she couldn't control and wanted to, unable to see ahead.

You knew you'd have to face up to it one of these days, she told herself, it just happened sooner than later.

50: TJ

Three hours before dawn, the corridors of the university dormitory were silent. Two students sat outside the room Kellen Sing had occupied before he quit the university and went underground.

"Strange," Summer whispered.

TJ nodded. Kellen Sing had several places where he slept. Franco Valdez had been accompanied this night by a young woman ostensibly infatuated with him. Later, she'd sent word to the palace that Kellen was in the dormitory room. TJ thought that it was a perfect hiding place for Kellen Sing. No one would think to look in the room he'd used as a student where other students were available to warn and protect him.

TJ and Summer stood in the shadows at a turn in the corridor. So far, they had not been seen. Both were dressed in nondescript cloaks with hoods so, if seen, they wouldn't be recognized.

Most of the corridor lamps had been extinguished and they moved quietly through the shadows. Summer stepped to the far side of the corridor and paralleled TJ.

The two students seemed to be dozing until one of them snorted and brought his head up curiously.

Summer beat TJ to his student by half a step and his hand chopped into the side of the guard's neck before the student could raise his arm to protect himself. TJ found a pressure point on the drowsing student's neck and he went from sleep to unconsciousness. Both guards slumped in their seats.

Summer tried the door and found it bolted from the inside. He looked at TJ. TJ nodded. Summer stepped back, checked along the corridor, and shot his foot at the door. The pad of his foot struck the wooden door at the height of the bolt. A sharp snap echoed along the corridor as TJ went in grabbing the door before it could slam against the wall. Summer followed him and closed the door to a crack, looking out to see if the commontion had attracted any attention.

Moonlight from a window provided enough light for TJ to see.

Kellen was sitting up on the cot. "What? Who is it?" he paused. "Uh oh."

TJ grinned to himself. You'd think Sing could see in the dark. "Most people would stand for me," he said in a level voice.

"Oh," Kellen said, scrambling out of bed flustered and searching in the half light for his clothes.

TJ could see Kellen gaining control of himself, the transition from sleep to wakefulness complete. TJ saw Kellen freeze once while pulling on his clothes. He was using the mechanical actions of dressing to gather his thoughts and reason out his situation. At the momentary freeze, TJ could tell Kellen had figured out his situation. It was almost as if the boy could read minds. "He has it figured, Summer."

"Bright lad."

"He is that. He hasn't complained once. He also seems to have healed from his beating."

"What do you want?"

"He loses civility the more awake he becomes," Summer said.

"It occurs to me," Kellen said, "that a dictator who rules by decree doesn't need to be prowling in the middle of the night. Are you going to kill me?"

TJ didn't think Kellen showed enough fear to really think they would kill him. Of course, if they were going to kill him, they would have done so by proxy to keep some suspicion away from the palace. TJ read Kellen thinking those same thoughts. Kellen couldn't seem to figure it out. Why the King and the jester? A squad of soldiers would have accomplished the same task. But, TJ thought, one soldier might inadvertently talk.

"You are going to come with us," TJ said as Kellen finished dressing. "Your choice is to come quietly or come unconscious."

Kellen fastened his eyes on TJ's and didn't answer. TJ found the gaze unsettling. He felt compelled to talk to Kellen, to explain, to be gentle with the boy. The overwhelming urge disappeared as TJ shook his head and concentrated on his purpose.

Summer stepped up beside him and broke the spell, or whatever it was. "It's still clear, boss. Let's get him out of here." He looked at Kellen. "You gonna cooperate?"

Even TJ felt the blast of hatred. Kellen snarled, "I've seen you in action, Camp. I know what you can do."

TJ said, "You do exactly as we tell you, when we tell you. Summer first. Then you. Then me. Don't try to cry out." He nodded to Summer.

Summer checked the hallway once more and motioned. They went out between the two unconscious guards. Kellen stopped to check their respiration and TJ felt obligated to let him assure himself that they were still alive.

Then he pushed Kellen ahead. Once he touched Kellen on the shoulder when he thought the young man was walking too noisily.

At the intersection of the corridor with another which led to a side entrance, TJ felt a compulsion to let Kellen go but then regained his resolve. He sensed Kellen beginning to panic.

Summer cleared them and led off around the corner. Only an occasional lamp glowed dimly. Summer was around the corner and so was Kellen. As TJ stepped around the corner himself, he saw Kellen tensing and taking in a large gulp of air.

Before Kellen could cry out and push Summer away, TJ closed his right hand around Kellen's mouth from over his shoulder. With his left, he found the pressure point and Kellen fell, immediately unconscious.

Summer had turned swiftly and caught Kellen as he fell from TJ's grip. He ducked his shoulder and hoisted Kellen.

Soon they were outside trotting across soccer fields to the edge of the amaranth fields.

It was good to be active again, TJ thought. Hell, it was good to strike back at Sing, right or wrong.

They didn't have to run through the amaranth to arrive back at the palace before dawn, but they did so, the running becoming an unspoken contest. Neither was breathing hard and they traded off carrying Sing every thousand paces. TJ was glad it had rained recently and the engineers weren't flooding the fields for irrigation.

At the edge of the fields, they waited as a patrol passed. Their plan hinged on the fact that no one at all know they had kidnapped Kellen Sing.

They jogged to the river and followed it upstream to the palace. In the deep shadows of the palace which rose above the river bank they stopped.

Like all palaces TJ'd ever heard of, this one had a secret access. Monarchs needed to go places at times without being recognized. And TJ even had a swift sailboat, large enough for a party of twenty, concealed in a giant and fake drain pipe nearby for escape down the river if the palace were overrun. A staircase ran from the top floor, where the royal apartments were, down the northwest corner of the palace with access to every floor. Not coincidentally, Summer's apartments were directly below his and Gwen's and had access to the secret stairs.

TJ was holding Sing so Summer went behind some shrubbery and swung the counterbalanced section of the wall open. TJ ducked and entered and Summer swung the wall-section closed, struck a spark to a lamp's wick, and led the way upstairs.

At his apartments, he worked a catch and stepped into a closet blowing out the lamp. Directly above this closet was TJ's own access to the secret stairway: the concealed room where sat Jean-Claude Lafitte Fitzroy's transmitter.

"In the inner bedroom."

They entered through Summer's bedroom. Through another door was a similar bedroom, unoccupied, but deeper within his chambers. TJ dropped Kellen on the bed and thought the accommodations too good for him. But if they put him in an ordinary prison or jail, or even the old-fashioned and unused dungeons beneath the palace, word would get out.

"Strip him," TJ said. "A naked man is a more vulnerable man."

When they had done so, Summer got a chain with an ankle clamp, secured one end to the lamp holder above the bed, locked the clamp around Kellen's left ankle, and pocketed the key.

TJ surveyed their work as Kellen showed signs of regaining consciousness. "You or I could pull that off the wall, but not Sing."

Summer grunted. "Hope this solves the problem."

"It won't," TJ assured him, "not right away. It might even aggravate it, I don't know. But passions cool over time, and maybe the movement will die."

"You did not kill me because of my sister," Kellen said, eying them both.

"Perhaps," TJ said.

"Goddamn whore," Kellen said.

"Perhaps not," TJ said. "We just might need you alive to quell a riot or two."

"Yeah. Like hell."

"Sing," Summer said, "watch your mouth when addressing the King. Understand?" He continued when Kellen did not reply. "Actually, never mind what you think, we aren't murderers. Although we could have killed you or ordered it done. I could kill you right now, dump you out the window into the river and fall asleep inside a minute. You need to understand you're dealing with grown men now, not fire-eyed children."

"Screw off, Camp," Kellen said and TJ thought that he'd known Sing wouldn't buy the line Summer had fed him.

"My, my," TJ said mildly, "didn't the Webbines teach you patience, too?"

Kellen reacted as if he'd been bitten by a snarv. He suddenly realized he was naked and scrambled to cover himself with bedclothes.

Summer was looking at TJ. "That explains a lot of things, TJ."

"I never was an expert," the King said, "but I observed enough to know what was going on. And tonight, alone in the silence, he tried to sway us mentally somehow. It wasn't hard to figure out from there." He looked at Kellen. "Even now he tries." He made a fist and darted it at Kellen who cowered back. "There. Be advised, Sing, I can tell when you're doing that thing. Each time you try it on me, I shall break one of your teeth."

"Me, too," Summer said. "Fingers."

"That ought to take care of that," TJ said. "Now, young man, tell us of the Webbines. Are they backing your plan? Or is it 'they'? I need to know."

Kellen looked sullen and did not answer.

Summer pulled out a knife and tested the tip with his thumb.

TJ held up his hand. "Kellen, I am not going to torture you. But I will tell you something. I understand a man goes mad during the third day of thirst." He pointed to an inner room. "Inside there is a bathroom with running water and with field rations of sheepaloe jerky. Your chain is now long enough to reach inside there for whatever you need. If you do not cooperate, I will shorten your chain. I don't expect you to last more than thirty-six hours. Now do you wish to speak?"

"One Webbine," Kellen said. His answer was the least possible threat case and thus worth his while to admit, TJ thought.

"I'm inclined to believe him," TJ told Summer. "What Kellen has done does not square with how the Webbines operate—to my knowledge. They flat ain't like that. I'd guess an outcast, a renegade." He turned to Kellen. "Name?"

"A:alpha," Kellen said.

Too quick an answer, TJ thought. "Shorten the chain, Summer."

"Wait. I lied. It's O:omega."

TJ would have liked to talk to O:chacka about this and resolved to do so if the opportunity arose. "I think he's telling the truth."

"Two dissidents, two rabble-rousers, caused all this trouble?" Summer asked.

"Appears so. Never can tell how much drive a fanatic's got. The question is why. Why, Sing? What have you to gain?"

Kellen spat at him.

"Personal animosity," Summer observed.

"The thing about his father?"

The silence hung there tangibly. TJ and Summer stared at Kellen.

Kellen spat at TJ again. "And my mother, too, you sonovabitch!"

Summer nodded knowingly.

TJ thought about it. Kellen had lost his parents. TJ reflected on the irony of it all: he, himself, was losing—or had lost—all or most of his sons, and maybe a daughter or two. Mike and Gil and the rest were dying and going through pure hell to encounter Webbines. Kellen had not endured any hardship whatsoever, yet knew more about Webbine aura-control than probably any man alive. Certainly more than TJ had learned while at the Home Grounds. The more he thought about it, the angrier he became.

He grabbed a handful of Sing's hair and jerked him upright. He twisted Kellen's hair in his hands causing his head to go back and stretch his neck.

TJ stared in his eyes, ignoring the minor panic of attempted aura-control. "You don't call me names, Sing. You have given nothing to this land, you have only taken. You blame your parents' deaths on me and, I guess, the wars. Well, they killed *my* father. Or contributed to and supported our enemies, which is the same thing. It has been Shepherd misfortune to die goddamn near every generation for this land. And you accuse me?" For a moment his anger caused him to consider killing Kellen Sing right then. And Kellen read that intention immediately. He shivered and cringed as if he expected the death blow to his neck to come now.

Summer put a restraining hand on his shoulder. "TJ."

TJ held his position for a moment, then pushed Kellen roughly aside. "You're right, Summer, he's not worth it." While his methods did not include murdering his opponents, he thought about it seriously this time. A good manager and politician has no need of murder—no matter how tempting. What would he have done if Summer and Mike weren't infatuated with Rebecca Sing? He decided he didn't want to answer that. But both Mike and Summer were worth more than a million Kellen Sings, so Sing's death wasn't even worth considering, no matter how attractive it would be to see this vindictive twerp swing from a gallows.

Then he had an inspiration. The idea was so good that the decision came simultaneous with the thought. Kellen Sing would be a problem no more. Put him where he would do Thomas Jefferson Shepherd Rex some good. It would be expensive, but it would be worth it in its own right—not just for Rebecca Sing.

Summer saw that his anger had subsided. To Sing, he said, "All right. Your chain stretches to the bathroom. You can bathe, do whatever you want. Your food is in there, also. The window is heavily barred, but also it hangs over The Howling Volv. No one will hear your cries, so save your breath."

TJ saw that Kellen was still shaken from reading his aura. He smiled to himself. He felt better than he had for a long time. Sing's naked body had paled significantly. He reminded TJ of the belly of a slug—he didn't have Rebecca's darker color nor any of her attractive freckles.

"And Sing?" TJ added, his voice low and threatening. "Should your tame Webbine come around," he jerked his thumb at the window, "you tell him to stop interfering in my business. O:omega? O:omega has broken the unspoken noninterference agreement. You tell him I shall brand him. I want him the hell away from here." He turned and strode out not waiting for an answer. Summer blew out the lamp and followed. Kellen Sing had no need of light.

51: O:OMEGA

He rose from the river shaking off the excess water. He climbed the river bank while inflating himself.

Kellen's aura had changed and had not been difficult to locate. O:omega had never experienced terror in an intelligent creature. He'd vicariously experienced terror when he observed lesser animals attacked, killed, or devoured by greater animals—that had been part of his training. It was part of the balance of nature and thus necessary.

But Kellen's terror? That was much more personal, something to which he could relate. Kellen's aura had been flashing for a while now, and O:omega had determined that Kellen was finally alone.

Inflated now, he rose slowly into the air, a touch here and there on the stone walls of the palace sufficient to send him upward toward the opening from where Kellen's aura flowed. The window was unlighted, yet he knew Kellen was awake.

/Kellen?/

"Here, oh, Sweet Jesus, here I am."

O:omega heard the clank of metal. He peered through the bars. /You are detained? Forcibly?/

"Yeah,"

O:omega read depression and desperation in Kellen's aura. He expanded his own aura to meld with Kellen's, to infuse some comfort.

"Ah, I needed that. They got me, O:omega. I've been sitting here with nothing to do but think. No matter what happens, I'm through. But I no longer care. Can you get me out of here?"

O:omega tried to wrap one of his webs around a bar. His attempt was clumsy and his web's hold was awkward. His natural secretions oiled the bar and made it that much more difficult to hold. /Observe, Kellen. I can barely maintain a grasp. And my brittle bones are unable to provide opposing muscle strength sufficient for the task./

"Yeah, I figured. Well, it was worth a try. They'll kill me next time, I know it."

/Why would they kill you?/ O:omega couldn't fathom this.

"Don't pretend you don't understand. You know what we were doing and you were aware of the consequences."

/I never understand, Kellen. Human ways are alien./

"Alien? Want me to tell you exactly what Shepherd told me? The Trekmaster told you to go away, else he'd brand you. What does that mean?"

/'Tis a fact I am not familiar with the concept./

"Burning with hot metal."

/Ah. Permanent, perhaps, deflation. I would have to survive on land only./ He thought a moment. He didn't know if he could use the aura-control to stun or kill an intelligent

316 James B. Johnson

being as he could a snarv or flashworm. It just wasn't done, had never been done. /Yet the Trekmaster threatened me thus?/

"You got it."

/Kellen, your aura indicates blind lashing out, much violence./

"Don't be coy with me."

/This side of you offends me./

"Fickle bastard." Kellen shook his chain in frustration.

O:omega read the anger and frustration and senseless madness for revenge in Kellen's aura and was aghast. He didn't know any thinking being was capable of such thoughts, much less of similar actions, though he did understand academically about the humans' warlike past and their proclivities toward violence. It was one thing to know, another to experience.

He saw his own nebulous designs of striking back at the Webbine elders dissolve in Kellen's overwhelming hate. Those old fools were just as bad as humans! Could they solve a problem? No. Would they listen to the females who deserved a voice? No. His fears about Kellen had been finally realized. He'd know Kellen had the capacity for exceeding their joint plans. But he had hoped against hope.

O:omega became sad as he extrapolated from what he knew. A mood of depression overcame him as he saw no finite answers. The Webbines should change and they wouldn't. A damning enigma.

His alliance with Kellen had failed. He had failed at every opportunity. O:Omega began extrapolating his own future and discontinued before completing the computations. There was really no future for him.

"O:Omega?"

He released his purchase and a breeze swirled him lazily over the river.

"O:omega?! I'm sorry!"

He began deflating and sinking toward the cold, cold river.

"Don't leave me."

He sank into the waters, sank to the bottom in emotional depression, not even caring to reconfigure to aquadynamic.

52: REBECCA

Now she was really mad at Kellen. Rebecca Sing strode angrily toward the palace, down Shepherd Avenue almost as fast as she had run along the adjoining walls one night.

Finally she had moved to show Summer Camp what she was made of. And now Kellen threatened to ruin her whole plan.

He'd disappeared.

Well, by God, she was going right to the palace and get it straightened out. Valdez and his freaky friends had bothered her. Constables had bothered her. Padres had bothered her. Attorneys' representatives had bothered her.

Where is Kellen? they all wanted to know. Suspicion was rising that the King had done something to her brother. Valdez had been at the palace and demanded to see the King and been rebuffed.

Was Kellen's disappearance some ruse of his to blame the King and begin a new round of confrontations?

She walked on to where the road narrowed significantly to enter the palace grounds. The massive gates were just in front of her.

"Hey! Rebecca!" Franco Valdez rose from a squatting position along the wall. "Wait for me!"

She paused, not knowing what to do.

"You are going into the palace?" he asked.

She bit back a retort and nodded.

"May I go with you?"

She resumed walking to the gate. "Why?"

He coughed and shrugged.

They reached the palace gates. Rebecca nodded to the late afternoon shift of guards. By now, she was well known among the Gyrenes.

Two of them smiled at her and moved to intercept Valdez. "No entry," one told him.

"Aw . . ."

317

The guard who spoke looked at her. "He's been here for three days. Entry no longer authorized."

So Franco had pestered the palace as much as he'd bothered her. She smiled back and continued.

Valdez turned back, hesitated, then shouted, "Find out what they've done with Kellen!" He waved a pair of thumb drums. "Look!"

She didn't indicate she'd heard. She was mad at Kellen for disappearing. She was mad at Mike for keeping her worried. She was mad at Summer for being so attractive and assuming.

Well, she'd done something to show Summer. He'd find out soon. She was challenging him on his own territory. She couldn't conceal a ray of glee and anticipation and several Gyrenes at the inner entrance thought her smile was for them and beamed back at her.

She realized how important political connections were when she reached the King's inner reception office without being challenged. It appeared that there were more guards about today than usual.

"I'm looking for Summer Camp," she told the King's secretary.

Soon Summer came out of the King's inner office dressed in his jester's outfit, makeup in place. He wore a surprised expression. "Hi," he said. He led her into the VIP waiting room and offered her a chair.

She refused, shaking her head. "I'll get right to it, Summer. Kellen has disappeared."

"Oh?" His expression was bland, but it was difficult to tell nuances under all that makeup.

"Everybody and their uncle have been after me. None can get any official help in the search for him and none can get access to anyone in authority in the palace to plead a case."

"Valdez is persistent," Summer said.

"Franco claims two students guarding Kellen were assaulted and Kellen kidnapped."

"Valdez speaks too much."

"Right. And Summer? Valdez speaks a lot. By now the whole city knows Kellen is missing and Valdez and his crew are blaming the King. Word is spreading like a fire in the fields."

"I'm aware of that."

Summer certainly was acting wooden about this whole

thing. Did he know Kellen's whereabouts? She looked him straight in the eye and he averted his glance. Am I so tied to this man, she asked herself, that my empathy can tell when he's evading the question?

"Is my brother all right?" she asked.

He shook his head sadly. "Come with me."

As they left, he told the King's secretary, "Going to my quarters. Don't let the boss go anywhere without me."

As they walked down a busy corridor, Rebecca said, "Now that you've ruined my reputation, where are you taking me? Is Kellen there?"

"You'll see."

He led her up two floors by the wide, common ramps. At the end of the third-floor corridor, the double doors to his apartments stood closed.

"You weren't kidding," she said. "My reputation is in trouble."

He shrugged.

She smiled and said, "How about *your* reputation, Summer?"

"There ain't none."

"Not when I get done with you tonight, there won't be."

"What?" he paused at the door.

"You come to the Double-M Club tonight and see."

"See what?" he demanded.

She shook her head and pointed at the door. "Are we going in there or are we going to stand here and talk all afternoon?" Was Kellen inside? If so, it didn't make much sense. Summer finally dropped his curious gaze from her. The Double-M Club was for members only, and the membership did not include women. She really had him hooked.

He opened the door, surprisingly, with a key and motioned her ahead of him. She found herself in a comfortable living room area, large and airy, but giving little indication of any use. She followed him silently down a hall and into his bedroom which showed more signs of occupancy than the outer room. She glimpsed a closet through an open door, inside of which were more weapons of all kinds than most constabularies possessed. The room was neater than she would have expected from a single man. And there were several of the permaplas books she'd heard about on a shelf over his bed.

She was confused and hesitated.

He grinned at her obvious discomfort. "You're safe from me—now." He went ahead of her through another door and stepped inside motioning for her to follow.

In the semidark room, she saw a man scramble to cover his nakedness with sheets.

"Kellen!"

Summer pulled curtains aside from the window and the room lighted nicely.

Kellen sat up and she saw the chain extending from the lamp holder above the bed to his leg under the covers.

"Rebecca," he said knowingly. "Sold any brothers to the enemy lately?"

She turned to Summer. "Why is he here, here in your chambers?"

Summer hesitated. "So no one would know we've got him."

"With the ugly mood of some of his followers, it doesn't matter. They assume you have him, or have killed him."

"But they don't know, Becky."

"Rebecca." She thought. "Why didn't you kill him?"

Summer looked directly at her. "Because he's your brother," he said bluntly. "And it's possible we may have a use for him later." His face drooped a bit, the effect heightened by the flour-white makeup. "You, too, think we are murderers?"

She sighed. "No, Summer. I don't. I think you can and would if you had to, but I don't think you are."

"Thank you," he said, voice cold.

"I'm sorry, that's what I think." She crossed her arms and turned her head.

"Well, goddamn, look at this!" Kellen's voice was accusing. "A lover's spat, right here. Hey, don't forget me, I'm chained right in front of you."

"Oh, shush, Kellen."

Summer stepped forward and leaned over Kellen. "I am here to assure your sister that you are in good health. I have put myself in her hands. If she speaks of this, the King is in big trouble because of me. And you might thank us for helping save your life, Sing. Too many people were using you there at the end. Your death as a martyr was preordained and would serve as an assault on the King. I am trying to tell you your life was a short-lived thing." He grinned evily. "And even now, should we let you go, those elements which had been using you would probably kill you just for what you *might* have told us."

"I don't believe you, Camp."

"He could well be telling the truth," Rebecca said.

"I am, believe me," said Summer. "How does it feel to be a loner now, Sing? You are now condemned by both sides. Perhaps you are acquainted with the feeling from your dealings with O:omega?"

Kellen recoiled.

Rebecca looked her question at Summer and he explained about the outcast Webbine. "It explains a lot of things," Summer finished.

"Is it true?" she asked Kellen.

He was silent.

"It is true, then. Why, Kellen? Revenge? Our parents are dead now, the past is gone. Milvin chose the matter of his own death by fighting against Crimson Sapphire. It is history now."

Kellen's eyes blazed, his words a controlled fury. "Shepherd himself, Thomas Jefferson Shepherd, King of Bear Ridge, Trekmaster, bastard, personally beheaded Milvin Sing."

Rebecca took his words like blows.

Kellen continued. "You've heard Shepherd's sword has been called Widow-Maker?"

"I can't believe you," she said hoarsely. But she did believe him, what he said had to be true. It answered so many questions.

Summer had his comforting arm around her. "How do you know this, Sing?"

He spat. "An eyewitness."

"Get me out of here, Summer."

"Bitch!" Kellen screamed. "They've subverted you, too! Whore! Traitor! Get out. I disown you, fool goddamn sister. Leave me alone!"

Summer closed the inner door and she sank onto his bed.

He stood in the center of the room and said, "I'm sorry."

She felt drained. She wanted to cry, but couldn't. She felt physically exhausted. Her shoulders sank and she looked at the floor. "Why does it have to be this way?" she whispered.

His voice was equally low. "I don't know, Rebecca." Something in his voice made her look at him. His face was tortured. "If it means anything, I didn't know. About TJ and your father."

"I believe you," she said.

"It could have been me," he told her. "I fought at TJ's side."

It was then that she knew. The questions were answered. Her growing empathy with Summer told her that he had not known the King was the one who killed Milvin in battle. It also told her that he was genuinely sorry. His tortured clown's face told her he cared and that he thought he'd lost her now with the new revelations.

She stood, a difficult physical feat, walked to him, and took his head and pulled it down to the joint of her shoulder and her neck. His eyes were wet—not teary, just wet—with disappointment. "It's not your fault, Summer." She surprised herself at her own strength. "You can tell me how you feel," she said.

"I can?" He turned his head and a long, heavily made-up eyelash brushed her cheek.

"If you still want to after tonight," she said, gaining strength. His arms tightened around her and she disengaged them. "You have to get back to work. I have parents to mourn and practicing to do."

"Practicing?"

"You'll see tonight at the Double-M Club. The show starts late, be there, okay?"

"Count on it." His voice was normal again, his emotions under control. But she could tell he was curious.

As she left the palace, Franco Valdez ran after her shouting questions. She walked on, refusing to answer. In a few minutes, a soldier stopped Franco from bothering her and she walked home.

Summer had taken her to the Double-M Club as his guest. That had occurred not long after he'd rescued her from the riot in the park.

The Double-M Club was a members only eating and drinking saloon. All the members were men.

Except on special occasions, the rules allowed members to bring women guests to dinner, for a drink, or to watch the nightly entertainment.

Like most people, she'd heard of the Double-M Club, but had paid no attention. Summer had surprised her by taking her to dinner there. They'd first had a drink at the bar where Summer introduced her around. He had dressed almost formally, without his makeup or costume. The men in the bar knew him and accepted him, which was strange for she didn't think many people at all knew of the real Summer Camp. Another thing that surprised her was that they all seemed to be aware of all things political. When introduced as Rebecca Sing, eyebrows went up a little, but that was all the reaction. A Sing with the King's right-hand man? Remarkable to most people, but acceptable to these. And, unlike the general public, each member seemed to know Summer was the King's closest advisor and friend.

Another thing that had surprised her was the composition of the club. Sure, some nobility—they were obvious. By the time she'd catalogued vaqueros, Gyrenes, soldiers, officers, padres, farmers and merchants all as legitimate members of Crimson Sapphire's most exclusive club, she'd figured it out.

Even the bartender held the Muster Medallion. The entertainment that night hadn't been impressive, three men playing instruments and singing.

She hadn't wanted to spend all the gold she'd gotten from selling the farm, so the next day she returned to the Double-M Club and auditioned for a job. Kellen wasn't the only musical Sing. She played the six-stringed lutar and sang. The "Sergeant-at-Arms," who was really the manager, hired her on the spot. It had been obvious that her talent had landed her the job. She wouldn't have gotten it because she was Kellen's sister—except that her date with Summer had made her acceptable.

Tonight was her opening night.

She was nervous. Her first performance. Yet she was determined. She'd unbraided her hair and let it fall naturally to her waist. She wore loose black trousers—as part of her statement—and a matching blouse. Her outfit gave the impression of being a pair of pajammas.

She sat on a taller bar stool, back to the wall of the raised platform on the other side of the room from the bar, right foot under her left thigh in a position carefully designed to make her look casual.

The dinner hour was almost over and single men and groups of men drifted into the bar. She was surprised at the number who escorted women. A vaquero grinned devilishly at her, obviously not expecting to see her, but liking what he saw. She returned the smile.

Her fingers stroked the lutar strings in a repetitive pattern and she began humming lowly along with the music. She'd started early and thought that this way she could work up to her songs and be rid of the nervousness by the official start time. She reviewed her plans. Sucker 'em in, then say what she had to say.

A padre waved a mug of beer at a table with three nobles and sat down with them as they began a game of cards.

She reached up on the wall to the side of her and turned down the lamp. She didn't wish to be obtrusive.

An occasional puff of smoke rose from a patron like morning mist from a stream. The noise level rose and fell, and she felt more comfortable. Those in the bar had accepted her background music. In a moment it would be time to begin. She took comfort in the thick, rough-hewn ceiling beams.

The bartender had offered her a drink before she'd climbed the platform, but she'd refused—and now she regretted the decision.

Almost time.

There! Summer walked in—and the King was with him! Neither was dressed formally; they could have been well-to-do merchants. While no one in the room made any effort to rise for the King, there was a general acknowledgment of his presence. Several waved, nodded heads, or raised their glasses. The King smiled and nodded back, shook a few hands, and took a table with Summer who was watching her curiously. Rebecca was certain that the manager had told them about her.

Her thumb increased the pace on two low strings and people began to watch her.

"This one's called 'A Soldier's Refrain,' " she said simply. Her fingers played along the strings as she cleared her throat quietly.

Hands and feet,
   Swords and assegais.
One Soldier's defeat,
Another's way to die.

The Finger of God
   Or an Assegai?

Well it's certain they can't fly,
   Though they might try.
Fly one day they may,
   If TJ has his way.

The Finger of God
  Or an Assegai?

Hands and feet,
Marching to the beat . . ."

It was a chanted poem rather than a song. As she performed it, Rebecca could see that it pleased them, these men recalling long ago battles. She could make up verses to the simple rhyme scheme for hours. When she finally became comfortable playing the lutar and singing in front of this audience, she finished.

The applause started slowly and built. It wasn't a sustained applause, simply one which recognized her effort. She understood that she was supposed to provide unobtrusive entertainment so the patrons could talk and drink and socialize. They were acknowledging her now because she was new and her material had gotten their attention. She planned on using that initial attention.

The applause died and they waited to see what she'd do next. She'd catered to their military background, the fact that they all wore the Muster Medallion. What new and unusual material did she have next?

"A song now," she said into the silent void. She had all their attention. Gambling had stopped and only the bartender moved about; nothing new from the platform would ever surprise him. Her fingers slowed the beat on the lutar. "A ballad," she told them, " 'A Womans' Cry.' "

"Out of the confines of the cooking
  shed
From that she has done fled.
Her Vaquero's a dashing man
And his name is Red.
But now when he calls,
She refused to fall and spread
For she's done and bled once too often
  for *his* pride
But now she lasts and only fasts
  For a woman of her own is she
  It's hard, but fine, just to be
free

They chew tobacco
  And drink wine
And want to love you
  And say the line
Now JUDGES are we
  Changes are coming
We will be free
  To chop the tree
  The rotten tree of time-worn
tradition
And may come the time
  of certain perdition
All the bells will chime
The Trek will fade pale
And the Queen shall have made
The land into a swale
For no more do we wade
Into the waters out of our depth
  For the river she has leapt

To save face?
No!
To take our place.
So!

  For a woman of her own is she
  It's hard, but fine, just to be
free!"

The audience this time was stunned. Every eye in the place watched her. She'd challenged them all, and done so right in front of Thomas Jefferson Shepherd.

She strummed her lutar softly. She knew Summer wasn't really for male dominance, but she wanted him to know how she felt, and this was her way, although a bit melodramatic, of saying. "Okay, Summer, here's how I feel." Now she knew why she'd left Lonestar. She tried to act casual as she thumbed strings. The silence stretched. She hoped they didn't think her a fanatic, another Kellen spearheading another cause. She just had something to say and had said it. Maybe that was one of the things which had attracted her to Mike in the first place: he was more emotionally tuned to people and would probably appreciate her efforts more than would his father—or Summer. Would they never respond?

Summer Camp began applauding, the sound not loud in the crowded room. There was no murmur. She even had the bartender's attention.

Summer approved!

Time seemed to drag and no one had yet joined Summer. Eyes went from her to him. Rebecca could see some of them digesting her words and intent.

Summer doggedly continued his applause. King Thomas Jefferson Shepherd joined in and stood. Then, as if in accord, many of the women guests of the Double-M Club members stood and joined the King. Summer stood, too.

A vaquero rose grinning and applauded; alongside him a Gyrene sergeant pounded his table with the hilt of a dagger. A few applauded grudgingly; they'd obviously liked the tune and melody, but not the message of the song. Rebecca hadn't known how they might react. But she barely noticed the crowd's reaction. Her eyes were attached to Summer and his half smile.

She sang several more traditional ballads, and played a couple of instrumental numbers on her lutar. The atmosphere of the bar gradually relaxed and conversation resumed, as it was supposed to, throughout the room during her performance. She wondered if her job was in jeopardy because of the lyrics of "A Woman's Cry." On reflection, she doubted it since the King had reacted so positively.

When it was time for her to take a break, she went to Summer's table. The King was at the bar talking to several other members.

Summer rose to greet her. "Well done, Becky."

"Rebecca. And you're just saying that."

"Nope. I mean it. Cross my heart, hope to die, stick a pin in my eye."

"Okay, then. Buy me a beer, fella?"

As they sat, he waved two fingers to a waitress.

"Thank you for your support, Summer."

"You performed amazingly well considering the personal tragedy or two which hit you today." He looked studiously at her. "You were trying to tell me something, not just pitch a message at a bunch of old soldiers."

"You aren't so old."

"Not too old for you?" he asked, casualness completely gone from his voice.

"Not one minute," she said, surprised at herself for being so calm.

Summer visibly relaxed. "Mike?"

"I hope he is safe. I worry about him. He needs someone strong to help him through. Someone who will compliment his gentleness." Rebecca Sing covered Summer's hand with her own.

The waitress brought their beers.

Rebecca glanced around and saw the King looking at them while talking to General Vero. On a whim, she smiled directly at him and caught him by surprise. He grinned back.

Summer's fingers were massaging the underside of her hand. "I feel constricted by the formality of this place," he said.

"Me, too," she replied. She felt lighthearted and happy. A strange feeling for her, she thought, whose brother had been kidnapped and incarcerated by two men in this room, and whose father had been beheaded by one man here and had been fought against by many of those here tonight.

She didn't feel a conflict.

"What time do you get off work?" Summer asked.

53: TIRANO

ARMY EN ROUTE TO MANEUVER LOCATION AT PLAINS OF BURIAL. PALACE GYRENES REMAIN, BUT YOUR FORCE SHOULD BE ABLE TO ACCOUNT FOR THEM. KING AND PARTY TO DEPART LAST MINUTE. SPONTANEOUS VIOLENCE IN WAKE OF SING'S DISAPPEARANCE TAPERING OFF.

Tirano mentally rubbed his hands in joy. Everything going as planned. Look out, Shepherd, here I come. He tapped out his reply.

LOOKS GOOD. IMPERATIVE TO KEEP SHEPHERD IN CRIMSON SAPPHIRE FOR OUR ARRIVAL AND AWAY FROM ARMY TO REMOVE HIM FROM ACTION. IF HE IS WITH THE ARMY HE WILL BE ABLE TO ORGANIZE RESISTANCE, AND OUR WEAPONS SUPERIORITY WILL BE INSUFFICIENT TO HANDLE

TREKMASTER 329

THE ENTIRE ARMY AT ONE TIME. SAME REASON-
ING APPLIES TO OTHER MEMBERS OF HIS FAMILY
AND HIGH RANKING STAFF. REPLY.

He knew TJ's reputation and that the fool would never
surrender while at the head of his army. Tirano's plans
hinged on immediate removal of the Shepherd family and
his advisors and upper level managers.

I CANNOT GUARANTEE KEEPING KING ETC. AT
CRIMSON SAPPHIRE. PRINCE MICHALE AND BAS-
TARD KINGLETS ON TREK WITH NO RETURNEES
YET. QUEEN AND QUEEN MOTHER KEEPING LOW
PROFILE WHILE TREK IN PROGRESS. GENERAL
VERO TO DEPART WITH KING. ANOTHER UN-
KNOWN IS KING'S ADVISOR CAMP. IT IS NOW MY
CONTENTION THAT CAMP IS HEIR APPARENT
SHOULD NONE OF TREKKERS RETURN.

"The Jester?" Tirano asked aloud and only his pet bird
was there to hear him. "The jester?"

SAY AGAIN RE JESTER?

He fidgeted while waiting for the reply. On the whole, the
balance was going against Shepherd. Dissension among the
people. Alienation of segments of the population. TJ shoving the Federation down the people's throats. His own experience had taught him most people operated under the "What
have you done for me lately?" principle.

CAMP DIRECTED MATTERS DURING KING'S RE-
COVERY. ALSO RUMORED THAT CAMP AND KING
SINGLE-HANDEDLY QUASHED HUK REBELLION
WE INSTIGATED. WHISPERS OF RUMORS THAT
CAMP HAS HIMSELF ACCOMPLISHED THE TREK,
BUT AM UNABLE TO CONFIRM. MY PERSONAL
OBSERVATION IS THAT CAMP IS NO LONGER THE
BUMBLING COURT FOOL, EVEN IN PUBLIC. REC-
OMMEND HE BE HIGH ON IMMEDIATE ELIMINA-
TION LIST.

Tirano thought about the jester for a moment. But his
presence was merely a minor hindrance. Tirano had an
inspiration.

TO PRECLUDE SURPRISES, ARE YOU ABLE TO
PREVENT OR INTERCEPT THE RETURN OF ANY
TREKKERS SHOULD THEY SUCCESSFULLY COM-
PLETE THE TREK?

Not a bad idea once you thought about it—he wondered

if the Prince had the strength and mental ability TJ had to live through that horrid medieval Trek.

PLENTY OF YOUR GOLD REMAINING AND PLENTY OF UNDERWORLD THUGS AND DISSATISFIED ELEMENTS FROM WHENCE TO RECRUIT AMBUSHERS. THERE IS ONLY ONE DIRECT ROUTE TO RIDGES THROUGH DAWN'S EDGE. TASK SHOULD BE SIMPLE ENOUGH. MAJOR PROBLEM REMAINS KEEPING KING ETC. HOME FROM MANEUVERS.

There had to be an answer to that problem. He chewed on a knuckle and had an idea.

PERHAPS POISON IN ROYAL FAMILY'S FOOD NIGHT BEFORE DEPARTURE.

Not a bad proposition, Kill 'em off before he arrived. Might be safer.

THAT OPTION ALREADY CONSIDERED. WILL ATTEMPT SAME IF OPPORTUNITY ARISES. BUT DO NOT THINK FEASIBLE. WITH ALL THAT IS GOING ON, NONE OF THEM EAT TOGETHER ANY LONGER. PLUS WE RUN THE RISK OF POISONING GOLD. AND FAILURE COULD BE TRACED TO ME. MUCH PARANOIA HERE AMONG STAFF. YOU AND YOUR TROOPS WILL PROBABLY HAVE TO FACE KING AND GYRENES.

Goddammit. All this fine-tuning was ruining the fun of the whole thing. But he realized the spy was correct. On second thought, a mental picture of Shepherd and his pitiful force being overwhelmed by Two Tongues troops brought a smile to his lips. He tapped his reply, caressing the keyboard.

CONCUR. BAD POLICY TO CHANGE PLANS AT THE LAST MINUTE. LAST ITEM: REMOVAL OF FED ENVOY'S POSSIBLE INTERFERENCE STILL NECESSARY. DESTRUCTION OF HER COMM GEAR MANDATORY. WE CANNOT AFFORD TO GIVE HER A CHANCE TO CALL IN FED ASSISTANCE FOR ANY REASON. HANDLE CAUTIOUSLY FOR WE ALSO DO NOT WISH TO GIVE ANY CAUSE FOR DISAPPROVAL OF OUR APPLICATION EVEN THOUGH WE PRESENT THEM WITH NO CHOICE IN THE MATTER.

Indeed it was fortunate that Two Tongues was reviewed (and passed!) before Bear Ridge got its turn. Tirano reviewed his communications with Bear Ridge and was satisfied that the last minute details were taken care of and all parts of the plan were falling in place. As far as he could tell, he'd covered all the contingencies. It was pure inspiration that had led him to think of killing off TJ's son when and if he returned. Another blow to TJ—if Shepherd found out about it before he died himself.

54: MIKE

While Mike rested, A:alpha inflated himself some more and floated up the cliff face. Mike watched him as he touched the rock occasionally, thrusting himself upward, Mike's rope dangling below him.

A:alpha reached a rock outcrop and clumsily looped the rope around the base. Mike reflected that he would be able to travel up twice as fast if the Webbine's webbed "hands" were more agile and could tie the rope instead of draping it.

A:alpha deflated and sat on the rock to provide a safety point should the rope slip.

Mike grasped the two ends of the rope and began walking up the cliff, hitching the double strand under him as he went.

As he neared A:alpha, he wondered if the Webbines had performed this service for any other Trekkers. He tried to think the concept and project it, but found he couldn't communicate as well as A:alpha. He pulled himself over the lip of rock and said, " 'Pha? Have any of your people done the same for any other Trekmasters?"

/Negative, Mike. Conditions did not warrant such action./

Mike nodded. He was still uncertain about A:alpha's role, but thought maybe the problem would work itself out. He was comfortable with the Webbine, more comfortable than with most people.

The return journey thus far had made a mockery of his Trek east over the ridges. Right now they were just below a summit on Teddy Bear Ridge. And while he was tired, he was not exhausted. He determined to shave again when they stopped for the night. They'd practice aura-control again. He enjoyed melding auras with 'Pha. He'd reached a new inner awareness within himself.

Which led him to reexamine his own intentions. Should he challenge his father for the throne as he'd originally intended?

A:alpha floated off again and Mike waited. A wind blew him away and Mike tugged on the rope to reposition him on the cliff.

He doubted that he could best his father in combat. Which led to another interesting question: should they actually fight for the crown, would his father kill him? Or merely disable him? Mike had no doubt that TJ would put what he thought was the good of the kingdom above the well-being of his son. Were it otherwise, TJ would have outlawed the Trek.

But any kind of challenge to his father would be divisive to the kingdom.

What would Sharon think?

Maybe there was a compromise position. Could he be peacemaker between Kellen and the other dissidents and his father? He wasn't sure. He'd changed some on the Trek, that he knew. Some things had lost their seeming importance. One thing he'd learned of himself and about the world lately: there were no absolutes.

A:alpha beamed and motioned for him to climb, and he did so, the going easier so he didn't have to rely on the doubled rope so much. Even though he was tired, he felt a reserve of strength in his legs. They were almost like his mind. On the eastward Trek, they'd been worn to the end of their strength and ability. Then the rest and regaining of strength with the Webbines had seemed to rebuild them, give them an extra dimension of ability. He was reminded of basic training for soldiers where the drill and combat instructors worked the recruits to a frazzle, leaving only their spirits intact, and then rebuilt them physically while reorienting their thinking to the army way. The Trek was as much or more mental than physical.

Jeez, it felt good to be alive.

Quit evading the question, he told himself. What are you going to do? He recalled something TJ'd said one time, and the meaning took on new significance. "Son, you'll find there are three sides to every question: your side, their side, and the right side."

So whatcha gonna do, Mike?

"Beats the hell out of me," he answered himself and A:alpha's aura showed surprise and an aura-query. "Not worth discussing," he said, and wedged himself in a small vee-shaped crevice.

With little trouble they descended the western slope of Teddy Bear Ridge and found the valley where he'd left his mounts.

He found carcasses instead. Snarves or volves, he thought. But then his aura felt another, familiar presence, and he jogged until he found them: Gil's horses. Two of them. A paint and a gray. No pack animal. Well, Gil had been more interested in speed. He recognized the animals and used his aura-control to calm them. Though skittish, they'd fed and watered well. Mike searched around in the logical places for Gil's saddle and equipment and found the pack—Gil probably saw no reason to hide it.

He ate some of Gil's dried rations and decided to leave immediately.

He saddled the paint and climbed on.

/Mike? What about me?/

"Take the other horse and come on. Oh. Don't you want the saddle?" He'd put his own saddle on the gray.

/This is a strange beast with which I am not familiar,/ 'Pha complained.

"Just climb on him and follow me."

The gray snorted and shied away from the Webbine when A:alpha approached.

Mike grinned and thought about the picture the two would make, Webbine riding horse. He turned his head aside to hide his face.

/It pleases me that you find mirth in my discomfiture./

A:alpha's aura expanded and encompassed the gray. The horse immediately quieted and let the Webbine approach. A:alpha inflated himself and rose slowly in the air. The horse stomped again and 'Pha strengthened his aura. The animal quieted and A:alpha drifted over his back and settled awkwardly on the saddle.

"Grab the reins like this," Mike said. "He'll follow me."

A:alpha awkwardly took the leather into his "hand" and queried, /What next?/

"Start him with your heels or webs or whatever you got down there. He'll keep up with me."

A:alpha looked his distaste at Mike and melded more with the horse. The gray started off without A:alpha urging him too physically.

Mike tried the same and felt his horse's surprise. Though the animal existed on a lower plane than Mike could interpret, he could read basic desires from the animal, like thirst and tiredness and wariness.

As he hurried to catch up with A:alpha he reflected that aura-control techniques had other uses and would be worth investigating—once he had his problems cleared up. He found he didn't need to guide his horse but for an occasional mental nudge.

/Whee!/

Mike glanced back to see A:alpha floating above and behind the gray, being towed through the air by the reins.

/Experience of a lifetime. Akin to riding a dolphin in the oceans./

Mike stopped and rigged a rope so that the gray's reins wouldn't be pulled by A:alpha's wind resistance. He tied the reins to his own saddle horn.

One afternoon, they were riding in their accustomed position of Mike on a horse and A:alpha cavorting about in the wind above the little party, when A:alpha beamed at him.

/I sense danger./

Mike guessed they were within a day's ride of Dawns' Edge and making good time on the established trail.

"What is it?"

/Humans./

"And dangerous?"

/Affirm./

Mike searched the spectrum and sensed nothing. Of course, A:alpha was much more accomplished than he was.

He worried whether to take another route or to simply wait out the danger. While he thought about it, he got Gil's crossbow and loaded it. He loosened his sword.

/They are near./

Mike began to detect something, but he could not read the danger. Just auras of men.

They rounded a bend in the hilly terrain and came upon an encampment. Mike heard a shout and saw six men scramble for their weapons. He projected friendliness. People were too jittery these days.

"Hi," he shouted. "We're alone." Although he had to admit that a Webbine towed airborne by a horse led by a human was a strange sight.

A tall, lanky man tugged at his beard and stepped out. "Prince? Prince Michale?"

"Yes?" Mike was suddenly worried. Something didn't feel right. He tried to read his first human aura and read the danger A:alpha had seen. But it was difficult as all their auras were swirling and mixing. There was one other, more threatening . . .

/Mike!/

Mike followed A:alpha's aura-surge to a rock behind them and a man fell as the shock hit him. His crossbow had twanged as he went down and the quarrel struck harmlessly aside.

"What?" 'Pha's aura showed confusion and doubt. It ran through the spectrum of colors and levels.

"Get him!" shouted the one in front.

Mike jerked his mind back to the six men in front of them.

Three lunged at him and he shot one with his crossbow. He kicked his horse in the ribs and knocked the other two onto the ground. He threw his crossbow at the bearded man and drew his sword.

He fended off a sword attack and felt the horse quiver as a bolt struck the animal next to his right knee. The horse screamed, reared up, and took a sword slash on the shoulder.

Mike tumbled off, rolled on one shoulder and came to his feet with his guard up. The paint was down pawing the air with his hooves and screaming. The reins between the paint and the gray snapped and the gray jumped and ran off.

Then anger took over and Mike charged them. He parried one man, whirled and took the bearded man by surprise, his sword cleaving under his beard much as TJ's had into Yoji in Nihaoma.

He leaped and imitated Summer, disorienting another man, and pierced him through the heart.

He sensed another falling from a stunning aura-blow by A:alpha.

The two remaining men stood together, shock and fear on their faces. They began edging back toward their camp and their horses.

Mike said, "Why?" in anguish and ballooned his aura and tried to lance it into them as 'Pha had done. One of them reeled at the mental blow but managed to keep his feet and raced after his now running companion.

"Let 'em go," Mike said, more to himself than to A:alpha.

He looked around and found A:alpha perched on a small hillock inspecting a crossbow bolt which was sticking through the web on his "foot."

" 'Pha!"

/I am all right, Mike. See to your horse./

Mike felt the paint's pain and quickly scooped up a crossbow, loaded it from a fallen quiver, and shot the horse in the heart. He had to steel himself to the final cry and aura-extinction.

He'd been too busy while fighting to notice if the men's death throes were broadcast. He shut that possibility out of his mind with the thought, Am I going to feel mental deaths as well as see people die? Could he ever observe another execution? And what about sick people, people dying from disease and illness? Was he doomed to accompany them through their deaths? He pushed those thoughts aside.

As he went to A:alpha, he heard two horses and turned his head to see the last two ambushers ride off across the plain. They had determined he was Prince Michale and then attacked. Much to think about.

He bent to inspect A:alpha's wound. The bolt had cleanly pierced the web between his digits. The skin there was thin, but tough. He broke the fletched end off the quarrel and slid the shaft smoothly out. He tossed it aside.

Then he noticed that 'Pha wasn't really paying attention to him. The Webbine was looking at the two men he had slammed with his aura.

/Never before have I killed any intelligent being. The closest was a flash worm./

"They're dead?"

/I felt there was no time to judge the proper amount of energy, so they received the full amount./

Mike sat down heavily. He remembered hacking away at the Ethnarch's palace in Nihaoma, killing several. "I had the same reaction." And Gil. Never, never forget Gil.

While he knew the killing was for their survival, the fact remained he had killed. Humans. /Intelligent beings/ as 'Pha had aptly put it.

Adrenaline deserted him and a lethargy overcame him. He felt depressed. Was life to be always like this?

He sensed 'Pha's aura. The Webbine was terribly depressed, too. Mike could tell that the tremendous impact of killing had affected A:alpha to the point of total revulsion and dejection. It was as if his heart were crushed. His aura

wavered and Mike began to understand the Webbines and
their nonviolence. Another piece of Webbine character revealed and, oddly, Mike was able to see more clearly why
the Webbines were the way they were.

His own reactions were so similar that he found his auara
melding with that of A:alpha.

It occurred to him that the Webbine ability of mental
blows—aura-attack?—at which he had shown little apti-
tude, unleashed within a human would be a vast power,
maybe even too much power and responsibility for one man
to handle. But his experience told him that he would have
to rise many levels of awareness to be able to accomplish
this thing that A:alpha had done with his aura. Mike didn't
think he could ever gain that level. Or would even try.

But the melding with 'Pha helped them both, he realized.
They were both learning at the same time, exploring their
own selves and each other. He found few barriers *now*
between them.

/Such bonding is unusual,/ A:alpha observed.

He decided against burying the attackers and searched
their camp for food.

What would Rebecca think of him now?

Or Sharon?

55: TJ

Sharon Gold was steaming mad at him, and Summer was
only aggravating the situation.

"Gonna shout at me about bedrooms this time, Sharon?"
Summer asked. Summer had been inordinately cheerful of
late.

Sharon glared at him. She turned her gaze to TJ. "Well?"
she demanded.

"Looks like somebody fought a volv in here and killed
it," he said.

They were in Sharon's rooms in the guest wing of the
palace. Not ten minutes before, Sharon had stormed into his
office and demanded an explanation.

"What are you up to now, TJ?"

Summer no longer hid behind his jester's disguise for Sharon and had merely nodded to her.

TJ had been afraid that she'd somehow discovered Kellen in Summer's suite. He rose. "What are you talking about?"

"You could very well have done it," she said. "I just have to find out why."

"Done what?"

"Ransacked my rooms. Destroyed my communications gear."

"Uh oh," Summer said. Summer must be thinking the same thing.

They'd accompanied her back to her suite. All five of the rooms had been torn up. Furniture was left alone, but all drawers had been emptied on the sheepaloe skin rugs, most of her clothing tossed about, cushions and pillows and mattresses sliced. On one wall, a painting of the Finger of God had been smeared with blood—animal blood, he guessed—and a message was written across it.

THE HELL WITH THE FED.

On a bedroom door BEAR RIDGE DOES NOT WANT THE FED was printed sideways in large crimson letters.

GO HOME TO THE FED WHERE YOU BELONG, STAY OUT OF BED WITH SHEPHERD appeared on a counter in the bathroom.

Now they stood in the living room. Sharon pushed smashed electronic equipment around on a table. "I never thought to lock it up. Why should I?"

"Your communications set?" Summer asked.

"My only contact with the Federation and the sector fleet."

"But why?" asked Summer.

TJ was thinking furiously.

"That's what *I* want to know." Sharon's voice was full of disgust.

"You think we had something to do with this?" RJ asked.

"Could very well be," she admitted, but doubt was creeping into her words.

"The evidence would seem to indicate otherwise," TJ said.

"Misdirection."

"Why would we do this thing?" he asked.

"Look, *Your Majesty*, I already know about the ice-needle guns. You didn't requisition them from the royal armorer.

They are illegal, proscribed. And there is the fact of your marvelous, mysterious recovery from a fatal poisoned arrow—quarrel or whatever you call them." She paused and looked crafty. "It is possible that you would have me held incommunicado for some equally obscure reason. One that I don't understand now, but would later."

"No." TJ said. "We have nothing to hide."

"Oh? Where is the source of your weapons?"

"There were only two of them. Summer and I . . . had them for emergency use only."

"I saw evidence of them at Dawn's Edge also," she said adamantly.

He glanced at Summer. Summer nodded. TJ wondered what to tell her. "Like I said, emergency. Men were in that schoolhouse. Trying to kill me—and Mike and Summer—with crossbows out of our reach. We used the ice-needle guns then and in Nihaoma only."

"Yeah, sure." Her tone was now bitter.

"I didn't notice you complaining in Nihaoma," Summer said.

"No, and I hadn't intended to, either, damnit."

"Sharon," TJ said, "there is obviously much more politics involved in this Fed acceptance business than either you or we know." He pointed his finger at her. "You are aware of my personal commitment to joining the Federation. Would I jeopardize our chances by such foolish tricks?"

"I hadn't thought you would. But how do you explain this?" Her arm swept wide, indicating all the rooms.

"I don't. Yet. Summer?"

"Way I see it, boss, is there is no reason to tear up the rooms. Except to mislead."

TJ nodded. "Go on."

"While there are fanatics about, only one significant thing occurred here: destruction of the comm equipment."

"Right," TJ said.

"So the question is, why would somebody not want Sharon to be able to communicate with the Fed or its navy?"

"Exactly," TJ replied. "And since Sharon accused me first, it stands to reason that whoever did this is my enemy more than hers."

Sharon asked, "Another attempt to block your membership?"

"On the surface," he said.

She appeared mollified. "Well, I'm inclined to believe you."

Summer began to pick up clothing. He held up a pair of panties and grinned at her. "Good taste. Hi-tech?"

Sharon snatched them from him and threw them through the bedroom door.

"Summer," TJ cautioned.

Summer took a deep breath and stuck his hand out to Sharon. "Peace? Way I figger it, we're even, unless you make another bedroom crack."

Sharon didn't take his hand. "Temporary alliance."

He nodded.

TJ didn't know what to do about the hostility between them. He wasn't sure the clash was totally serious, but . . . Summer had been acting like a young man in love, and Sharon had been totally businesslike, but withdrawn, since the incident in Nihaoma. Could the kidnapping and subsequent imprisonment have affected her more than she let on? After all, she wasn't from Bear Ridge and might not be used to hardships. On the other hand . . . "Sharon, I can't help but recall your contribution in Nihaoma. You killed Commander Luis Taruc with a vengeance. I thought you were one of us."

"I thought so, too." Her voice cracked. "I was ready to forget about a couple of inconsistencies like ice-needle weapons."

She's fighting to maintain her calm, TJ thought. Something happened there between Westginny and Nihaoma. He stepped over and put his hand on her shoulder. "Want to talk about it?" Her look told him she knew what he was talking about.

Summer turned away and began picking up pillows.

Sharon looked into his eyes for a moment and shrugged. He saw the soft inner core in her eyes, a vulnerability he knew she had even if she'd never shown it. "No. I don't want to talk about it. It's something I've come to grips with and will have to live with. It's over." Her tone hardened. "But I was ready to be on your side. It's difficult staying neutral."

He dropped his hand. "Yeah. Can you repair your equipment?"

She shook her head. "It leaves me with my wristcomp." She waved her arm and TJ remembered what she'd done with it in Nihaoma. "I can do a couple of electronic tricks with my wristcomp data base, like shortrange comm, send emergency signals, locate local electronic signals; but I can't communicate long range."

Summer said, "Do they expect you to check in?"

"Not on a periodic basis," she said.

"Which makes this mess more of a mystery," Summer said.

"But a naval ship is scheduled to pick her up when she completes her review," TJ pointed out.

"So why doesn't somebody want me to be able to talk to the Federation or the navy before then?"

"I don't know—yet," TJ said. "What's different about now as opposed to before or later?"

"Mike's gone," Sharon said.

"The army's gone for maneuvers," Summer said.

"And Kellen's disappeared," TJ added.

"I'm almost finished with my formal review, save for the maneuvers," Sharon said.

Summer looked at him.

"Yeah, Summer. Put all that together with the kidnapping from Westginny and the assassination attempts. There is a knowledgeable hand behind those things. Somebody who knows where the royal family is, somebody with access, probably, to our security files. Somebody familiar with routines . . ."

"A traitor," Summer said.

"Right. Anyway, add it all up. Army gone, only palace Gyrenes here. All of us preparing to leave Crimson Sapphire. Perfect time for a coup."

"Could be," Summer said noncommittaly.

"You don't think so?"

"Maybe, maybe not. I kind of thought we had everything under control, what with Kellen . . . ah . . . gone, now. While I'm certain that the individual groups dedicated to the removal of the Shepherd family would jump at any opportunity, we have no evidence of anything like that. You'd have to organize on a scale so big that we'd doubtlessly hear something about it. And we ain't heard nothing. Kinda strange."

TJ nodded and sank to a ripped cushion on a couch. "This smacks too much of a plot. But the elements don't make sense. Nobody's tried to kill me in weeks. Sharon has a deadline in which to report, but that's in person, not by comm."

Both were watching him now.

He went on. "Then it stands to reason that, considering all we've discussed, that this plot or traitor or whatever, knows full well we're going to be traveling soon for the Plains of Burial and the army maneuvers. Something to take advantage of. It's just for us to figure out how they will use it."

"TJ," Sharon interrupted suddenly. "Stay here. Don't go to the maneuvers."

"Why?"

"You could be ambushed en route, killed."

Summer laughed.

Her look was withering. "I feel it, I feel something."

Summer said, "Nobody can catch TJ in the open and best us and a squad of Gyrenes. Remember Nihaoma?"

"Stop playing the macho warrior and think, Summer Camp," she demanded.

"It occurs to me," Summer said, "that whatever threat is here, it is not so much of a threat when the King is personally leading his army, never mind where that army is."

"That would be my reasoning," TJ agreed. "So it just doesn't make sense." He thought for a moment. "Besides, Sharon, our presence at the maneuvers is mandatory."

"Don't you see, somebody *knows* that, TJ!" Her hand crashed onto the table smashing something tiny, made of metal and glass that TJ couldn't even begin to identify.

"Sharon's got a point, TJ," Summer said seriously. "Somebody could be waiting for us to leave to mobilize dissident elements."

"For what purpose?" TJ asked. "No group on the whole of Bear Ridge can stand up to the army—which is currently gathering. That fact couldn't escape plotters."

"But these plotters must have some kind of plan," Summer said, rummaging through a cabinet. "They couldn't have gone to all the trouble and expense they have for mere disruptions and inconveniences."

"Hey," Sharon said, "what are you . . ."

"Ah," Summer said, holding up a bottle. "All this talk makes me thirsty." He opened up the bottle and took a drink. Then he held it out to TJ.

TJ shook his head.

Summer offered Sharon some. She surprised TJ by accepting and drinking from the bottle.

Summer nodded appreciatively. "Good girl. That decides me. TJ, I agree with Sharon. Something stinks, and it's predicated on the maneuvers. Which means you are vulnerable, somehow, en route. Or," he held up his hand stopping TJ's reply, "if that ain't the case, then it's predicated on you *not* being in Crimson Sapphire."

Sharon took another drink, coughed, made a face, and said, "That's what I think." She looked sourly at the bottle and passed it back to Summer.

He took it and started to wipe off the neck, then obviously thought better of it and took another drink. He looked at Sharon. "We'll make you a citizen of Bear Ridge yet." He turned to TJ. "Here's my recommendation. The plot is probably based on timing, if history is any indication. Let's send a runner to the army and tell them to practice. That the maneuvers have been postponed for a few days. Then we either stay here, or ride off and circle back, one or the other. Then wait and see what turns up."

Sharon nodded enthusiastically and held her hand out for the bottle. "The more you drink, the more sense you make, jester."

TJ thought that what these two suggested could not hurt. Summer had spies out looking. Alfred had spies out looking. If anyone wearing a Muster medallion heard a whisper, he'd inform the palace immediately. It still didn't make sense.

Summer and Sharon were trading the bottle frequently now, as if they were having a drinking contest.

The only thing that made sense was that the attack would come to his vulnerability and he didn't know where that would be. He wasn't vulnerable, except personally, to any threat which could be mounted on Bear Ridge.

Sharon giggled.

Any internal threat.

An external threat.

"Tirano!" TJ said aloud.

"What?" Sharon said.

"On Two Tongues," Summer said.

"It's a long walk," TJ said.

"What are you talking about?" Sharon asked.

"Tirano. Tyrannical Tirano. He could be behind this."

"He sure doesn't like you," Summer said. He pulled another bottle out of the cabinet. "Here," he handed it to

Sharon. "Did I ever tell you about the time one young king stole the lovely Gwendlyon from Tirano?"

"I heard the story from Mike," she said.

"Oh."

"But I see what you're getting at, TJ," Sharon said, peeling off the wax sealant. She tilted the bottle and drank. "Ah, better. But Tirano's already been through the review checklist and *passed* it. He has nothing to gain."

"I know," TJ said. "Even Tirano's too smart to jeopardize his chances."

"If you can get ice-needle guns," she went on, "then Tirano can do something illegal, too. But that would entail a great expense," she giggled again, "just to pay you back for the bird guano incident."

TJ smiled to himself remembering. "That all may be true. But my basic point is that perhaps there is a threat we've missed. Somewhere, something, somebody."

Summer took the bottle and drank. TJ watched the invisible contest between Summer and Sharon. One way to solve your problems, he thought, drink 'em out. Get drunk instead of fighting. Maybe we could learn a lesson from these two. Summer surprised him. Summer doesn't drink this much this quick. Yet Summer can hold his liquor better than most people. Rebecca Sing. Summer was happy with the world. It pleased TJ until he thought of Mick—make that Mike. If he lived, Rebecca Sing's defection would hit him hard.

He rose and held his hand out for the bottle. Summer handed him his. TJ took a drink and the sour mash didn't assuage whatever it was he wanted assuaged. He gave Summer back the bottle. He paced. He was missing something, something significant. But what was it? Just paranoia?

Sharon hiccuped. "Summer?" She pointed through the open bedroom door to the bed. "Would you get that box and bring it here?" she asked casually. Her voice was sweet.

"Sure," Summer said. He went through the door and knelt on the bed. He lifted a small wooden box. "This it?" he called.

"Summer get out of my bed!" she shouted, laughing.

Summer dropped the box and came back into the living room. "Damn it, TJ, she got me again." He grinned. "Maybe we're even—*now*."

The two began drinking again.

TJ shook his head. Obviously, this party had passed him by. "I'll set a guard outside day and night."

She sobered slightly and nodded. "Okay, if you think it's necessary."

"And I'll have Alfred send servants to clean up the mess."

"Alfred Theadministrativegenius?" she asked.

"Huh?"

"Jeesh," Sharon said, "if I've heard that one time, I've heard it a million times. I thought it was his last name."

Summer grinned and handed her the bottle.

TJ shook his head and left.

56: MIKE

It was midday when Mike and A:alpha rode into Crimson Sapphire.

They came in from the east and Mike couldn't help notice from the beginning that something was wrong. The army barracks and parade grounds were deserted.

Bearpaw Avenue, which, with others, converged on the palace, was not thronged with people.

He didn't understand. His apprehension increased. What was he going to do? He was exhausted from the long ride—and the Trek. He wished he had thought to take clothing from the ambushers' camp. His clothing was in no shape for him to be seen in public. Perhaps they shouldn't have bypassed Dawn's Edge. They could have rested there. But something told him to avoid towns and communities.

An old woman and a teenager were pulling a cart. When they saw him on a bandit's horse with a baby cheshire clinging to his shoulder followed by A:alpha swinging lazily above the gray, they stared in amazement. Then the old woman must have realized what it meant and she began applauding. The kid just watched. Mike nodded to them.

He scanned Bearpaw Avenue ahead. Normally, this thoroughfare was used by soldiers going and coming from the barracks area. Where could they be?

Then the thought hit him that they might be gone for the maneuvers.

Thank God!

If the army was gone, then his father must be gone, too!

The inevitable confrontation could be postponed. Relief washed over him like the cold wine he was anticipating. His confidence rose and was echoed in his aura. A:alpha acknowledged the change, but did not query why.

But why weren't more citizens about? By his reckoning, it was a regular workday.

A beggar sat beside his bowl and watched them pass cynically, only raising a hand in acknowledgment.

A padre stood frozen in shock.

Mike guided his horse down a back road to enter through the side entrance of the palace.

As he neared, he told A:alpha about the palace.

A:alpha melded auras with him, sharing his apprehension. /Many humans are there./

"I sense their glow," Mike said. He didn't understand.

Was TJ there?

His mother? What would he say to her?

And Sharon. He reached up and rubbed the cheshire on its furry forehead.

57: TJ

TJ had never seen the Gyrenes so edgy. Summer was staying unusually close to the throne.

It was midday and open court session. The throne room was as crowded as he could recall ever having seen. He'd considered canceling the court session, but had needed to give the appearance of normalcy.

Also he wanted to quash the challenge to his crown which he knew was coming. Among the nobles and the padres were those who wore the Muster medallion and word had reached him of an alliance between the leaders of both groups. This court session should be their only formal opportunity to end his reign—though if he won here, nothing was to preclude them from continuing their alliance to unseat him. Except that he intended to render the ringleaders powerless.

One way or another.

After this challenge was resolved, he could ride off to the Plains of Burial and join the army, finish the maneuvers, and get on with life and Federation membership.

Word must have gone out, for the crowd rivaled a coronation in size and importance. An air of expectancy had raced through the city yesterday and this morning.

Padres, Roaland Cruz' supporters, clustered together. Nobles overflowed their reserved section. Aisles were clogged. He'd been told the crowd extended outside and packed the courtyard.

Well, hurry up and make your challenge, he thought. I'm ready.

Felicia and Gwen were there, Gwen still weak and withdrawn. Not for the first time did TJ regret what the Trek had done to mothers and fathers of Trekkers. Gwen, at his side, tried to give him a reassuring smile, but her preoccupation made it a feeble attempt.

Alfred was completing the opening ceremonies, shouting rules and formal procedures for petitioning the King. Though, in actuality, petitioners of rank were generally allowed to go first having prearranged it with the herald.

Summer plopped casually at his side, sitting cross-legged and staring up at him. When he spoke, only TJ could hear. "Behind the padres. Remember Franco Valdez? With him are many of his and Kellen's ardent followers."

With his eyes, TJ acknowledged Summer's report and Summer slid down two steps from the throne.

The bedlam quieted somewhat when Alfred finished.

TJ saw Sharon with Felicia in the royal box to the side. She looked like she had a hangover. Summer cartwheeled past her and TJ saw a glint of teeth from Sharon.

"First order of business," Alfred stated in a voice calculated to silence the crowd, "Lord Franz, President of the Forty, speaking for himself." He paused. "And Chief Padre Cruz wishes to address the throne along with LORD Franz."

Cruz arrived on his bowed legs before Franz did. Surprisingly, Franco Valdez accompanied him. He remembered Valdez from what seemed a long time ago. Give the man credit for guts, he thought.

The three stopped in front of him. The great hall quieted.

"State your case," Alfred intoned, distaste obvious in his voice. TJ noticed for the first time that Alfred wore a sword. Alfred? TJ thought that maybe he ought to take this challenge more seriously.

Franz stepped a pace in front of the other two. unlike his usual habit of conservative dress, his clothing was colorful, but formal. Trying to change his image? "I . . . we, challenge your right to continue your rule, Highness," he said, abbreviating the proper form of address.

"Go on," TJ said in a disinterested voice. Sure, I've done this plenty of times before, Franz, you bore me. Or so he wanted Franz to think. Was Franz the traitor? Possibly. But Franz had jumped too soon, he thought, probably at Cruz' urging. And that didn't show the kind of intelligence he was giving the traitor credit for.

"The kingdom is no longer being ruled safely and effectively," Franz said. "Illegal disappearances. Riots. Dissension. You are ignoring custom and form when you decimate the ranks of the nobles and disregard the Church. Additionally, you disregard the wishes of the people by forcing this Federation on them. . . ."

TJ reflected that everyone kept telling him what "the people" wanted, except for "the people" themselves. He interrupted Franz. "You wish me to abdicate. In favor of which successor, Franz?"

A murmur ran through the crowd and was quickly hushed. This was it, they were thinking. The grand confrontation. The battle for power.

Franz and Cruz were taking their one great opportunity, the one time when the army was not present. Too bad, TJ thought, I kind of liked the adversarial relationship with Roaland. I'd already decided to strip Franz of his titles and land. Maybe Franz had guessed.

Casually, he glanced around. Gyrenes had been positioned in balconies with clear lines of fire into the nobles—if necessary. Some Gyrenes, not in uniform, were placed in public seats close to the nobles. Franz had no chance.

Since TJ'd known this was coming, he'd had the opportunity to quell Franz' incipient "rebellion" outside of formal court, but had chosen not to do so. It was his contention that the confrontation should be done publicly to clear the air. "Good political savvy," Summer had said.

"How would that successor be chosen, Franz?" His voice took on steel and he saw doubt growing in Franz' eyes.

"By the popular acclamation of the people," Franz said, pushing ahead even though realization of failure must be running through him. Obviously, he hadn't thought TJ would let him get this far.

"Do you wish the entire royal family to step aside for you, Franz?" TJ asked softly, "Or just myself?"

Franz didn't answer as he probably hadn't thought that Gwen and Felicia should be considered.

"Would you be that successor, Franz?"

"If the people so desire."

"Ha!" said TJ. "Are you willing to take the Trek, Franz?"

Franz looked at Cruz. Then it became clear to TJ. Franz was not the fool he'd thought. Franz knew full well that TJ, sooner or later, and most likely sooner, would strip Franz because of his opposition. Thus he'd made a legal claim in open court session—hopefully remaining safe by going public and not giving the King legal reason to take his lands and imprison or execute him. Nice thinking, TJ admitted. Franz had cornered himself and this was his only way out. Probably encouraged by Roaland Cruz.

Cruz spoke up. "The Church would have a say in affairs, Sire, as we had in the past. We would return to basic values. And we would not jump helter-skelter into some off-world franchise further diminishing the role of the Church." He paused and looked *devious*. "We are prepared to recommend the end of your rule should you not drop this Federation matter at once, and bend your efforts to shoring up the Faith and no longer ignore the majority and their need to return to the fundamental and moral laws of God and the Church."

TJ thought, not for the first time, that Roaland could write bureaucratic policy. Then he saw the surprised look of panic fleeing across Franz' features. Ah, that explained it. Cruz had urged Franz to do what he had done, then deserted him! Cruz had just bargained TJ his support if TJ would drop his bid for Fed membership! Brilliant move. Cruz was a worthy opponent who could survive any political infighting—and probably enjoyed being on the razor's edge of that fighting.

TJ grinned acknowledgment and was rewarded by Cruz' slight smile.

"And you, Sr. Valdez?"

"The people, Your Majesty," TJ groaned inwardly, "would have a voice in their destiny, as often related by *our* leader,

Kellen Sing. We also petition you to release Kellen Sing in the name of humanity. And . . ."

"Enough." TJ held up his hand to stop Valdez. Was everybody whose name ended in a Z against him today? But he had to give Valdez credit for determination. He decided to remove one problem. "Herald," he directed, "have two Gyrenes escort Sr. Valdez to the dungeons and take him through the entire basement of the palace. Then take him to the constabulary jail in town for a tour." He turned to Valdez. "I want you to assure yourself and your friends that Sing is not there."

Valdez looked bewildered and began to speak, but two Gyrenes stepped forward and urged him away. Valdez looked wildly at Cruz for help, but the Chief Padre could do nothing.

He saw Cruz thinking. He knows, TJ thought, that I've outflanked him. How's he going to remove himself safely?

"Sire," Cruz said, "it's this Federation business. Let us stop the foolishness and get on with rebuilding life on Bear Ridge. In that instance, the Church would be more than willing to ask the Church members worldwide to support you."

Further undercutting Franz, TJ thought.

"I decline your invitation," he said. "Best insure your Church members support *you* first." To Franz, he said, "I deny your challenge and I shall maintain my rule."

A scattered applause rose throughout the room contrary to court etiquette.

TJ smiled his approval. "Further, I declare you no longer of the nobility. All titles held by you are rescinded. All property confiscated and the proceeds from sale will be donated to 'the people' in place of regular taxes until such time as no funds remain."

Silence. Then applause and cheers.

Franz stood before him a broken man.

TJ could see it in his face. Franz' hand was slowly going for the hilt of his sword. There was no way he could win, and TJ knew that Franz knew. So, it followed that Franz was going to commit suicide right here. but TJ couldn't allow it—and not just for political purposes. He needed to find out if Franz was the traitor, or knew of the suspected plot. After all, this couldn't be all there was to it.

Summer must have seen the same thing in Franz and reasoned as TJ himself had, for he tumbled up, knocking Franz down.

No one laughed. As embarrassing silence followed as Alfred and several Gyrenes escorted Franz out.

TJ saw Roland Cruz edging back to the Padres' section, trying to be unnoticed.

TJ smiled. "Well," he said jovially, "does anyone else wish to challenge me for the crown?" His voice dripped with authority and sarcasm, playing to the crowd. "Has anyone here taken the Trek and can prove it?"

"I have," rang a voice from a side entrance.

TJ saw the look of bewilderment cross Cruz' face as he stood and looked.

"Michale!" came Gwen's startled whisper.

And a Webbine.

58: MIKE

Mike stood there with thousands of eyes on him. He'd answered the King's question. Was he going to challenge him for the throne?

A:alpha radiated confidence in him.

Mike started forward and saw surprise as people noticed A:alpha behind him. 'Pha's aura changed to one of slight anxiety. Not only was he unused to humans, he was unused to this many humans. He'd inflated himself for internal breathing and followed Mike for lack of anything else to do.

Gyrenes stared at him, the new situation beyond their comprehension. Where did their loyalties lie?

As he approached the stairs to the throne in eerie silence, Alfred stood back, divorcing himself from the proceedings. Alfred would not take sides.

Like a shadow, Summer flitted to his father's side. Mike read the commitment to TJ in his aura. Should this turn into a confrontation, Mike knew he would never prevail in a one-on-one combat with the King—and would have to deal with Summer Camp if he bested TJ.

How had he gotten himself—them—into this situation? His Trek-forged confidence and toughness wavered momentarily, but that streak of obstinacy which had sent him on the Trek resurfaced, compelled him to continue to the throne.

He strode decisively forward and climbed the wide stairs without looking down.

With every eye in the throne room on him, he stopped two levels below his father and extended his hand.

He opened his fist and the light struck his small crimson sapphire. It sparkled there for all to see; the coruscation almost an echo of his wildly rainbowing aura.

The hall was deathly silent and he felt in command of the situation.

His father, grayer in beard and hair than he remembered, was struck dumb by his appearance. A:alpha beamed encouragement to him, but the Webbine didn't understand all the history and thus the undercurrents.

He was afraid to look at his mother, so he let his glance slide to . . . Sharon sitting with his grandmother in the royal box. Sharon exuded joy, presumably at his safe return, but then her aura showed worry as she registered the impact of his arrival. She hardly noticed A:alpha.

His eyes were drawn toward his mother. She was pale and weak, and her aura shouted fear. Was she afraid for him or her husband? Suddenly, Mike realized that she would lose, no matter who prevailed in the coming confrontation. He saw it from her viewpoint: after years of being in the middle between him and his father, she'd thought her son dead on the Trek, but now that he'd returned alive, she was in another quandary—he, or his father, would emerge victor from the challenge; the loser, whether dead in combat or escaping alive from some other form of the challenge, was still the loser and therefore disgraced in the kingdom, unable to participate in events in his rightful place.

And, Mike thought, he'd placed her in this position by his poorly conceived rush to become a Trekmaster.

He'd been through an ordeal and now he was putting her through one just as bad, maybe worse.

TJ's breathing was harsh. "So you are a Trekmaster?"

Mike looked down at his crimson sapphire, gaining confidence. "My credentials." His mind screamed, What am I going to do?!

He read a fleeting moment of pride in his father's aura.

"The others?" the King asked.

Mike shook his head. "I buried Gilbert Trevan."

His father slumped back against his throne. Well, he'd known it when he sired all his kinglets.

"Wasted," TJ said.

"Yes."

He had not known what he would do when he returned. But the situation he found shouted at him to take his inevitable part in it. He'd so far been unable to control himself. His impulse had forced the situation.

He asked himself if he had challenged for the crown.

Not specifically, but his words seemed to imply that he had.

What would he do if he got the crown?

A better job, no doubt. But he knew before anything else, this bitter conflict between his father and himself must be resolved.

His father's eyes were boring into him, searching for his soul, his intentions. He built a barrier in his mind and lanced back involuntarily, his aura ballooning too much at the last.

TJ's face showed surprise. A veil fell across his mind and was reflected in his aura coalescing around him.

Mike extended his aura some more and TJ fought the onslaught clumsily, but effectively.

Mike strengthened his aura and funneled it directly at his father. TJ's natural shield shattered, and Mike attacked his basic core. TJ reacted as if dealt a physical blow, yet some barrier, something Mike recognized from the adversity of the Trek, leaped into place to withstand his attack.

TJ tried to attack Mike mentally, but could not do so effectively; his natural ability was strong enough, but without training he could not lance the way Mike could.

The crimson sapphire still in his open hand augmented his efforts. It flashed with the expenditure of mental energy.

For the first time, Mike saw his father's own crimson sapphire, much larger than the one from A:alpha, lodged in the top of the throne. It was flashing brilliantly, dazzling him, hindering his attack on the King.

Suddenly, Mike knew what TJ had inside him. That thing, that drive, that inner conviction which had made him King of the entire planet.

That trait frightened him. He'd rather face the ambushers again, even the Trek again. The fabric of his father fought him, fought his attack, maintained its position over the more practiced Mike.

Mike knew he could not duplicate his father's experience, experience which contributed to TJ's ability to withstand his probes, his lances.

Quickly, he switched tactics and emoted love and friendship and compassion. TJ's barricades stretched, not knowing how to deal with this development. While reshaping his aura, he remembered he'd vowed never to use the aura-attack again.

His father was bending to his tremendous outpouring of good will. A:alpha sensed what was happening and mushroomed his aura into the battle, acting as a catalyst, geometrically expanding Mike's emotional attack. Mike knew that A:alpha wasn't necessarily taking sides; he was simply trying to reunite the two on a higher emotional plane so they could get on and solve the problems. A:alpha was acting in the Webbines' interest.

TJ was wavering; the balance was on Mike's side now. His father gave a little, surrendered some mental territory. Mike pressed his advantage. TJ fought it, not knowing what it was, but wary of it nonetheless.

While TJ was untrained, Mike saw that he had an intrinsic, atavistic grasp of aura-awareness. Maybe TJ *was* the toughest man on the planet.

Yet Mike's efforts were paying off. His father's mind was becoming susceptible to his emotional appeal. An opening appeared, TJ's aura became receptive, red of battle and orange of caution dissipating.

In a flash, Mike considered gathering his mental strength and lancing another, and this time deadly, attack, into his father. It would severely wound his life-force. He pushed aside some obscure message from A:alpha.

His father was fading!

Ready . . .

He felt tentatively with his aura, trying to finesse his father, and they remained locked thus for what seemed an eternity, neither one gaining or losing.

Then his mother collapsed. Her aura sank dangerously into purple-black. She rolled off her throne and fell to the floor, her forehead making a flat sound on the tiles.

TJ dropped his mental guard immediately and rose to go to her aid.

Mike saw his chance, TJ's barriers down, finally. He poised to strike through dropped defenses . . .

Then he knew he could not take advantage of the situation. He thrust guilt aside and ignored A:alpha's pleading aura and rushed to his mother's side.

As he leaped up the remaining stairs, he felt drained. He didn't know how long they'd been locked in that bizarre combat, nor was he aware of the audience in the throne room.

Summer stopped him before he reached his mother's side. Summer's eyes searched his, and Mike read the infamous /killerman/ aura. Summer would kill him should he threaten TJ during this time. Mike reassured Summer with an aura blast and pushed past him.

His father had his mother in his arms and was running down the stairs to the rear exit.

Mike stood, uncertain what to do. He looked at his crimson sapphire which now merely reflected light. He looked at the top of the throne and the life seemed to have gone out of TJ's crimson sapphire, too.

59: SHARON

It was almost evening and she was going mad. More than a full day since the confrontation in the throne room and no one told her what was happening. She hadn't been invited to eat with any of the royal family nor had any been available to talk. And she was afraid to disturb Mike herself. She suspected Gwen had not recovered yet, since the servants whispered and tiptoed about in the halls.

A quiet knock interrupted her thoughts.

"Yes?" she opened the wooden door to her suite and there stood Mike. She noticed the Gyrene guard still on duty.

"Hi," Mike said, and held out a tiny cheshire cub. "For you."

She snatched it from him. "Mike!" The cub snuggled warmly into her hand, its double tail snaking around her thumb, and made a mewling sound.

Mike had changed since yesterday. He was cleanshaven, had on fresh clothes, and looked rested. He had a haircut.

But his eyes wore a haunted look. He seemed older than she remembered him. Maybe it was the quiet intensity about him.

She couldn't help but think of yesterday and his dramatic entrance into the King's court. Even following the events of Franz' challenge, he'd still generated excitement. Everything about him had been ragged: his clothes, his hair, his two-day growth of beard, his features. Until then, she hadn't quite believed the outrageous tales about the Trek. She'd always thought TJ a throwback to earlier and harsher times. Now Mike seemed more like his father with a worn outer shell, but a new inner strength and clarity of purpose—oh, what purpose!

Mike had stood in front of his father and all of Crimson Sapphire holding out his jewel. She had almost seen the sparks fly between them as they were frozen in that strange tableau.

"I've bathed," Mike smiled.

"Oh. Come in." She caressed the cheshire and led Mike into the living room. She kept her eyes on the floor, embarrassed at her own feelings, suddenly awkward in his presence.

Her apartments had been cleaned up and damaged cushions and curtains had been replaced. She'd dumped the electronic components of her comm equipment into its case. Maybe one day they could put it in a Fed laboratory and discover evidence of who wrecked it. But she didn't think it would be important then.

They sat down, she being so careful she accidentally sat on the arm of the couch and bumped down on the cushion. Oops. To cover, she asked, "Where's the Webbine, Mike?" She'd truly like to interview the "mysterious inhabitant."

"He's in The Howling Volv. Food and rest and recreation."

Another uncomfortable silence followed. "Um, how's your mother?"

He shrugged. "Still very ill."

His problem compounded, she realized. It wasn't enough that he had to resolve who gets the crown, but one way or the other, Gwen would suffer. "What will you do, Mike?"

He avoided her gaze. "I don't know, Sharon. I thought I did, but now I don't. Maybe go off somewhere and rest and read?" He paused and looked at her, eyes pleading. "I thought I wanted the crown, I wanted to be King and right wrongs, guide the kingdom to its proper destiny. But now I don't know. Events have taken on an inertia of their own and I doubt I'd have much impact." His voice trailed off and she wondered if Mike won, what would happen to TJ? Wither up and die, more than likely, she answered her own question. Thomas Jefferson Shepherd could fill no position but King. There was no other role on the planet he could play.

She saw he was holding back. "Is that all?"

He shook his head. "I'm not certain I want to be King. It's lost its allure. It's not worth all the trouble and pain and anger and anguish and . . ." He stopped and slumped back.

But she'd felt the fire come back into his voice. There was something else underneath that he wasn't letting out. And she had to get it out of him, if not for his benefit, for hers. "Um, Mike, ah, have you talked to Summer?"

Mike flashed a grin. "He told me that you had thrown him out of your bed. I was jealous."

"That scoundrel. But that's not what I was referring to." Then she heard the echo of his words in her mind: "I was jealous." She had to suppress her feelings and push on.

"Yeah, I know. That other, well, I accept it. It's over." His face fell. "Not that there was ever much of anything there in the first place."

She could tell it hurt him to say so, but maybe it helped him to admit it. Summer and Rebecca Sing. Quick, girl, change the subject before we both die of embarrassment. "Did Summer tell you about the . . . highly placed traitor?"

He nodded. "We already know that the ex-Lord Franz is not the one, nor does he know who is." He told her about the ambush east of Dawn's Edge. "That ambush rather confirms what you-all thought."

She nodded. "TJ speculated on the possibility of, well, off-world, maybe hi-tech, interference. Council politics, maybe."

"You know what I wish? I wish I could read minds like you hi-techs read electronics and all. Then I'd just walk around and find out who's the traitor and why they're doing what they're doing."

He obviously still cared for the kingdom and the royal family, his differences lying with his father only.

"Maybe between A:alpha and me, we could dig out the traitor." He went on to explain auras and aura-control techniques. Sharon vowed to talk to A:alpha in depth or die trying. "We can read auras, but not minds, and . . ."

Sharon thought, So that's how the battle was waged in the throne room.

"That's it!" she interrupted. His earlier remark about jealousy had clouded her mind. "Maybe, Mike. Listen. Suppose there is hi-tech interference, just like we speculated. The agent here who is acting the traitor has to communicate."

"Yeah? I don't think I or 'Pha could pick up electronic transmissions."

"But I can!" she said softly.

His eyelids lifted.

She pulled her sleeve up and snapped the ornamental cover off her wristcomp. She tried to remember the sequence of instructions to get the durn thing to act as a signal finder. She couldn't, so she tapped in the request to her data base and it told her. Her fingers touched the tiny spots on her wristcomp, setting that program into the work section. Since the wristcomp could act as an emergency beacon, or transponder, it had also been designed to *locate* other emergency signals on different frequencies. Thus it would act as a direction finder for any signal.

It beeped.

Both she and Mike jumped.

She held her wrist as level as she could and a tiny arrow solidified on the screenface. "That way!" she said harshly. "The darker the arrow, the closer we are, though it's not supposed to be calibrated this fine—it'll show the darkest if the signal is in the area of, say, the palace."

"There's a signal coming from the palace, here?" he demanded.

"Yep." She recycled it in case of a false reading. She stood and turned 360 degrees to insure it was reading correctly. "All tests positive."

"Let's go!" he said. His excitement was contagious. He loosened his sword in its scabbard. Before the Trek, he'd never carried his sword in the palace.

Out in the corridor, she stopped to recheck the direction from which the signal was coming. "It's a very strong signal, more powerful than my own comm gear."

They took a corridor that led across the entire palace. They went toward the throne room and then up two more ramps. "This is difficult, Mike. The screenface is not three dimensional to show ups and downs." In the open country where the direction finder was designed to operate, the source would be obvious.

She stopped in front of a door. "This is it, near as I can figure."

She saw the stricken look on his face. "What's the matter, Mike?"

"Summer's room."

"Oh, no." She realized it, too, now that she wasn't following the arrow. "I've never really used the DF before. Maybe it's a false reading."

"Let's see." He tried the door. "It's locked! That's unusual in itself." He hesitated, then knocked. "Nobody's home." He glanced down the corridor the way they came.

Sharon did, too, and saw nobody. The corridor ended here, against the outer wall of the palace.

Mike drew his sword and jammed it into the doorframe just above the lock. His arm strained and the wood shattered. He pushed in.

They stood in the spartan living room.

"That way," Sharon said and led him into Summer's bedroom, bore left and stopped in front of a closet. "In there?"

Mike scooped a lamp off a table and lighted it. They went into the closet, an oddly large closet. Uniforms, civilian clothes, jesters' outfits. Weapons, from swords to assegais. Mike rummaged around. "Nothing."

Sharon tilted her wristcomp and tried to figure it out. "According to this, we're right next to it. Ah, there. It's above us."

"A false ceiling?"

"Beats me."

Mike stepped outside and brought back a chair. He climbed on it and knocked on the ceiling with the hilt of his sword. In the corner, there came a hollow sound. He ran his hand along a seam. "A catch. Like a drap door, I bet."

Grit fell and a panel dropped into his hands. He swung it free on its hinges. "Well hidden," he said. "Hand me that lamp." He stuck the lamp into the dark opening, stretched to look, then set the lamp on the level above and swung himself up. His head reappeared, ghostlike in the shadows. "Sharon, you've got to see this."

She climbed the chair and he grasped her under the arms and pulled her through.

They stood in a small, cramped room. A chair. A table. On the table sat a black metal box. A white light flashed rhythmically next to an unlighted red light.

"A transponder," she said immediately.

"What's that?"

"A simple unit. Self-contained power pack. Long lasting. Sends a signal. That's all. And it is signaling now. It doesn't make sense."

I don't know that I understand," Mike said. "Summer Camp?"

"Me neither. Where are we?"

"Above Summer's rooms. Could he be the traitor? I've heard whispers of secret passageways, and I know of one or two. But I've never heard of or seen this room. From the layout, it almost has to be on the floor above, perhaps adjacent to my parents' rooms."

"A perfect hiding place, then."

"Sure is. Let me see if I can find another exit." He took the lamp and began inspecting walls. "I can't believe Summer is the traitor."

"It is rather farfetched, Mike. While you . . ." she hesitated.

"While I what?" he was at the back wall.

"While you were gone and troubles mounted, there were rumors that Summer had taken the Trek long ago and was to be TJ's chosen successor if you didn't return."

"Difficult to believe."

"Is it really, Mike?"

"Nope. Nothing makes any sense today . . . ah, got it." A section swung aside, revealing a dark and dusty landing and stairs leading downward. "Now this makes more sense."

Sharon chewed on a thought. "But if Summer was to become King, why should he be the traitor, too? Maybe we ought to search his rooms while he's gone."

"Good idea. Let's hurry." It was the work of a a moment to pull the trap door up and clip it. Then they went out on the landing, closed the panel behind them and walked down the stairs. Mike found a release on the landing below and they were back in Summer's closet.

Mike returned the chair and Sharon took the lamp and went into an inner chamber.

"Oh, my God. Mike, come here."

Mike hurried to her side, sword drawn. "Un oh,"

Kellen Sing was wiping sleep from his eyes. Sharon saw that he was chained to the wall above the bed.

He shaded his eyes. "Who . . . Mike! Is that you?"

"Kellen,"

"Mike! You made it back! You're a Trekmaster now. By God, we'll win yet. Get these damned chains off me."

Sharon drew Mike back. "Has anyone told you what's going on?"

"In his briefing, Summer said only that Kellen had disappeared. We were pressed, he had so much to tell me. I . . . I didn't read his aura to see if he was telling the truth—you've got to close your mind sometimes, or you're overwhelmed. Something to get used to," he finished lamely. "I had called Summer my friend. Selling us out. My mind tells me one thing, my heart another."

"He took my sister from you, too, Mike. Please, God, Mike, turn me loose!" Kellen seemed to concentrate.

Sharon saw Mike smile, frown, and concentrate himself.

Kellen fell back on the bed as if struck physically.

"Kellen?" Mike's voice was dangerously low. "How is O:omega these days?"

"You know? God, the power you got . . . I never dreamed."

"You never thought, either," Mike's voice accused, low and deadly. His nose wrinkled.

Sharon smelled the unwashed body odor, too. She had too much to think about and couldn't concentrate.

"Come on, Sharon," Mike said, "let's go find Summer and have it out. I'll bet he's with my father." He doused the light, led her out, and closed the door behind them.

"Mike!" Kellen shouted. "Don't leave me! Mikemike-mikemike! You son of a bitch!"

Mike slammed through the door into the outer corridor and didn't bother to close it behind him.

As they hurried down the corridor, Sharon's bewilderment increased. "Who is O:omega?"

"I'll explain later."

She had to run to keep up with him. They went up the ramp to the next floor. What was going on? Something was driving Mike, something she'd never seen in him before. Mike brushed by the sentries outside the royal chambers. They went quickly through the outer rooms into the lounge where they had all waited while TJ was unconscious.

The Queen's bedroom, while adjoining that of the King, had its own entrance from the lounge.

The door was ajar. Mike motioned her back and peeked around the corner.

60: MIKE

Mike did not need to visually check, but did so out of habit. He saw his father, Summer, and his mother. His mother's aura was weak and whirled randomly.

He drew his sword silently and lunged in.

Before TJ or Summer could react, he was in front of Summer with his sword point lodged against Summer's neck. Through the corner of his eye, he saw Sharon come in hesitantly behind him.

Summer's cool, deadly eyes gave nothing away, but his aura echoed dangerously. "You're quick, Mike."

A compliment. Big deal.

TJ was rising from his wife's bedside. "Explain yourself, Michale. Do so quickly."

"Treachery," said Mike.

"No!" TJ lurched for him.

Summer held up his hands to halt the King. He raised his chin to avoid the point.

Gwen moaned on the bed.

Sharon stood, aura flashing confusion.

"No!" TJ said again. "Drop the sword, Mike," he commanded, voice ringing with authority.

He did not do so. "Father, I do not come to claim the throne." TJ relaxed a little. "Not today, anyway. We've discovered an electronic whatchacallit, transponder, above Summer's rooms."

"And that makes Summer the traitor?"

"Along with Kellen Sing chained in his inner bedroom. Don't you see? He kidnapped Kellen to stir up trouble with Kellen's followers. You heard Franco Valdez yesterday . . ."

"So what?"

"Father, you don't understand."

"*I* kidnapped Sing—with Summer's help."

Mike felt his resolve melting. Was there more here than he understood? Damn sure had to be. His sword arm drooped a little and Summer inched his head down. "The transponder?"

"Mine," said the King and his aura told Mike what he said was the truth.

He let his sword tip fall to the floor then thought better of it and replaced it in the scabbard. "M'sorree, Summer."

Summer rubbed his neck and looked at the spot of blood on his hand. He looked speculatively at Mike. "You've grown some, Mike."

Sharon looked relieved. Me, too, thought Mike.

TJ explained about the transponder. "Sharon already knows we got two ice-needle guns from smugglers."

"Why is the transponder transmitting now?" Sharon asked.

TJ looked guilty. "It occurred to me that whatever I did with Kellen Sing might alienate . . ." He looked at Summer.

"It's okay, TJ."

"Might ruin the relationship between Rebecca and . . ."

"Me or Summer," Mike finished.

"Right," his father said.

TJ was concerned about him! "So?" he prompted, voice level.

"So I couldn't very well jail him or kill him. Worse, I couldn't leave him free to preach his populist demogoguery against me. So it was simple: I'm going to employ the smugglers to take Kellen Sing to Two Tongues where he can be a thorn in Tirano's side."

Summer was grinning.

Mike went over to the bed. His mother's eyes were open. He pushed a wisp of hair off her forehead and she smiled weakly at him. "I'm glad," she said, "you understand."

He nodded. He couldn't think of anything to say. TJ went through his own bedroom and Mike saw him enter the small room with the transponder. He flicked a switch and the light went off. "See?"

Mike rose and nodded.

Sharon was standing next to Summer, watching also. "It's your turn to throw *me* out of a bedroom."

Mike felt comfortable for the first time since his return. His mother was okay, and he wasn't fighting with his father.

Sharon was putting the ornamental cover back on her wristcomp and TJ stepped from the little room, snapped his fingers and went back inside and flipped the switch on again.

Sharon looked again at her wristcomp and then through the bedroom door at TJ. "Did you turn that off momentarily?"

"Yes," he called.

"I was still getting a reading."

Mike saw her face and his blood froze. Summer tensed.

"Turn it off again," Sharon directed.

TJ did so, closed the room and came back into the Queen's bedroom.

"I've got another signal!" Sharon said. "If it's comm gear, the agent can turn it off when he's finished transmitting."

"Mike," TJ said, "you and Summer. Take some Gyrenes."

"Right. Let's go."

He followed Sharon out of the room, Summer on his heels. It occurred, then, to Mike that his father hadn't called him Mick since his return. And TJ'd stayed with Gwen and let him and Summer go after the traitor. He trusts me with important missions, Mike thought. Maybe TJ was going out of his way to make a point. He recalled that TJ hadn't really been worried about jeopardizing Federation membership and the Council seat when he confessed to the transponder in front of Sharon. Was she an ally? He wanted her to be, badly.

Of course, TJ had been up most of the night at mother's side and maybe he was tired . . . nah, not TJ.

The electronic trail led them to the housing in the rear of the palace where some of the higher officials, such as Alfred, resided.

Summer had picked up three roving Gyrenes along the way. All had their weapons out.

Sharon stopped in front of a door. "This is it."

On the door was a medical symbol.

"You know who," Summer said.

"Yeah," Mike replied. "It figures. Damn it all!" He knew Nora resented him and held a grudge against his father for the aborted affair. But this much hate?

Summer tried the door quietly. It was locked. Sharon stepped out of the way and Summer's foot lashed into the door, smashing the locking mechanism and all six rushed in.

The surgeon's reception area was vacant, but Mike spotted a light down the hall and ran that way. He burst through a partially closed door.

Nora Ahimsa rose to a half crouch. On a table in front of her was a compact piece of electronics equipment, with a screen and buttons and keys.

He read her aura. Violence washed over him. He also read the deadly purpose in her motions—as Summer must have. She snatched a needle from a solution in an open vial and slashed at her own throat.

Summer was too quick for her, catching her arm before the needle made contact.

Sharon went to the small console. "Selfcontained power source, of course. An older model, but not yet outmoded." She pointed at the screenface. "I've never seen that language. Code?"

Mike leaned over her shoulder. "Those letters. Yaqui written in Norteamericano, more than likely, as that is part of her heritage. The others, some sort of Indo-European, if I recall my studies." He hadn't really believed that delving into ancient permaplas books would ever pay off, but here it was—though he certainly couldn't translate the words.

Summer had taken the poisoned needle from Nora and gave her into the grasp of two Gyrenes. "Keep her safe. The King will want to interview her soon."

He joined Mike and Sharon.

Sharon lifted a small book full of fine printing. "A translation dictionary. Serbo-Croat."

Summer scratched the cut on his throat. "Serbo-Croat, now where . . . Tirano! By God, Tirano!"

Mike read Summer's aura, alarmed at the flashing danger signals. "You mean. . . ?"

"Invasion."

Sharon said, "It fits. It fits our speculation perfectly."

Summer went to Nora. She stood limply in the grasp of two Gyrenes. Her face was twisted in hate. Mike didn't want to read her aura as he didn't want to know the emotions of his mother's half sister.

Summer said, "When, Nora, when?"

"Soon, you damn clown!" Her voice lashed out and stung Mike. She looked venom at him. "It'll be the end of you Shepherds, too, and I'll see it. Ha, you Shepherd whelp. Heir to a conquered kingdom." Spittle dripped from the corner of her mouth.

Summer squeezed her shoulder. Her long red hair seemed lifeless.

Mike moved next to him. "When?" he asked softly. He strengthened his aura and locked onto hers. He might not be able to read her thoughts, but he could sense changes.

She didn't answer.

"Days?"

No response.

"Weeks?"

No response.

Her aura seemed to taunt him.

"Hours?" he asked incredulously.

Her aura screamed at him.

"That's it," he told Summer and withdrew from reading her aura.

"It's evening now," Summer said. "I'll wager dawn, or thereabouts." His face fell. "We're in trouble, Mike. The army is already down at the Plains of Burial."

"Yeah."

"Tirano had to know," Sharon said. "He went through the same checklist process on Two Tongues. So the invasion was planned for precisely this day when he *knew* the army would be gone."

"And," Summer finished for her, "Nora was smart enough to somehow con us into keeping TJ here. With only the Gyrenes to protect TJ, Tirano could capture or kill the King and remove the rallying point for the army. He can entrench himself here and establish position and be consolidated when the army returns."

"Or a different version of the same song," Mike said, realizing, but not saying aloud, that Nora had a legitimate claim to the throne—if all the Shepherds were dead, she could thus legally command the army. He saw that Summer and Sharon both understood this.

Summer turned to the third Gyrene. "It's too late to recall the army, but we have to try. Find General Vero, tell him what you've seen and heard here. Tell him I said to send the fleetest horses and riders to the maneuver area to recall the army. Forced marches, all that. Maybe we can hold out until the army arrives."

"Summer," Sharon interrupted. "Two Tongues has higher technology than Bear Ridge. If they can transport an invading force from there to here, they might possess energy weapons." Her face was pale, but her words and actions showed her involvement. "No wonder my comm set was destroyed."

"Well, it doesn't alter things," Summer said. "Go now," he told the Gyrene. "I don't want any of those horses to reach the army alive. Tell Vero that."

But the Gyrene was already at a full run down the corridor.

61: TJ

He'd told Gwen, "Now's the time I have to earn my pay,"
and a squad of Gyrenes had escorted him to the conference
room.

A council of war.

It had been years since he'd planned a battle, but the
thought processes were coming back as if it had been
yesterday.

Everyone in the room echoed his own grim determination.

Mike and Sharon were there, as well as Summer and
Manny and many other top officers and officials.

As he walked in the door, Alfred said, "Your Majesty,"
and all in the room rose.

"Thank you. Sit down. Alfred, report."

"Sire, evacuation of Crimson Sapphire and the palace is
just beginning. But it will be impossible to complete the job
before dawn."

"We have to try, anyway," TJ said. "General Vero?"

"Yes, sir. Messengers have been dispatched to recall the
army."

No way they'll get here in time. Manny looks older. Well,
none of us have gotten any sleep. Manny seemed to reflect
his own fatalism. No matter what happened, he knew that
Manny would never run, never abandon Crimson Sapphire
and the palace. Me, neither, he thought. Others can run to
fight again another day, but not me. "Strength report on the
Gyrenes."

"Right at a thousand, Sire."

Enough? Tirano must know their strength and should
planned accordingly. "What's the estimate of the enemy's
troop strength?"

Manny looked at Mike.

Mike said, "Six thousand." Six to one odds. Not counting
weapons superiority. Angry with himself for not anticipating
this possibility, he wondered where his famous ability to see

367

problems had gone. The Seven-P Principle. He vowed to never underestimate an opponent again.

The room was silent. So Nora had talked—or Mike had used his aura-control techniques.

"A:alpha helped," Mike explained.

"Where is he?" TJ asked.

"Trying to find O:omega."

TJ nodded.

"I'm sorry about Nora," Mike said.

"It wasn't your fault," Summer said. "No one guessed she had more poison hidden in her clothes."

A double blow to Gwen, TJ thought. First, the shock that her half sister was a traitor, and then the further news that she'd killed herself. Gwen had had many burdens lately and didn't need this one. Not to mention an invasion.

"Order of business," TJ said suddenly. "Prince Michale?"

"Yes?"

"Is it your wish to further pursue your challenge for the throne at this time?"

Mike glanced nervously at Sharon Gold. "Not at this time." His voice was formal.

"Good. We stand united." It was understood throughout the room that after today, it might not matter anyway. Thomas Jefferson Shepherd was to live or die with his kingdom today. Somehow, Mike's challenge didn't seem important now. He looked at Manny. "Have the Gyrenes got their full compliment of weapons?"

"Yes, sir."

"Open the armory to the public." Not that most people didn't have their own arms.

At his right, Summer coughed. "Uh, boss, I kind of already did that."

"Oh?"

Summer's hand dipped into his tunic and pulled out his Muster medallion. " 'Bout time for another muster. The word's gone out."

TJ nodded approvingly. "All right. Our strategy will be as follows: Prince Michale will lead a small party consisting of the royal family, namely Gwen and Felicia, and Ambassador Gold, Alfred, the Chief Padre and others of the Church, to join the army and provide leadership . . ."

"Like hell," Mike said. Alfred nodded agreement. Roaland Cruz smiled at the offer, taking it for what it was: a bargain for peace and compromise.

"We'll settle that between us later, Mike. The rest of the strategy is that the remainder and the Gyrenes will fight a delaying action. I will not allow an invasion of Crimson Sapphire." He was determined never to abandon the city. His city. His roots. The city in which his destiny had long ago been forged by men like Bearpaw and Trevan and Francisco Shepherd. He could not desert a legacy such as that. He was a Trekmaster. While he knew well that to run to live to fight again another day was sound logic, and the situation might even come down to that anyway, he was not going to plan on that. Mike could lead the army in guerrilla actions. Tirano obviously thought to catch them by surprise and eliminate the royal family. Except now, TJ had a few hours of grace—time to plan, time to prepare. "Now to the tactics. In what form will this invasion occur? He's got space transport and will obviously strike here."

"TJ? If I may?" said Sharon. He nodded. "I think we're all agreed that Tirano will land in the amaranth fields outside the city—those acres offer the best access to both the city and the palace. And the quickest."

TJ saw the irony. Tirano was going to use his future starport before he himself ever would. Tirano is rubbing my nose in it, he thought.

Sharon was twisting a strand of hair in her finger. "It is also my considered opinion that," she paused and breathed deeply, "if they do not bomb the palace or use ship-mounted energy weapons before or immediately after they land, then they haven't been given hi-tech weapons and will not be allowed to use any." To his unspoken question, she said, "The politicians involved at Fedcentral certainly don't want the kind of thing traced back to them. Tirano might also be, hopefully, overconfident about his muskets or whatever their armaments are."

"Flintlocks, matchlocks, pistol and shoulder weapons," TJ said. "Single or double shot." For the first time, he regretted not instigating the manufacture of that kind of weaponry himself. Making gunpowder was simple. But by the time he had the capability, Bear Ridge was consolidated and he was looking for Federation membership.

"If it rains," Summer observed, "Tirano's got a problem."

"I agree," TJ said. "More than likely, though, they'll have some fall-back weapons, like swords and crossbows."

"Awful cumbersome load for a soldier," Summer said.

"Especially when carrying powder and ball and ramrods and stuff."

TJ nodded. "You're right. And Tirano must be confident. Six to one odds, he doesn't have to worry. So, I'll wager perhaps a short sword for every man. Or a bayonet attached to the shoulder weapons." He looked at Roaland Cruz. "Padre, pray for rain, will you?"

"Yes, Your Majesty. Immediately."

"Sharon," he asked. "How do you reckon they will land? In shuttle craft? In ships?"

"I'd bet my next paycheck on ships, TJ. Six thousand men would take a whole lot of shuttle craft; transports are designed to land and disgorge men or cargo swiftly."

"Makes sense to me. But the ground out there is soft."

"That won't matter with stabilization pods and gyros."

"That's Tirano's problem, anyway," he said. "Anything else?"

"Yes," she said. "I used Nora's comm set and sent a message to the Federation Navy. They won't get it in time—I checked their schedule. Again the politics. The sector patrol is not within range—their routine has been cunningly designed so that they are effectively removed from any interference at this time."

"It is suspicious," TJ said. "They need someone new on the Council to clean 'em up." He tapped his finger on the table. "This should effectively ruin Tirano's chances at selection for that Council seat."

"Not at all," Sharon said apologetically. "The way the rules read, if he is successful here, he will automatically get the seat as he will rule both of the planets in the running for the same seat. And even though you might have an army opposing him in the outlands somewhere, he'll have the power here. Which is what he is counting on. It's not really a loophole in the system; it's just that the Council never has had this problem and didn't consider the possibility when it wrote the rules."

TJ was calm, cold, and calculating. He'd figured something like that. It was the final reason in his decision to remain in Crimson Sapphire and fight. "It's all academic, anyway."

"*I* told you this Federation business would lead to no good," Roaland Cruz said.

"You did that, Roaland. You did that." He paused and

tugged at his beard. "Everybody knows the situation. Manny, feed your troops and let them get as much sleep as possible. Alfred, continue evacuation of the city. Anybody with a family, best make your peace with them now. And Mike, get your party ready to go."

"Father," Mike said quietly, "you don't really think that Gwen and Felicia Shepherd would run out on Crimson Sapphire and you, do you?"

"Me, neither!" said Sharon.

He glanced his appreciation at her, though she was wrong. But he did respect his wife's and mother's wishes to remain. They were as dedicated to the kingdom as he was. "We'll see," he said noncommittally.

When the noise overwhelmed the land, it was just before dawn and TJ was still arguing with Gwen and Felicia and Mike. In fact, he'd already decided they wouldn't move short of his using force. And he was considering that option. But Mike wouldn't do that to his mother and grandmother.

"All right," he finally shouted. "Tell Cruz he's lost his escort."

Then the noise intruded. The earth shook. Weapons fell from walls.

"Going to have to move the spaceport farther away from the city," he told himself.

On the western side of the palace was a landing which overlooked the amaranth fields. He grabbed his weapons and raced for that place.

When he arrived, several people were already there. It was still dark, though a hint of dawn was showing over the mountains to the east.

He counted six great, sleek gray machines just now landing on the plain, squatting in the dark like menacing, mechanical monsters.

"That confirms it, TJ," Sharon said at his shoulder. "Those ships carry about a thousand each."

"They haven't bombed us yet," he said.

"Nor used missiles nor energy weapons," she said. "The crews aren't going to get involved, but you can bet they've got us on night view cameras right now."

"I hope you're right about the energy weapons," Summer said from the dark.

"Which maybe I can help," Sharon said suddenly. She

flipped the cover off her wristcomp and tapped at it. "There. Found their frequency." She put her mouth close to the unit. "Unidentified troopships. I know you read. This is *Federation Ambassador* Gold speaking. You are violating Federation code and law. I have recorded your energy emissions and am relaying them to the Federation Navy patrol which is already en route. I order you not to interfere. I also order you to turn off all systems and remain in place. Do not disembark any personnel. You will be held accountable and face the penalties. I shall recommend death."

TJ looked at her. Mike was standing right beside her.

"It was worth a try," she said.

Mike linked his arm with hers.

A Gyrene climbed the outside stairs to the landing. "General Vero presents his compliments and says that the Gyrenes are forming."

"Very good," Tj said. "I'll be there directly."

Glaring lights shot out from the transports and illuminated the area. TJ saw troops marching down ramps out into his amaranth fields.

Sharon spoke into her wristcomp again. "Troopships, I say again, I have identified you. Turn off all systems immediately."

The lights extinguished.

"I'll be damned," said Summer.

"Yep," said Sharon.

Dawn was rushing across the land.

"Troops still piling out," Mike said.

"There wasn't much chance of stopping that," Sharon said.

TJ knew it was time to go. He looked to his left and saw the dawn strike Crimson Sapphire. To the right, the river and the mountains were peaceful in the morning air. Behind him, within the palace, he heard shouts and quick movement.

Well, if it had to end, this wasn't a bad place for the end to come. He turned on his heel and strode down the stairs.

Dressed in full battle gear, TJ, Summer, and Manny Vero stood on a balcony overlooking the assembled troops. Helmets and chain mail glinted in the dawn's light. Assegai blades sharp enough to shave on thrust into the air from each soldier.

". . . we have the advantage, temporarily," Manny was saying. "We'll rain crossbow bolts on them from afar."

"That'll make them think twice," Summer said.

"Are their weapons confirmed?" TJ asked.

Manny nodded. "Just as we discussed. Scouts report flint-lock and matchlock type weapons."

"Not accurate at long distance," Summer added. "Nor as deadly as our crossbows."

"Did the scouts report transportation?" TJ asked.

"Some horses, none of the steam engines," Manny said.

"Stands to reason," TJ agreed. Tirano hadn't expected much resistance and would rather transport troops from Two Tongues than mounts or vehicles or cannons. He looked down at his Gyrenes. All were mounted. Not that in battle their mounts would survive, but it was another initial advantage.

Alfred climbed up the outside stairs to the balcony. "Sire, the evacuation of the city and the palace does not go well."

"It figures. Do what you can." TJ thought about stalling his attack. The delay would give Alfred more time for the evacuation. He looked off to the right at the mountains. A possibility of rain, but you never knew. From his position, he could see ranks of soldiers from Two Tongues forming. It would be soon. Had things gone right, he would have preferred to attack while the enemy was still forming. Perhaps contain them in the troopships before they offloaded. But no such luck.

He evaluated their chances. Not good. However, he knew the mettle of his Gyrenes. To the side, a few hundred men all wearing the Muster medallion prominently were seeing to their mounts and weapons. Here and there a padre or noble or farmer was stripping to battle gear. A formidable force in itself, all battle tested—but rusty and out of shape. At least they'd brought their own horses. Which was more advantage. Especially in the amaranth fields criss-crossed by the irrigation ditches. Horses would leap some of the ditches, while foot-soldiers would bog down. And horses could wade while the mounted Gyrene fought. The more he thought about it, the better he liked their chances. He turned to Summer. "My amaranth fields are going to be ruined."

"You can scratch the sluice-berry crop, too," Summer replied.

TJ saw the realization strike them both simultaneously; it grew between them like a balloon. He grinned and said, "Alfred?"

"Sire?"

"Send runners to the royal engineers. Open all the sluice

gates to the amaranth fields. Open them wide. Insure the downstream locks are closed so that no runoff escapes back into the Howling Volv. I would flood the fields."

As Alfred rushed off, Manny grinned. "I knew you were the boss for a reason, TJ."

TJ acknowledged the compliment and then realized Manny had never called him by his name.

Mike, Sharon, Felicia, and a frail Gwen came out on the balcony behind them.

TJ took Mike by the arm and stepped aside with him. Sharon followed. "Mike," he said, "you stay here and run things. That's my last word."

Mike started to speak but then said nothing.

"We're going to flood the fields," TJ continued. "In addition to bogging down Tirano's troops, the water should play hell with the powder for his weapons—and help them misfire, too." He paused and lowered his voice. "I charge you with one task, Michale. Get Bear Ridge into the Federation." He clasped arms with Mike. "If we don't win, you might want to fight a guerrilla war against Tirano. Anything can happen. The army is strong and will follow your leadership. You are a Trekmaster and know your duty."

"Yes, faith . . . TJ." Mike's return grip was surprisingly strong. Yes, Mike had learned well. He would make a fine leader. Was he not a Trekmaster?

"And take care of your mother, will you?" TJ released Mike's arm. He put his hand on Sharon's shoulder. "It's been fun, Sharon. Thank you. Help Mike get us into the Federation, okay?"

Sharon didn't answer. Her face showed inner strain. She was involved.

He turned and walked to Felicia. He hugged her. "Mind the store, mum."

The old woman looked ancient this morning, but the fire was still there in her eyes. "I am proud today, Thomas."

He went toward the stairs and Gwen. She was deathly pale and leaning against a wall for support. She was dressed formally, crown and all. "I'll be here when you come back," she said.

And now he was unable to speak.

She reached up and snapped something onto the chain which held his Muster medallion. He looked down and saw his crimson sapphire. It began to glow.

"For luck," she said. "I had it mounted in gold last night."

He thought inanely, I hope it doesn't make me any more of a target than I already am. He embraced her quickly, awkward with battle gear and weapons, and ran down the stairs three at a time.

As Summer and Manny followed, he saw three Webbines float to the balcony and land next to Mike. A:alpha, he knew. He recognized I:imbawe from a long time ago. The third? O:omega?

He went to his black stallion and looked back.

"Good luck, Camp," Manny said.

"We'll drink together tonight, Manny," Summer said.

Manny shrugged and went to his mount.

Summer stepped over to TJ. His voice was low when he spoke. "I regret it has to be this way, TJ."

"Me, too." TJ and Manny were to lead half of the Gyrenes each. Summer was to take the Muster comrades and they would attack the enemy in a three-pronged movement. "But this is the best plan."

"If it makes you feel any better," Summer said, "Mike will do the job we left behind."

"I'm not worried on that account, Summer. Not any longer." He checked Widow-Maker.

"Thanks, TJ," Summer said enigmatically.

TJ felt a surge of confidence. "Horse shit, Summer. You've already got us dead. Rebecca would never forgive me if I didn't get you through this."

"There's that, TJ."

TJ grinned. "You know, I suspect it's written somewhere that you and I will die together. As long as we're apart on the battlefield, we shall live to fight on."

Summer touched him on the shoulder and ran to his troops.

TJ looked up. All were mounted, waiting for him. A thousand Gyrenes. A couple of hundred extra men dressed for battle, but not in uniform; each wearing a Muster medallion.

He was the center of attention, all waiting for him to speak.

Movement on the walls and on the balconies and landings ceased. He felt the pressure of thousands of eyes and ears.

Casually, he stepped into the saddle and turned his stallion to face his troops.

"History will not forget this day," he said. "Let's go out and kill the bastards."

62: TIRANO

Tirano looked through his glass at the thousands of acres of prime farm lands that would this day be ruined. He saw the interwoven network of culverts, ditches, and trenches. The choice of landing site no longer looked perfect. But where else could he have landed his invasion force? There wasn't sufficient space close enough to Crimson Sapphire for the surprise attack.

Shepherd should be sweating blood by now, he grinned to himself. Then his thoughts immediately soured. That swine, Captain Shawn, had just deserted him. To hell with the Federation representative. Of course, it was all politics. He'd never really trusted Shawn all that much anyway.

He turned his glass onto the city of Crimson Sapphire. Larger than he remembered it. Lots of space here; unlike cities on Two Tongues, they didn't stack people on top of people.

He wondered what had happened to his spy. Caught? Probably. At any rate, her primary use was at an end. He scanned the palace. Now that was a *royal* palace. He'd live there himself, when he visited his vassal planet. There. Shepherd and his puny force forming up.

"We'll have to watch all those damned ditches," he told the gathered officers in front of him. "The land looks flat, but trenches run all over the place. Is all in readiness?"

"Yes, Your Majesty," replied his chief general.

"Well, I tire of waiting. Let us end this quickly." His arm went up, dislodging his special pet bird. "Our purpose is to capture or kill Shepherd and his family, and as many officials and officers as we can. To do that, we're going to have to overcome his palace guards." His arm still up, he paused.

The bird fluttered around his raised hand, squawking its displeasure. He finished, "As we planned, a frontal attack, encircling the palace. Just overwhelm them! And keep your powder dry!"

He dropped his arm in a dramatic gesture.

The officers raised their fists and chanted back, "Keep your powder dry."

They turned and marched to their horses and mounted.

Tirano went to his mount, a speckled gray. The bird landed again on his shoulder. He reached up and stroked its neck. The bird stretched its head backward to feel more of the scratching, its long and wide curved beak lifting into the air, seeming to point toward Shepherd. "Yes, my darling," Tirano said, "soon." Carefully, he set the bird atop the special T-frame constructed for the bird in place of the saddle horn.

He bent to scrape clay and dirt from his gleaming boots.

He was going to stay here in the lee of Shawn's ship and direct the battle.

He scanned the scene again. He estimated Shepherd's troop strength. Tirano had maybe five or six to one advantage. That was good.

What wasn't good was that Shepherd was leading his troops in this direction. Why doesn't the fool fight us from defensive positions in the city or the palace? God damn it! This wasn't according to plan. Shepherd should realize the odds against him—and our superior weapons.

Only a fool would attack. He realized guiltily that he and his generals hadn't worked out any tactics for open field battle. Shepherd, you cagey bastard!

"Smash them!" he said viciously.

He had to climb on his horse to monitor what was happening. The Bear Ridge troops came closer, spread over a wide front. They stopped and Tirano saw thousands of crossbow bolts lash into the sky and fall onto his troops. Fire back, fools.

Puffs of smoke rose from his front formations and a second later the ragged banging sounds of their weapons reached him. Ah, good. But the firing had little effect. Shepherd's troops were still too far away for ball and powder. No matter, soon they would close. Another volley of bolts from crossbows lanced into the front of his columns. Men were down now, how many he couldn't count. He was taking heavy losses. He saw men stumble in and out of ditches and water channels. What a goddamned place to fight a battle.

The two lines had not yet clashed and he tried to pick out Shepherd.

The attackers came closer and he saw them split into three wedges, all mounted, and bearing down on his troops.

There! Shepherd. Leading the middle formation, close to spearing into the Two Tongues troops and their wide, single formation. Shepherd had that damn sword out, his beard jutting in the wind, face grim. Old TJ has aged, Tirano thought. Serves the bastard right. TJ's black stallion was trotting and then moved into a canter. Tirano knew that the war horses would crush his foot soldiers.

He turned to a pool of generals and runners. "Have them aim for the horses, goddamnit, we'll get slaughtered."

A general nodded and sent a runner off. Tirano knew that they knew that their troops were sufficiently experienced to do so without being told.

The runner's horse splattered a little mud on Tirano's leggings. Absently, he noticed that this part of the field seemed to be seeping water. A minor irritation, he thought. He glanced at the sky. Just so it doesn't rain. He smelled powder on the quickening wind. He heard continuous shooting now and looked again. Shepherd and his men were close enough for the weapons to begin to take their toll.

The three Bear Ridge formations, looking puny in the distance, were almost to his lines. "Keep your powder dry," he said to himself.

He realized, then, what Shepherd was doing. He was going to die in a blaze of glory, not the ignominious death he must know Tirano had planned for him.

Not a bad move, Shepherd, but you'll be just as dead.

He urged his mount to higher ground, out of this mud. His glass caught flowing water in some culverts and canals about the periphery of the battle field. He wanted to be closer to witness the death of Thomas Jefferson Shepherd.

63: MIKE

"What is he waiting for?" Sharon asked. "The longer he waits, the better Tirano becomes organized."

"The fields to flood," Mike said. "But he doesn't dare wait too long, for the enemy is not going to stay spread out like that forever." I wish I could be out there with them, he thought. It's my place. As Trekmaster. As next King of Bear Ridge. As a Shepherd.

Sharon was looking at him. The breeze on the balcony blew her hair and she straightened it with her fingers. "I know what you're thinking, Mike."

"Oh?"

"The smart thing to do would be to stay here, just as TJ said."

"Do you think so, too?"

"Somebody has to run things when this is over."

She hadn't said it, but she thought they were all going to die. Father, Summer, the Gyrenes, everybody. She avoided his gaze.

I couldn't live with myself, he thought. "Would the remnants of the kingdom respect my leadership?"

Her face was drawn. "Mike, *I* don't want you to die." Her voice was hoarse.

"Thanks," he said, touching her face with his fingers. "You wouldn't respect me."

"Yes, Mike, yes I would."

I wouldn't, he thought.

The battle was far enough removed from the palace that they heard only flat, instant sounds of musketry. Sometimes many fired together, causing a ripple of unnatural sound. "We could use some rain," he said.

/Why?/ asked A:alpha.

"The enemy has weapons such that the powder and igniter sources . . . you can do it!"

Sharon was following this odd conversation with a bewildered look on her face.

/Sometimes,/ I:imbawe replied, /when conditions are ripe./

Mike saw that I:imbawe had an immediate grasp of the problem. "Now I understand about the weather during the Trek," he aloud.

I:imbawe's aura colored to admission. /It is necessary to the test of the Trek. At times./

"Try it. Try it now," Mike demanded. "Certainly you see the necessity."

/But we would contribute to the battle,/ O:omega said, flickering his eye-membranes rapidly.

/No,/ indicated I:imbawe, /we would be joining with the Trekmasters and the other humans of *our* world./

/'Tis true,/ A:alpha said. /Shall we meld?/

O:omega beamed instant agreement.

The three Webbines stood together and faced the mountains. Mike watched their auras join, meld, and expand.

Excitedly, he told Sharon, "They're going to try to make it rain!"

"How can they do that?"

"I don't know," he admitted. "I certainly can't. But they can, I think. Remember what I said about auras? They've linked." He went on and told her his theory about the weather on the Trek and other occasional odd weather occurrences.

"What a scientific gold mine," she said. "But how? How does a thinking creature affect something like the weather?"

"Beats me," Mike said.

"Some kind of energy interaction with natural lasers in the atmosphere?" she asked.

The clash of the two armies interrupted his thoughts. Time to go, he thought. Don't tell mother, just go.

Sharon interrupted his thoughts again. "Mike, do you realize that the Webbines' cooperating with you solves the problem? This means they are no longer a 'separate' people according to Federation guidelines. And since they can change the weather, the Federation scientific community will allow—no, demand—Bear Ridge be accepted to the Federation?"

He hadn't thought about it. "You might have to take that up with Tirano." TJ's dream so close, yet now, so far away. A dream is all it was. Not reality any longer. The only constant was death. His aura must have reflected his thoughts, for A:alpha spared a tiny bit of energy to bolster his confidence.

Just then, Alfred came out onto the balcony and pointed to the city. "Prince Michale, I want to show you this."

From Crimson Sapphire a steady stream of people flowed. Men certainly, but also many women. He could see that they were armed with whatever came to hand. Walking sticks, brooms, axes, assegais, crossbows.

"What are they doing?"

"Going to fight for what they believe in and fight for their land," Rebecca Sing said as she ran up the outer stairs lightly. She was dressed in tight trousers and a thick jacket. Her braided blonde hair fell across the crossbow strapped to her back. Mike counted three daggers in her belt. The always-ready smile tugged at the corners of her mouth. "Welcome home, Mike."

"Rebecca," he acknowledged.

Sharon moved next to him and linked her left arm through his right.

Rebecca smiled. Her freckles seemed to dance on her face. Mike felt the old attraction returning, dragging his attention from the battle raging in front of them. Involuntarily, his aura reached out to touch hers. He found her carefully neutral, determined to fight. Another intruded on his now heightened awareness. Sharon. He could almost read her thoughts from her aura. He felt his own aura being pulled to her, away from Rebecca. He turned and stared into her eyes and somehow they melded. He saw the sudden change through her eyes and her aura switched to scarlet and then to an outflow of emotions so strong that it surprised him. He found himself reciprocating as their auras cemented together . . .

And he knew it would be all right.

". . . we're going to go out there and help any way we can," Rebecca was saying.

He tore his concentration back to Rebecca and the battle.

"We're not very organized," Rebecca said, "but we'll do what we can."

"Wait," Mike said. "I have an idea. Alfred?" his voice rang.

"Prince?"

Mike saw the naked sword in Alfred's hand. Mike wondered if he, the Prince of the Realm, was going to be the only human male left in Crimson Sapphire not in battle. "Alfred, you go with Rebecca Sing. Take charge of the city folk. Do not let them go into battle for they would die swiftly and uselessly. Instead, have them circle the amaranth fields—the battle field. They are even now flooding and the rain will soon come." He glanced up at the darkening skies. Black clouds were beginning to boil over the mountains. He felt the force of the three Webbines' melded auras working, demanding. "With the rain and the flooding, no one out there will be able to move well. They will struggle in the mud to . . ."

"That's it!" Rebecca said. "It *will* work. Summer and I . . . well, those fields will flood quickly. Unmounted men will have the most trouble. They'll seek to escape."

"Right," Mike said, "the enemy will want to get to drier ground. They'll come out slowly, one by one, and you can overcome them easily." A brisk, cool wind swept the balcony. Hurry! his aura demanded of the Webbines.

Alfred was already running down the stairs to his waiting horse.

Rebecca looked at Mike one more time and ran after the herald.

"Things are looking up," Mike said with a hitch in his voice.

Sharon was watching the two forces come together. Mike looked also and his father's figure leading the attack could not be missed. Just like him. Right out there in front. Can I do less?

Sharon must have guessed what he was thinking. "An admirable figure, huh?"

"Yeah."

"His reign is remarkable if nothing else," Sharon said, "since he has all those women out there ready to fight for him."

Mike nodded. "He's won, then, hasn't he? Even if he loses the battle and his life, he's won."

She squeezed his arm. "We've all won."

Mike realized that almost everything TJ had done as King was now paying off—but not in the way he'd intended it.

"Who is that?" Sharon asked, pointing.

On the far side of the city, pouring out of the forest came mounted men riding hard. Two hundred, maybe, he estimated. "Vaqueros," he said. His own vaqueros from his herds. "They'll be here in a few minutes."

"Mike! No. Not you, too!"

"It's the only army I could come up with."

"All right, dammit," she said, snapping at her wristcomp and stretching a tiny filament to the ring on her forefinger. "I'm going, too."

"No! Don't sacrifice your position with the Federation."

"To hell with the Fed," she said. "Ma would never forgive me if I didn't do what I had to do."

"Sharon," he enveloped her with his aura, "I need your help. With me gone, no one is left to help Felicia and mother. You could do it. They aren't strong. You could save them. I saw you in Nihaoma, I know you can do it." He strengthened his aura until it was urging, demanding, showing his concern. She wavered. "We need your presence here, to monitor the ships should they choose to intervene. Think how much you can contribute. If we win, we'll need you worse than ever before, can't you understand?" *I'll need you, too,* his eyes pleaded. "Do it for me?"

"Yes," she said.

He grabbed her and kissed her hard. It was wet and clumsy—but it made him want something he hadn't known he needed. He tore himself away and ran down the outer stairs to the lone horse below, thinking already about flanking the enemy with his two hundred vaqueros.

64: TJ

After the first volleys, TJ raised his sword in signal and swung the black toward Tirano's lines. The fool had spread his soldiers in a broad front.

TJ checked behind him and saw that his Gyrenes had formed a wedge behind him. Off to the right and left, Manny and Summer were duplicating his moves with their own troops.

As he approached the enemy's line, he noted that some of them had mounts—mostly officers and NCOs, but many in the front line were mounted and poised to receive the Bear Ridge charge. At least Tirano had somebody who knew something about fighting battles. He saw that many of the enemy were almost finished with reloading their weapons. Some fired prematurely and a ball whanged off his chain mail. He winced as his shoulder injury pained him for the first time in weeks.

Just seconds to go before the collision with the enemy. He double checked his position, heading in the general direction of Tirano's battle command. That was the goal. Behead the enemy. Kill Tirano and maybe save Bear Ridge from Two Tongues' domination. He hoped Tirano hadn't changed and allowed any officer to get close to him in power so that there would be no immediate successor. If, he amended, this attack is successful. A grim game, he thought. Which of the three dragoons would reach Tirano first? Would any survive?

With perfect timing, his Gyrenes were spreading behind his point now. He saw Manny off to the left begin to draw ahead of his own group. TJ kicked his horse to a dead run and easily outpaced Manny.

TJ aimed the black at the biggest man on the largest horse in the solid battle line in front of him, and hunched his shoulders for the collision. Crossbow bolts still flew over his head and dropped into the massed Two Tongues troops. He smelled burned powder now, and the flat sounds of musket fire punctuated the roar of thousands of horses' hooves.

The black leaped a small irrigation ditch nimbly and they slammed into the enemy's line at full gallop. TJ was braced for the impact and saw his target scream as the black's shoulder crushed his leg against his horse. The black lurched, keeping his footing as the other horse went over, crushing foot soldiers and causing havoc with its kicking feet.

Suddenly, the noise was deafening. His teeth ached from the collision.

Those Gyrenes immediately behind him forced themselves through the opening he had created, enlarged it as the flying wedge drove through.

Ha! We'll teach these fools what Bear Ridge soldiers can do. As he selected a target, a musket ball smashed into his chain mail, stunning his chest. He saw that his Muster medallion was gouged and bent.

He slashed with his sword and opened a man's chest. Several foot soldiers were struggling toward him, obviously having been briefed to bring him down first. An empty musket clanged off his helmet and he ignored that opponent.

His foot lashed out, boot crushing a man's nose. Widow-Maker made another.

He urged the black forward, bowling over two men. The ground troops were swinging for the stallion's legs with their short swords, trying to incapacitate the animal. He leaped the horse forward into more foot soldiers. Most of the amaranth was trampled and the fields looked scythed.

They'd broken through the front lines and now were in the midst of the action. He saw that the speculation about weaponry had been correct: Tirano's soldiers now had no time to reload, so they were using short swords. But because of their numerical superiority, some could avoid hand-to-hand combat and load weapons for themselves and others. TJ burst through a group of the enemy doing just that. He decapitated one loader and sliced through a shoulder of another.

A Two Tongues sergeant on a wiry red pony charged at him, but the mount tripped on the lip of an irrigation ditch and went down.

TJ pushed ahead, forging the way for the Gyrenes. He didn't want to go too fast and leave them behind, but he knew that to go slowly would be to bog down and become targets in the center of a mass of the enemy. He hoped his timing was good, that the triple-fake-pincer movement was working. From a command viewpoint, it would look like the three separate Bear Ridge forces were thrusting into the enemy to a certain point, and then would turn and meet each other—his center dragoon splitting—ostensibly to crush the enemy in between and establish a center position. What they were really doing was spearing for Tirano and his battle staff.

He fended off a short sword and a crossbow bolt from behind him took the man in the armpit, eliminating the threat. Tirano's soldiers hampered each other as they strove to get at him. TJ's swing was free and strong. Body parts flew and blood gushed. Maiming was just as effective as killing in these circumstances.

A searing pain struck his unprotected left buttock and he spared a glance down. A dagger protruded from there. He continued his charge, attacking a mass of troops which surrounded a circle of musket-armed soldiers. Men and animals were down now, screaming and cursing and dying. A Gyrene next to him fell forward with an arrow in his back and TJ put his sword point through the culprit's right eye.

Momentarily, his sword became stuck in the shoulder and harness of one soldier as another attacked him. TJ wrenched the knife out of his buttock with his left hand and flung it at the attacker. His aim was true and that soldier toppled with the dagger growing out of his throat.

Two mounted men took that soldier's place, and TJ struck for their horses' heads, disrupting them. The black's hooves ground one of them into the muck below and he lost sight of the other.

He saw that his crimson sapphire was glowing brightly, blinking like a light.

For a few seconds, he was free. He noted clouds rolling in and checked the ground. The water from the culverts had begun to do more than trickle, it was flowing freely. As three Gyrenes pushed past him, he saw the fetlocks of their mounts were wet, but not yet covered. Would the sluice-gate plan work? And Cruz would justify all those years of political fighting if it were to rain soon.

The three Gyrenes went down in a ragged volley from another circle of musket firing. TJ led a charge into that group, trampling, hacking, slicing. He snatched an assegai from a riderless horse and hurled it, impaling the officer in charge of that group. Looking behind him, he saw that his Gyrenes were thinning out, but gamely staying with him. An arrow glanced off his saddle horn and he cursed, then, on second thought, grinned at his good fortune. Adrenaline pumped through him and he screamed a challenge riding down the side of a ditch, sloshing through rising water and coming up the other side, surprising a half-dozen men kneeling among sluice-berry bushes and aiming their weapons. He smashed into the end soldier and kept going. Weapons went off and the black screamed his fear at the unaccustomed sounds and smells. But the horse was trained and lashed out with his hooves, crushing at least one skull.

TJ wondered how long they'd been fighting. It seemed many hours, but it had probably been less than one. While the adrenaline surge had increased his breathing, he still wasn't winded. Hacking at one soldier on his right, he swept his left hand down and grabbed an attacking opponent on his left by the throat and lifted him over the black and tossed him at the soldier on the right. The black sagged at the sudden added weight, but kept his footing.

Smoke billowed from muskets and the tin-pan sound of

shots echoed over the combatants. Skies were darkening and he shot a thought for rain and his crimson sapphire glowed. He knew his Gyrenes were taking terrible punishment. He saw wounded Gyrenes fighting without heed to their wounds. His own left hand was wet with his own blood—from his buttock, he thought, until he saw the slicing cut just above his left elbow. He pushed his helmet back and wondered if they'd prevail.

The first stinging drop of rain hit his cheek. As he fought on, the rain increased, a light but steady rain, one which could increase in intensity. He saw flintlocks begin to misfire.

One of the last shots fired that day struck his horse in the throat and the black flipped forward.

TJ hit the muddy ground rolling, concentrating on keeping Widow-Maker in his possession. A fleeting regret passed through him then, one which told him he would have liked to put the black out of his misery. But he was too caught up in battle. The magnificent war horse would have to die in pain.

Soldiers rushed at him with renewed enthusiasm, swinging muskets and short swords. He had to be swift, jumping from place to place, remaining no longer than a second in each location so that crossbowmen couldn't have that moment to target him precisely. He stumbled in mud and two crossbow bolts crossed each other in the space he'd just vacated. Two Tongues troops weren't as proficient as his own, and misfired bolts and arrows struck mostly their own troops—one advantage of a smaller force engaging a far larger one.

He smelled blood now, and the mud beneath his boots ran red.

A man grabbed his beard with a wayward hand and TJ severed his arm at the elbow. Then he had to disentangle the fingers from his beard while the arm dangled against his chest. He swatted a young officer in the face with the arm before disemboweling him.

Temporarily, he became disoriented, not knowing which direction was forward. He knocked a crossbow aside and hacked at the crossbowman's stomach. He located himself.

He began making his way forward, driving three swordsmen ahead of him. Two more joined them.

He saw Manny Vero forcing his horse toward him, obviously bent on rescue. An enemy soldier had climbed onto the rear of Manny's horse and had circled Manny's neck with his arm. Manny held the man's arm, keeping a knife from his throat and all the while urging his horse toward TJ.

TJ tried to shout that he needed no assistance, but the noise overwhelmed his voice. One of the few remaining mounted enemy officers rode up beside Manny, planted his pistol against Manny's neck, and fired.

General Manuel Vero tumbled slowly from his mount, face burned by the powder, neck mangled by the shot. The enemy soldier still clung to him and fell on his own knife.

With a cry of rage, TJ began spinning, Widow-Maker slicing through the air slashing rain as well as soldiers. His glittering weapon killed three men before they could respond, and continued with the practiced swings, weaving a web of death around him.

The officer, apparently realizing he was the object of TJ's attention, tried to escape and was blocked by fighting men. TJ cleared his way through men fleeing in terror, striking them from beside and behind. He knew a single determination of death and retribution and saw without noting that the enemy feared his rage of destruction.

As if by magic, a small space cleared between TJ and the officer. The officer threw his now-useless pistol at TJ and drew his short sword. The man, whose long, black hair draped over his shoulders, charged TJ.

TJ jumped and screamed at the horse almost upon him, surprising the animal and causing him to rear in the air. One swift lunge of sword opened a great wound in the animal's belly, insuring it would not bear the rider away. TJ skipped in the mud around the sinking horse, and dragged the long-haired officer off the saddle. A wall of soldiers surged toward him then. He stood upon the neck of the struggling officer, flicked Widow-Maker once, and the officer's left eye came out on the tip. TJ flipped the eye at the advancing soldiers.

They understood his gesture, all right. He pictured himself in their eyes. They faced the one man they were supposed to seek out and kill over all others. And here he was, beard flowing, blood of their comrades dripping from him, his own blood staining his left side, covered with mud, eyes insane, and calmly popping out the eye of their officer.

With another deft stroke, out came the other eye and it, too, flew into their ranks.

With a stomp, TJ crushed the officer's throat beneath his bootheel.

He grinned at them, taunting them, reading the fear in their eyes.

Rain fell harder now, hindering his vision. Men and horses were foundering around him and he felt the water level at this place over his ankles.

He wondered how Summer was doing. Even though he'd made a flippant prophecy that Summer and he would die only if together, he wished they were together. They'd make short work of these Two Tongues clods.

A no-man's-land seemed to open in front of him. Two Tongues soldiers had never seen fighting like this, he'd wager. Fear had expanded from their eyes and was written on their faces now. He knew his Gyrenes were better conditioned than the enemy and their determination and superior fighting skill had to be discouraging to any opponents.

TJ stood between the two groups, still atop the dead officer. Water washed over the body.

TJ walked calmly forward into this odd eye of the battlestorm and knelt. He tugged off Manny's helmet and stroked his forehead. His hand came away bloody. He rose, raised Widow-Maker, saw the Gyrenes watching him, nodded to them, and turned and rushed the foot soldiers in front of him.

Mud sucked at his boots and he found running difficult. With the flat of his blade, he slapped the haunches of Manny's terrified horse, launching it into the enemy in front of him. He leaped swinging into the cleared avenue.

An occasional musket raised against him and failed to fire.

A group of Gyrenes moved up with him into this new engagement. They stood in the midst of massed enemy troops and fought. While the Two Tongues soldiers were game, they had not the skill and experience of his own Gyrenes. In one-on-one combat, it was a mismatch. Yet the Gyrenes were taking losses. TJ fought for a space against four opponents who were not nearly as proficient as he was. They tumbled one atop the other and TJ used the opportunity to climb to a vantage point.

Standing atop the bodies and surrounded by Gyrenes protecting him, he surveyed the situation. No semblance of military formation remained. Fighting was all around them. Rain alternated between quick, short squalls and steady light rain. Behind him, the fields were littered with dead and wounded. His Gyrenes had more than made up for their numerical disadvantage.

His crimson sapphire glowed more brightly. There, far over, through a lull in the rain he saw vaqueros.

Mike!

He felt a surge of pride. He watched the vaqueros for a moment, their cutting horses familiar with darting about, swerving on a spot. They were accounting for many more than their number, drawing off plenty of the enemy to the side.

Ahead on a slight rise, he saw a grouping of battle flags in the looming shadow of one of the transports and guessed that was the location Tirano had selected for his battle staff. Just like Tirano to stay out of the fighting.

There! Summer. On foot, leading mostly unmounted Muster troops, angling for the flags.

TJ jumped down from the pile of bodies, slipped in the mud, righted himself, and burst through the Gyrene circle.

They took up his cry and smashed into the enemy once again. A fighting wedge with the King in the front, they sliced through crumbling defenses with one goal in all their minds.

TJ waded through a waist-deep canal, cursing the water. It was hindering him as much as Tirano now. At least it had accounted for Tirano's weapons. Looking around, he could tell horses were no longer able to move freely. In fact, some were mired so deeply that riders had to dismount.

His right hand ached from wielding the sword, so he switched to his left and wiped water from his brow with his right.

He fought on, picking up an assegai with his right. The razor sharp blade and dagger point and long reach of the weapon made it as much or more effective than a sword. The enemy could not counter with any similar weapon and thus TJ and his Gyrenes surged forward in the rain and muck.

A squall caught them and he couldn't see much at all. Some of the fighting took on comical aspects as friend and foe alike were unable to maintain footing, to swing freely from a firm stance, to move well.

"I hope you ain't a prophet, TJ," came a voice from beside him.

"Summer!" TJ fended off a thrown musket, the crude bayonet at the end scraping his cheek.

And they were all behind him, TJ saw, the Muster troops,

medallions hanging muddily from neck chains. There were many fewer than when they'd started, just as his Gyrenes had bled and died along the way.

"What's your estimate?" TJ asked as he threw his assegai at an enemy officer.

"I'd have aimed at his torso, TJ, not his thigh," Summer said. "We've dealt them mortal blows, but we'd better get through with this soon, the mud and water are becoming impossible." Summer leaped and his lashing foot crushed a soldier's teeth. The man went down vomiting.

"Impossible for them, too," TJ grunted, making his way over a swollen ditch.

Summer bent, scooped a knife from the muck, and threw it at a colonel. "Missed."

TJ thought he wouldn't have counted a shoulder hit as a miss. "A colonel. We're close."

Summer paused and glanced behind him. "Manny and his troops joined with you?"

"Yes. But Manny's dead."

Then Summer was gone, running, skimming the top of the rising water, wrenching a sword from a soldier so that he now had one in each hand. He began spinning as TJ had, but faster and just as deadly. He wove steel around him and whirled into the packed and panicked enemy. Summer cut his way directly toward the battle flags and TJ followed, knowing the rest of their men would be right behind.

Soon he caught up, cut the leg of a crossbowman who was taking aim on Summer, and slipped and slid to his side.

Together they churned into the enemy killing, scattering, frightening them, a perfect compliment, Summer on the left, TJ on the right, just like years before.

TJ saw one he recognized as a padre choking a muddy soldier with his Muster medallion chain.

They attacked with a vengeance, crushing those in front of them. They seemed unstoppable and soon Tirano's troops were fleeing in front of them, refusing to fight.

A high kick from Summer deflected a falling axe and TJ had to throw Widow-Maker like a spear at another officer who was chopping a vaquero from behind.

As he retrieved his sword, he realized that the vaqueros had made it this far. Where was Mike?

Water level continued to rise as their wedge charged through the disheartened opposition. Now TJ was thigh-deep in a trench, slugging with the hilt of his sword upon some luckless soldier's head.

They ignored those of Tirano's men seeking to escape, for they offered no threat. Tirano's men couldn't seem to cope with the rain and the mud and the water in the trenches and crop rows. TJ saw several overloaded soldiers drowning in a culvert nearby.

With a clarity of vision that transcended his involvement in the battle, TJ knew that Mike was out there somewhere wreaking havoc with his aura. He felt the mental surges and read the increased fear of the unknown on enemy faces as they neared the command area.

Fighting was becoming almost desultory. Tirano's troops must be demoralized and, for the first time, he realized that he and his forces might win a major victory here today.

He noted that he and Summer were moving forward at a faster rate now. Ah, that indomitable Bear Ridge spirit. He thought about Gwen and the Federation and then clamped down on his mind and thought only of fighting.

He pushed ahead of Summer, slicing, weaving, stabbing, jabbing fingers at eyes while sword met sword.

A chill wind off the mountains eased the rain. Tirano's battle staff was just ahead. They appeared to be in a state of shock and dissaray. TJ determined to take advantage of their confusion. Some Two Tongues troops were beating on the hull of the nearest troopship, but nothing happened. TJ saw that the offloading ramps had withdrawn into the ships and there were no open entry ports. Perhaps Sharon was still prevailing over the troopships' crews.

He raised Widow-Maker again and called for a last charge.

His men must have felt his excitement, his confidence, for they pushed ahead with renewed energy. From off to the side, TJ saw Mike, still astride his horse, leading mounted and unmounted vaqueros toward the command position.

TJ flung himself at the retreating enemy, oddly smelling mud as if his nostrils were clogged. He realized the futility of battle as he always did near the end. He killed a man with a stroke that cleaved through the cross dangling from his chest.

He realized that Tirano's men were in a full retreat, going where, he did not know, nor, probably, did they. Only officers seemed to be clustered around this troopship. He went around a giant metal strut which sank into the mud and clashed swords with a colonel for a moment before finishing him.

The officers were trying to escape now, but it was too late. They had trapped themselves by not fleeing sooner. Horses broke legs in trenches and crop rows. TJ watched momentarily as Mike engaged a general and killed him with a swift, Summer-like blow.

Men flogged their horses trying to get them out of the deepening muck.

Still the water came.

Summer was stuck ahead, unable to extract himself from the waist-deep muck in a trench while gamely fighting two of Tirano's officers.

Gaining a foothold on the carcass of a horse, TJ launched himself over Summer's shoulder and bowled into the two men. Finding his grip, he held both under water until their struggling ceased. Then a Gyrene helped pull him and Summer out of the trench.

Summer grinned wryly. "Not much loyalty on Two Tongues." He cleaned the mud off his sword on the uniform of a fallen general.

"Let us find Tirano," TJ said.

Summer motioned. "There's a couple of generals over there," pointing at a pair floundering in a channel.

The carnage had almost ceased. Men merely struggled to free themselves from mud, and could hardly find time or effort to fight. He watched silently as his men mopped up Tirano's command area. Officers were beginning to regroup the Gyrenes to sweep the rest of the battlefield.

Mike rode up, splashing, and his horse mounted the bank where TJ was standing. He climbed off wearily.

"Looks like we won," Mike said. He'd lost his helmet and blood oozed from a scalp wound.

TJ nodded. He told Mike about Manny and indicated Summer who was holding the two generals under water shaking his head to indicate he hadn't been able to locate Tirano.

Summer rejoined them. "No luck."

The rain lessened to a drizzle, then practically stopped. The clouds still hung heavily over the battlefield.

"Tirano is running for his life somewhere," Summer said.

"He won't get far," Mike said, and told them about Alfred and Rebecca and the townspeople intercepting escapees at the edge of the amaranth fields.

Gyrenes began to fan out, leaving the command area to check the rest of the battlefield. Vaqueros swept in another direction. Muster troops arranged themselves in defensive position near TJ. Many were the apprehensive looks given to the looming presence of the silent troopship.

"Mike," TJ said, "could you find Tirano's aura?"

"I could try, but I don't know him," Mike said.

Clouds began to blow away and TJ saw the setting sun light the macabre scene. Had the battle lasted that long? He looked toward the palace and thought he saw figures standing high on the balcony watching, but it could have been a trick of his imagination.

Gyrenes were going to individual enemy soldiers and officers stuck in the mud and disarming them. There had been enough death this day.

"There!" Mike said abruptly and pointed.

The sunset seemed to paint this water-world with blood.

A short man dressed in the garb of a common Two Tongues soldier sat on a speckled gray becoming more and more stuck in the mud and water of a channel. The horse was panicking, swinging his head to and fro. The rider swung a whip against its neck mercilessly. A strange frame in the shape of a T rose from the saddle.

"Reckon we should offer a hand?" asked Summer, obviously not yet understanding.

"No," said TJ.

Summer looked at him strangely. "A common soldier?"

"Tirano," TJ said and felt the chill in his own voice.

The horse reared, sending waves from itself, and the rider fell aside. Still in a panic, the horse continued to scream and paw at the air. The gray stepped into a deeper section and disappeared.

It reappeared for a moment, and Tirano was caught up in the lashings of the T-frame.

The horse went under again, dragging Tirano with it. Tirano's head surfaced seconds later, his face showing the effort of struggling to free himself from the drowning horse. Tirano's head disappeared underwater. Then he surfaced again, gasping for air, and looked directly at TJ.

Tirano's hand reached out for rescue.

TJ watched calmly, knowing Tirano had seen and recognized him.

Tirano's hand begged for help.

TJ stood as if stone.

The horse dragged Tirano under again. The water boiled with its death throes.

Tirano's hand remained above the water, clenched and jerked for a moment and then was still.

A strange looking gray bird with a curved, broad beak swooped from the sky and settled down on the hand, shaking water from its feathers.

TJ looked at Mike and Summer and turned and walked away.

EPILOGUE

TJ stood in the bubble on the top floor of the tallest building on Federation Central. The bubble darkened from the sun as it made its route *the wrong way* across the sky. Nor could he become used to the three moons and their seemingly random paths.

He saw that he was the only one in a bubble. While many of the higher floor suites, from about the one and a half kilometer point up, possessed bubbles in which to view the city, he was the only one whom he'd ever seen use their own bubble. He and the Bear Ridge Federation Council delegation, that is. He wasn't afraid to stand on nothing two kilometers high. He rather enjoyed it.

The top floor of the building revolved so that Council members could see each portion of the sprawling city—though most of them displayed the scene on their walls instead. TJ guessed the rotation increased their vertigo and acrophobia. The city stretched from the center point of the Council building into a cross-patched design. Quaint waterways and patches of green parks reminded him of amaranth fields. His favorite section was the portion of the southwest in which the architecture resembled giant stingbees' nests.

A soft tone told him someone had entered his office inside. He checked the time on his wristcomp and read: 42. No, that was his pulse rate. Time: 1445. He had no appointments. He sighed and stepped through the soft membrane into his office. The membrane closed behind him.

Summer was sitting on the edge of TJ's desk looking at the diagram he'd left on the wall. It was an enlarged representation of the diagram appearing on the recessed screen in his desk.

"Everything go okay?" TJ asked.

"Sure, TJ. I:imbawe, needless to say, is as happy as a cheshire cub in its mother's tails. Becky and Gwen are showing him around and they'll be up later for the formal Council introductions."

"Rebecca" TJ corrected automatically.

Summer ignored him. "He appears to be adjusting fine."

"Better than I am," TJ grunted.

Summer went to a cabinet. "Drink?" He was dressed semi-formal. TJ momentarily regretted the loss of his jester.

"Why change now?"

Summer poured sour mash into tumblers and gave TJ one. "According to I:imbawe, Mike hasn't made any major mistakes yet."

TJ nodded and was glad he didn't have to oversee Bear Ridge as it leapt into technology. Change would sweep the planet; farseeing men and women would adjust. Others would ride the crest of upheaval and have to be dragged from trouble. Well, as long as Sharon Gold was there to help him, things should go more smoothly. And A:alpha. Among the three, they ought to be able to manage the internal affairs of Bear Ridge. Not to mention Felicia's advice. One of these days Mike would have to decide the fate of the Trek. Mike—was he to be the Last Trekmaster? TJ had confidence in his son. He was already acclaimed a fine King of Crimson Sapphire and Bear Ridge. He wondered if Sharon would accept the title of Queen when the transition period was over. Oh, well, not his problem.

"Punch up a chair, Summer, we have some talking to do."

Summer shook his head. "I don't like those things." He scooted up on TJ's desk and crossed his legs. He looked at TJ expectantly.

"I've decided about Two Tongues."

"I told you before," Summer said, "administration ain't my style."

"I don't agree, but I won't force you into it. I need you here, anyway. Alfred . . ."

"Alfred Theadministrativegenius?"

"Sure. Mike needs his own people to run the kingdom the way he wants. Alfred can reorganize Two Tongues." TJ held up his hand to forestall Summer's comment. "And no, I haven't decided whether to keep Two Tongues as my own private fiefdom."

"You just don't want to deal with Kellen Sing again."

TJ grinned. "Right." A memory struck him. "I feel naked not being armed all the time."

"Not me." Summer patted his sleeve and thigh.

TJ grinned thinking of his own concealed weapons. "Me neither."

"So what's so important now? For a change we can rest. No pressing problems, no threats, no intrigue, no battles, no padres, no Treks. Life is looking good, TJ. So what's next?"

"The Federation."

"What?"

"The Fed."

"That's what I thought you said."

TJ strode to the wall and indicated the diagram. "This is the organizational chart of Fedcentral and the Council. Up here are the Council members, me on the end. Mostly policy and legislative functions. Now, this dotted line to the administrative section shows that the Council itself hasn't got strong control over the actual work of the Federation. Administrators and bureaucrats are really running things even though Council members are treated like gods. And look at all these other lines. Dotted. Heavy. Light. Color coded. What a mess. Nobody could possibly know what's what. Now the problem is to get a handle on . . ."

Summer groaned. "Give us a break, will you?"

DAW

**THEY WERE THE ULTIMATE ENEMIES,
GENERALS OF STAR EMPIRES FOREVER OPPOSED—
AND WORLDS WOULD FALL
BEFORE THEIR PRIVATE WAR...**

IN CONQUEST BORN
C.S. FRIEDMAN

Braxi and Azea, two super-races fighting an endless campaign over a long forgotten cause. The Braxaná—created to
become the ultimate warriors. The Azeans, raised to master
the powers of the mind, using telepathy to penetrate where
mere weapons cannot. Now the final phase of their war is
approaching, when whole worlds will be set ablaze by the
force of ancient hatred. Now Zatar and Anzha, the master
generals, who have made this battle a personal vendetta,
will use every power of body and mind to claim the vengeance of total conquest.

☐ **IN CONQUEST BORN**   (UE2198—$3.95)

NEW AMERICAN LIBRARY
P.O. Box 999, Bergenfield, New Jersey 07621

Please send me the DAW BOOKS I have checked above. I am enclosing $_____
(check or money order—no currency or C.O.D.'s). Please include the list price plus
$1.00 per order to cover handling costs. Prices and numbers are subject to change
without notice.

Name _____

Address _____

City _____ State _____ Zip _____
Please allow 4-6 weeks for delivery.

DAW

DAW PRESENTS STAR WARS IN A
WHOLE NEW DIMENSION

Timothy Zahn
THE BLACKCOLLAR NOVELS

The war drug—that was what Backlash was, the secret formula, so rumor said, which turned ordinary soldiers into the legendary Blackcollars, the super warriors who, decades after Earth's conquest by the alien Ryqril, remained humanity's one hope to regain its freedom.

☐ THE BLACKCOLLAR (Book 1)   (UE2168—$3.50)
☐ THE BACKLASH MISSION (Book 2)   (UE2150—$3.50)

Charles Ingrid
☐ SOLAR KILL (Sand Wars #1)
He was a soldier fighting against both mankind's alien foe and the evil at the heart of the human Dominion Empire, trapped in an alien-altered suit of armor which, if worn too long, could transform him into a sand warrior—a no-longer human berserker.

(UE2209—$3.50)

John Steakley
☐ ARMOR
Impervious body armor had been devised for the commando forces who were to be dropped onto the poisonous surface of A-9, the home world of mankind's most implacable enemy. But what of the man inside the armor? This tale of cosmic combat will stand against the best of Gordon Dickson or Poul Anderson.

(UE1979—$3.95)

NEW AMERICAN LIBRARY
P.O. Box 999, Bergenfield, New Jersey 07621

Please send me the DAW BOOKS I have checked above. I am enclosing $_____
(check or money order—no currency or C.O.D.'s). Please include the list price plus $1.00 per order to cover handling costs. Prices and numbers are subject to change without notice.

Name _____

Address _____

City _____ State _____ Zip _____
        Please allow 4-6 weeks for delivery.

DAW

A GALAXY OF SCIENCE FICTION STARS

☐ **TERRY A. ADAMS Sentience**   UE2108—$3.50

☐ **MARION ZIMMER BRADLEY Hunters of the Red Moon**
                          UE1968—$2.95

☐ **JOHN BRUNNER More Things in Heaven** UE2187—$2.95

☐ **A. BERTRAM CHANDLER Kelly Country**   UE2066—$3.50

☐ **C.J. CHERRYH Cuckoo's Egg**   UE2083—$3.50

☐ **GORDON R. DICKSON Mutants**   UE1809—$2.95

☐ **CYNTHIA FELICE Double Nocturne**   UE2211—$3.50

☐ **C.S. FRIEDMAN In Conquest Born**   UE2198—$3.95

☐ **ZACH HUGHES Sundrinker**   UE2213—$3.50

☐ **CHARLES INGRID Solar Kill**   UE2209—$3.50

☐ **TANITH LEE Days of Grass**   UE2094—$3.50

☐ **BOB SHAW Fire Pattern**   UE2164—$2.95

☐ **E.C. TUBB The Temple of Truth**   UE2059—$2.95

☐ **JACK VANCE The Book of Dreams**   UE1943—$2.50

☐ **A.E. van VOGT Null-A Three**   UE2056—$2.50

☐ **DONALD A. WOLLHEIM (Ed.) The 1987 Annual World's
Best SF**   UE2203—$3.95

Write for free DAW catalog of hundreds of other titles!
(Prices slightly higher in Canada.)

NEW AMERICAN LIBRARY
P.O. Box 999, Bergenfield, New Jersey 07621

Please send me the DAW BOOKS I have checked above. I am enclosing $_____
(check or money order—no currency or C.O.D.'s). Please include the list price plus
$1.00 per order to cover handling costs. Prices and numbers are subject to change
without notice.

Name _____

Address _____

City _____ State _____ Zip _____
Please allow 4-6 weeks for delivery.